Wrecking Us, Saving You

Leaona Luxx

Dedication

To you ~ my reader…thank you for your continued support. I'm humbled.

WRECKING US, SAVING YOU

Author's Insight

When I started this journey, I was told to 'write what you know'. Well, that's family. I know families. After my first two books in The Cove Series, I moved to the next series with every intention of coming back to Chord's story.

I knew it had to be special because I needed to redeem The Cove Series. It was my first love and closely reflects my family. Lea is my middle name, Malone is my husband's grandfather's name and Lloyd, my grandpa.

I waited and wrote until the perfect cover came along. I'm different. Yeah, I know you noticed. I always have a cover and blurb before the story. It drives me and the words from the character's themselves.

Chord and Sarah's story is one of redemption for more than just them. This is my redemption. I wanted, no, needed a BIG BOOK, one that yells for it to be seen. Their story is heart-wrenching and one that can be seen in anyone's family.

Open your heart and let them in, you won't be disappointed.

Lea~

1

Sarah

Sitting in my room, I'm playing with my old rabbit when a loud sound echoes from the living room. Standing, I tiptoe over, easing my door open, cringing in hopes it doesn't creak. I peek out just as the banging makes the walls vibrate again.

I stretch my neck to see if my mom's door is still shut. I chew on my nail, trying to decide if I should answer it or not. Knowing if I do and it's someone she doesn't want to see, I'll get in trouble. But if it wakes her up, she'll be mad anyway.

I sprint to the door like a church mouse, hurdling clothes and boxes still in the way from our move. The door shakes again with a hammering fist. I stop long enough to peep out the window to see who it is.

WRECKING US, SAVING YOU

A woman with long black hair stands on the stoop. Her blue suit is pretty, but when I notice the papers in her hand, my belly flips. "Oh, no," I whisper as I hurry to unlock the door.

I can hear my mom coughing in the other room, I know I'm running out of time. I jerk the door open, rushing through it, shutting the door behind me. My eyes wide, I hold my breath as I wait for her to speak.

"Sarah?" Her brow furrows as I quickly nod. She squats in front me, offering me her hand. "Hi, I'm Maggie." My eyes flicker from her face to her hand as it hangs in the air for me, but I don't take it.

"What do you want?" My legs unsteady, I keep watch behind me.

Her eyes narrow, a smile plays on her lips. "Well, I'm here to talk to your mom. You, sweetie, should be in school."

My mouth pops open, my mom isn't going to like this. "She worked late last night, she's still sleeping," I answer with our old standby story.

"Well, I'll come in and wait for her to get up." She grins. I shuffle my feet, racking my brain to come up with an excuse to get rid of her.

"She'll be asleep for hours. If you want to give me the papers, I'll make sure she gets them," I plead with a weak smile as my stomach flips.

"You're a bright little lady, Sarah, but I have to speak to your mom." Just as I'm about to come up with another excuse, the door swings wide. I jump, turning to find my mom glaring at us.

She squints as her yellow hair flies wildly around her face when she steps out on the porch. Her eye makeup is smeared down her cheek as she straightens her tank over her belly.

"Sarah, get in the damn house," she grumbles, pulling me by my shirt as she turns her venom on our not so welcome guest. "What the hell do you want?"

8

"Are you Lisa Smith?" Miss Maggie asks as she squares her shoulders.

My mom snarls as she takes a drag from her cigarette. "What of it?"

"As far we can tell, you've been here for two weeks, and Sarah needs to be in school," she explains. "Unless you can provide an excuse for her absences."

Mom blows her smoke in the lady's face. "Well, we just moved here. I ain't had time to get over there to enroll her."

"I have her paperwork. I can also give you the bus schedule, she can start tomorrow." Miss Maggie digs through her papers.

"Oh, good." Mom rolls her eyes. "Sarah, get over here and get your school stuff."

Maggie's face grows soft as she kneels to talk to me. "Sarah, the bus runs at eight. The driver's name is Amy and it's bus number one-five-eight-nine. Your teacher is Miss Stafford," saying as she points to the paper. I nod, hoping to hurry her along.

"Do you know the room number?"

"I'm sorry, I don't. I'm sure someone will be able to show you once you're there." She rubs my arm.

"Alright, what else do you need? I'm sure her old school has already sent everything over there," Mom spouts.

"I believe they did," saying as she stands, "considering I found you."

"Wonderful, I guess that's all you need then." Mom wraps her fingers around my wrist, pulling me with her.

"Sarah, if you need me," Maggie says in a flurry as my mom shuts the door in her face. "Your teacher can help." I hear her muffled voice yell from behind the closed door.

WRECKING US, SAVING YOU

My hand begins turning red as her grip tightens. She slings me around, tossing me like a rag doll onto the couch. "What in the hell are you thinking answering the damn door?"

"I-uh, thought I was helping."

"Helping? Why in the hell would you think that?" She leans down, getting in my face. I tremble, knowing she's getting mad. Real mad.

"I'm sorry, momma," I stutter. "I won't do it again." Even though I see it coming, the pain of my punishment rests on my cheek. She's in my face again, her long black nail pushing on my nose.

"Don't fucking do it again." I snub as tears flood my eyes. "Now, get outta my face," she snarls. I scurry past her, escaping to my room.

I examine my face in the mirror of my broken jewelry box. Her print blazes on my cheek as I dry my face with my shirt. I sit, snubbing, in the back of my closet. It's dark but I prefer it in here than any other place.

In my own world, I can pretend to be on an adventure. Hiding away from the monsters trying to take me. I can pretend to be a princess, locked in a tower, waiting to be rescued from the dragon.

I learned early to stash some cereal and crackers in my room, I never know when I'll be stuck in here for hours at a time. I check the bag with the light that's streaming through the crack in the door.

Sometimes, there are bugs in my food. I even had a mouse once but, Mom killed it. We haven't lived at the house long enough for anything to be in here, that's usually when they make us move.

"Sarah!" Mom yells from the other room, making me jump. I slide the door open, crawling out as fast as I can. It's dark out now. I stumble through my room, hurrying to her. I walk into the kitchen to find her at the front door.

"Are you leaving?" I watch as she slathers on red lipstick in the mirror by the door.

"Yes"—she cuts her eyes at me—"and if you know what's good for you, you'll not answer the door while I'm out." She rubs her lips together before turning to me. "I'll be back later. You need clothes for tomorrow, find some."

I pick my nail until she's out the door, locking it once she's gone. I turn to the kitchen to find some food. I search the cabinets, finding a jar of peanut butter and a box of crackers.

My belly growls as I slather on the creamy goodness, thankful for the soda in the fridge. I eat in a hurry, so I can find my clothes and shoes for tomorrow. Mom hasn't turned the water on yet, so it's gonna be hard to find something clean.

My jeans are an inch too short, and the shirt I have is a wrinkled mess. I pull at the blue shirt after hanging it up, in hopes of straightening it out. I check the buttons to make sure there's enough of them.

Digging through a box, I find some sneakers, a tad too small and one needs laces. I find another string, it's a little too short but I'll make it work. I don't even look for a backpack or school supplies, I know I don't have any.

I wander around the kitchen looking for something to brush my teeth with. "Maybe Mom has a bottle of water?" I run to her room, terrified of the dark but even more afraid she'll catch me.

I slap at the light, squinting as it comes on. Immediately, I spot a half bottle on her nightstand and another on her sink. I scurry to the kitchen, grabbing a cup. I take half of the bottle on her sink and a little more from the one beside her bed. "She'll never miss it." I smirk, proud of myself.

I hide it in my bathroom cabinet, putting toilet paper in front of it to keep her from finding it. I dust my hands, putting them on my hips. I have no idea how I'll wake up in time tomorrow.

"If I go to bed now, when Mom comes home, I can stay awake and won't be late for school." I climb into bed, pulling my blankets up to my neck. I toss and turn, trying to get comfortable when a light catches my attention.

I left the light on over the stove. She'll be furious if it's still on when she comes back. The trailer has two bedrooms and two bathrooms, a living room and a kitchen with the bedrooms on opposite ends.

I slide from the bed, easing over to my door. I peek through the crack, searching the space. I run full stride to the light, my feet slapping against the floor. I push the chair over to the stove, biting my lip as I look over my shoulder. I flip the switch as I jump from the chair.

The room is pitch black, not even a light from outside shines a path. I hurry as fast as my feet will carry me, tripping over obstacles as I dive into my bed. I scurry to cover my head, waiting for the monsters to come.

I stick my head out of the blanket, checking to see if I can breathe without screaming. I spot a bright star twinkling in the sky. I grin as one of my favorite songs come to mind.

"Standing next to her is like standing next to a thousand suns, not a cluster of stars could outshine; I knew that a part of her belonged to the world, but the world that is within her, is all mine." It's all I know of the song, so I repeat it until I fall fast asleep.

What feels like minutes later, a crashing sound startles me from my sleep. I tremble with fear, waiting for the monsters to grab me. "Settle down, big guy. We don't wanna wake the neighbors." I hear my mom giggle.

"Hell, fuck 'em. I just don't want to have to deal with my girl." A bright light shines from the kitchen, and my mom walks through to my room.

"Girl? There's a little girl here?" The words come out rough and garbled.

12

"Shhh. Yeah, she's asleep," Mom says as she closes my door.

I lay as still as possible until I hear her bedroom door shut. I take a deep breath to slow the flip flops in my belly. I hate it when she brings weird people home, especially men. I toss and turn, doing my best to not fall back to sleep.

As the sun begins filtering through my window, I know morning isn't far behind. I creep to the bathroom to brush my teeth, washing my face as best I can. I have just enough water to get everything done.

I search drawers and boxes trying to find a brush, with no luck. I gather my hair as best as I can and wrap a band around it. After I dress, I walk out to the stoop and wait.

When I see other kids walking to the bus stop, I know to follow them. I notice some of them look like I do. Their clothes are wrinkled, shoes mismatched, and hair that sticks up in different places.

I step onto the bus to find much of the same, and there's no one to sit with. I take a seat a few rows behind the driver and settle in; my belly rolls, and I think I might have butterflies in it.

"Hey, sweetie"—the driver looks at me through her mirror—"what's your name?"

My eyes flicker to her, I'm not sure I should answer. I smash my lips together as I consider telling her. I bite the corner of lip buying time. My tummy doesn't feel weird, and it always does when something isn't right. "It's-uhh..."

Her face softens as she tilts her head. "I need to write it down in my book, that way we can make sure you get home."

I take a deep breath. "Sarah, with an h, Sutton."

"Well, hello, Sarah, with an h, Sutton. Nice to meet you, I'm Amy." Her mouth stretches wide as she winks at me.

I sit quietly, watching other kids get on the bus and find seats. No one offers to sit with me, but I'm used to it. Back home, no one really liked us. Other mommies would tell their kids to stay away from me.

WRECKING US, SAVING YOU

As the bus comes to a stop, I stare out the window to the large, brick building in front of me. It's bigger than anything I've ever seen before, making my belly feel funny. I pick my nail as the others get off the bus.

"Are you okay?" The words, soft and sweet, draw my attention. I turn to find the driver leaning over me. "You alright, baby?" I nod, my eyes cut back to huge red box out the window. "Want me to walk you in?" she asks.

I bounce my head up and down, turning to look at her with wide eyes. Her face lights up as she smiles at me. She takes my hand, warming it with hers. Pieces of white hair mixed with brown fall around her face.

Miss Amy leads me through the big double doors of the school. There's an open door on the right, filled with several desks and people rushing around. "Hello, Miss Amy." A lady with red hair laying in curls, waves. "Who do you have with you?"

"This is Sarah Sutton. She rode in with me from The Horseshoe Mobile Home Park," she replies.

"Thank you for walking her in, I'll take her from here," the lady says as she walks around the end of her desk.

My driver squeezes my hand. "Ashley will take you to your room, and I'll see you this evening." There's a pang in the pit of my stomach.

"Alright, Sarah." Ashley reaches for my hand. "Let's get you to your class." We enter the hallway as kids hurry to rooms on either side. "Your old school sent your information when your mom left a forwarding address. That's how we knew you would be joining us here at Millbrook."

We come to a stop in front of an opening to a room, the door has a small pane of glass in it. She knocks on the door numbered One Two One. "Miss Ashley"—a lady with long black hair smiles at us—"who do you have with you?"

"This is Sarah, she's your new student."

"Hello, Sarah. Welcome to our kindergarten class. I'm Miss Stafford, it's nice to meet you." She waves. "Come on in and we'll find you a seat."

I release Miss Ashley's hand, plodding over to the teacher's desk. "May I have your attention please?" She clears her throat for the room to grow quiet. "This is Sarah, and she'll be joining us. Everyone, please make her feel welcome."

I look around the room, decorated in reds and yellows with Clifford the Big Red Dog all over the walls. I hear snickers from the back of the room and notice two girls whispering.

Most of the room greets me with smiles. As I scan my eyes toward the back, I notice a waving hand attached to a boy with brown hair, smiling. I think I can see all of his teeth his mouth is so wide as he bounces in his seat.

"Sarah, why don't you take the seat next to Chord." I glance at her for more instructions, unsure of who Chord is. "He's the one jumping up and down, when he needs to take his seat, Mister Hamilton." She points down to signal him to sit.

I drop my head as I zigzag my way through the students. I come to a stop in front of the grinning boy. "Hi, Sarwah. I'm Chorwd." He straightens a desk next to him. "You can sit herwe." His eyes are a blue I've never seen.

I step around him, dropping into the seat. He sits on the edge of his chair, trotting his leg. "You shouldn't stare, it's unbecoming."

"What's unbecoming?" He wrinkles his nose.

I narrow my eyes when I realize, I don't know. "I'm not telling you."

He shrugs and reaches for the papers being passed around. "Please take one. This is your spelling words for the week," Miss Stafford says.

15

WRECKING US, SAVING YOU

"Here you go, Sarwah." Chord hands me a sheet, smiling. I've never had anyone be so nice to me.

"Be sure to write your name at the top of the page," the teacher adds.

My eyes flicker across the desk before I scan the room. "I have one you can have." I turn to Chord, his hand outstretched with a pencil.

My brows pulled low, I slide it from his fingers. "Thank you."

I'm busy writing my name when I hear more giggling. I glance up to see several pointing in my direction. They point at my shoes, whispering. My stomach lurches, I already hate it here.

Chord

"Finish your breakfast, it's time for the bus, baby boy," Mom says, patting my back. I look up at her as she loads the dishwasher, her black hair piled on top of her head.

I gulp down my milk, wiping my mouth on my sleeve. "I gotta get more pencils!" saying as I jump from my chair.

"Hurry up, I'll meet you at the door with your backpack," she shouts as I run from the room. "Thayer, let's go, love."

I push the heavy door open to my father's office, hurrying over to his large, cherry desk. He works from home as much as he can, and he always keeps extra pencils for me in the top drawer.

Pulling it open, I grab a handful, smiling when I see the blue raspberry PushPop he left for me. It's the reason I need pencils, we just don't tell Mom. I chuckle at our secret as I shove the candy into my pocket.

17

WRECKING US, SAVING YOU

"Chord, here comes the bus!" Mom yells as I hear my sister stomping down the stairs.

"Brother, you're going to miss it!" Thayer screams.

I slam the drawer shut and take off out of the room. Turning the corner, Mom stands at the entrance with my bag in her hand. I take it from her as I rush out the door. "Thanks, Momma."

"Have a good day!" She waves from the steps as I board my ride. "I love you!"

Next year, I'll be riding to school with my big brother, One. I can't wait to ride in his car, he's the coolest. The other night, I heard my parents saying that once One graduates, he's talking about going into the military. I hope not.

As the driver parks in front of the school, I grab my backpack and walk to class. Miss Stafford is busy writing on the board as we put away our things. I find my seat just as Miss Ashley from the office, walks in holding the hand of a girl.

She has yellow hair and big, blue eyes. My belly flips when she makes eye contact with me. There's an empty seat on my left, so I wave to get her attention, but she keeps looking at the floor. Miss Stafford tells her to sit beside me, which makes me smile bigger.

"Look at her hair." Marissa snickers.

"Her shoes!" Kelly says, pointing at them. I fist my hands, hitting the desktop. My face is burning up. They're the meanest girls in the class, I don't like them at all.

Sarah takes the seat next to me, and I can't help but notice her shoes are dirty and the laces don't match. Her hair is kinda up, but you can see it has tangles in it. She's so pretty. "Here you go," I say, laying our spelling words down on her desk.

She looks from me to her desk. The others continue to laugh at her, and I grit my teeth wanting to tell them off.

18

"I think she stinks." Marissa pinches her nose.

"Her clothes are dirty too." Kelly curls her lip as she scowls at Sarah. I glance at her when I realize she doesn't have a pencil. I have plenty, so I give her one.

"Thank you," Sarah responds and my belly does a froggy hop. The next thing I know, I'm smiling at her like Goofy. I can't stop myself, she's so pretty she makes my belly hurt.

When class begins, I help Sarah with her books. The teacher finds her a locker, even though Sarah doesn't have anything to put in it. I give her some notebook paper to do her work on. She doesn't talk much but that's okay, I don't want to talk to the jerks around here either.

After lunch, we get outside time. I play close to Sarah, as she sits on a bench by herself. I'm working on the courage to go up to her when Marissa shows up. "My mom says people like you are trailer trash." Sarah's shoulders slump.

"Where's your dad work?" Kelly asks.

Sarah mumbles, "He doesn't."

"Does your mom even comb your hair?" Marissa spits at her.

Sarah sighs, as if she's heard it all before. My hands shake as my face turns hot. I can't take it another minute. "Shut up, Marwissa, or I'll tell everyone you pee the bed," I snarl.

Marissa's face grows bright red as she steps toward me. "You wouldn't."

"I would and I'll tell everwyone that Kelly sucks herw thumb," I growl, pointing at her.

"I'm gonna get you, Chord Hamilton." She balls her fist up tight. I ready for her to hit me but, instead of lashing out at me, she turns and pushes Sarah off the bench.

WRECKING US, SAVING YOU

Kelly bursts with laughter as she turns her attention to Sarah. "Now she's even dirtier." They run away as I rush to help Sarah.

"Arwe you okay?" I reach for her hand, her eyes filled with tears as they flicker from my hand to my face. She grips it as a shock races through us.

I jerk my hand away, shaking it as we giggle. "You shocked me!"

"You did it to me, Chord!" She rubs her palm on her shirt. We stand there, looking at each other.

Still shaking our hands, she sits back down and I plop beside her. "Don't pay any attention to those girls, everyone knows they're stupid."

Sarah shrugs. "I don't care." I would believe her, but she's still looking at the ground. "My mom was asleep when I got ready this morning, I couldn't find a comb."

"Sarwah, where do you live?"

"In a trailer with my mom." She bites her nail as I swing my legs.

"What about your dad? Does he live with you?"

Her lips press into a thin line as she tilts her head back. I mimic her, squinting at the sun in the sky. "He's in heaven," she says with a sigh. There's a sharp pain in the middle of my chest.

"My brother's dad is in heaven."

Her head spins, eyes wide. "You have a different dad?"

"Yeah, me and my sisterw, Thayerw. But my momma says, 'We'rwe all family and that's all that matterws.'"

"I want a family," she murmurs.

"You don't have anyone to love you?" I ask as the pain around my heart increases.

"Mom says, I'm not worth loving." She shrugs.

As the pain increases, I rub my chest. "My momma says everwyone deserwves love."

"Not me, I don't believe in it." Her mouth twists. "But I don't have a family either, so what do I know."

"You can be a parwt of my family." A small smile plays on her lips. "Do you wanna go swing before the bell rings?"

She nods. "Okay." We spring from our seats, running full tilt. We swing until the bell rings, ending recess. We walk silently down the hall to our classroom. The afternoon passes quickly, and soon, we're readying to catch the bus.

"Do you know where my bus is?" Sarah whispers to me.

"I'm not surwe, but Thayerw will know," raising my brows, I explain just as the bell sounds. "Follow me, we'll ask."

"Thayer's your sister, right?" Her brow furrows.

I nod with wide eyes. "Yeah, my big sisterw."

Sarah follows closely behind me as we hurry to find Thayer. She always waits on me before we load the bus, I guess to make sure I don't miss it. I see her just outside the entrance, waving.

"Is that her?" Sarah asks as we get closer .

"Yeah, that's herw." Thayer looks just like our mom, she's beautiful.

"Do you have everything?" she asks as we approach her.

"Yes, but can you help Sarwah find herw bus? She's my frwiend, I told herw you would." The words spill from my mouth like a waterfall as Thayer smiles at Sarah.

"What's your bus number?"

Sarah averts her eyes, mumbling her words. "One five eight nine."

WRECKING US, SAVING YOU

"Fifteen eighty-nine?" Thayer's eyes narrow as she scans the line of yellow machines. "There"—she points. "Chord, go wait by our bus and I'll make sure she gets on." Thayer takes Sarah by the hand.

"Bye, Sarwah." She smiles as I wave.

"See you tomorrow, Chord."

As soon as I'm home, I run straight to my room. Looking through my desk, I gather a new pencil sharper, paper, and folders. Swinging the closet door wide, I search for my old backpack.

"I wonder if Sarwah likes Batman?" I mumble.

"Whatcha doin', little dude?" my brother, One, says from the hall.

"I have a new friend, Sarwah," I say as I walk past him and into our shared bathroom.

"Oh, really? She pretty?" He winks.

I frown as I scour the vanity drawers for a brush. "Yeah, she has yellow hairw."

"A blonde, good choice, although I prefer strawberry blonde." He chuckles. "Are you planning on playing beauty shop?" He leans against the door as I gather some of Thayer's hair ties.

"She doesn't have a comb. Marwissa and Kelly made fun of herw hairw." I shrug. "And herw clothes."

One holds his hands out to stop me. "Let me help you carry these." I fill his hands with everything I can find for her hair. One follows me back into my room, watching as I stuff the bag.

"You givin' her that?" He motions to the backpack.

"She doesn't have one."

"Let's take a break and go eat, Mom has dinner ready." One rubs my head as we stand. He throws me over his shoulder as we walk down the stairs. One's twelve years older than me, Thayer's two years.

"There you two are, we were about to start without you." Mom waits for One to put me down before fixing my plate.

"Loverboy was packing a bag for his girlfriend." He tickles my side, sitting down next to me.

"She's not my girwlfrwiend, Sarwah's just my frwiend."

"What are you talking about?" Mom asks.

"Tell her, she won't get mad," One encourages me.

"Sarwah's new and she doesn't have stuff, so I'm taking herw some of mine."

Mom's eyes dart from mine to One's. "Chord, that's good of you. Can I ask what you're taking or still needing?"

"Well, she needs girwl stuff and a backpack. The girwls at school were making fun of her 'cause herw hairw wasn't brwushed but only 'cause she couldn't find something to do it with."

"Okay. What kind of girl stuff?" Thayer joins us.

"Hairw bows and a brwush. I gave herw a backpack and some school stuff too."

"Tell you what, let's eat and after we clean up, then I'll help you find some things. Maybe Thayer can help her with her hair tomorrow?" Mom lays her hand over mine, and I immediately feel better.

I wait with Thayer by the front doors until Sarah arrives. She walks with her head down as she enters the building. I'm so excited for her to see what we have for her, I can't wait another minute.

"Sarwah." Her head snaps up as I greet her with a smile. "I have something for you, but Thayerw's going to help."

"What is it?" Her brows drop low, and I shift my feet and glance at my sister.

WRECKING US, SAVING YOU

"Let's go to the restroom, and I'll show you." Thayer ushers her to the restroom.

I go on to class, hoping Thayer hurries, I can't wait to see Sarah. Just as the bell rings, Thayer waves at me from the door. Sarah's smile lights the entire room as she walks past gaping mouths. My heart thunders in my chest.

Sarah's hair is smoothed into a ponytail with a braid on one side. Her bright blue shirt matches her eyes and her sneakers are new. The denim jacket Thayer picked out for her is wrapped around her waist.

"I got the worwksheet for you," I say as she walks by to put her new Powerpuff Girls backpack in the locker.

After dinner last night, my family talked about things Sarah needed or, at least, what I thought it was. Mom went out with Thayer and bought Sarah the bag, some clothes, and a bunch of other things. Thayer's going to help her every few days with her hair and give her a new shirt or whatever she needs.

Sarah slides into her seat, still smiling as she whispers, "Thank you." My belly froggy hops, though I think she means 'thank you' for the sheet.

"Class, we're going to the computer lab this morning," Miss Stafford announces. "Please put away your things and line up at the door."

"Come on, Sarwah, I'll show you what to do."

"Sarwah… Sarwah… Sarwah, can't you say her name right, little baby?" Marissa teases as she turns to join the class line.

"Shut up, Marwissa."

"It's not my fault you talk like a big baby." She sticks her tongue out at me, making my face turn red as I growl.

"It's not our fault you're ugly and mean!" Sarah spouts, making me giggle.

"I'm gonna tell the teacher." Marissa narrows her eyes.

"Go ahead, she already knows you're ugly," Sarah snarls.

Marissa grits her teeth. "I'm gonna pay you back, just you wait."

We start down the hall, and Sarah grabs my arm. "Call me Sutton. It was my dad's name, and I like it better."

"Okay." I stare at the ground as my cheeks glow bright red.

"Only if you want to, I like the way you say my name." Sarah's eyes are soft as she smiles.

"I like Sutton, it is easierw."

"Chord," Sarah pauses, "are we best friends?"

I smile as my heart flutters. "We arwe. Foreverw." She takes my hand as we skip to the computer lab.

From that day on, we're inseparable.

Sarah

Nine years later…

"Mom." I pause, waiting for her response. "Mom." Still nothing. She lays there as if she's dead, and I find myself wishing it were true. "Mother." She begins to rouse, no way am I going in the room with that man in bed with her.

"What?" she grumbles from the bed.

"I'm gonna spend the weekend with Thayer, so I won't be home after school tomorrow." It's six in the evening and she's still in bed. Apparently, this jerk doesn't work either.

"No, you're not. You're only going over there for that brother of hers, and I'm not taking care of a baby if you get knocked up," she slurs, rising from the bed as the body next to her begins to stir.

26

"Eww, Mom." I storm away from the room so I can finish packing my bag.

"I said, you're not going. That's all you do anymore is stay at that house." She props herself against my door.

"I like it there," I mutter. "You're never home on the weekends anyway."

"You're spending too much time there, I don't like it."

I spin on her, trying to hold my tongue. "Since when do you care what I do?"

She pushes from the wall, stepping closer to me. "I don't care, you're here because you have to be."

I tighten my fist and try to contain my anger. "Why do I have to be? If you don't want me, I can leave."

"Do you honestly think 'Richie Rich' or his family wants you? You're a toy to them, something to dangle on a charm so they can show people what they do. 'Look, we saved some poor, trailer trash. Aren't we wonderful?' You're such an idiot."

My face flames as anger builds deep inside. "You know *nothing* about them."

"Like you fuckin' do! That boy will use you like every other guy, if you don't wise up." Her face pinches up, making her grow older by the minute.

I narrow my eyes. "No, he won't." *I'm nothing like you.*

"Whatever, you're not going anywhere until you're eighteen."

I bat my eyes, holding back the wetness. I've known my entire life she hated me, but hearing it is a different story. "That's all I've ever been, isn't it? A check."

"A thorn in my side is more like it, but yeah—so what the fuck?" She gets in my face, spitting her words at me, "You're not going anywhere until I say so."

27

WRECKING US, SAVING YOU

"I just want to spend the night, I'm not going to stay." Tears well in my eyes.

"No, you spend too much time over there as it is," she snarls, turning to leave. "And clean the damn kitchen."

I grab my hair, pulling it at the roots. "I hate you," I breathe just above a whisper. I bite my tongue as I stomp to the kitchen. Cleaning up after her drunken night of partying burns my ass.

As I empty the sink to start the dishes, my mom's 'bed buddy' joins me. "You might want to wait, she's in the shower."

I push the faucet completely open. "Maybe it'll chill her attitude."

"Shew, you sure do have your momma's temper." Duke's saccharine words nauseate me.

"I'm nothing like her," I growl.

I watch him as best I can as he pulls a beer from the fridge, popping the top to take a long drink. "You sure as hell look like her from back here, honey."

The hair on my arms stands on end as I hear him take a step closer to me. "I look like my dad."

He chuckles, his breath sweeping over my shoulder. "Trust me, from back here, you look nothing like a man."

"Mom will be out soon, maybe you should go wait on her in the bedroom." My breath hitches as I send a silent prayer up.

He takes another step toward me, and I shudder from his proximity. "Of course, your mom's ass has never looked this good."

I hover over the sink, hoping he'll get the hint. "She's been in there awhile."

"So, tell me, Sarah, you ever been fucked?" My stomach rolls as I try to think of a way out of here.

"Leave me alone."

His body heat singes my back as he steps closer to me, agitating the contents of my stomach. He sweeps my hair from my shoulder, revealing my neck. "I bet you taste even sweeter than she does, don'tcha, baby girl. You ever had that tight little pussy licked?"

I press my stomach into the sink, holding back bile. "She'll be back any minute."

"The more the merrier; besides, I've never had a mother-daughter duo." He grinds his dick into my ass, and I tighten my fist, ready to take aim.

Gritting my teeth, I throw a sharp elbow into his ribs. "Get away from me or I'll scream."

Bile rises in my throat as his hand wraps my neck, pushing me forward as he lays over my back. "There ya go, I like it rough, ask your mom."

"What in the hell do you think you're doing?" Mom asks from behind us.

Duke releases me, backing up slightly. "It's all good, we're just playing around."

"I'm fourteen, asshole." I push my way past them, hurrying to my room.

"What the fuck? Do you want her?" Mom yells, but not because of his treatment of me.

"She's one hot piece of ass, Lisa." He chuckles. "And probably a hell of a lot less trouble."

"You're a piece of shit."

"Maybe, but she's fucking hot." A slamming door echoes through the place as my own crashes opens.

"Get your shit and get the hell out." Mom glares at me. I grab my bag, half full, stepping around her. "Don't come back until Monday."

WRECKING US, SAVING YOU

Her words stop me in my tracks. "What bothers you more, that I'm my father's or that I'm competition?" I walk out, slamming the door behind me before she can answer.

Jumping from the porch, I sprint to the end of the street. Cutting through the trees, I continue to run. If it gets dark, I can't find my way. There's a little country store at the intersection; if I can make it there, they'll let me use the phone.

I spotlights in the distance just as I hit a small clearing. I'm so caught up in getting there, I don't pay attention to where I'm going and stumble over some brush, falling. I lay there, palms burning, knees, undoubtedly scraped, as my long-held tears begin to flood my face.

"What did *I* do to deserve this? Huh?" I scream, allowing the built-up tension to release like a dam.

The sky grows darker, reminding me I've laid here long enough. I sit up, inspecting my scuffed hands and trying to clean the blood from my knees as best I can. I stand on shaky legs, plodding through the field until I make it to the other side of the tree line.

The store is bustling as people stop to pick up last minute items before getting home. I step through the door, scanning the crowded shop. I spot the person I need to talk to coming from the back.

"Ann?" She's about my height with curly brown hair; her family owns the store. Though she's older than me, we've become good friends.

"Sarah, are you okay?" Her eyes dart from mine to my legs.

"Yeah, I fell in the clearing," I stammer. "Can I use the phone?" I ask as I bite my nail.

"Of course." She smiles as she grabs the phone, reaching it to me. "Let me get you a wet paper towel."

"Thank you." I grimace, dropping my bag to the floor before dialing the number, silently praying someone answers quickly. Three rings later, my heart sinks in fear there'll be no one there.

"Hello." A lady's voice echoes through the receiver—Elise, Chord's mom.

"Hi, it's Sarah. Is Thayer around?"

"Yes, she is. Just one second." I hear rustling over the phone. "Thayer, Sarah's on the phone."

"Hello, sister. What's up?" Thayer sounds so much like her mom, my chest tightens as tears begin to build again.

"I-I need a ride"—I swallow hard—"and I know we were planning on me staying this weekend, but I need to stay a few extra days."

"Where are you?" she asks without hesitation.

"The general store before my house."

"We're on the way." I gasp, no way do I want to see Chord like this.

"Don't bring Chord." I wipe away the trailing tear. "I'll explain when you get here."

"Mom is coming with me, okay?" She pauses.

"That's fine." I squeeze my eyes tight. "Thank you."

"Stay there, we're on the way." Her words of reassurance do little for the heaviness in my chest.

"Thank you, Ann. Someone's coming to get me."

She takes the phone, laying it down. "You're welcome here anytime." I return her smile, grabbing my bag to find a place to wait outside.

I stand, just under the awning, waiting for Thayer and Elise. I watch as people come and go, families taking care of one another. I can barely remember my dad anymore. The memories I do have, I hold close.

Every night, he would tuck me in with a song. I sing it when life hands me more than I can handle, and with my mom, that happens all too often.

"Standing next to her is like standing next to a thousand suns, not a cluster of stars could outshine; I knew that a part of her belonged to the world, but the world that is within her, is all mine," I whisper the lyrics as I bat away the falling tears.

A blinking light draws my attention. Rubbing my eyes, I focus on Thayer as the car stops in front of me. "It's dark out here, you should've waited inside," she says as the door opens.

"I'm okay, I wanted to get outta everyone's way."

She pulls me into a hug before yanking on the handle to the backseat. "Thanks for coming. I'm so sorry to impose." I sink into the cool car.

"You're not an imposition, we love having you." Elise glances at me through the mirror. "You know I love having you around and then there's Chord." She waggles her brows.

I glance at Elise as she smiles at me through the mirror. "Oh, yeah. I mean, we are best friends."

Thayer whirls her head around, wide-eyed. "Sure, because I look at you the way y'all stare at each other."

I side-eye Elise, my stomach tightens at the thought of Chord. "Stop it."

Thayer laughs. "We all can see it, you two need to admit it."

"Never." I giggle.

We ride in silence to their home, set just off Glenwood near downtown Raleigh. I never thought about it when I was younger, as we moved from trailer park to apartments back to mobile homes, but Chord's family has money.

We live on the wrong side of the affluent neighborhood and just inside the school district. Chord's been by my side since kindergarten, and we're best friends. The things my mom said about him are so untrue.

And Thayer, she embarrassed me talking like that in front of their mom. Chord and I are not like that with each other. I mean, I love him and I know he loves me, but there's nothing more between us. His family is my family, one I've never had.

"I hope you're hungry, dinner should be ready soon," Elise says as we drive through the gates to their home.

The four-bedroom, five-bath home sits just behind a circle drive lined with trees. The white two-story has a large entry with mahogany double glass doors. The blues, grays, and whites blend well with the built-in bookshelves and fireplaces.

The laundry room is bigger than my bedroom, and the family room is the size of our trailer. They even have a home theater and a patio that's equipped with a fridge. But they've never made me feel like I don't belong here.

"I am, but I need to clean up first." I wince as I touch my bloodstained knee.

Thayer swings the front door wide. "Go on up to my room and I'll grab the first-aid kit."

Elise tugs at my hand. "Let me see, Sarah."

I pull my brows low, hating that she's making a fuss. "I'll be fine once I clean it up."

She bends in front of me, inspecting my knees. "Thayer, be sure to get the antibacterial ointment. Why don't you jump into the shower, just to make sure all the dirt is out, sweetie."

WRECKING US, SAVING YOU

My chest tightens as I peer down at her. Why can't my own mother be this caring? My breath hitches, trying to hold back the beckoning tears. "I will."

Elise straightens, wrapping her arms around me. "Take your time, we'll wait."

"Is that Sutton?" Chord yells from the other room. My stomach knots with the thought he'll see me like this. Wide-eyed, I shake my head at Elise.

"Go, I'll keep him busy." Her face glows with her smile.

"Thank you," I murmur, turning to take the stairs two at a time. I push the door to Thayer's room open, dropping my bag by the bed. I hurry to the bathroom, stripping as soon as I hit the door.

I twist the faucet, allowing the water to heat as I strip. Stepping into the gush of hot water, I relish the warmth on my cool skin. I wince as it runs down my legs and over the torn flesh.

Slowly, I lather the soap over the rough surface of my palm. As the dirt washes away, so does the sting of the cleansing. Working my way down to my legs, I scrub away the debris.

Gently, I stroke my kneecaps, clearing the dried blood from the marred surface. I suck air through my gritted teeth as the sting grows and the water runs red. "I suppose this is the metaphor for my life." I chuckle, trying to stop the tears.

"Sarah?" I jump from the knock at the door.

"I'm almost done."

"I wanted to make sure you have everything, I'll leave the first-aid kit on the nightstand," Thayer replies.

"Alright, thank you." I turn the shower off, drying quickly. I'm sure they'll be waiting on me to eat dinner.

I bandage my knees, dressing as fast as I can. I pull on my sweats and a baseball tee, knotting my hair on top of my head. I carefully navigate the stairs, making my way toward the kitchen. They rarely eat in the dining room, it's always the breakfast table.

Sure enough, I find them huddled together by the bar, waiting on me. "I'm here, sorry it took so long." I chew the inside of my cheek.

Chord spins on his stool, smiling. "No worries, we're just hangin'." I wrap my hand around my stomach as it flips and flops as though butterflies are playing in it. I'm stunned at how tall he's gotten as he stretches his long legs out in front of him.

"Umm, good," I stammer as he brushes past me with his broad shoulders. There's more definition in his torso, like his jawline. A tingle spreads through my body as I take his scent in, what in the world?

Thayer squeezes my shoulder, "Let's eat," saying as she tugs me with her to the table.

We join Elise, Cal, and Chord at the table. I sit between him and his sister. It's like every other dinner I've had here, but this time, when Chord looks at me, the hair on my neck prickles.

Chord nudges my thigh under the table, whispering to me, "Are you okay?"

Chills race over my body as I choke out a response, "Yeah, just tired."

"Thayer said you fell, I hope you're okay." He glances down at my legs.

My face flushes, I'm just not sure why, so I shrug. "A few scrapes, I'm good."

Then it happens—he winks at me, and my heart thunders in my chest. His blue eyes sparkling. "Good, I'd hate it if my best girl got hurt."

My heart races, as it has so many times before, but this is different. We've always went with 'best friends', knowing we mean

35

more to each other. Being best friends is great, being in love is everything.

My eyes flicker around the table, I know I can't tell him. It would ruin this, the only family I've ever known. And what's worse, my mother would be right. I'd fall for him and in the end, I'd still be the girl from the wrong side of the tracks.

Two years later…

"Hurry up!" I shout from the bottom of the stairs.

"We're coming, shithead," Thayer yells.

I roll my eyes at her term of endearment. "I'm goin' on out."

"Fine," she screams from her room.

I yank my towel from the rail, throwing it over my shoulder as I walk through the house to the pool. It's the last day of summer break, and I want to relax. It's my sophomore year, I'm taking all advanced placement classes—there'll be no time to slack.

I toss my towel on the patio and dive in head first. I lap the pool before finally hearing someone call my name. "Brother!" Thayer screams, stopping me mid-stride. "May I introduce, Sarah Beth Sutton."

WRECKING US, SAVING YOU

"What are you talking about, I know who Sutton is." I splash at her.

"I know you do, but not like this. I'm sure the other boys will enjoy this too." Thayer winks.

She slips to the side as Sutton steps from the French doors. She's wearing a multi-colored blue and white bikini with ties on the side of her hips. The top has a ruffle that falls over her biceps with lace, but nothing can hide her full breasts.

Her blonde hair is piled high, wisps falling around her collarbone. My mouth goes dry when she licks her lips, her lids hanging low as she watches me. I'm not sure if I'm the predator or the prey, but I'll be damned if I care.

I follow the curve of her hips down her toned legs, and she curls her toes tipped in pink. My chest is heavy, making me struggle to breathe. Sarah's always been beautiful, but suddenly, she's breathtaking.

Damn. Why are we sixteen? Then again, no way in hell does Sutton look sixteen. I don't like it. I mean, yeah, I love it, but won't other guys? "Are you gonna say something? I look stupid, don't I?" she mutters.

I side-eye Thayer, trying to hide my reaction, but I can tell she's already nailed me by the smirk on her face. "I mean, it's cool." I shrug.

"I think she's freakin' hot." Thayer joins her, holding her phone up in front of them. "Smile." They put their heads together, twinning for the picture.

"Hush! Chord might gag at the thought of me being pretty." Sarah narrows her eyes as they glisten from the sun's reflection. They're as blue as a Carolina sky.

"Chord knows what's hot and what's not." Thayer giggles.

"*Chord* is right here, ladies." I splash at them as they lather on lotion. "Aren't y'all coming in?" Please, come in. I'm not sure how

38

long I can last before blowing my load watching Sutton rub her body down.

"Nah, we're gonna work on our tans," Thayer says as she sits on the chaise lounge. Sutton continues to rub lotion over her hips and down to her ass cheeks. My pulse races as my blood pressure rises.

Before I can regain my senses, I mutter, "Sutton doesn't need to work on a damn thing."

Her eyes snap to mine, her mouth agape slightly. "Excuse me?"

I blink several times, trying to shake the fact I said that out loud. "What? Nothing. Just work on your tan," I growl.

"What crawled up your ass?" she snarls.

"Nothing." I dive under the water, praying it helps my growing hard-on. What in the hell is wrong with me? She's my best friend for Christ's sake. I reach the other side of the pool, gasping for air.

"Chord?" Her soft voice startles me, and I jump, making her giggle. "I'm sorry." Her brows are pulled tight.

"No, don't be." I lick my lips as my eyes drop to her cleavage. "I'm just daydreaming."

"About?" Asking, as she treads water. She's never been more beautiful as she is right now.

I shake my head. "Stuff. What's with the Spanish Inquisition?"

She bites her lip. "You know what? Forget you." She splashes me before turning to swim away. I watch as she climbs from the pool then settles in her seat. She shoves earphones on and lays back.

I grit my teeth, trying to think of a way to talk to her, but before I can, a ball smacks me in the side of the head. "What the f…" I snap my head around to find my brother standing on the edge, smirking at me.

"You little shit. You were gonna cuss." He folds his arms over his chest.

WRECKING US, SAVING YOU

"What are you doing home?" I push up from the side, dragging him into a hug.

"No way am I gonna miss Thayer's first day of senior year." He punches me in the arm.

I roll my eyes, "She's not a princess."

"Dear Lord, don't tell her that, she'll be ruined for life." He chuckles. "So, what'sup with you and Sarah?"

He follows me over to my towel, sitting down in the chair where it laid. "What do you mean?"

His eyes float from me to her and back. "Dude, she's crushing on you."

"No way." I shake my head, trying to bite back my grin.

"Hard." His eyes fall below my waist, before looking away. "Like you are her."

I hang the towel in front of me, face blazing with heat. "Fuck you."

"You better watch that mouth, Mom will tear you up." His brow cocks. "She likes you. You like her. It happens."

"We're friends, that's all."

"Friends make great lovers." He winks.

"You're gettin' on my nerves, man."

He slides to the end of the chair. "I'm just sayin', beautiful girl like Sarah will get plenty of attention."

I shift my feet, throwing the towel around my neck. "Yeah, that's what I figure."

"You ain't my little brother if you let that go down." He tilts his head. "Surely, you're not gonna let another man at her?"

A thunder rolls inside my chest. "Shut the hell up, One."

He snickers. "I do believe you're sprung."

I cut my eyes at him. "Yeah, I know. But what if you're wrong and she doesn't like me the way I like her?"

"You'll never know until you try." He stands and takes a step toward the house. "Or you can ask your sister."

My brows shoot up when my mouth pops open. "Ohh, yeah."

"Come on, little man." He nudges my shoulder just as Sarah stands, adjusting her bottoms over her plump backside. I shift my stance. "And close your mouth."

One walks in front of me, laughing his ass off. I, on the other hand, am adjusting my junk. Again. "Shut up."

"Ladies, may I bring you a beverage?" One pauses to ask.

"Yes, please!" Thayer squeals.

I follow One into the kitchen, and he grabs some bottles of water and pop. "I'll take Thayer's."

"Seriously?" I cringe as my chest tightens.

One leans against the counter. "Hold up. What's the problem?"

I pound my head on the wall. "I don't know. Sh-she makes me nervous now." Sweat beads on my forehead.

"I can see that." One purses his lips. "Why? You've been best friends forever, she's still the same girl."

I peek over his shoulder, spotting Sarah. There's a pounding in my ears as my mouth goes dry. "I've always loved her, but now it's different."

"Still the same girl." He smiles. "Just continue to be her best friend, respect her, and let love grow."

"What if we ruin everything?"

He looks over his shoulder. "I don't know much about love, but I do know she's always been here and it's not because of the food."

WRECKING US, SAVING YOU

I watch as she laughs with Thayer, she's always had the best smile. "True. I mean, who wouldn't want all this?" I motion to my body.

"Alright, stud, let's go." One pats my back with a laugh.

I open the door to the sound of giggling, and I'm completely entranced by the sight and sound before me that I trip on the rug, falling into Sarah's lap. Water bottle in her cleavage and pop can on her side. "Ahhh, cold!" She jumps, bumping my head with hers. "Oh, my gracious. Are you okay?"

I look up into her twinkling eyes, "Sorry, I..."

"Dude, I'm sorry." One chuckles. "I didn't mean to trip you." As if I didn't know it already, my big brother is the best.

"No worries." I push off from the side of the lounger, sitting at her feet. "It's all good." One nods with a wink, and I think I played that smooth.

"Too bad the rug tripped your ass." Thayer bursts with laughter. One frowns, shaking his head at her. I cut my eyes at Sarah, her cheeks are rosy colored. Great, she's embarrassed for me.

"Are you laughing at me?" I narrow my eyes, watching her squirm.

Her eyes flicker to Thayer. "Uhh, no. No, I wouldn't do that."

I stand, circling the chair to stop at her side. "I think you were." I cock my brow.

Her eyes wide as they cut to Thayer, I see my chance. I slide my arms under her, picking her up and throwing her into the pool. "Chord!" she screams just before she hits the water.

"Why do boys think that's funny?" Thayer huffs.

Sarah bobs out of the water. "Oh, paybacks."

"You'll have to catch me first!" I dive into the lower end of the pool. We hang out for the rest of the day, deciding to cookout later that evening. Sarah spends the night with Thayer, like she always has the first day of school.

When the bell rings, I rush downstairs, looking for Sarah. She's stunning today. After searching the halls, I'm about to give up when I run into Thayer. "Hey, where's Sar...Sutton?"

"She's out front, but I need to warn you..." My stomach knots. "Randy has her cornered."

"Cornered? Does he... like her?" My blood boils as that knot turns into a monster. A green-eyed one.

"Yes." I press my lips into a thin line, nodding. "Chord, you need to tell her."

"Tell her what? Not to be with that jackass." I grind my teeth.

"That you love her." My breath stops as I drop my head to meet her eyes.

"I'm afraid, but I'm more scared of losing her. I need to find her." I push past my sister, hauling ass through the doors.

What am I going to say? That I love her? I've always loved her, I can't think of a time I didn't. Yes, we're best friends but, to be honest, the first time I laid eyes on her, I wanted her as mine.

I'm not sure what that means at six-years-old. I do believe kids can see beyond a person's face. Hers was perfect, but there was something more about her that told me, this is it. She's your always.

I've tried talking myself out of this for years. I've fought wanting to kiss her, to tell her she's mine. Never did I think I might lose her. I guess I was hoping she'd just realize this is more than friends—it's love.

WRECKING US, SAVING YOU

I scan the area, spotting them next to the big oak tree. I can't stop myself, I put one foot in front of the other until I'm running toward her. Sarah's eyes lock on mine as I get closer.

Coming to a complete stop inches from her, I stand there, fighting the burn in my lungs and the pull of her heart with mine. I drag a deep, ragged breath in, wrapping my hand around her back, holding her against me.

"Chord?" She searches my eyes as I harness the ball of nerves twisting in the pit of my belly. Her eyes glisten as she trembles in my arms. This, it's meant to be.

I take her lips, pressing them against mine as an explosion of light flashes behind my eyes. The heat builds between our bodies as her soft lips work with mine, as if we've done this a million times.

I sweep my tongue over her plump, pink lips as she opens them freely. I tangle her hair in my right hand, molding her body to me. Her tongue swirls around mine, coaxing a long-awaited groan from me.

In the distance, I can hear catcalls and whistles. But it's a throat clearing that pulls me from her lips. "Hey, guys. You're drawing a crowd," Thayer chirps.

I unwillingly release Sarah's lips and place a light, soft peck on the swollen pucker. Laying my forehead against hers, I give her my heart. "Sarah, I'm sorry it's taken me so long to get here."

"I would've waited a lifetime." Her warm breath floats across my lips.

"I'm not sure when I fell in love with you, but I promise to never stop."

Sarah slowly lifts her lids, her eyes finding mine. "You called me Sarah."

I run my nose against hers, reveling in her touch. "You've always been my Sarah, even when you were my best friend Sutton."

"I'll always be yours." Her lips collide with mine as chills race over me.

Thayer coughs again. "Y'all, you're gonna get busted."

"She's right, we'll pick this up later." Sarah sighs. I twist our fingers together, tugging her to my side.

"Oh, Randy." I extend a fist. "Sorry, man."

Randy bumps my fist. "It's all good."

"Gracious, I'm glad that's over with. Y'all were killin' us." Thayer laughs, bringing me up short.

"What?"

She looks from me to Sarah. "We've all known you two were gonna end up together."

"Was it that obvious?" Sarah pinches her face up.

Thayer wrinkles her nose. "Yeah, pretty much."

I turn to Sarah, and her face flushes with the realization. Leaning in, I place a soft kiss on her lips. "They could've said something, saved us all this time."

She giggles against my mouth before breaking away. "Sounds like we have lost time to make up for, right?"

"You better believe it." The light dances in her eyes as I move in, taking her lips again. I don't think I'll ever get enough of her.

We walk to class, hand in hand, spending the rest of the day passing notes and flirting. We have all but two classes together, making the day go faster. I know nothing's changed yet, my heart tells me everything has.

I find myself staring at her throughout the day. I thought I knew everything there was to know about her, so why I am seeing her so differently? She's kind, even when she thinks no one is watching.

"Penny for your thoughts?" she whispers.

WRECKING US, SAVING YOU

I rouse from my daze. "You. I'm thinking about you and just how amazing you are."

"Do you have any idea what you mean to me?" She glances around the room, checking to see if there's an audience.

"Tell me." The tip of her tongue sweeps between her lips, drawing me to them.

She scoots closer, leaning in so her breath brushes past my ear. "I love you." Her words knock the breath out of me. My heart stutter steps as I see forever in her eyes.

"The girl who doesn't believe in love, is in love?" I murmur against her cheek.

Her fingers tangle with mine as she squeezes. "You make me believe anything is possible."

We break apart as the bell rings, bringing the best moment in my life to an end. I grab my backpack, throwing it over my shoulder before taking her books in one hand and her hand in the other.

5

Sarah

Two years later…

"Do y'all have any plans for Chord's birthday?" Thayer quirks her brow, smirking.

"None that I care to share, unless you want to hear about the cake I'm baking him?"

She giggles. "I can't believe he's eighteen already, time flies."

"Tell me about it! We're seniors, I'm so ready to go to college," I huff.

Thayer's brows knit. "Has your mom asked what your plans are for college?"

"You're joking, right? You know she doesn't give a shit about me. I'm ready to run as fast as my feet will carry me. I'd leave now, if I could." I crash onto her bed.

47

WRECKING US, SAVING YOU

"It won't be long, this year will fly by, I know mine did." She joins me on the bed.

I roll to my side, propping up on my hand. "Do you like Clemson?"

Her smiles grows wide. "I love it! I love being home, but I'm on my own and love the freedom."

"Ughh, I can only imagine." I sigh, falling over.

She pats my arm. "Soon enough, hang in there."

"So this party your mom is throwing, is she inviting a lot of people?" I nibble on my nail.

"Just family; with me leaving and his birthday, she wants it to be us." Thayer slides from the bed, standing in front of her suitcase.

"How much more do you have to pack?" I sit up, still chewing on my nail.

She walks over to her closet, searching through the racks. "Not much, I need to go shopping for a few things."

"Do you care if I tag along? I want to pick up one more thing for Chord."

She spins, hands on hips. "Duh! Since when do I shop without you?"

"Never." I jump from the bed. "Let's hit it."

"Alright"—she grabs her purse—"we'll stop downstairs and tell Mom."

I step out into the hall and am suddenly grabbed from behind. "Shit! Oh! You scared me."

Chord's arms are wrapped around my waist, his face buried in the back of my hair. "Listen at that mouth." I spin in his arms, smiling.

"I'll be with Mom." Thayer rolls her eyes as she slips past us.

"You like this mouth, so why are you complaining?"

Chord's sly grin warns me of his mischief, but not before I can stop him. "I've got you now."

His lips smash mine as he lifts me, stepping back into his room. He turns, closing the door with his free arm. Pushing me against the door, I wrap my legs around his waist.

Chord's shoulders are as broad as a barn now, I can't even get my hands around his biceps. He's not just shot up in height over the last two years, but he's muscle-bound as hell. Makes my mouth water.

He releases my lips for a brief second. "What are you doing? Your momma is gonna flip shit if she catches me in your room!"

He smirks and everything south of my bellybutton tightens. "I've dreamed about pinning you to this door." His nose travels down my jaw, to my neck where he nips at it. The scruff on his chin tickles as it prickles me.

I lick my lips as my mouth dries. "Oh, yeah?" I groan.

"Yes, I have. It's getting increasingly harder to keep my hands off you," he growls into my neck.

My breath becomes ragged, and I struggle to speak. "I-I think… maybe, yeah… I think we sh-should, you know…do this."

Chord stops cold, and my heart pounds in my ears as I wait for his response. "Are you sure?" He leans back, searching my eyes. "I can wait, baby. I can wait as long as you need."

I swallow past the knot in my throat. "I know we discussed waiting until we get to college, but…" I wet my lips. "I don't want to wait. I want you, in every way."

He holds me close, sweeping my hair over my shoulder. "And I want you the same way, but there's no way in hell I'll have your mom saying I'm using you. I can wait."

WRECKING US, SAVING YOU

I take his face in my hands, pressing my mouth to his. "I know, but we've been together two years, we're planning to get married, and college is an entire year away."

"I can wait, baby. You're more important than my hard-on." My mouth drops open at his frankness. I slap at his chest as we chuckle.

"Well, thank you." I kiss his tender lips.

"I better let you go before they come looking for us." He releases his hold as I drop my legs to the floor. Tiptoeing, I place a kiss on his cheek.

"I won't be long, we're only going for a few things. Besides, I want you ready to roll after the cookout your mom has planned." I slap his ass before turning to the door.

"Hey, now." He winks.

"By the way, where are we going tonight?" He narrows his eyes at me.

"It's a surprise." Smiling at me with his lopsided grin. "Just be ready, beautiful." I practically float down the stairs with a smile on my face, but apparently, that's not the only thing on my face.

Thayer's eyes bug out as I turn the corner. I stop dead in my tracks, cocking my brow. "Your shoe's untied." She points, rushing over to me. I bend over, checking my Chuck's laces. They're fine but before I can raise my head, Thayer's pulling me down.

"Your face and neck are blood red, did he try to eat you alive?" I try to stifle my laugh, but I end up snorting, making us burst into laughter.

Thayer springs from the floor, grabbing her purse. "We'll be back in a bit, bye." She wraps her hand around mine, dragging me out the door, laughing all the way.

We hit the mall wide open, stopping at every shop until I get a chance to sneak in a gift for Chord. "What'cha got there?" Thayer eyes my bag.

I wrinkle my nose. "Nothing, really." I avert my eyes to keep from telling on myself.

"Would it have anything to do with tonight?" She elbows me.

My head is shaking before I can utter a word. "Nah, it's nothing like that." Again, I window shop as we walk, doing my best to keep her at bay.

"Sarah, you're one of my best friends. I know you love Chord, I'm only wanting to make sure you two are safe." She nudges me with her shoulder.

I roll my eyes; the jig is up, I might as well come clean. "How did you know?"

"You've been together for two years, you're crazy in love, and your planning to go to the same college. It's easy to deduce—you're sleeping together." She smiles coyishly.

I sigh heavily. "We haven't, yet. I told him I wanted to, but I'm not positive we will."

She nods knowingly. "I understand, even for two people who have been together for a while, it's a big step."

"It is." I pull her to the side. "I'm on Depo and have been for a few years, my mom made me. I know it's not a reason to do it but, for the record, I want to spend the rest of my life with Chord." I take a deep breath.

"As long as you've both thought about it and he's not pressuring you." She takes my hand.

"Oh, no. He would never, he's the kindest person I know. And, Thayer, I know we're young. So many people would tell us to wait but we know this is it for us. It's me and him, no one else."

51

WRECKING US, SAVING YOU

She stares at me before a grin pushes her brows up. "I know. He loves you too. Just be safe, nothing's foolproof."

"I promise, we don't want anything to mess up our future." I wrap my arm around her, continuing to the car.

Sitting in the corner of the patio, I take in the Hamilton family. Chord's parents, Elise and Calder, are so loving. One is the epitome of the doting big brother, I actually thought it was just Thayer he treated like that, but it's his baby brother too.

Thayer beams as her brothers tease her, knowing she's their princess. She loves them unconditionally. I can't help but to be jealous from time to time, my heart's desire is to have a family. Chord tells me all the time, I already have one.

"Hey, you okay?" Chord wraps his hand around the back of my thigh, squeezing it playfully.

I work on pulling the wrinkles out of my forehead. "Yeah, I'm fine. Are you having fun?"

He gives me his most mischievous grin. "I am, but we could be having more."

"Such a perv." I wink. "But I'm down."

His eyes sparkle with playfulness. "I'm so ready to go down."

My mouth hangs open with his words, recovering only to slap at him. "You are so bad. Oh my gosh. I bet my face is blood red." I place my hands on my cheeks, hoping to cool them.

He chuckles as he leans in and whispers, "I'm sorry, I didn't mean to embarrass you," as he places a soft kiss on my nose. "Wanna get outta here?"

I bite my lip, nodding. "Yeah, I do."

"Give me five minutes." He presses his lips to mine as all those butterflies take flight.

I watch as Chord sits next to One, and Thayer blocks my sight as she joins me. "I'm assuming One's gonna help cover."

I cut my eyes from her to Chord and his brother. "No way. Oh, no. Please tell me you're joking?" I start chewing my thumbnail as I watch them talk among themselves. Chord glances at me, shifting in his seat.

"One will call him out, I bet money they're having 'that' conversation." She giggles.

"Good Lord. Please say it ain't so." A flash of heat races through my body. "I'm gonna die now."

Thayer's full-on laughing now. "It's all good, he's probably giving him the 'talk' and making sure he knows what to do."

I slam my head into the back of the lounger. "Yeah, kill me now."

"Why on earth would I do that?" I squeeze my eyes together. "Go ahead, I'm ready. Just do it."

"Not a chance, gorgeous." Chord's lips are on mine before I can respond. I open my eyes to find him hovering, his eyes twinkling. "Come on, let's hit the road."

"I'll be right behind you." One throws his hand up. I turn to him, eyes wide.

"He's, uh, letting me spend the night," he murmurs in my ear. I nod, waving at Thayer as we head out.

He holds the door to his Durango open for me; it's black as night but shines under the street lights. One meets him at the front of the SUV, mutters something, and pulls him into a hug.

He waves at me before jumping in his truck and pulling out in front of us. Chord slides into his seat, driving in the same direction as One. I'm not sure if the nervous feeling is from what we're about to do or the fact his brother may know.

We follow him around the corner and through a light. Two streets down, he pulls over with One in front of him. He unbuckles his belt, reaching for the handle.

"What's going on?"

"We need a place to sleep." He smirks at me before jumping out and running up to his brother.

Chord grabs a rectangular case from the bed of the truck, followed by a couple of sleeping bags. One meets him, taking another bag out. They walk around Chord's SUV, placing everything in the back.

"Y'all be careful and be good." Chord side-eyes me before narrowing them at his brother.

"We'll be fine, just headed out to Jordan Lake to spend some quality time together."

"What the fuck ever, take care of her." He wraps his arms around Chord, giving him a big bear hug. "Happy birthday."

One walks around to my side, making me fidget in my seat. He jerks the door open, leaning in to pull me into a hug also. "Love you, sister. Y'all be careful."

"Love you and we will, I promise to protect him from the woodland creatures." I giggle.

"Someone needs to." He laughs. As One walks away, I get a sick feeling and wrap my arms around my stomach. My mind wonders as to why he's being so protective.

Chord jumps in, buckling his belt. "You ready?" He looks over at me as I offer a tight smile. He takes my hand, shaking it slightly. "What's wrong?" He pauses. "I told you, I'm in no hurry. We can wait and just spend the night together. The first of many in our lifetime."

I tremble, not from his touch but my swarming thoughts. "I-I'm just thinking…"

He twists in his seat, staring at me until I face him. "Talk to me, or there's no reason for us to be here. We're in this together, always have been."

I suck my bottom lip in, chewing on it as I try to decide if I should say it. "Does One think I'm not good enough for you?"

He blanches as his mouth hangs open. "What?" His brow lifts. "Why would you ever think that, did he say something?"

I'm waving him off before he can go on. "No, he's been nothing but wonderful. Your entire family has always treated me good."

"Then why would you think that?" His body grows stiff.

"I don't know." I shrug. "He just kept talking to you, like he was upset. Did you tell him?" I drop my head, picking at imaginary lint on my shorts.

WRECKING US, SAVING YOU

Chord tugs on my hand, but I'm reluctant to look at him. When I do, he gives me a sweet smile. "No, I wouldn't share our private information. He assumed, since I asked him to be my alibi. As far as everyone knows, you're going home and I'm following him to spend the night at his place."

"So he knows?" I rub my forehead.

"He talked to me about protection, making sure I respected you, and..." he side-eyes me, "...that I make sure you're comfortable and... satisfied, if anything were to happen." He grimaces as I fall back into the seat, covering my face as it glows bright red.

"Oh my god. I'm dying!" I scream. "I'll never be able to face your family again."

"Sarah... Sarah..." Chord pulls my hand free, bending to get in my face. "I plan to do all of that because I love you. If the conversation is too much to talk about, it may be a good sign that we're not ready."

I rub my sweating palms on the seat, tilting my head. "I have faith in nothing. I'm unsure of everything, but there's one thing I know without a doubt—I believe in us. When I have no one or nothing, I turn to you and my heart is home."

Chord leans in, taking my lips with a desire so heated a fire sparks deep in my core. I fist his hair, smashing his mouth to mine. His tongue swirls over mine, and I'm lost in the heat building between us.

I fight for air, breaking our connection. "Come on, let's go."

He releases me, buckling his belt. He takes my hand in his after turning the truck on, returning to the road. The park is dark by the time we get there, but Chord's thought of everything.

"I'm gonna leave the Durango's lights on while we set up."

I slide from the SUV, following him to the back. "Hand me something."

He does a double take. "I've got it, this stuff is heavy."

"Didn't we just talk about being in this together?"

He stares blankly for a second. "We did, you can carry the sleeping bags." He reaches in, handing me the bags.

"By the way, you do know how to put a tent up, right?" I quirk my brow.

His eyes grow wide. "It doesn't just pop up?"

My mouth goes slack. "Please tell me you're joking."

He narrows his eyes. "Who do you think put the tent up for all those years in the backyard?" He flexes his arms. Wowza, he's built so fine.

"You did not! No way!" I snicker as I pick at him.

"I did with One or Dad's help, they knew we loved it. Where else could we hunt ghosts?" He chuckles, making me laugh as I walk toward the camp area.

"True, but today, I'm all the help you're getting…" I hesitate, glancing over my shoulder, "…and I don't plan to hunt ghosts."

We double time setting the tent up, we toss the air mattress in, waiting for it to fill up. I roll out the sleeping bags, tossing the pillows on top. Chord fixes our camp light after handing me the cooler and snacks.

Chord peeks in. "You all set?"

"I am." I smile.

He hits the lock on the truck and crawls in, joining me on the bed. "It's a little chillier than I thought it was gonna be. Are you warm enough?"

My tongue sweeps over my lips, looking at him from under hooded eyes. "I'm kinda hot actually."

He drags his eyes down my body. "I can see that."

WRECKING US, SAVING YOU

I can feel my cheeks redden, mimicking the fire in my lower belly. "You can?"

He tucks a strand of hair behind my ear before caressing my jaw. His thumb rubs over my cheekbone. "Since the day I met you, you've been the most beautiful girl I've ever laid my eyes on."

His lips brush against mine as I release a breathless moan. "I've loved you for so long, but I never imagined having you."

"Why would you think something like that, Sarah?" he asks, kissing me softly.

"I'm not worth it, I'm not good enough for you." A tear rolls down my cheek as I admit my deepest thought, my fear.

Chord's lips press into my cheek, drying it. "You're my soul mate, you'll always be exactly what I need."

"I love you." I fist his hair, smashing our mouths together.

His hand slides around my back, pulling me closer. When his tongue sweeps over mine, I gasp, giving into him. Our bodies tangle as the heat grows between us. Panting as we melt into one, kissing as if we never had.

I tug his shirt, pushing it up his back as I hitch my leg around his waist. His hand runs from my knee down to my ass, groping it as he begins to grind into me. My soaked panties stick to my shorts.

I thrust my hips into his every push, our tongues fighting for the same resolve. We break as I rip his shirt over his head. I gasp as I run my hands down his hard torso to the button on his jeans.

I peek up at him, his eyes watching my every move. When he glances at me, I can see the war in his eyes. "No more waiting and wanting, I need you, now."

Chord's mouth crashes to mine as I work his jeans open, reaching in to fist his cock. This time, he's the one moaning. "Are you sure?"

I lick my lips as I stroke him. "Oh, yeah. I'm positive."

"Let's get you outta these clothes." He sits up on his knees, pulling me with him. I tug my shirt over my head, revealing one of two of his presents. "The fuck, Sarah?"

My simple, white lace demi bra is just the beginning. "Present one." I raise my brow, leaning back on my elbows, I shimmy from my shorts.

Chord's gaze blazes a path down my stomach to my matching panties. He sighs heavily as the fire behind his eyes ignite. "Damn, you're the most beautiful thing I've ever seen," he says as he runs his hand over my pussy.

My legs spread of their own accord as he slips his finger under the lace. He sinks into my wet center, rubbing my swollen clit. I buck from the mattress, digging my fingers into his biceps. "Chord," I beg, breathlessly.

His eyes meet mine when he slides two fingers into me. My mouth hangs open as I clench around him. I push at his jeans, trying to peel them from him. He leans over me, placing his mouth on my breast.

Sweeping the tip of his tongue between my flesh and the material, the warmth from his mouth ignites the spark in my belly. Heat spreads over me when his tongue glides over my hardened nipple.

He rises, leaving me wanting and cold. Stripping his pants, he takes his shorts with them. I get my first full look at Chord. His abs tight, legs hard, and his cock bobbing with heaviness.

I follow his every move as he crawls between my legs, sitting close enough his cock brushes against me. His eyes once again on mine. I know what he's asking before he says a word. "Yes, I want this." I sigh. "I take the shot, Mom made me start a few years ago."

"I came prepared, in case." He holds a condom between his thumb and finger.

WRECKING US, SAVING YOU

My eyes flicker between it and his face. "It's up to you, I've never done this and never will with anyone else." He drops the foil package as he presses his mouth to mine.

"I feel exactly the same way, Sarah." His lips are on mine as his thighs push my legs open wider.

I gasp as he slowly slides into me, the intrusion burning as it stretches me. Chord never takes his eyes off mine, even when he pauses for me to adjust. I wrap my leg around him and with a final push, he breaks through.

My breath hitches as the pain registers, and Chord stops, watching me closely. "Am I hurting you?" I close my eyes, taking in the moment.

The pressure of his cock filling me astonishes me as to how well we fit together. I nod, biting my lip. "No, you feel so good."

He withdraws slightly, slowly, before sliding back again. The drag, branding me with each push and pull becomes easier. His bump pounding into my grind. I throw my other leg around him, squeezing as his pace picks up.

He takes my mouth with a groan as a bright light flashes behind my eyes, biting my lip as I climb my orgasm. I moan as Chord grunts, groaning with one last thrust. We lay there, tangled together, sated and fascinated.

His breath warms my neck as I try to calm my racing heart. When his cheek rubs mine, I force my eyes open to find him staring down at me. "I love you, Sarah Beth Sutton."

I kiss his sweet lips but can't help myself. "Now you say my full name."

He shakes his head. "Whatever, I love you."

"I love you." He takes me in his arms, holding me close as he rolls to his side.

LEAONA LUXX

Sleep takes me fast for the first time in my life. I can't remember when I've ever felt safer or more at home. I want to spend the rest of my life right here next to Chord.

7

Chord

New Year's Day—Four months later

My phone buzzes just as the light turns green. I hit the speaker. "Hello."

"Mini-me, what the hell are you doing?" He wishes.

I come to stop at the next light. "Fighting traffic. What's up?"

"Where you been?" The sound of the ocean fights for time with his deep baritone.

"Dropping Sarah off at home, if you can call it that," I grumble. "Her mom is a piece of fucking work. I don't know what I'll do if she hits Sarah again, I swear, One, I hate her."

"I hear ya, not much longer and we'll all be outta there," One grumbles.

62

"So you're going? Does Mom know yet?" I wait, knowing he's fighting his own war at the moment.

"I'm gonna come by this evening, let her know my plans."

"You want to know what I think?"

He chuckles. "I'm not sure I have a choice."

I swallow past the knot in my throat. "It's time to get the hell away from Raleigh. Your crazy ass ex has put you through enough, and you deserve a chance to be happy."

He's quiet for the longest time. "What do you think I should do with the company?" he murmurs.

I pull into our driveway, turning off the Durango. "One, it's your business. Your dad left it to you and you know Dad loves you. He'll help any way he can, but it's time to stop allowing other people to dictate your life."

He huffs, "Aren't you the little brother?"

"I am, but I'm also the smartest." I laugh. "Seriously, do what you want. Keep it with the right man as supervisor, start a smaller business down there."

"The smart-assed, maybe." I laugh harder. "Maybe I should call Dad."

Cal is my father, but One's stepfather. His dad died before he was born, leaving his company to my brother. Being twelve years older than me, some would think we wouldn't be close, but that's not the case.

"Weren't you thinking of going residential and allowing the commercial to stay here?"

"I was," he sighs, "but I'll still have to learn the entire business. I wouldn't mind doing both down here."

"Well, it sounds like you've got a plan and Dad's just the guy to help. You know he loves you just like he does me and Thayer."

WRECKING US, SAVING YOU

"I know. So y'all still going to Clemson?" He's asking about Sarah too.

I smirk, thinking of getting her away from her horrible life here. "We are! Actually, we can't wait. The sooner May gets here, the better. We're gonna spend the week with Thayer, hunt us a place, and start our life together."

"You're gonna live together before you get married? Good luck telling Mom," he grunts, amused. The subject of marriage still stings him. I pray one day, that changes.

"Sarah refuses to marry me right after high school or I'd do it now." I sigh. "She wants us to grow and make sure we can make it. I think she's afraid but using the excuse we're too young."

"Look, I know you think I'm completely against marriage, I'm not. I do, however, agree with her. There's no harm in waiting, if y'all are meant to be, God'll make a way." A shiver washes over me, I suppose he's right.

"I know, I just want to protect her." I rest my head back. "I really do love her, there'll never be anyone else."

"I hear ya. Four years or less, I think Sarah's got it right," he chirps up. "Maybe, two years living together and then y'all can get married."

"That's a thought. So you comin' home tonight?"

"Tomorrow, I need to check a few things out now that I know what I want to do." He sounds better, more upbeat.

"Alright, be careful."

"You be careful, you know what I mean." His voice is low.

"Dude, do not go there. We're good."

"I'm just sayin', if you ever need money or help buying anything, let me know. No questions asked." I shake my head, he's terrible at being sneaky.

64

"I know this is your way to find out my business, but you're the one who told me to keep my private life with Sarah between me and Sarah. So thanks, but we're good."

"Huh, you do listen." He chuckles. "Okay, love ya, little shit."

"Love you, brother." I end the call, itching to text Sarah but I wait. It's just knowing that I can call her when I want to now, that I love. Just as I slide from my seat, my phone rings again.

"What the fuck now, man?" I answer without looking.

"First, you shouldn't answer your phone that way, you never know who it might be. Second, I'm not a man. I'd prove it, but I'm not there. And third, I think you already know I'm not a man since you left my thighs sore last night." Sarah's voice drops with each word, leaving her sounding sultry and freakin' hot.

"Who is this?" I can't hold in my laughter as she screams my name over the phone.

"Chord Averette Hamilton," she growls. "I'm gonna kick your ass."

"I'm kidding! You know you're the only woman not related to me with my number."

"Am I? I'm not so sure about that," she huffs.

"Yes, you are." I pause. "It's good to hear from you."

She giggles. "You just dropped me off, but she's not home so I wanted to talk."

"You can call anytime."

"Yeah, I thought so. My gorgeous man bought me a cell for Christmas. I think he wants to keep tabs on me," she whispers.

"He's a smart man, as beautiful as you are." I walk in the door, taking the stairs two at a time. Shutting the door behind me, I hurry to my bed.

WRECKING US, SAVING YOU

"I hate I'm here," she grumbles as I make myself comfortable.

"Me too." I turn my face into my pillow, where her scent still lingers. "I can smell you on my bed."

"I can't believe Thayer didn't wake up, you were making so much noise." She laughs again. "Thank God your parents' room is on the other side of the house."

"Oh because you were so timid," I tease. "Let's talk about something else or you're gonna have to talk sexy to me so I can handle this thing."

"What in the hell? You are such a perv, calm yourself." Sarah has no clue how many times I've done it to the sound of her voice. She's hot as hell, and a man's gotta do what he's gotta do.

"I hate you're there alone, but I'm happy she's not home."

She sighs heavily. "I know what you mean, I wished she'd stay gone."

"You could come live with us." I chew on my lip, knowing what she'll say.

"She'd never let that happen, it's gonna be hard to get away from her after graduation. She thinks she owns me until July." She's quiet, making me worry.

"We'll get outta here, I promise. Whatever I need to do, as soon as we graduate, we'll run away if we have to, but you'll not be there another minute to be treated bad," I growl through my teeth. I wasn't raised to hit a woman, but her mom makes me want to find an excuse.

"You promise, Chord?" She sniffles, breaking my heart into a million pieces.

"Me and you, forever."

"Thank you, I'll never be able to repay you." Her breath hitches.

"Repay me? Sarah, I love you, there's no debt." I sigh heavily. "My love comes freely, it always will."

66

"I love you, I do." She hiccups with a giggle. "Oh, yeah. Please remember, I have to get my shot tomorrow."

"I remember, it's in my phone from when you set the last reminder."

"You still have my birth control dates in your phone?" Her voice shakes.

"I do. It's not just your responsibility." I clear my throat. "Which is another reason I should be driving you to the Free Clinic. I'd prefer you go to the doctor closer, but you also won't let me pay for it."

"You make my heart pound. I'll be fine. It's downtown and then school. I'll be done before you know I'm gone." She sighs. "I love you."

"I love you, most." The phone goes silent and with it, my heart sinks.

I hate leaving her there, alone or with her mom. She brings the trashiest people around; they're drunk or on drugs and wander into Sarah's room as she sleeps. They've woken her up, arguing. It's a shit show at best.

I wanted to put her on my phone plan, but if her mom finds out she'll take it from her. Because leaving your daughter alone without any way to get help is the right thing to do. She's even thrown away clothes we've bought Sarah.

I decided this Christmas, I'd get her a Go Phone. Inexpensive and easy to hide, giving Sarah a little peace of mind. I can get to her in under six minutes if needed or she can call the police, neither an option before now.

I lay there, thinking about her and our future when my phone vibrates with a text.

Night, love you. ~S

My heart races at the realization she's thinking of me too.

WRECKING US, SAVING YOU

Good night, love you most.

I toss and turn until late, I'm not even sure when I fall asleep. I slap at the alarm, trying to wake up. The minute my phone vibrates I force one eye open to say hello to my girl.

Mornin'. ~S

Good morning, gorgeous.

How'd you sleep? ~S

Horrible. How was your night?

She's still not home. ~S

When are you leaving?

Seven thirty. Should be at school by ten. ~S

I hate I can't take you.

I'll be alright. Love you. ~S

Text me. Love you most.

I drag ass to the shower, hoping it'll wake me up. I'm dressed and out the door by seven. I hate being here without her, it doesn't feel right. I think the longest we've ever been apart has been a weekend.

But that's changed now, we spend every weekend together and several weeknights. She hates going home, there's a different guy every week. They've hit her and hit on her. Lisa's usually too inebriated to care.

I sit in homeroom waiting to hear from her. Sure enough, I get the notification.

I'm here. See you soon. ~S

Please be careful.

Will do. Love you. ~S

Love you most.

LEAONA LUXX

That girl wrecks my soul, I love her so much. I hate she went by herself and that I let her ride the bus. When Thayer's home, she gives her a ride but Sarah was afraid someone would see us. Like I care?

The morning drags by, and I'm having trouble concentrating. With each class she misses, my concern deepens. This is the exact reason I should've gone with her, needless worrying. By lunch, there's still no word from her. I'm starting to freak the fuck out.

Hey, where are you?

Everything alright?

Sarah, I'm getting worried.

Baby, you okay?

Nothing. I've texted every ten minutes and haven't heard a word. I know it sounds extreme, but she's never taken this long. The clinic is in a rough part of the city, what if something did happen?

By two that afternoon, I'm full-on freaking the hell out. There's still no word, she hasn't answered one text. And all I can think of is driving to her house. I have to know if she's alright.

The bell rings, and I spring from my seat. I full out run to my SUV, jerking the door open so hard it looks like it's about to come off the hinges. I dial her number as I start the vehicle, no answer.

I call Thayer, not giving a damn where she is. I need to find Sarah. "Hey, brother."

"Thayer, have you talked to Sarah?"

"Well, hello. And no, I haven't." She pauses. "Wait, I think she called, but I was in class." I wait, trotting my leg so hard my Durango shakes. "Yeah, she called around twelve thirty. It doesn't look like she left a message."

"What about a text? Did she send you anything?" My voice trembles as I rush my words.

"No, no texts. What's going on, Chord?" Her voice is low and calm. For now.

"She went to the clinic, it was time for her checkup. She wouldn't let me drive her, she was afraid someone would see us. What the fuck? Where could she be? I should've taken her." I fist my hair, slamming my head against the seat.

"Calm down, give me a minute and I'll see if I can get in touch with her. In the meantime, ask Mom or even One." Thayer's words are a little more rushed than before, she's worried now. Good, it's not just me.

"Fine. Go." I end the call, immediately dialing Mom.

"Hello, love," Mom answers in her sing-song way.

"Mom, Sarah had an appointment today, then she was supposed to be at school by ten or so. I can't find her, has she called you?"

"No, Chord. I haven't heard from her. Where'd she have to go?" I squeeze my eyes tight. I'd rather not have this conversation but to hell with it, Sarah's more important.

"The clinic downtown, she had to get her birth control."

There's a brief silence before she speaks. "I would've taken her, she shouldn't go down there by herself."

"I offered, but she was worried people would talk. For Christ's sake, I don't care. Mom, we're sleeping together, we have been for several months." There, said it. I don't give a shit about anything but finding her.

"Chord, I've raised three, I know what sex is and who's having it. I'm proud of you both for being proactive." I'm speechless. "Let me call and see if they will tell me anything. I doubt it, but I'll try."

"Thanks, Mom. Thayer's trying to text her, I'm gonna try One."

"I'll call you. Love you." Mom ends the call before I can. If Sarah only knew how much we all loved her. I hit speed dial for my brother.

WRECKING US, SAVING YOU

"Hey, what's up?" One answers on the second ring.

"Sarah's missing. She had an appointment downtown and was coming to school after, she never showed. Has she called you?" I stutter through half of my words, I'm so panicked.

"No, nothing. What about Thayer or Mom?" His voice is rough, then a door shuts.

"They haven't heard anything, why do you think I'm checking with you? I'm going to her house, I have to know if she's okay."

"I'm still in town." His truck revs up. "I'll be home in ten."

"I'm still at school, I'm leaving now." Thayer beeps in. "Hey, that's sis."

"Let me know." One sounds as freaked as I do. My head feels light making me sick at my stomach. We all know this isn't Sarah, she would never do this.

"Talk to me."

"Nothing, brother. Are you sure she was coming to school after?" I know Thayer's trying to help, but so help me—I can't with this.

"Yes, I'm positive. You know she would tell me," I growl.

"Okay, alright. Just double checking." She sighs. "What are you doing?"

"I just turned onto the highway, I'm hauling ass to her house."

"Please be careful, you know how Lisa feels about you," Thayer warns me with good intentions.

"Fuck her, like she gives a shit about Sarah," I bark at her. "I'm sorry. I'm fucking scared."

"Brother, I'm scared too. But you have to calm down, you're not gonna do her any good being this upset." She tries to calm me as best she can, but it's not helping.

"I know!" I yell as the light turns green, and I spin my tires.

"Chord, slow down. You'll not be any help if you wreck." Her voice wavers as my stomach takes a pitfall.

I turn into her mobile home park, driving straight to her place. I shove my stick into park, licking my dry lips. "I'm here, give me five." I don't even let her answer before hanging up and jumping from my SUV.

I scan the area, looking for anyone who can tell me anything. Nothing, it's like no one's home. I take the steps two at a time. Pounding on the door the second I can. No answer.

I walk around the trailer, checking doors and windows, but there's no sign of anyone. I rub my forehead, my heart racing. I close my eyes, trying to regain my senses. "Go home, maybe she'll call," I convince myself.

I drive the long way home, searching every bus stop and bench in the city. She's nowhere to be found. There's still no texts or a call. I've never been so pissed and frightened at the same time in my life. "Please, Lord, let her be alright. She means… everything to me." I wipe the fledgling tears away as I make my way home.

I'm not even parked before One's at my door. I shake my head. "She wasn't there, One." When my brother wraps his arms around me, I allow my fears to take me, and I cry.

"She's gonna be alright, we'll find her." He pats my back, trying to calm my trembling body.

"Chord," Dad calls my name, helping me to pull myself together. "We can't make a formal report until tomorrow. Come on in, let me write down what you know."

"Baby boy, come in, you're a mess." Mom slips her arm around my waist as One releases his hold.

"I know something's wrong, I can feel it." I stumble through the door.

WRECKING US, SAVING YOU

We spend the rest of the evening going over everything I know. Her texts, where she was going, and the last time anyone heard from her. It was Thayer, she called my sister last. I'm a little surprised as to how I feel about that fact.

Watching as the sky turns dark, my body quakes with fear. Sarah hates the night, with good reason. I try to keep my mind busy, thinking of what could be happening to her has me freaking out.

I pace the foyer, waiting as Dad's friend to arrive, he's a detective. I refused to go to school today. It's been twenty-four hours since I've heard from Sarah. I couldn't even sleep last night, so school isn't a priority.

I sprint to the door when I hear a car in the driveway. "Hi, I'm Chord. Thank you so much for coming." I'm shaking his hand before he can get out his door.

"Good to meet you, I'm Detective Eddie Long." He nods and I back up, giving him space to move.

"Hey, Eddie. Thank you for coming, I see you've met Chord." Dad stands at the door as I show him in.

"I did." He takes my dad's hand. "Where we doing this?"

"This way." I point to the family room where everyone is, even Thayer. She drove back home early this morning.

An hour later, the detective has all of our information and he's on his way to find out what he can. "Fair warning, she's a minor and without the police or a court order, I may be limited to what I can find out."

"I understand. I hate it because her mom doesn't give a shit about her." I swallow past the rising nausea.

We wait for what feels like hours, hoping to hear anything. Sarah still hasn't called or texted me, it's like she's vanished. I jump when the house phone rings. I run to answer the phone, putting it on speaker.

"Hello?"

"Hi, this is Eddie. Is this Chord?" His voice is monotone.

"Yes, we're all here. Do you know anything?" My stomach knots as I bite my lip.

"Here's what we know and please remember, I called in a few favors, so this is top secret," he explains.

"Meaning?" I don't have it in me to play cops.

"We broke more than a few laws." I smirk, that's cool with me. "Sarah did arrive at the clinic. She was seen by a provider and left around ten yesterday morning. The hit from her cell showed she was at or around a bus stop near the clinic."

"Wait. So she didn't call a cab?" I rub my temples, allowing the information to sink in.

"No, she did not. She took bus 211 south and got off around Lake Wheeler Road." His neutral tone is driving me insane when suddenly, it hits me.

"She went home?" I shift my feet, racking my brain as to why she'd go home.

"It looks that way. Her cell hit off a tower near there when she called Thayer." Then why wasn't she there when I went after school?

"I drove by yesterday, no one was around." I fist my hands, praying the pang in my stomach goes away. I can't shake the feeling that I'm never going to see her again.

"The place was still dark when we checked it. I'm sorry, but that's where her trail ends." His words cut through me like a knife, my chest constricts, and I struggle to breathe.

"No. There's no way in hell she'd ever leave me, something's wrong. I'm telling you!" I hold my head as my world spins outta control. "I can't breathe, I need some air." I bolt for the front door.

WRECKING US, SAVING YOU

Pacing, I begin to feel sick. Bile rises as fast as my feet will carry me to the edge of the grass where I lose the contents of my stomach. I clean my mouth with the back of my hand.

"No." I shake my head vigorously. "She wouldn't leave me. I'm telling you, I know her better than anyone. She didn't run away or disappear on her own. I just know it."

I check my pockets, finding my keys. I bound for the Durango, pulling away before One can get to me. "Chord! Wait!" he yells as I drive like a bat out of hell to her house, running lights and losing my shit all the way there.

Turning into the park, I race to her place. Slamming on my brakes, I slide to a stop. I'm out of the door shortly after coming to a rest. I leap onto the porch, banging on the door until I rattle the windows.

I spin, looking around to see if I can find anyone to talk to. I jump from the front porch, running around the back. My heart pounds in my ears as I rear back and kick the fucking back door in.

"Sarah?" I hurry to her bedroom, she's not there. "Sarah!" There's a bedroom on the other end of the mobile home. I rush to search the room, there's nothing in her mom's room.

I walk back to her room, searching for any sign of her or that she was here. "Please, Sarah. Tell me something." I lift her blanket, checking her bed. In the corner of the room are the clothes she had on Sunday. I step over her textbooks laying on the floor.

"Textbooks?" I bend down, moving the pile. "I know for a fact she had these in her school bag." I gasp, "Her phone." I pick it up, checking to see if there's anything on it. "Fuck, it's dead." I fall onto her bed, my hands in my hair as I cry out, *"Please, tell me something!"* My words are laced with venom as the most horrific images race through my mind. I stare at the contents of her backpack splayed on the floor in front of me. I kick the stack of books for taunting me.

76

A white envelope sticks out from the side of her biology book. I rub my eyes with my palms, trying to see clearly. I squint to make out the word, and my heart sinks. I fall to my knees, reaching for the paper.

My name is clearly written on the front in her handwriting. I try to slow my breathing as my palms begin to sweat. I carefully open the sealed letter, pulling it free. Unfolding it, I close my eyes and send up a prayer.

I focus on the words, and my hands tremble. Two paragraphs in, I scramble from the floor, running to the opened back door. I vomit until I dry heave. My head spins with the words she's written on notebook paper.

"You should've called me!" I cry out, knowing she's gone and there's not a damn thing I can do to help her.

I pull myself together enough to go back to her room. I pick the paper up and grab her phone. Trudging to the Durango, I gather myself for a few minutes before I can drive away. I don't care what anyone thinks of me, I'm broken.

"I know this wasn't your choice, Sarah."

Numb, I don't know how I manage to get home. I'm standing at my front door, broken and defeated. I reach for the knob as it swings wide. I stare blankly at One, lost and confused. I open my mouth, but nothing comes out.

One steps toward me, wrapping me in his arms. My legs buckle as the world goes black. I can't breathe. I want to die. Without her, I have no meaning. No true north to find my way back.

Present day—Six years later

I whip into the first spot I see. I'm in a hurry and need to hit the road. My brother asked me to stop by his office, so this better be fast. I push the door open, tripping the chime. "Hey, where you at?"

One walks out of the back hall, holding his newest daughter in his arms. "Hey, brother." Sliding my sunglasses on top of my head, I follow him to his office. He turns, handing my niece over. "Five minutes, I'll grab your paperwork."

"Tierney looks just like Lea, strawberry hair and all. Don't you, baby girl?" I coo at the precious bundle in my arms.

"She is, attitude and all. You wake her up, you can take her with you." One glares at me over the paper he's holding.

"Where is Lea?" My sister-in-law is a superpower, badass all the way. She's exactly what One needed.

"The twins had well visits. No way the newborn is going to a clinic with other kids possibly sick." One peeks up at his snoozing daughter.

"Do y'all do a roll call at dinner? Or do you have a whistle you blow and they come running?" I snicker, picking on my brother has become an art form.

One narrows his eyes. "Smartass. We have six kids, six. Not ten or twelve, six."

"Technically, you have nine." I add his daughters-in-law as I run my finger over Tierney's tiny hand. "And if Lea hadn't stopped you, who knows how many y'all would have." I waggle my brows as he flips me off. I pop my mouth open, pretending to be offended. "Not in front of the baby."

He starts to say something when the phone rings, he grabs it on the first ring. "Malone Woods." He's all professional as he cuts his eyes at me. "She's out of the office, but I can leave her a message. Will do, thank you."

"Thayer coming in?"

"Yeah, she's dropping Holden off to Mom." At this point, my family took 'go forth and multiply' way too seriously. "Hadlea said this is what's left to be delivered. She'll be there Tuesday to set you up." He hands the paper to me to look over.

"Looks good." I tap the paper on the chair arm. "Is it weird I have a big house but no family?"

"I don't think so." He takes the list from me. "How much longer do you have until you hear about your real estate exam?"

"Any time now, I'm getting excited."

"It'll be good to have you. Being your own boss is great—less bullshit, more beer." He raises his brows with a smile.

WRECKING US, SAVING YOU

"I'll keep that in mind." I know I worried everyone, taking so long to decide on a direction in life. So I sucked it up and pretended to move on.

"Where you off to tonight?" he asks as he sends a text.

"Charleston, Alden's playing down there. I thought one last road trip before the real work begins."

"Don't run into any trouble down there, if you're gonna drink, don't drive." Always the big brother.

"Yes, mother." I snicker. "Speaking of running, I'd better hit the road." I stand as he shuffles a few things on his desk.

"One more thing…" His eyes flicker from me to the paper. "Eddie sent a monthly report."

It takes me by surprise, causing me to catch my breath. I swallow past the lump in my throat. "And? Nothing?" He shakes his head. "You know, you'd think I'd get used to hearing it." I rub my chin, trying to steady myself.

"I don't see why you would, it wrecks me every time." He stands, moving to my side. "Don't let it get to you, there's always another day."

"Yeah, I know." I kiss Tierney's head and lay her in his arms.

"Be good and stay away from trouble. You pick them like I used to. Love ya."

"I did it right once, that's the only chance I get." I lean in for a quick hug. "Love y'all."

I head to my SUV, ready to get on the road when Thayer pulls in beside me. "What's up, darlin'?" I throw my arms around her, hugging her tight.

"You leaving already?" She pulls back, straightening my shirt.

"Yeah, I'm headed down to Charleston. Gonna hang out with Alden for the night, I'll be back tomorrow."

"Be careful." She pats my chest. "Love the new ride." She jerks her head toward my Land Rover Discovery.

"I do too, but Tiffany calls it a 'Spoiled Brat Mobile'."

"She's such a bitch." My mouth pops open, making her giggle. She's never liked any of the girls I've dated. But then again, I haven't either.

"She is," we say in unison, laughing.

"I'll call when I get back, I need to come see Holden. Tierney gave me the feels." I clutch my chest, smiling.

"Sounds good, love you." She waves as I slide into my seat.

I return her wave. "Love you."

I pull onto Highway Seventeen, taking Sixty-five until I hit the interstate. I'm about two and a half hours away from Charleston. We moved to Cherry Grove my senior year, following One when he decided to move here.

Thayer joined us after she finished Clemson. She married One's best friend, but not before getting engaged to Walker Pennington. Fun times, I tell you. Hardy's a good guy though, he loves Thayer and Holden.

I'm staying at The Belmond Charleston Place. It's about twenty minutes from the venue, but it's the best in town. I settle in, Google directions to the club, and check my messages.

When my phone vibrates, I can't control the eye roll. I know who it is, and I hate answering it. "Chord Hamilton."

"It's about time. I was beginning to wonder if you were ditching me," Alden yells through the phone. The music in the background is blasting.

"I apologize about that, I'm working on emails."

"It's all good, we're doing sound checks." The music stops in the middle of his sentence. "Sorry. So when you gettin' here?"

"Around nine, right before you go on."

"Sounds good. I'm leaving you a VIP badge at the front. Just tell them who you are and then head on up." He's excited. I don't blame him, this is a great opportunity for him. They say this club is one of the best on the east coast.

"Will do." I pause, checking the club's website out. "Let's check the Dungeon out after you're done."

"I hear you. I'm all about it." Alden's always up for anything, especially if it has to do with women.

Dungeons and Dragons is the up and coming club in the entertainment community. Its structure is built like an old Brownstone with a bar on the main floor and a strip club in the basement, hence Dungeons.

No one can decide if it's a marketing nightmare or ingenious, but it's definitely drawing a crowd. Prime real estate in the right district. I arrive a few minutes before nine, heading up to the second floor.

Alden's in his dressing room, so I hit him up. "Hey, man. You've got a packed house. You ready?"

I offer my fist for him to bump it, smiling. "Ready and willing. How ya doin'?"

"Good, I think this might be what you've been needing. It's a good platform, country or rock."

"Can't you just be my manager?" He cocks his head.

"Trust me, I'd already have you locked down. But it's not my thing, I'd have you in the bumfucked part of town." I laugh.

"I love you too." He winks as I shake my head.

"Get at it, I'm gonna grab a seat." I throw my thumb over my shoulder.

"Aight." He holds his fist out to me. "Let's crash the Dungeon after."

"Sounds like a plan. Do work." I pat his shoulder and head downstairs.

I met Alden Beck through my sister's ex, Walker Pennington. Alden's been working the club and bar scene for a few months; he's good. Someone needs to sign him and stop dragging ass.

I film a few songs for Alden to use as demos and enjoy the rest of the show nursing the same drink I got when I walked in. I've never been much of a drinker, but I play the part.

Alden works his way through the crowd toward me after he finishes his set. "Great job, man. I got the good stuff, you should get picked up."

"Sounds awesome." He throws back the drink in his hand. "You still up to checking out downstairs?"

"Hell yes, I'm ready to check out some ass that won't drive me crazy. Well, not in a bad way."

We're checked at the top of the landing, the steps are well lit but the further down we go, the darker it gets. The smoke machine is working overtime as lights flash to the beat of the music.

The medieval theme is carried throughout with cuffs and chains hanging from the walls. The stone tables are surrounded by large wooden chairs. The bartenders dressed in hooded capes with leather vests.

Dancers are placed strategically around the room with the main runway down the center. With the smaller areas, it gives a more sophisticated vibe. The ladies aren't totally stripped, some are topless.

It's packed, leaving us with only one option for seats. First table to the right of the runway, it's tucked next to the bar. Easy to watch, hard to be seen. It's not grouped with other tables, so no personal show, just the runway.

"So, what'cha think?" Alden asks as he motions for a waitress.

"I can see the draw, they've got a good thing here."

"Drink?" He points to the brunette standing to the side of the table. She's wearing a black leather corset and a lace high-low skirt.

"Yes, I'll have an Old Fashioned." She winks at me as she takes my order.

"Jack and Coke." Alden elbows me with a smile as the waitress sashays away. "Damn, she's got more junk in her trunk than treasure in her chest."

I burst into laughter, cocking my brow at his saying. "What the fuck? That may be the worst analogy ever."

"Nah, dude. It's fire." He touches his arm, shaking his hand as he pretends he's hot.

"Whatever helps you sleep at night."

The music switches, drawing our attention to the stage. Post Malone's *Rockstar* blasts through the speakers as a gorgeous redhead takes the runway. She rocks on a chair, grinding and swaying her hips.

Her hair flows down her back, swinging with every pitch and roll of her body. Her neck is elongated as she thrusts her breasts forward. She stretches her legs around the chair, squatting. Her ass is prime real estate all on its own.

She's wearing a black vest with rhinestone panties, her breasts strain the buttons. But not for long. She stands, ripping it open to reveal a rhinestone string bra. Her nipples peek out from the side of sparkling thread.

She works the stage, spinning on the pole, bumping and grinding the floor, sliding across it like it's wet glass. Every man in the room is all eyes on red. I've got to say, she's giving me a reason to stare.

She bites her full bottom lip as it turns crimson, picking and choosing who gets to watch her licking the red and swollen pout. Her body moves like she's making love, closing her eyes when she can.

"Fuck me, please," Alden murmurs.

"Damn straight." He elbows me with a shit-eating grin. When her eyes meet mine, I shudder. Chills raise the hair on the back of my neck. My blood begins to boil, rushing through my body like a wildfire. I'd know those blue eyes anywhere.

I spring from my seat, knocking it over. Dazed, I lose my footing as I shuffle back, catching myself against the wall. My chest tightens, leaving me breathless. I steady myself again as my head spins and I spiral out of control.

"Chord, you alright?" Alden stands next to me, but he sounds a million miles away.

She freezes, caught in a time warp. I narrow my eyes, trying to calculate what kind of hell this is and if it's even real. Her eyes incinerate me, she knows it as well as I do. A sudden coldness builds deep in my core.

She spins, rushing from the stage without finishing her routine. I push the table to the side, running after her. "Stop!"

A fire coils in my gut. "Damn it, stop!" I dodge the security guard, grabbing her by the arm. A current courses through my veins, stinging us both. The word rolls off my tongue, blistering me as it falls from my mouth.

"*Sarah?*" Her name, once a hymn to my soul, now a curse on my lips.

She looks over her shoulder, cutting her eyes at me. A heavy feeling roots me to the spot. My skin crawls as a tingle creeps over me. When she turns, I gasp, staring deep into her eyes.

"I-I'm sorry." Her eyes glisten, leaving me speechless. The one person I thought I would never see again stands in front of me. I'm already gone.

"You disappeared." I shudder from our proximity. A tear rolls down her cheek, and my chest is so tight as I struggle for air.

WRECKING US, SAVING YOU

"Sutton, you alright?" A big, broad and brooding man glares at me as he stands beside her. He has no idea what I'm capable of at this moment.

She nods, swallowing hard. "Yeah, he's with me." She looks toward a door, motioning for me to follow. "Outside." By god, you better believe I will.

"What the fuck? Where have you been?" I growl from behind her.

She steps through the door, peeling her wig off. Her blonde hair sealing the deal, halting me in my tracks as the door slams shut. "I said, I'm sorry."

"Oh, okay." I throw my hands in the air. "Good to see you, let's catch up sometime. What the actual fuck, Sarah?"

"I can't explain right now, please. I have one more set, I need to get changed." Her voice quivers as she moves toward the door, but I slap my hand on it, slamming it shut.

"*It's been six years!*" I clasp my hands behind my head. "You left a letter." Bile rises in my throat, but I grit my teeth, pushing it back down. She won't look at me, her face pinches up. "You said…things." I fight the urge to take her in my arms, holding her like I used to.

Her tears run wildly as she fights them, batting them away with her hands, nodding through my every word. "I did. I need to explain, but I can't right now. Please, I promise you. I'll tell you everything, but not right now."

"Tell me this, you at least owe me that. I deserve to know." Anger etches on my face as it turns red, and a pounding fills my ears. I tremble with every word. "*Tell me.*"

"Yes, I was." Her body vibrates as she breaks, and her hands cover her face.

Those three words scorch my ears as a sinking feeling grows in the pit of my stomach. "You were?" She nods as my head whirls, and I stumble back. She reaches for me, but I flinch from her touch.

LEAONA LUXX

She gasps, her eyes wide and wet with tears. "Chord?"

I tug at my shirt as I struggle for air. A thunderous rumble rattles my chest. I bury my hands in my hair, reeling. My mind goes blank. "I need to leave." I turn my back on her for the first time in our lives, and I run.

I drive the two and half hours back home. It's five in the morning when I pull into my garage. I trudge into the house, still numb. Emptying my pockets on the table, knowing my phone is full of texts.

I need to send Alden something, I left him with no word. "I'll deal with that in the morning," I say as the events of the night replay in my head.

I walked away. Said nothing. Just like she did all those years ago. I asked her about the letter, and she wouldn't take the time to explain it. Any of it. She stared at me like I was the ghost. Words she had written have torn me apart for years.

I rub my face, frustration growing. "She acted as if I was the one who disappeared. Plans we made, gone. She ripped them all from us. Never gave me a choice in the matter. Just like she did tonight!" I yell and grab a glass from the table, smashing it against the wall.

LEAONA LUXX

The room spins, stopping at the stairs. I run up them to my bedroom. Boxes are stacked all over the space. "I have to find it." I slap at the switch until the light glows overhead. I shift and move this box and that one.

I open one lid, spotting the one I need, and pull out the old shoe box. I step back, dropping onto the bed. I run my hand over the top, tracing the letters of her name with my fingers. This is the Sarah I remember. Here, in this box.

Lifting the flap, I push it open. Picking up her phone, I rub it as her face flashes in front of me on the day I gave it to her. We were so happy that Christmas Day, she was thrilled to get her phone. "You loved this damn thing."

I charge it, scanning the calls and texts from that day. My mom, Thayer, and One all called and texted her multiple times. Sending concern, offering help, and giving love. Every call or text from me, I told her how much I loved her.

Tears fill my eyes as they move to the letter laying in the bottom of the box. The envelope is worn, crumpled from the hundreds of times that I've read it. The days I've crushed it in my hands, broken from the words on the paper.

"This is the last thing I heard from you." I take it out, unfolding it carefully. The ink has run in a few places, tears smearing it. The edges torn and wrinkled from the years of wear. I close my eyes as the sound of my heart breaking reverberates in my ears.

I can still see her face as I drove away that day, she was beautiful. Her eyes, the way they sparkled the last time I held her in my arms. I can hear her moans from my touch. The sound of her beating heart as she slept next to me.

I close my eyes, forcing the tears from them. I dry my face with the back of my hand, needing to read this again. I swallow past my memories as they knot in my throat. To this day, I feel each word as she writes it.

WRECKING US, SAVING YOU

Chord,

I want you to know that I love you. I'm afraid by the end of this letter, you'll not understand how much you mean to me. I need you to believe, you are my life. Without you next to me, I would never survive.

The love you give me makes me whole. Some may never comprehend a love like ours, thinking we're young and inexperienced. But not everyone has the kind of love you give, nor will they ever.

I'm shocked, my world shaken. I hope you can help me, that we can work through it. There's no easy way to say this and if there's a better way, forgive me because I'm lost. I'm pregnant. They tested me before my shot and again when I questioned it. This isn't how I wanted you to find out, it's wrong.

I have no one else, Chord. I know I can't make it on my own. I have no fight left in me and don't know where to begin. I'm so sorry, I've messed everything up. Forgive me, I never meant for this to happen. Please, I need you right now.

I love you,

Sarah

"You broke my heart." Crumpling to the floor, I weep. For us, the child, and what might have been the last six years. Our lives irrevocably changed forever. Moments lost, memories never to be had. Lives torn apart, hearts shattered.

I watch as day breaks, screaming as it crashes through my window. I sit up, folding my letter back into the perfect form. I place it on my nightstand, I never want to forget.

I pick up the pieces of my life and stand as I push myself to move. My head pounds from the events, the words, her. I plod to the kitchen, making coffee to give me some sense of being.

My phone pings, and my eyes glare at the clock on the stove. I hit my head on the wall, turning to grab my laptop. I fire it up, yanking my phone from the table. I send the video and information to my email.

Pouring a cup of coffee, I shoot Alden a quick text. I ask him for no questions right now, that I'll explain a little later. I'm bitter and mad as hell. She should've told me, said something to me about what she did.

That was my child too. Rage fills me as a tremor rocks my body. My blood boils as anger coils tight in the pit of my stomach. I have to know, I deserve to know about my child. I stare at my phone, debating my next move.

I shoot a quick message off to the last person I ever thought I would ask for help from—Walker Pennington. I jump into the shower, dressing as fast as I can. I'm no sooner downstairs, then my phone rings.

"Hello."

"Chord. It's Walker. How can I help you?" I'm a little surprised he's up this early, but I know he has ghosts as well as I do.

"I have a problem and no one else I can trust. How soon can we meet?"

"I'm here now." I check the time.

"Ten minutes?"

"Knock on the side door, I'll meet you there." I release a sigh.

"Thank you." I end the call, steady myself on the counter, slowing my breathing. My heart hammers against my chest. "Here goes nothing."

Grabbing my keys, I'm out the door. I park on the far end of his building, out of sight. Tapping on the door, Walker meets me to open it. "Come on in."

91

WRECKING US, SAVING YOU

"Thanks for meeting me."

"You sounded desperate." Walker points to a light on at the other end of the hall.

"I am, but it's Saturday; I appreciate this." He nods at a chair in front of me, I sit, rubbing my palms over my jeans.

"It's fine, Chord." He sits across from me, ready to take notes. "Now, how can I help you?"

"It's Sarah," He raises his brows. "I found her."

"Wow. That's great, isn't it?" His brows furrow.

"I've never told another living soul what I'm about to tell you." At the time, I couldn't bring myself to disappoint another soul like I did her, so I kept it to myself.

He leans in, resting his hands on his desk. "Alright."

"When Sarah disappeared, she was pregnant." I blow out a slow, steady breath.

He rubs his chin. "Did she leave for that reason?"

"I'm not sure." I stand, plodding across the floor. "I didn't get a chance to ask her. We argued. Well, I argued, she cried." I rub the back of my neck.

"What about the baby?" His eyes dart to mine.

"I don't know." I give a half shrug before running my hand through my hair. "I was mad. I yelled at her. When I asked her about the letter she left for me and the fact that she was pregnant, she replied 'I was'."

"I see." He leans back in his seat. "So why are you here?"

"*If* I have a child out there, anywhere, I want to be the baby's father. I wasn't given the chance to decide if I wanted a child or if..." I trail off, my face reddening as I ball my fists up.

92

"Alright. First things first, you need to find out what she did." He straightens in his chair. "If she aborted the child, you obviously have no recourse. If she put said child up for adoption, we may be able to petition the court for visitation or even custody."

"Aborted? She would never have an abortion." The thought alone maddens me. I set my jaw, gritting my teeth.

"Are you sure?" My hands shake with fury, and I'm about to punch him.

"I know damn well. Sarah was my soul, I know her. No way. She might have put the baby up for adoption." My stomach turns with the thought.

"That's a guess. Her mom was a piece of work, and you don't even know if she had prenatal care; she could have lost the child." He tilts his head, lacing his fingers in his lap. I feel lightheaded, what has she gone through? And by herself.

"You're right." I sigh, sinking into the seat. I clasp my hands when they begin to shake at the possibility that she could have lost the baby. And I wasn't there for her or our baby. "Now what?"

"Talk to her." He stands, walking around his desk. "Ask her what happened and listen."

"I don't even know where she lives." I cross my arms, trotting my leg. "I know she's in Charleston."

"And your P.I. couldn't find her after all these years?" He's right, why couldn't he find her? "Where did you find her?"

"Dungeons and Dragons, she's a fucking stripper," I spit with disdain, rubbing the back of my neck.

"Hold up,"—his face hardens—"what's wrong with her being a stripper?"

"Come on, she shouldn't be there." The thought of men staring at her and God only knows what else—it sickens me.

93

WRECKING US, SAVING YOU

"I graduated with several, women and men, who paid for their college doing the same thing. There's no shame in working for a paycheck. You know, not all strippers are prostitutes or on drugs." He glowers at me, shoving his hands in his pockets. Damn.

"You're right." I lean over, covering my face with my hands. "I was an asshole. It's one reason I was so angry, she shouldn't be there. And the fact she was so close but never tried to find me."

"You had a detective who couldn't find her." Walker cocks his brows.

"Fuck. I have to go find her, which means, I'm going back to the club."

"Sounds like it." He pauses. "A word of warning: stay calm, listen to her. You have no idea what she's been through."

I nod, drying my hands on my pants again. I reach for his hand, not knowing what to say. "Thank you."

"Anytime." Walker takes my hand. "Let me know if or how you want to proceed."

"I will. I appreciate this." I turn to leave, but he stops me.

"Chord, just one thing." He hesitates. "Why didn't you go to One?"

"No one, Walker. I've never told anyone about that letter."

"You kept it all these years?" His brow furrows.

"It's all I had." I drop my head, and the pain lays heavy on my soul.

"When you talk to her, make sure she knows you still love her." He offers me a tight smile.

"Ha! I think that ship has sailed, man." The words shatter me as they roll off my tongue. I have no doubt everyone knows I still love her. Well, not everyone. "Thanks."

Starting my SUV, I turn onto Highway Seventeen, heading back to Charleston. I arranged another night's stay this morning. I knew I was going back, I left my things there with my abrupt exit.

I hold my phone, trying to make up my mind if I should make the next call. I need the only person who'll listen and not ask a million questions. I press dial and wait. "Chord, what's up?"

"I need you to listen to me, ask few questions and have my back." I roll my shoulders, popping my neck.

"Alright." I hear shuffling, then a door creaking. "Are you okay?"

"Physically, yes. But I'm not gonna lie, I'm a fuckin' mess." I run my hand through my hair. It's been a long time since my heart has beat this wildly.

"As long as you're not hurt, we'll get through this." His voice is smooth, calm. I would've never made it after Sarah left had it not been for my brother. He got it. He knew I was broken.

"I found Sarah. She's in Charleston." My breathing's ragged, my head still spinning. "I'm not sure about anything. We had an argument, and I left."

"So you talked to her?" He remains calm, helping me to.

"I did, well, that's a lie. I yelled and demanded answers from her." I roll my eyes, I was an asshole.

"Damn, do you think she'll see you again?" I scratch my head, I'm not sure I deserve the chance.

"I'm going back to try to talk to her again. If she'll talk to me, that is."

"Is she doing alright?" One whispers.

"From what I could tell, yes." I sigh. "I never gave her a chance to talk, actually."

WRECKING US, SAVING YOU

"You've got to remain calm. If you don't, all this time you've waited on her will have been for nothing." He's dying to say so much more. And ask more.

"I have things I've never told anyone about us, One. I still can't, I need her side of the story first."

"If you need me, call. I will come to you, anytime."

"I will, promise." He's a good man and the best brother.

"Stay calm and remember, she's still Sarah. It's been awhile since you've talked, but at least you've got the chance to talk again." I shake my head, he's so right. "Don't be a shithead, love you."

"I always wondered why you two called me that, it was loud and clear last night. Love you, brother."

I stand on stage as the lights come up slowly, Rihanna's *Love on the Brain* pulsates in the room. I step into the light, taking the pole in hand as I swing. I work my body along the metal support.

Spiraling down the pole, I come to rest on the floor. I slowly climb to my knees, swinging my hips. Wrapping my hand around the shaft, I spin around it. Grinding and thrusting to the sultry words.

The entire time I'm dancing, I'm thinking of Chord. His face spoke volumes last night, and it devastated me to have him see me this way. I wish I had another choice, but there is none. Not for someone like me.

As I finish my set, looking through the smoke and lights, I see him. The wreckage still fresh on his face. I avert my eyes, trying to avoid him altogether will be impossible, but for now, I can.

WRECKING US, SAVING YOU

I traipse from the runway, making room for the next show. I plod down the steps, whispering to my friend. "He's here." I glance around the room, waiting for him to come to me. I'm so sure this is the best idea.

"What do you want me to do?" Luke is my best friend, he's been my ride or die for five years now. "I'll throw his ass out if you want me to?"

Chord stares at me, and I know my time is up. Inclining my head, I roll my eyes toward Chord. "Yeah, I'm not so sure that'll work."

Chord stands, working his way through the crowd toward me. Everything happened so fast last night, but I didn't miss what a tall drink of water he's become over the years. His rugged good looks floors my best friend.

"Damn, girl. That's him?" I sigh heavily, thinking of how many times my lips have touched him. And where. "You're flushing. Should I fan you? Oh, girl. Calm it down over here."

"Stop it." I play slap at him as my eyes flicker back to Chord. His shoulders were always broad, but he must've gained four more inches in his span. His shirt is pulled tight over his pecs. He's several inches taller also.

He smiles as he approaches, and I'm seventeen again. The luckiest girl in the world. His smile still makes my girl parts tingle, and I squeeze my thighs together, chewing on my bottom lip. His deep voice raises the hair on my arm.

"Sarah."

"Chord," I say his name on a sigh, earning me a sharp elbow. I wince, netting Luke a stern glare. "This is Luke."

His eyes dart from me to Luke. "Can we?" He gestures toward the back.

"Yeah, let's take it outside." I cringe at my choice of words. "I mean, it's private." I roll my eyes as I turn to the back door, and Chord follows me closely.

"I prefer this top to the other one," he grunts from behind me. I'm wearing my favorite costume. It's a blue and purple butterfly, outlined in black with a matching thong.

"Thank you, it's my favorite." I open the door as he slides his hand over my head, holding it for me. The door shuts behind him as I lean against the wall.

He runs his hands through his dark brown mane, just the way I used to. "I don't know where to start." He shakes his head, his frustration palpable. "I'm sorry. I hate that I was rude and angry. I showed my ass last night."

His words bring me up short and my shoulders sag, knowing I'm the one who let him down. I war with what I know I have to do and what I want to do. In all the years we shared, we've never argued.

"No, Chord." I wrap my arms around myself, hiding from the man who's seen more of me than any other ever has. "We were both wrong." I can't look at him. "And you're right, we need to talk. But not here and not for five minutes."

"I agree." He releases a long breath. "Since when can we not talk?"

"Seriously? Can you believe we just had our first argument?" I shift my feet.

"I thought the same thing." His mouth falls slack. "You tell me when and where, I'm there."

"I would say we could get some breakfast, but we need a little more privacy." I tighten my grip around my stomach, holding down the butterflies that are always around when he is. "Are you staying close by?"

He narrows his eyes. "I am."

WRECKING US, SAVING YOU

"Can I meet you there?" I pinch my lips between my fingers, doing my best not to bite my nails. "Unless your wife would care?" He shakes his head on the word 'wife'. "Girlfriend?" Again, there's a quick shake of his head.

"I'm alone." He inclines his head, as if he's trying to tell me something.

I nod. "How about I catch a ride and come there?"

"I can wait, take you with me." He smirks, drawing my eyes to his mouth. Getting exactly the response he wants from me—heat.

I sweep the tip of my tongue between my lips, watching as he ignites. Now, it's my turn to smirk. "That works for me." I pause. "I have one more set. I'll tell Luke not to wait for me."

His brows knit together. "Does he give you a ride to work?"

"We live together."

He averts his eyes. "I'm staying at the Belmond, in case you want to tell him where you'll be."

"Yeah, I kinda need to do that." I wrinkle my nose as he nods.

"I'll be waiting out here." He shoves his hands in his pockets.

"You don't want to come back in? I don't mind." I hold my breath, wanting him to stay close for some ungodly reason.

"I do," he grunts. Ah-ha. I raise my brows, he's not happy I work here. Join the crowd, Chord.

"An hour? Where can I find you?"

He jerks his head toward the street. "Black Land Rover."

No doubt the most expensive one they make. "Like I said, give me an hour."

I reach for the door but his hand is already there, pulling it open and holding it until I'm inside. I glance back at him, my heart racing.

"Thank you." His brow furrows, then he gives me my favorite smile. *You're fucked, Sarah.*

I finish my last set, hurrying to get dressed as I give Luke the basic details. "He's staying at the Belmond. I'm not sure how long this is gonna take. We have so much to talk about. How do I look?"

"Like a girl still in love." Luke fixes my jacket in the back as I slide it on. "I want you to be careful, Sarah. You haven't been around him in years, he could be a different person."

I turn on my best friend, pinning him with a glare. "What the hell does that mean? You don't know him, he's good to the core. What happened between us had nothing to do with him, it's all my fault."

"I'm just saying, people can change and you don't know him anymore." He holds his hands up. "Ask yourself one thing, where in the hell has he been? He owes you that much."

My forehead wrinkles. "You're right. I need to take my time, ease into this. I might not want him back in my life." A chill runs over me with the thought of losing him forever. At least I had the hope of having him for all these years.

"Breathe." Luke takes my hands in his. "Feel him out, see if you can still trust him."

I nod. "Good idea, I need to be cautious." We walk out the back door, arm in arm. At the end of the building, I spot his SUV. Chord rolls down the window, waving.

"He's rich alright." Luke side-eyes me. "Good looking and money, was he good in bed?" Luke snorts when he laughs.

"Seriously? Gross! I'm not talking to you about that." I push away from him, crossing the street to Chord. I pause in the middle, turning to Luke. "Hey!" When he turns to look at me, I smile, nodding until my head is about to roll off my shoulders. He bursts into laughter.

"What was that about?" Chord asks as I open his door.

"Huh?" I play innocent.

WRECKING US, SAVING YOU

He narrows his eyes. "Nothing, I guess." He puts the SUV in gear. "To my place?" He cocks his brow.

"Yes, please." I hold my breath. "But… no funny stuff. It's been a long time, we don't even know each other anymore," echoing Luke's words of advice.

Chord does a double take before smirking. "Sarah, I'd know you in the dark. I've already proven that fact. We haven't changed. Our lives have, but you're still *my* Sutton."

Chord takes his time driving to the hotel. The silence is almost deafening, and I can't take it. "So what brings you to Charleston?"

"A friend," he replies as a sharp pang twists in my gut. "I came to watch Alden."

Why does that make me feel better? "He's good. Were y'all friends in college? "

"No, he's a friend of Thayer's ex. We just hit it off. He's a cool dude." He shrugs.

"Did you go to Clemson?" I pick at my cuticles as my stomach turns thinking about all the plans that we made, that he went on to do.

He side-eyes me. "No, I didn't go." My breath hitches as he pulls up to the front of the hotel. Sliding from his seat, he tosses the attendant his keys.

He rounds the front of the truck and once again, I'm seventeen and lusting for the hottest guy in school. He's in all black with a gun metal colored hooded leather jacket. Damn, I could eat him alive.

Opening my door, he offers his hand. I take it, grabbing the hem of my skirt to hold it down. His eyes smolder as they run a path up my legs and that old, familiar pang is back. I clear my throat, hoping to dispel my lust.

"Thank you." I peek up at him through my lashes, trying to hide my desire for him.

102

His hand lands on the small of my back, sending a jolt to my core, as the doorman holds the door open. "Thank you." Chord nods.

We wait by the elevator, watching the numbers tick down. I fidget as he sighs heavily. The ding of its arrival sends a wave of chills over me. Chord slides his hand behind me once again, guiding me inside.

The elevator jolts when it begins to move, causing me to lose my balance. I throw my hands out to steady myself, one on the wall and one on his thigh. Shit. I freeze when he tenses, his muscle growing harder under my touch. Which only heightens my arousal.

"I'm sorry. So sorry." I straighten myself as my pulse races full throttle.

"You're fine...okay. It's okay." He turns his head, cracking his neck.

We come to a stop, and I'm first off the elevator. Chord's hand spreads wide in the center of my back, and my body reacts with a shudder. How in the hell can his touch still drive me insane? Damn if I know. I'll be damned if I care.

He slows, stopping in front of the penthouse. I quirk a brow when he flashes me his sly grin. He swings the door wide, stepping to the side. "Ma'am."

"Thank you." I throw a playful backhand into his stomach, meeting rock hard abs. My mouth goes dry, so I decide to put some distance between us. I make a beeline to the window, gazing at the view. "It's beautiful."

I feel the heat from his body before I hear him join me. "It is." My eyes dart to his, he's staring at me, not the view. "How long have you been here?"

I whirl around as he gets right to the point. I take off to the couch on the opposite side of the room. "Six years, there about."

His brows pull low. "How long have you worked at the club?" He mumbles something as he takes his jacket off, joining me on the couch. I'm shocked to see he has tattoos on his arms, which makes me wonder where else I'd find them. I turn to him, tucking my legs under me. I can't look at him, so I fix my stare on the couch.

"Close to five years. I started before the new owners took over," I say absentmindedly as I trace the pattern on the material. "It's not something I was excited to do, but I needed money."

"I don't think either of us thought this is where we'd be six years ago," he huffs as the old pull tugs at my heart. We've always been connected in some way.

"Ain't that the truth." I quirk my brow.

He shrugs. "The sad truth but yeah, the truth nevertheless." He stands, wandering to the fridge. "You want a drink?"

"Do you have a water?"

He pulls out two bottles. "I do, I still drink it more than anything," he says, handing me the bottle.

I nod with a crooked smile. "Yeah, me too."

He plops into the couch, kicking his shoes off. He faces me, curling his legs under him. His eyes meet mine and a thousand words are spoken. My heart seizes. "Where did ya go?"

"Mom." I shrug as tears spring to my eyes. "As soon as I got home that day, there was a knock on the door. I hesitated answering it, knowing it had to be bad news but finally I did. Two big guys pushed themselves in, started searching the place. I tried to stop them but a third man came in.

"He grabbed me by the throat, pinning me to the wall, told me he would kill me if I screamed. He kept asking me where my mom was, had she been there and with who. Then he ran his hand under my dress, threatened to rape me if I didn't tell him where Mom was. I'm not sure what changed his mind, but I was hysterical and couldn't stop crying. They decided to leave, telling me they'd be back." My stomach turns, cringing as I think of what could've happened. I swallow past the knot in my throat. I was so scared, not knowing what they'd do.

"Later that evening, she came home in a panic. Dale, the current flavor of the month, was selling coke for some drug ring in town. He and mom had a party with it instead of selling it. They got fronted some more by another guy and ran off with it.

"She was screaming at me to pack a bag, but I refused. We fought until I ended up running to my room. I thought if I could get in there, I could climb out the window and run. I tried to lock the door, but Dale forced it open. Mom came in, dumped my backpack out, and told me to grab what I could. I fought with her again. I was afraid she'd find my phone.

"I knew if I had to leave, I could take it and call for help. But Dale was ready to go and tired of us fighting. He came barreling in the room, hit me and busted my eye open. I had no more fight in me. I was afraid I'd end up killed." I shudder at the memory, knowing this is the easy part of the story. Thinking about it has my chest aching.

"Dale dragged me to the car, and they took off. We didn't stop until we crossed the state line. Mom knew she needed to switch addresses for the checks from my dad, so we had to settle down every few months. But then, they'd get paranoid and we'd move again." I take a long drink from my bottle, my mouth bitter with the details I left out. I tremble as my eyes fill with tears. I need to tell him, but I'm terrified he'll leave.

"Son of a bitch. I knew you wouldn't leave without telling me, I knew it." His hands shake as he laces his fingers.

"We ended up here because their money ran out. I turned eighteen, and she was done with me." I fight the bile rising as my lip quivers.

"I've looked for you." His face is marred with hate and regret.

Gasping, I clutch my chest. "You did? When?"

WRECKING US, SAVING YOU

"I've had a private investigator the entire time, we looked everywhere." He picks at invisible lint on his pants. "I just got an update Friday. You disappeared off the face of the earth, how?" He holds his breath, his brows pulled low.

"I had to change my name." My heart plunges as I watch realization dawn on him.

"Fuck." He runs his hands through his hair. "Sutton."

My old nickname rattles me to the core, and my heart pounds in my ears. "Yeah, I made Sutton my first name."

"What the fuck? Why didn't I think of that?"

"Are you mad at me?" Panic sets in as I'm hit with a pang in the pit of my stomach.

"Damn straight, I'm mad as hell." He rubs his hands on his thighs.

"It's not like I had a choice, Chord. I've never had a choice as to what life hands me." I point at my chest.

He rubs his forehead, his face growing red. "I know, I'm not mad at you. It's that all this fucking time, I should've guessed."

"I sent you letters." My voice quivers as my anger grows. He's not the only one allowed to be mad, I was alone too. "You sent them back or someone did." I glance at the ceiling. "Honestly, I wasn't surprised. It's not like we were supposed to be together in the first place."

"What in the hell does that mean? I loved you like I've never loved another person. We were perfect, and everyone knew it," he growls.

"Why would my letters get returned? Are you sure someone in your family didn't do it? Or maybe, a girlfriend?" I level him with a glare.

"My family loves you like they do me, and you damn well know that. It took a long fucking time before I dated again." He points a

106

finger at me. "And what letters? I don't know a damn thing about you writing me." He folds his arms across his chest.

"I wrote you several times a week. Even when they came back, I tried again. For years, I sent those fucking things, for nothing. No response, not even a 'leave me alone'." I jump to my feet, getting in his face. "They all said 'Return to Sender' so what the fuck was that about?"

"Return to Sender?" He cocks his head, and I'm caught up in his blue eyes. I look away, trying to keep my head straight. "Where did you send them?"

"Your house, where else?" I growl as his shoulders sag in defeat.

"We moved after you left, in February." He shakes his head. "I couldn't stand to be at school without you. The questions and gossip were more than I could handle. I graduated from South Brunswick." He falls into the couch. We're both wracked with hurt and disbelief.

"With One? Y'all went down to be with him." I chuckle, not believing the fucked up'ness of the situation.

Sarah

Pressing forward, I settle in across from him again. I need a little more from him before I can give anymore of myself. "So we've been chasing each other this entire time. What does that mean?"

"It should've never happened, but it's done now. All that's left are broken pieces of us." He stares out the window as dawn rises. We've spent many mornings watching the sun come up, but none have been like this one.

"Is there someone special?" I bite my nail, studying his face, hoping there isn't.

"Huh! No." He blows out a long breath. "I mean, I've dated."

"Of course. You're single and handsome, why wouldn't you?" I fidget, turning away from him. What was I thinking, asking a question like that? He's amazing, no doubt he's had women.

He touches my knee, until I look at him. "None were ever you. Once I realized I was trying to fill the place you left, I stopped because I knew it would never happen."

"So nothing serious?" I avert my eyes, not wanting to know the truth. He runs his finger over my foot, tickling me. "Stop, you know I can't stand that."

"There it is." He smiles at me. "I was afraid life had taken it from you."

"Taken what?"

"Your smile." He shakes his head. "No, I've never been able to get close to anyone else."

"Oh. I thought..." I wave off my thoughts. "Nothing."

"You thought you were replaceable? Not a chance." He cringes. "If you mean sex, yes, there were a few. Such a waste of time."

The image of another woman in his arms crushes me. "I get it, you were lonely. You didn't know if I'd ever come back." I pull my knees up, wrapping my arms around them.

"Lonely? I wished it were that simple." He leans over, hanging his head. "Fuck. I feel like I just told you I cheated on you."

Tears well in my eyes, I feel the same way. "Not possible, we weren't together. I understand, I do." I gulp, swallowing the rising bile.

He turns to me, fear written on his face. "Did you, you know?"

I shake my head, fighting my tears. "No, I couldn't." I watch as he berates himself, his mouth forming a thin line. "It's different for girls, I guess."

"No, I guess you wouldn't have." He turns, facing me. "They meant nothing, Sarah. I promise you, I've only ever loved you."

"Chord, stop. I can't do this right now. Besides, is it even possible to still feel this way after all this time?"

WRECKING US, SAVING YOU

"Who the fuck writes the rules on love? I don't give a damn what anybody thinks, I know how I feel. How I've always felt about you." He reaches for me but I deny him, moving across the cushion from him. We sit there, silently, for the longest time.

"You're right, you've always been right here, Chord." I lay my hand over my heart. "No one else has been here." He moves to my side, our shoulders touching, watching the sun. After some time, he breaks the silence.

"I know it sounds insane. Hell, I often thought I was crazy waiting, but nothing else ever felt right. It was never you, never our love." His forehead wrinkles.

"Now that, I understand."

"Could you not call?" He tilts his head.

"I tried but you must have already moved. Mom stayed pretty close, waiting to see if she was gonna get killed or get me killed. I didn't have a chance at first."

"So what did you use as a last name? We searched for Sutton surnames."

My stomach knots, I know what's coming. I swallow past the lump in my throat. "Hamilton. I used Sutton Hamilton." I clutch my belly, it feels like a rollercoaster.

"You used my name as your last name?" He rubs the back of his neck, releasing a heavy breath. "Wha-what happened..." I close my eyes, refusing to face him. I'm about to crush him with the truth.

"The baby?" My words are no more than a whisper.

Tears flood our eyes. "Yes. You left a letter, said you were pregnant, and there's not been a day I haven't thought about you both."

"I was, Chord. I never meant for you to find that letter, I was shocked when you mentioned it. I wrote it with the intention of giving it to you, but I knew in my heart that's not how I wanted you to find out." I fight to dry my face, but there's no hope of that.

"I shoved it in that book to keep Mom from finding it. When I went for the appointment, per doctor's orders, I had to do a pee test. When she came back, she was holding it. I was shocked it was positive, so I asked for a blood test.

"I waited another hour before she came back with the same result. I lost it, told her there was no way. She explained that the days I missed because of the holidays, when they rescheduled my appointment, had to have been when it happened."

"Thanksgiving?" To my surprise, he remembers.

"Yes." My voice quivers. "I can't believe you would know that."

"All I've had was time to think." He glances away. "Did you...your mom, did she make you?" This is it, no more holding back. Six years of hell and the truth comes down to this one moment.

"When Mom finally took time to pay attention, she realized I was pregnant but it was too late to terminate. I took another beating for that, and you damn well better believe if I hadn't been pregnant, I'd have beat her ass." I tremble with the memory, wiping my face with the back of my hand.

Chord's hands are fisted on his knees. "Did she hurt you? Or the baby?"

"No, Chord." I lean in, taking his hand in mine. I take a deep breath and pray he'll understand. "I kept the baby, we have a son. He was born on a morning, just like this, on August twentieth."

His lip quivers as his long held tears break free. He slumps over, the gravity of my words crushing him. He's lost so much time. I slide my arm around him, holding him as close as possible.

"I've been so afraid you lost him. Or had to give him up. Knowing I wasn't here to help you. I'm so sorry you went through this alone." His words are broken as he tries to breathe through his tears.

111

"No, no. Chord, we couldn't do anything." I lay my hand on his face, pulling him to look at me. "I named him Silas Jordan Hamilton." He pulls my hand to his mouth, kissing it.

"Silas, it's perfect." He smiles. "We have a son? A son. And he's healthy?"

"He's amazing. The best thing I've ever done, aside from you." My tears fall as fast and hard as his.

"Where is he?" He hesitates. "With Luke?"

I nod. "Yes. Luke has been incredible to us. We would've never made it without him."

"I understand."

"I sent ultrasounds in the letters. Updates on us both, I still have them. I'm so sorry this is how you found out. I never imagined finding you again." He reaches over, timidly drying my tears.

"You're not to blame." He ducks his head, making me look at him. "I've always known if you could've come home, you would have." I nod, drying my face on the back of my hand. He grabs a box of tissues, handing me one.

"I promise, I would have. I wanted you with us."

"I wanted to be here." He holds my hand, caressing it. My heart beats wildly as it takes the reins. Can this even be happening?

I glance at him. "Would you like to meet him?"

His eyes narrow, blinking rapidly. "Can I? I mean, will he be okay? What will he think? Will Luke be okay with me coming over?"

"Hang on, do you think Luke and I? I told you there's been no one else." He cocks his brow. "He's gay."

"You said you live together. I thought maybe he held a torch. He's gay?" Chord's face scrunches up.

"We do and no, never. Obviously, I'm not his type. When my checks stopped, Mom disappeared. I knew Luke from the apartment building, he saw me sleeping in the stairwell after I got kicked out of our place. He invited me to stay with him.

"Luke worked at the club and helped me get a job there, washing dishes at first. After Silas was born, we got a bigger apartment. One of the many reasons I started dancing, we needed the money."

"You took that damn job to take care of our son?" His eyes glow with anger. "No fucking way this is happening. I can't believe this shit."

I scoot closer to him, laying my hand on his cheek. "No, Chord. Don't do this to yourself, we didn't do this. And I would've done anything to take care of our son because he was your son."

He presses his hand into mine. "It kills me to think of what you've been through, Sarah."

"We made it." I shrug.

"You'll never do without again, I promise you that." He wraps his hand around mine, making my chest ache.

"Come on"—I stand, pulling him with me—"let's go see our son."

His eyes gleam. "Our son."

Sarah stands at the door of her apartment, keys in one hand, my hand in the other. "You ready?"

I tremble. "As I'll ever be."

She drops my hand, unlocking the door. "Honey, I'm home," she calls out as I step in behind her, almost hiding. She turns to me, nudging my shoulder. "Come in."

The pitter patter of bare feet on the floor warms my heart. She kneels beside me as I sit on the couch, and a blue-eyed, brown-haired baby boy darts around the hall corner.

"Momma, you're home!" Silas yells as she catches him, running full steam ahead into her arms.

"I am. Did you miss me?" Sarah kisses his cheeks, hugging him tightly.

He leans back, "I did but Unc said you'd be home soon."

"Have you eaten breakfast?" she asks.

He shakes his head. "Just a bowl of cereal."

Sarah giggles. "And we know that's not enough for you, right?"

"Nope, 'cause I eat as much as my daddy." He's all cheeks when he says it. I gasp at the reference to me. Sarah forgot to mention they talk about me.

"Yes, you do." She playfully swats his behind. "How about we talk for a minute and then we can go get some real food?"

"Okay." His eyes dart to me and narrow as he studies my face. The corner of his eyes crinkle, glistening as we come face to face. "He looks like my picture, Momma."

"What picture is that?" My eyes are wide as I lean down, getting on Silas' level. Silas traces my eyebrows and down my nose with his finger.

"The one Momma gave me, beside my bed." Silas' eyes dart from mine to Sarah's. He wraps his hand around mine, pulling me from the couch. "Come 'mere."

I turn to Sarah as she stands, and we follow our son through the house. She trails behind, giving us space. Silas jumps on the bed, bouncing to the head. I kneel beside the table where the picture sets.

"See, he's got brown hair and eyes like yours." Sarah sits on the side of the bed with Silas. I pick up the picture, gawking. I turn to her, my forehead wrinkled.

"I found it in the front zipper of my backpack. I was hoping to find my phone, but I found our Christmas pictures instead." I ease over, sliding onto the bed on the other side of our son.

"You kept it, all these years?" Her eyes glint as she stares at it, memories flooding her mind, as they are mine.

WRECKING US, SAVING YOU

"No duh, I kept it." She brushes Silas' hair out of his eyes, avoiding mine. "I had a five by seven made for him, so he would know his dad."

Silas frowns, his mouth pulled to the side. "What's wrong, Momma?"

She pulls Silas into her lap, looking him in the eyes. "Remember when I told you that one day your daddy would come find us?" He nods. "We talked about how much he loves you, even though he didn't know you were here?"

"Uh-huh, I rememberw." Silas tilts his head, listening.

My heart beats so hard, I think it may implode. "Well, he found us."

"Why are you crwying, Momma." He wipes her tears.

"It's happy tears, baby boy." She holds him close, and he glances at me. "That's him in the picture." She points at me, and Silas studies me.

My eyes well up. "I'm sorry I didn't get here sooner." Silas twists his lip between his fingers. Sarah watches as I hold my breath, offering my hand for acceptance.

Silas cranes his neck, gauging Sarah's reaction. She smiles at him, glancing at me. He turns to me, laying his hand in mine. "Momma said you'd come."

I wrap his little fingers in my hand, and my eyes well with tears. "We have a lot to catch up on, you think you could show me the ropes?"

"Yeah, we can play carws and you can go to the parwk with us." My sweet boy already owns his daddy's heart.

"I'd like that, thank you."

"How about we go get some grub?" Sarah says, tickling Silas.

"Pancakes!" he yells, making me laugh.

"Pancakes it is." I stand, holding my hand out. "Wanna ride?"

"I mean, if you're offering?" Her eyes smolder as a frenzied desire jumpstarts in my core. Yeah, my mind went there.

"Don't even joke." I focus on Silas. "How about a piggyback?"

Silas wraps his arms around my biceps. "Okay!"

Sarah scrambles from the bed, slipping behind me. She jumps on my back, and I reach for her thigh. "Like this, Silas." I pick Silas up and begin walking, adjusting my hand on her ass.

"Chord, put me down. You can't carry us both." Luke stands in the kitchen, smirking.

"Lock those legs, sister. I think he's got it handled." He gestures to my hand on her ass and sips his coffee.

"Wave bye," I say as she locks her legs around me.

They both wave with a smile. Luke lays his hand over his heart. "Y'all are killing me, bye."

"Hold on," I say as we start down the stairs.

Her eyes bug out. "Chord! I'm too heavy, you can't do this."

My hand squeezes her ass. "I got you, just keep those legs where they belong. You good, Silas?"

"Yeah, Momma's making a funny face." Silas giggles. Little does he know, I'm in heaven with my hand full of her ass and her grinding into my back.

"Momma's fine." I chuckle, giving her ass another squeeze. "Just fine."

She presses her lips to my ear. "Still thinking your hand is permanently attached, huh?"

"No, ma'am. I'm just offering a helping hand." My laugh tickles Silas, and he giggles with me.

"Hey, what are you laughing at?" She stretches over my shoulder to poke at Silas.

"He's funny." He points at me and I tighten my grip, earning me an inaudible moan.

"Yeah, he's a riot," she says as I release her ass to push the door open.

"For the record, my tickling skills are amazing." I chuckle, crossing the street with them in tow.

I stop at the backdoor, allowing Sarah to slide down my body. She stands to my side as I stare at the SUV. "What?"

"Does he need a car seat?" My voice shaky, I feel like a jackass for not knowing.

Sarah's face glows. "Oh, yeah. Let me grab it." Her hand caresses my forearm before she bolts across the street. She pulls a seat from a car. Jogging back, she says, "Here, it's from Luke's car,"

"You know, I'm gonna need a shopping trip. There's things I want to give y'all." I avoid eye contact, unlocking the doors and standing Silas up. I set the seat in, buckling it down. I help Silas in, pulling the harness around him. I'm thankful for my nieces and nephews now, car seats are the devil.

"What's that?" He points to the black box on the back of the seat.

"That's a DVD player, buddy. You can watch movies on it while we ride." I pause, do they not have one? And then I realize, I have no clue what he likes. Who he is? Feeling lightheaded, I steady myself on the car door. I stare at Silas as he smiles at me. "What do you say, after we eat, we go buy a few."

"Can we? I want all the superhero movies." He gives me a thumbs up.

I shut the door to find Sarah watching me. "You're taking all of this incredibly well, you know that?"

118

"Isn't this what we planned?" I shove my shaky hands in my pockets, hiding them. "Sarah, we didn't cause this. We would've done it with age anyway. I know we've changed, but you're still my best friend, that never has changed."

Her mouth curves into a smile. "You've always been so sure about everything. How you are now, I have no clue."

"Not everything, just us." I wink. "May I?" I open the door for her as she climbs in.

I jump in, smiling like a loon. "Where are we going?"

"Down this street and over to Washington." Sarah lifts the corner of her mouth when I raise my brows at her directions. "What?"

"How about you drive since you know where we're going." I hold the keys up.

"I can't." She winces. "I don't have a license."

"We'll make a road trip outta it." I wink at her, watching as she eases back into the seat.

A few wrong turns and we pull into the restaurant. I help Silas out as Sarah hangs near behind; it's as though she's allowing me to have time with him. I already have no clue how to leave them.

We're seated and order when my phone rings. I glance at it. "It's One. Hey, brother."

"Hello. People are starting to ask questions, I wanted to check in before your phone is lit on fire." His voice is low, Lea's close by.

"I'm good. We're having breakfast, catching up." I smile at Sarah as a line forms between her brows.

"I'm assuming she's there, since your answers are clipped. When can I tell everyone to expect you?" I watch as Sarah shifts in her seat, averting her eyes.

"Actually, I haven't asked how long I can stay." Sarah's eyes snap to mine, and I shrug. "Hang on just a second."

119

WRECKING US, SAVING YOU

Muting the phone, I touch Sarah's hand. "I don't want to overstay my welcome, but I'm not ready to leave without you."

She waves me off. "You can come and go as you want."

What in the hell is going on? "Sarah, what's wrong?" She lowers her head, I unmute the phone. "Can you give me a few and I'll call you back?"

"I can do that." He sighs. "I know something's up, I expect a call this evening. Love you."

"I love y'all."

I end the call. Reaching for her hand, she pulls it from me. When our food arrives, Sarah doesn't say much. So I talk with Silas, "Hey, buddy. Who's your favorite superhero?"

"Thorw," he replies with big eyes.

"Thor's cool. What grade will you be in this year?"

"First but Momma said we might have to move." He looks toward Sarah as I begin to trot my leg.

"Why are you moving?"

She avoids looking at me. "School district, but I haven't decided on anything yet. We have a lot to consider."

"Is there anything I can help with?" I push my sleeves up as it dawns on me I need a shower.

She purses her lips. "No, nothing to concern yourself with." The fuck you say?

I sit up straight, leaning in. "What's going on, Sarah?"

"Nothing. Are you finished, Silas?" He nods as Sarah stands. Wiping his mouth, she helps him from the seat and walks toward the door.

I toss the money on the table, following them outside. I catch up with them as they're about to cross the street. I reach for Silas' hand only to have Sarah pull him away. I begin to tremble as I glare at her.

She helps him into the seat, shutting his door. I wrap her wrist, pulling her to the back of the SUV. "What the fuck is happening? You tell me I have a son one minute and take him from me the next?"

"I don't want you to think you owe us anything, you can visit whenever you want." She folds her arms across her chest.

"Sarah." I wait. "Sarah." She glances at me. "Talk to me. It's me, just us."

"You just got here, now you have to leave. I understand you have a life, I guess I thought, maybe... I don't know." She rubs her palms into her eyes.

"I'm here now."

"But for how long? Believe me, I know I sound ungrateful. Unreasonable even. I'm afraid, aren't you?" She runs her hand through her hair, and all I can do is stand there because I get it.

"You're damn right I am." My pulse quickens when I take her in my arms. "We've always figured things out, and we can work this out."

"I know, I'm fine. I just hate thinking of you leaving." She pulls away, and I immediately feel cold from the separation.

"I need to run by and grab my suitcase. Let's go grab some movies and head back to your place." I walk with her to the door, holding it open until she's settled in.

We stop by the Belmond long enough for me to run up and grab my things. On the way back to her place, we run in Target, getting every superhero movie and cartoon we can find.

"You're spoiling him." Sarah snickers.

WRECKING US, SAVING YOU

"I plan on spoiling you both, just give me some time." I peer at Silas in the rearview mirror watching Thor. We're sitting in the SUV, letting him finish it while we talk.

"How long will you be gone?" Sarah picks at her nails as she stares out the side window.

"I have to check on my license and set a few things up. And I need to drop my keys off to Lea. Maybe three days." I side-eye her.

Her head whips around. "Who's Lea?"

"One's wife. You've missed so much." I nudge her leg. "Do you remember One divorcing Monty?"

"Oh, yeah. Thayer wanted to rip her hair out." She grins.

"He met Lea, she's amazing, you'll love her. Get this, they have nine kids. Nine." I laugh when her mouth hangs open.

"Nine?"

"Yeah, Lea was a single mom. She has three boys, two daughters-in-law, and one has a girlfriend. Then, she gets pregnant with One's twins and they just had another daughter. They're like their own tribe or something." Her eyes now match her mouth. "And she's a Sarah, Hadlea Sarah."

"How many of each? Sarah's a good name."

"Umm, wait, I need to count." We laugh. "Four boys and five girls. Nine, I'm telling you. And Thayer, wow. So she hooked up with Hardy. Do you remember him?" She nods. "Okay. They broke up, and she got engaged to Walker. On the day they were getting married, she left him and went back to Hardy. They have a son now, Holden."

She covers her mouth, staring out the windshield. "Silas has ten cousins. He'll be so happy."

"He'll definitely love playing at Mom and Dad's."

"How are Elise and Calder?" She shifts in her seat, facing me.

"They're good. I think my family took losing you as hard as I did, Sarah. They'll be thrilled to meet Silas." I glance at him in the mirror.

"You didn't tell them anything?" My chest tightens. I wanted to, man did I ever need someone.

"I couldn't." I drop my gaze. "It was our business, we always kept that between us. It took me a long time to even talk about you."

"I've told Luke and Silas everything about you. I think Luke believed you were a figment of my imagination." She giggles. "He appreciated said imagination the other night."

"Appreciated what?"

"You." Her nostrils flare as she gives me a once over. "Although, my memory didn't do you justice."

Desire floods my body when she licks her lips. "I can say the same thing. That, silver beaded thing 'bout gave me a heart attack."

Her eyes shimmer from the radio light. "It's getting late, maybe we should take him in."

I turn to Silas, and he's fast asleep; we've talked for hours. "I'll get him, let me set my bag out." I lift our son from the seat, turning to find Sarah has my bag. "I can get it."

"I've got it. Watch your step." She points to the curb.

I follow her in, laying him in bed. "Does his clothes need changed or will he wake up?"

"Did you ever wake up easily?" She smirks, laying a t-shirt on the end of his bed.

"I can think of a few times, I rose to the occasion." She bumps me with her hip.

"Ya know, our child is in the room." She rolls her eyes.

"He has no clue what I said. Can I help?" I nod at the shirt.

WRECKING US, SAVING YOU

"Sure, I've never tag teamed him." We work Silas' clothes off, replacing them with a night shirt. Once he's tucked in, I can't resist kissing his sweet face.

"I'm pretty sure he's perfect." I sweep his hair from his forehead, gazing at him. "Thank you, Sarah."

She hurries from the room, sniffling. Closing the bedroom door, I follow her through the apartment. She's leaning against the kitchen sink when I find her.

"I'll never be able to make up for the time you've lost with him." Her bottom lip quivers. "I hate you had to see me that way the other night, I hate doing it."

"You were doing what it took to care for Silas. I don't think any less of you for it."

She huffs, "I saw you, Chord. The look of disgust on your face spoke volumes."

"You don't know nothing. It wasn't what you were doing or what you had on."

She leers at me. "Then what was it? Because from where I was standing, it was repulsion."

I spin on her, pinning her against the sink. Her perfume invades my senses, and I lean in, running my nose over her jaw. "I hated they were looking at you. Gawking at what was mine."

Her breath hitches as she presses into my cheek. "What was yours?"

I brush her lobe with my lips. "Is mine." My hand is in her hair before I can stop myself, and I angle her face up. Staring into her eyes, our lips only an inch apart. A sound at the door makes us jump.

Luke walks around the corner. "Hey, folks. What's up?" Sarah whirls around, running water in the sink for dishes. I lean against the counter.

124

"Nothing, we're just doin' dishes." She keeps her head down, and Luke quirks his brow at me. I have nothing, so I shrug.

"How'd your day go?" He eyes me skeptically.

I nod. "Good. We had a good time."

Sarah turns enough to prop up on the sink. "Yeah, I'd say it was good."

Luke's gaze moves between us, finally, glancing at my crotch. "It looks like it was about to be real good."

I hang my head as Sarah bolts from the room. I glance up, meeting Luke's smirk. "By the way, this may not be the time, but I want to thank you for helping Sarah and Silas. It means more than you'll ever know."

He takes a seat at the table, and I follow his lead. "For the longest time, I thought the poor thing was delusional. Stories on top of memories of you two and how you've been friends for the longest time."

"I know her better than anyone, although she's been with you the last five years and there's things I need to learn about the time I've missed, I love her." I say as Luke places his elbows on the table.

"What are you thinking? Do you really believe, like she does, that you two can live happily ever after?" His face reddens as he presses me.

"Why can't we?"

"It doesn't happen, ever. Sarah can't live some fairytale. She has responsibilities. Is your plan to be a part-time daddy, a weekend here and there?" He balls his hands on the table. He thinks he's getting mad, he ain't seen nothing yet.

"No, I don't plan on being here like that."

He smirks. "That's what I thought."

WRECKING US, SAVING YOU

"I plan on marrying her as soon as she's ready. That has been our plan for twelve years. Yes, even while she was gone, I made plans for us." I lean forward. "I'm going to give her everything she deserves, everything I promised her."

"You're still in love with her, after all these years?" He tightens his lips.

"I never fell out of love." I straighten my back. "It sounds insane, I can understand why people would think that, I do. But all these years, did she lose hope? Did she stop believing in us? Was there a time, she ever doubted my love?"

His face softens, relaxing his hands. "No." He shakes his head. "You two share a rare thing, I've never seen anything like it. Don't fuck it up."

"I'm gonna do my best. I've dreamed of this day for six years, nothing prepared me for it. I'd be a damn fool if I said I wasn't nervous because I damn well am. Even scared, she means everything to me."

"You know, you've both changed, it takes time to adjust. Learn one another again." He cocks his head.

"I hear ya. I'm trying to take my time, I am. She's just so amazing, everything I've ever wanted. I have no plans of ever hurting her or Silas. I love them, they're my life." My heart hammers against my chest. It may appear we have no idea what we're doing, but destiny knows all.

14

Chord

"Sarah?" I can't believe this shit. "Sarah?" I hope I don't wake Silas up, I forgot to grab a towel. There's a light tap on the door as it cracks open.

"Hey, what's up?" Sarah says softly through the opening.

I poke my head out of the curtain. "I need a towel."

She giggles. "Oh, let me get you one."

I step out onto the rug, taking a step toward the door when Sarah bounds through. Our bodies clash, and my arms wrap around her as the towel falls to the floor. She grasps my biceps, sending shock waves through my body .

"Your towel," she murmurs with hooded eyes. And there it is, just like chemistry, our intense attraction flares like kindling.

127

WRECKING US, SAVING YOU

"I'm getting you wet." My pulse purrs to life as she sinks her teeth in her lip.

"Yes. So wet," she says with a ragged breath as her eyes dart to the tattoos on my body.

Her lips mere inches from mine, as her heart beats beneath my palms. Our gazes locked, time stands still. I see my life in her blue eyes. "Sarah, I need you to leave."

She nods, trembling. "Going. Now." I release her, and she backs into the door and it shuts. Her eyes roam my body, a frenzied desire igniting us both.

"Sarah…" Her eyes snap to mine.

"Going now." She jerks the door open, glancing over her shoulder as she closes it. "Glad to see drinking all that milk paid off for ya."

"I got your milk, lady," I mutter, fisting my hard cock. "I know dude, I know."

I slip into my clothes, brushing my teeth to remove the fur coated on them. Thank fuck I didn't kiss her. I shove my things into the bag and head to the couch. Sarah's sitting in the chair next to it, pillows and a blanket stacked beside her.

"I hate you're going to sleep on this old thing, it won't be comfortable," she says as she chews on her nail.

"I'll be fine." I drop my bag by the door. "I appreciate y'all letting me stay. I need to give One a call, let him know what's up."

"You want me to step out?"

I slump into the couch, patting it. "No, I want you to move that sweet ass over here. Why are you so far away to begin with, actin' like we're strangers."

She quirks her brow. "I think we've become reacquainted at this point," saying as she sits beside me, holding a book.

"What'cha got there?" I ask, pulling up One's number.

"Silas' baby book, I thought you might like looking through it." Her eyes sparkle with the mention of our son.

"I'll make it quick." I hold up my phone, hitting the call button.

"Man, I'm about to kick your ass. What is going on?" One growls as he answers.

"Hey, good to hear from you." I laugh. "I'm good, gonna stay the night with Sarah. I'll be home sometime tomorrow afternoon."

"Is she coming with you?" One's still speaking quietly.

I turn to Sarah, raising my brows. "I haven't asked."

"Why the hell not?" He has a point. "Is she close?"

"Right beside me, why?"

"I'd love to say hi, we've missed her." One's voice cracks.

"One wants to say hello." I put the phone on speaker and her forehead creases.

"Hey, One." Her words no more than a whisper.

"Sarah, it's so good to hear your sweet voice. How are you, baby?" Her eyes glisten.

"I'm okay." She swallows. "I hate I left the way I did."

"As long as you're okay, that's all that matters." One sighs.

"Like I said, I'll see you later tomorrow."

"I guess I can take a hint. Sounds good, brother. Love you." We can hear the sound of a cooing baby in the background.

"Give the babies a kiss for me. Love y'all." Sarah's gaping openly at me. "What did I do?"

"You haven't changed, none of you. I thought your family would hate me, after all these years." She twists her lip between her finger.

"I told you. So what's in this book?"

She scoots closer, leaning into me so that we're shoulder to shoulder. "Silas. His life to date, basically." She giggles, opening it carefully.

"He's so tiny." I move in to examine his newborn photo.

"Tiny? Tell that to my hooha." She giggles. "He was eight pounds and ten ounces, not small in the least."

"Your what? Hooha?" I laugh. "I guess he wasn't so small." Silas' name is written below the picture. "Jordan, huh?"

"I loved the name Silas but Averette didn't sound right with it. That's when Jordan Lake came to mind, Silas Jordan." She grins.

"I agree, so much better." We turn the page to his birth certificate, and I run my finger over his footprints.

"His foot is huge." My chest swells thinking of him.

"Remind you of anyone's you know? Try keeping him in shoes, it's a never ending process." She laughs.

"Sarah Sutton Hamilton?" I glance at her. "I thought you changed your name?"

"Mom had fake stuff made. I have a birth certificate and social security number with the fake name on it. It was so we could move around and get jobs. When I gave birth, I used this name. It's a tiny white lie but it was never caught." She winces.

"I see, they thought you used your middle name." I nod as I notice no father's name is given.

"We weren't married, so I couldn't add your name." She grips my hand. "Again, I'm sorry."

"Stop, please. I think you've used 'sorry' enough in this lifetime." I squeeze her hand, smiling at her.

We spend a few hours going through the album. She kept a lot of his things, documenting anything she could. Closing the book, she peeks up at me through her lashes.

"I didn't want to miss anything." She chews her lip.

"I love it, thank you."

"Oh gosh. It's three in the morning, I need to let you get some sleep." She slides to the edge of her seat, placing the book on the table. "Silas gets up early too, so we should get some sleep." She stands, crossing the room. Pausing at the hall, she turns to me. "You'll be here, right?"

"Right here." I toss the pillow behind me. "If you leave the door open, you should be able to see me."

She glances to the door. "Yeah, okay. Goodnight."

"Night." I wait for her to go in before settling down.

I toss and turn all night, the thought of leaving them tomorrow wracking my nerves. I stare at the album Sarah made for Silas. I've never given consideration to what would happen if I found her. I assumed we'd be together.

Sitting up, I pull the book open, taking my time to study each picture. Sarah is still the most beautiful woman I've ever met; eighteen years hasn't changed my feelings for her or her beauty.

I can't leave them.

The sun dawns, streaming through the window. Sarah's blonde hair is radiant, she's angelic. Silas snuggles her, his wavy, dark brown hair sticks up like twigs in every direction.

He's cocooned in the blankets, leaving Sarah in her sleepwear. Her legs bare, the shirt is pushed up her stomach, leaving her round bottom skimpily covered with white cotton.

"You know, voyeurism is illegal in the lower states," Luke whispers from his door.

"Fuck, you scared the shit outta me." I step toward him. "Do you ever sleep?"

"As much as you do."

131

"I've got so much shit in my head right now, honestly, I stopped sleeping years ago." I rub my hand over my face.

"I suppose about six." He gives me the once over. "Just ask her, you know she'll go."

"She'll go where?" Sarah asks from Silas' door.

"Y'all gonna give me a heart attack, sneaking up on people. Damn." I rub the tightness in my chest.

She giggles, walking closer. "Seriously, go where?"

"Home." She blinks rapidly, rooting me in place. The silence sits in the pit of my stomach like a rock. I knew it was too soon, what was I thinking?

"Silas too?" I could count the hairs on the back of my neck as they stand on end.

"We're a package deal." I give her a lopsided grin as I count the beats of my heart pounding. Her glossy eyes gives me hope.

"If you're sure?" She nods, trying to convince herself. I'm already there.

"Positive. How can I help y'all get ready?"

"We need to pack a few things. What time do you want to leave?" She bites her lip.

"Last night?"

She laughs. "I'll get our suitcase, then I need to get him up; he didn't bathe last night."

"He's fine, I can help."

"Really? Alright. Now, where to start?" She spins on her heels, heading to Silas' room.

"Grab a suitcase and you start packin', I can help Silas shower." My stomach flips over and over. Like I know how to bathe a kid?

132

"Silas, wake up. Baby Boy, rise and shine." Sarah rubs his back, rousing him up.

"Good mornin', Momma." He rubs the sleep from his eyes, and my heart thrums.

"We're going to Chord's house for a few days. Would you like to go?" she asks him as he stares at me. He gives me a boyish smile, and I wink at him.

He scrambles across the bed, leaping from the end toward me. I catch him on the fly as he throws his arms around my neck. "Let's do this."

"Shit! You scared me, Silas Jordan." His eyes grow wide, and his mouth hangs open as he turns to me. I mimic his face.

"Momma said a dirty word." His eyes dart to her.

"I've heard her say worse." Sarah's face flames as she turns her mad mom face on me.

"Chord, so help me." She points at me. "Silas, no more jumping. You two get in there and get cleaned up. I'll pack our bag."

Silas' lip puckers. "We're in trouble."

"It's okay, I've been in trouble with her before." I wink.

"How'd you get out of it?" His brow quirks.

I can't stop my smile as it broadens. "I'll tell you when you're older."

Sarah's face is a deep red as she narrows her eyes at me. "You are in so much trouble, just you wait."

"Uh-oh," Silas and I say in unison as we giggle. I take a step back to leave the room, but Sarah looks up at me and I hesitate.

"What?" She stands straight, her hands on her hips.

"What do I do?"

She quirks her brow before it dawns on her. "Turn the shower on, double check it for the temperature before letting him get in, then just wait on him. Remind him frequently what to wash, boys tend to let the water run on or splash in and call it a bath." She giggles.

I shrug. "Sorry, it's new."

"You and me, we got this."

Chord

"Are you okay with stopping to see my family?" I glance at her to make sure she's not opening the door so she can jump.

Her head nods a few seconds before she answers. "What about Silas?" Her fingers go immediately to her mouth. I reach over, taking her hand in mine.

"They'll be happy to see you both." I lay her hand on my thigh. "I just need to call, let One get everybody there."

"I'm scared. Like, freakin' out." Her hand trembles against my leg.

"We can wait."

She turns to me with her shy smile. "Always thinking of me, you're too good to me. We can do this." She laces her fingers with mine, making my pulse race.

135

"I want to prepare One, he should know." I kiss the back of her hand, returning it to my thigh. Picking up the phone, I give One a call.

"'Bout damn time, what's up?" One's like a mother hen at times. Or is it Mother Hubbard?

"I'm about an hour away. Is there any way you can get the family together over at Mom and Dad's?"

"You know I can, but why? They'll want to know." He's right, I still make him sweat it.

"I don't plan on telling this story a hundred times. Call everyone, even your tribe." I snicker.

"Fine. An hour?" he asks.

"Yes, please. I know it'll take that long for you to load your bus of kids up." I smirk.

"Asshole. We'll be there." I drag a deep breath in, gathering my courage.

"One, I'm bringing Sarah."

"That's great, seriously. Why do I feel a 'but' coming?" He knows me too well.

"We have other news. I want to tell everyone at once, but I need someone to be prepared."

"I'm listening." My stomach knots.

"When she left, she was pregnant, but she had no choice but to leave. We have a son. I found my family, One." A wave of emotion crashes over me—fear, anger, happiness, and love. Sarah reaches over, rubbing my thigh.

"Chord, you were so devastated when she disappeared. I wondered about this, your tenacity to keep looking. Your love never wavered, I admired you for it." One's voice cracks as I try to get myself under control.

136

"I love her even more now. I know it sounds impossible, but I've waited all this time and now I have them."

"I'll read the riot act to everyone, tell them no questions and reassure them that you're doing good." One sighs. "And congratulations, little brother."

"I knew I could count on you, thank you." He ends the call.

"How are we gonna tell them?" She puts her other hand in her mouth.

"Do I need to tie you up?"

"Excuse me?" Her eyes are wide when I glance over.

"Your hands, you're chewing on them. Should I tie them together to make you stop?"

"I'm sticking with tie me up and you can take it from there." She waggles her brows. I grow rock solid as heat rumbles through my body.

"You're gonna make me wreck." She grabs her belly, laughing loudly. "You're not even right." Her eyes dance when she reaches over, smashing her palm into my face.

"Poor baby, I'm sorry." She forces her bottom lip out, eyes wide, trying to look innocent.

I hold my face, pouting. "It's on. I have three days' worth of stubble. That hurt like hell."

She sticks her tongue out at me, and I pretend to go for my zipper. Her mouth pops open as I laugh this time. "You are terrible."

"Stick that tongue out again, baby." I adjust my cock. "I got something for it."

"I know you do." She swivels in her seat, peeking at Silas. "Thank fuck he's asleep."

"Sarah!" She slaps her hand over her mouth.

137

WRECKING US, SAVING YOU

"Not even a week with you and my sailor mouth is back." She narrows her eyes.

I plaster on my shit-eating grin. "I like it dirty, baby." She slaps my arm, her mouth hanging. "Hang on, I need to get my zipper."

"I refuse to talk to you another minute." She puts her palm up toward me, spinning around to stare out the window.

"Minute's up." I gig her in the side, and she squirms, trying to get away from me.

"What am I gonna do with you?" She snatches my hand, holding it to her chest.

"That'll work for now."

She releases my hand, pushing it away. "You're driving me crazy."

"You like it."

"I love it. Now watch the road." My heart races when she smiles at me.

Pausing at the gate, I enter the lock code and wait for them to open. My parents' home comes into view with a host of cars in the drive. "Looks like everybody is here."

"Wow. How many people are we talkin' about?" Sarah's eyes bug out as she takes it all in.

"One's older kids drive, so it's still just those I told you about." I pat her leg.

"So what's your plan, Stan?" She bites her lip with a nervous giggle.

"Want me to go in and give them a little warning? You can wake Silas up and talk to him. Maybe prepare him for the number of people."

"I like that, sounds great." I jump from the seat, waving as I walk around the bumper to the front door.

I take a ragged breath as I turn the knob, strolling into a houseful. "Hey, y'all. Where is everybody?"

"Kitchen!" a chorus of voices calls out. I stride into the room and heads turn.

"Is everyone here?" I scan the room as Mom comes to stand at my side. "You might want to sit down, Mom."

"We're all here." One leans against the counter.

I take a long, deep breath. "I went to Charleston Friday night to support Alden, and while there, I found Sarah." Gasps fill the room. "Now, I know y'all have a million questions but there's plenty of time. She's with me. We have several things to tell y'all, but I want to first ask you to give us time. We're still working through some things. I'm gonna go get her."

A low rumble fills the room as I jog back out to get the two loves of my life. Sarah's standing beside Silas' door, fidgeting. "You're perfect, the both of you. You ready?"

She blows out the breath she's been holding and my stomach knots. "If the butterflies in my belly would settle down, I'd be good."

I help Silas down, and we take his hands, one on each side. As we enter the kitchen, Silas slips behind Sarah. I never thought he'd be as nervous as his mom. He clings to Sarah's hand, hiding.

"Hey, y'all." Sarah waves. My mom is the first to run to her, pulling her into a big hug.

"Oh, Sarah. Honey, have we missed you. You look amazing." She hugs her again as Sarah battles her falling tears. Silas peeks out, gasping. "Oh, who do we have here?" Mom squats, getting on eye level with him.

He steps out from behind Sarah, and Mom's eyes shoot to mine on a gasp. "I'm Silas."

"I'm Elise, it's so nice to meet you." She offers her hand, and he takes it with a grin. "Is this your mom?"

"Yes, Sarwah is my momma." Mom falls to her knees, knowing in her heart what doesn't need to be said. But Silas says it anyway. "And Chorwd's my daddy."

Mom tweaks his belly. "You look exactly like your daddy at this age, it's uncanny."

My dad staggers to my mom's side, kneeling. "It's good to meet you, Silas. We're your daddy's parents, your grandparents."

Silas glances at Sarah, who nods at him. "Hi." He takes my dad's hand, shaking it.

One walks over with Harlyn in his arms, wrapping her in his free arm. "Hey, Sarah."

"One, it's good to see you. I'm assuming she's one of your *nine.* Tell me he's kidding?" Sarah giggles, tickling One.

"I had lost time to make up for after that other mess. But I have to say, you and little brother have the scoop of the century." He smiles, hugging her again.

Thayer watches from the chair in the far corner. Her lips pressed into a thin line. Sarah tilts her head, shuffling her feet. Thayer stands, slowly making her way over. She lays back, waiting for Mom and Dad to give Silas room.

Thayer leans down to him. "Hi, Silas. I'm your Aunt Thayer, Chord's sister. I was your momma's other best friend when she was growing up." Her eyes flood with tears, and Sarah gasps, falling against me.

I wrap her in my arms. "Give her a minute, baby."

"She hates me," Sarah whimpers.

"No, not possible." Thayer glances at Sarah, her face wet. She rises, coming over to us.

"You owe me one helluva talk, sister. But first, you better hug me like you've missed me." Thayer's lips tremble with each word.

Sarah can't hold back, she throws her arms around Thayer and hugs her hard. I pull my hand free, quickly feeling a tug on it. I look down, Silas.

"Is Momma okay?"

I bend down, picking him up. He's getting big, but I haven't held him and I'm gonna make up for lost time. I hold him close as Thayer and Sarah hold each other. "She's good, buddy. Are you hungry? Come on, Daddy will find you something." I step around the girls, walking toward the kitchen.

"Chord, what does he need?" Mom rounds the counter.

Silas locks his hands around my neck. "I'm gonna hang back here with him. I think he's a little freaked."

"Well, if he decides he's hungry, the fridge is stocked, get him whatever he wants." She pats his arm, and he peers at her.

"I've never had a grandmother." Mom's eyes cut to mine, and I shake my head. Her eyes glisten, glancing at Sarah.

"Love her heart, life's been so cruel to her." Mom rubs my back. "To you all three."

"We're gonna be fine, aren't we, buddy?" I kiss Silas on the head. "So what do you think you want to call my mom?"

"What do you mean?" Silas pulls his brows low.

"Grandma or grandmother?"

"I like grandmother." Mom smiles at him.

WRECKING US, SAVING YOU

"That's perfect, your cousins call her that too."

"Momma said I have ten cousins." His eyes wide, he stares at Mom.

"You do, come with me and I'll take you right over there to meet them." Mom holds her hand out to him.

"Can I go?" He peeks up at me, chewing his nail, just like his mom.

"You sure can, they're right over there. When you're done, come back and I'll fix you something to eat." I set him down.

"I will." He takes Mom by the hand, and they slowly walk over to the others.

I lean against the counter, watching Thayer and Sarah. Both still crying with their arms wrapped around each other. One wanders over to stand beside me, looking over the room.

"How you doin'?"

"Good. Shocked." My chest tightens as I watch my mom, holding my son. "Beyond blessed. How did I ever get so lucky. I not only found the love of my life, but I did it twice. And though she has no clue, the extraordinary gift she fought to give me, I can never thank her enough for him."

"I have to admit, I sometimes wondered if once you found her, if it would be over. You know? She'd have moved on or maybe you'd fall in love. Standing here, seeing you together, the way she keeps an eye on the both of you. You watching them. It's obvious you're still in love."

"It's impossible, is that what you're about to say. To warn me, we've both changed and it may be ridiculous to try to work it out?"

"Chord, just because couples get married, doesn't mean they stop changing. We all do it, constantly; it's life. With each new situation, we grow." One pulls his hands free from his pockets.

142

"I know that, I do. I understand it's been six years and we've changed. And yet, we haven't. Love doesn't stop because people change. You grow apart when you change and love stops. If you love someone, you work through the changes."

"I'll be damned." One shakes his head. "You never cease to surprise me. You're a helluva good man, and you deserve this, Chord. You worked hard to have your family. I'm damn proud to say you're my brother."

"I just want them to be proud I'm her husband and his father."

"They already are but you keep thinkin' that way, you won't fail." He hauls me into a bear hug. I've never been so emotional in my life.

"Man, all these feels are fuckin' killin' me." I rub my chest over my heart.

"Yeah, the love of a good woman and a brood of kids will do that to you." He laughs, elbowing me.

"That explains why you've went all pansy on me."

He points in Lea's direction. "You see that amazing woman over there?"

"Yeah, I see her."

"She lets me have sex with her anytime I want. I'll be her fuckin' pansy any day." He fake punches me when I chuckle.

"I see your point," I say as I stare at Sarah. "Maybe she'll turn me into one."

"Only if you're damn well lucky." My big brother and I stand silently, watching our family.

I stand in the kitchen observing Silas. He's playing with his newfound cousins, One and Lea's children. Six are older and three younger; you'd never know he was the odd man out. They've taken him under their wing.

"Are you trying to number them instead of remembering their names." I snicker when Chord nudges me.

"How does she do it? She makes it look effortless. She moves from child to child, sometimes holding two and talking to one or the other way around. I'm wore out just watching her."

"Lea makes everything look easy, but she'll be the first to tell you—she doesn't know what the hell she's doing, but she's loving them as she does it." Chord laughs. My heart hammers as I gaze at him.

"I feel like I'm in a dream, this can't be happening." I step closer to him, needing to feel his warmth.

"Surreal. I have no other words for the last few days." He lays his arm on the counter behind me, and my pulse races. We keep doing this freakish dance of I want to give you time and space to throw me down and fuck me now.

"Hey, y'all. I hate to interrupt, but I wanted Chord to know; your deliveries have been made, but I thought I'd give you a few days before setting up," Lea says, smiling.

"Shit, I completely forgot. That sounds good, thank you." Chord's brows knit.

"What did you buy now, sweetheart?"

"A house and some furniture." His mouth curves into a smile.

My jaw drops. "You what? When?"

"A few months ago, I had One's company build it. Lea and Torrie, a friend of ours, do interior design." He fidgets. "We'll work out a day this week."

"That works. I wanted you to know before you walked into the garage full of boxes. We did get the other things taken care of for you, so y'all should be set up." She rubs her hands together.

"Where is said house? Close by?"

"Over by One and Thayer. Our lots adjoin, not too close because there's plenty of property." He gives me his lopsided grin. I love it.

"Were you going to invite me to see it?"

"Ding, ding, ding. There you go, girl." Lea high-five's me. "I can't believe he didn't tell you."

"First off, she didn't ask. Second"—I cross my arms—"I feel as though there's no winning here."

"Not at all." Lea and I laugh.

145

WRECKING US, SAVING YOU

"Come on, I need to get you home." His eyes snap to mine, and a warmth spreads through my chest. "Or my home. I mean, our home. The house. Let's go to the house."

Chord gives up, brushing past Lea as she chuckles. "I love it. I've never seen him so nervous."

"He's painstakingly easing into everything we do." I sigh.

Lea's brow cocks. "And you're not sure which you want him to do. Take it slow or full steam ahead."

"Am I that obvious?" I wrinkle my nose.

She shakes her head. "No, not really. I own a t-shirt from living there with One."

"Thank fuck, I was beginning to worry." I blow out an exaggerated breath. "One minute, I'm thinking we have plenty of time and the next, I'm afraid we've wasted enough time."

"What's your heart tell you?" she asks.

"Walk your ass to the edge and take a leap. It's the love of your life, don't hold back."

"Here's the thing, we tend to listen to our heads and that's good. Sometimes our hearts need so much love, we're ready to get it anywhere. So we fool ourselves into believing this is it.

"Our heads, on the other hand, think rationally. It's too soon, too fast, or not the right time. The thing is, we listen to it because people tell us it's what's right. But what they don't say is we should do what's right for us. It's our happiness, why do rules apply?" She shrugs. "They wouldn't for your child, so why do we apply them to ourselves?"

I'm gob smacked. "Wow. You're good."

"Oh hell, no I ain't. I've lived, made mistakes, allowed others to dictate my life, and then I met One. How lucky are we? Two of the most intelligent, caring, kind hearted and fuckin' sexy assed men are

146

in love with us. High-five, girlfriend." She throws her hand up, and I slap the hell out of it.

"Well, I certainly can see why Chord thinks so much of you."

"He sleeps on a bed of lies, don't believe a word the little shit says." She winks at me with a giggle.

"Did I hear my name?" Chord saunters toward us as we burst into a fit of laughter. "What?" He stands there, confused.

"Nothing, sweetheart." I pat his chest as One steps out from behind him.

Lea giggles. "Damn, you've got the hang of this already."

"One, you better get your woman. I think she's been filling mine full of lies." Chord narrows his eyes at Lea.

"Yeah, I'm right on top of that." One slides his arm around Lea, dragging her to him. He leans in, teasing her lips before taking them hard. He releases her, and I swear she swoons. And so do I.

"There you go, you tell her." Chord pats One on the back.

"You keep kissin' me like that, I might consider having another baby." Lea's eyes smolder as One's nostrils flare. Damn, their attraction is palpable.

"In that case"—he turns to the room—"let's wrap this shindig up, people." We laugh so hard, I can't breathe.

"Seriously, he's a mess." Lea play slaps One on the arm. "We do need to get our bunch to bed."

"One, where's your whistle?" Chord ducks One's punch.

"Keep it up and I'll tell them what you agreed to earlier." One shakes his finger at him.

"Alright, boys. That's enough for today." Lea wraps her arms around One. "By the way, you never picked out bedding for the bedrooms, just the master. You might want to grab some."

WRECKING US, SAVING YOU

"Okay, thanks, my love." Chord kisses her on the cheek.

"Get the fuck off, you've got your own. Put those chicken lips on her." One jabs Chord a few times.

He shakes his head with his mouth turned down. "She won't let me."

I raise my brows. "Won't let you what?"

"Put my chicken lips on you." He puckers his lips out, coming at me.

I throw my hands in the air, holding him off. "Arghh, no." Chord takes me in his arms, and I begin to tremble. He searches my eyes, then releases me.

"Not yet," he murmurs. "Soon and I won't ask."

My feet hit the ground, but I still feel as though I'm levitating. "Well, just tease a girl, why don'tcha."

"They want us to work for it, Sarah. Don't do it, take control," Lea mutters as she gazes into One's eyes. "Oh, to hell with it. You're on your own."

"See y'all tomorrow." One grins as he fist bumps Chord. Chord glances at me, a grin plastered on his face.

"Was I right? Lea's amazing, just what he needed."

"They're so in love." Chills race over me.

"Let's head out." Chord takes my hand. "I can't wait for you to see the place. We also need to stop at the store and grab a few things."

"Sounds good, if we can pry our child from your parents' arms."

We gaze at his family, each taking turns to say goodbye to Silas. Heat radiates through my chest as I witness the love my son is receiving, unconditionally. Come to think of it, this family has always given their love freely.

"What are you thinking about?" Chord cozies up next to me.

I swipe the tear from my face. "This family. The incredible love y'all give and the fact I have it in spades. I've never thanked you for loving me all this time."

"Yes you did." He takes my hand in his. "When you told me you loved me and when you gave me him."

"When I loved you?" I cock my head.

He bites his lip. "Are you saying you love me?"

"I'm saying we'll discuss it later."

Silas runs up to us. "Momma, are we going home?"

"We are, you ready?"

He nods. "Yep, I'm hungry too."

"Well, come on and we'll go grab some food and supplies." Chord takes his hand and leads him toward the front door.

Elise and Cal walk us to the door. I don't think they want Silas to leave. Us, not so much. They're already doting grandparents, Silas is so blessed. They make plans for later in the week, hugging him again as we leave.

Chord pulls out of his parents' gates, turning right. "Store first, food after?"

"Sure." I shrug. "Silas, what do you want to eat?"

"Pizza!" he yells from the back seat.

I open my purse, hoping to be discreet, I count my cash while in the wallet. Two hundred and fifty, but I'll need groceries when we go back. I'll need to watch what we spend, but pizza is doable.

Chord's eyes dart to me. "What are you doing?"

"Aren't you supposed to be driving? You have a terrible habit of not watching the road," I admonish him, trying to distract him.

"You're not spending your money, period." He scowls.

WRECKING US, SAVING YOU

"I'm not here to take your money."

A light catches us, and as he stops, he turns on me. "You're not taking my money. I invited you here, I want to take care of you for once."

"Like a vacation?" I tilt my head, pissing him off even more.

His jaw sets. "Is that how you feel? This is a visit, a vacation."

"I'm used to planning and budgeting, that's all I was doing." I lie, there's no way I can tell him what my heart is hammering about.

Things are quiet as we walk into the big box store. Chord takes a deep breath, ready for a fight. "I'm not sure what his favorites are, can you please help me?"

"I'll help you, Chord." Silas is his saving grace, I agree because of him.

"Yes, we'll help, and I'll give little resistance."

He quirks his brow. "I think I'd forgotten how stubborn you can be, and I think I like it."

"Remember that feeling when we checkout." I raise my brows with a smirk.

Chord grabs a cart, shaking his head. "Silas, let's go find some sheets." They walk ahead of me, and I watch as they talk. They play and joke all the way through the store.

"That's it." Silas is hugging the bedding before Chord can get it off the shelf. Chord grins, picking at him.

"You're positive this is the one you want? They have Wonder Woman or even Spiderman." Silas' brows pucker as he shakes his head.

"No, I want this one." He tugs at it.

"Dude, they have Batman too." Chord places the package in the cart.

150

Silas' head whips around, giving me his boyish grin. I glance at Chord, he's also wearing his. I roll my eyes. "It's a lost cause."

"What is?" Chord's brows knit.

"You two. I'll never win another argument."

"I didn't know we were arguing." He bumps my shoulder with his.

"I'm not use to having help, and I didn't come here for you to do everything for us, Chord. I've always paid our way."

He licks his lips and everything south of my naval screams. "I know you didn't, you've never been that kind of person. But neither have I, why should you pay for things I invited you to do?"

"It's what I know, how I do things." I fold my arms.

He stops, staring at me. "How about if you suggest it or it's a quick 'we need this', you pay for it. The bedding and supplies for the house, I get because I'll need most of it anyway."

"I can agree to that."

"Look at us, adulting and shit." Chord pushes the cart into me with a smile.

"You seriously need to learn to drive, you're all over the road."

"I keep getting distracted by beautiful women." There it is, the spark that's always made problems for me.

"Well, you need to tell them your old girlfriend is here and they need to stop until she leaves." I walk away, glancing at him over my shoulder. He stands there, his jaw set. My belly knots, maybe that was a low blow.

We finish shopping, grabbing breakfast and snack foods. I don't argue when we checkout, but I think I broke him. Chord hasn't said a lot since my jab about women. Maybe I took it too far.

WRECKING US, SAVING YOU

We swing by for the pizza then head to his place. He turns off the highway into a residential community, not far from his parents' home. The houses range from modest to amazing, I gasp at a few. They all have the beach feel with a weathered color palette.

"This is One and Lea's." He points to the right. "And Thayer and Hardy's"

"They're neighbors, their houses are amazing. And you're right, plenty of land to separate them."

He turns a right and then an immediate right. The tree-lined driveway opens to a large Craftsman two story home. Dark gray with white trim and the garage on the side. It's not until Chord reaches for the garage button that I realize where we are.

"Welcome home." Chord's eyes gleam.

I bite my lip. "You mean, welcome to your home."

He releases a heavy sigh. "Fine, welcome. We'll get this stuff in and I'll toss his things in the washer while we eat."

"You can do laundry?"

He nods as he parks. "I can and I do."

Chord jumps out, unlocking the door. There's boxes piled everywhere. I help Silas out, turning to grab some bags. We follow Chord through the door, from the mud room into the kitchen. I'm awestruck, the open floor plan showcases a great room with a wall of windows on the back side of the house.

I wander over. In the distance, you can see the ocean. "The view sealed the deal for the plans. I couldn't resist looking at this every morning."

"I'd say." I bite my lip as I spin around, taking in the rest of the place.

"I'm gonna throw his sheets in, the plates are in the cabinet." He jogs toward the way we came in. I walk over, peeking through to him. The laundry room is to the left of where we came in.

"Momma, I like it here," Silas whispers.

"Me too, baby boy. Me too." I get to work finding plates and glasses to set the table.

"I need to pee." Silas' eyes are wide.

"Chord?" I walk toward the laundry with Silas in tow. "Chord?" As I look for him, I find a half bath. "Oh, here ya go." I push the door open for Silas as he hurries in.

Chord steps in the mud room. "What's up?"

"Why do you need all of this?" I sound more harsh than I mean to.

He shrugs. "I can't explain it. Or, at least, I can't without you thinking I'm crazy."

"I've already made that discovery."

"You were always in my thoughts and plans." His eyes drop to the floor.

Silas opens the bathroom door, smiling. "I'm done, let's eat, folks." We chuckle. My eyes flicker to Chord; he looks so disheartened. I feel the same way.

"Here we go, there's three bedrooms. It has its own bath, and the other two have an adjoining bathroom. The master is straight ahead." We stand at the top of the stairs, looking around.

"Can I pick my room?" Silas' eyes are wide.

"Any one you want."

"You might want to reconsider, he'll want the biggest one." Sarah giggles.

I purse my lips. "I didn't think of that, besides his sheets won't fit the bed in there." I walk over, flipping the lights on to all the rooms.

Silas runs from room to room. "Hey, baby boy. Let's take this one, leave that one for regular guests." Sarah pulls him to the one at the front of the house with the adjoining bath.

"I love it!" he yells when he runs in.

"The bed is a full, and there are towels in the bathroom. I'll run down and get his linens."

On my way back up, I toss Silas' sheets on his bed, finding him in the tub. I walk around, looking for Sarah, to find her in the master. She cuts her eyes at me when I walk in.

"Sorry, just learning the lay of the land." She shrugs, staring out the window.

I lean against the wall. "No worries. I want y'all to feel at home."

Her eyes dart to mine. "Please, stop."

"Stop what, Sarah? Saying this is your home? That I want to take care of you both? Stop being in love with you because it doesn't make sense to other people that I'm still fucking madly in love with you, all these years later?" My heart pounds against my chest.

"Yes." She sighs. "I can't let myself get caught up in all of this."

"All of what?" I push off the wall. "Wait. You don't want me, do you? Not like I want you, right?" She spins on me, her eyes wet. "Fuck. I-I'm sorry, I thought." I wheel around, rushing downstairs.

I pick up the kitchen, waiting around on the rest of Silas' bedding. Once it's done, I take it upstairs, finding them both curled up asleep. I toss the comforter over them, then I turn toward the door and feel a pull on my hand.

"Chord?"

I wait. Nothing. I take another step toward the door, and her grip tightens. Turning to look at her, she peers up at me. Her eyes pleading, but for what?

"I don't know what you want." Her eyes flutter closed. I kneel beside the bed, and she rolls toward me. Our faces, inches apart. She opens her eyes, filled to the brim. "I don't want to push you. I don't want you to leave. I also don't want you to stay if you don't want to. I need you to decide or, at least, give me some direction."

WRECKING US, SAVING YOU

Her hand cradles my jaw, and I lean into it, craving her touch. Her love. "Right now, I don't want you to let go."

"I never have." I press my lips to her head, leaving her to sleep.

I turn the hall light off, continuing to my bedroom. Electricity shoots through my hand, her touch sending me spiraling. I turn to find Sarah, her chest heaving. The roar of my heart coming to life reverberates in my ears when I step closer to her.

"Kiss me," she breathes.

"I won't ever stop."

"Kiss. Me." She laces our fingers, and my eyes flicker from them to her eyes.

"Only if this is forever."

Her teeth sink in, turning her lip crimson. "Forever is all I want. Always have."

I tighten my grip, hauling her to me. Our intertwined hands land on the small of her back, and I slide the other into her hair at the base of her neck. I tilt her head back, sweeping her jaw with the touch of my lips.

Her audible moan sends me into a frenzied desire. I brush her lips with mine. She sighs, giving me my opening. I slide my tongue between her soft lips. Swirling it over hers, slipping it around as they tangle and fight through the fire.

I release her hand, grabbing her hip as I press her body into mine. Her fingers knot into my hair. Our mouths melt together, no longer misunderstanding what the other is trying to say.

Right now, we know exactly what the other needs. My cock pushes against her stomach as I nip at her lips. Her nipples, hard, push through her shirt. This is the life I've longed for. I take her mouth hard, devouring her.

"Momma?" The sweetest voice in the world rips us apart. She lays her forehead against mine, struggling for air.

"Yes, baby boy. I'm here." I release my hold, our hands wrapping our wrists, stretching as far as we can until we let go. She walks toward our son, glancing over her shoulder. She leaves me, for now.

I'm up and down all night long. I traipse across the hall each time my feet hit the floor. I can't stop myself, I need to make sure they're still here. I lean against the door, watching them sleep.

Silas may be his father's mirror image, but he sleeps like his mom. I cover my mouth, thinking of the times I woke with her knees in my back or elbow in my ear. She'd always apologize, but I didn't care.

She needed to touch me at all times, and I was okay with that. I mean, who wouldn't be. Then she was small but was built like a teenage boy's wet dreams. Having my baby made all her curves pop.

Damn, what a handful they are.

Her eyes snap open, startling me. "That's a little stalkerish, dude."

"Sorry, the view is spectacular."

She rolls to her back, stretching, giving me a full view as her nipples do the same. "This bed is heaven." She yawns, sitting up. Her hair is knotted and sticking up in every direction.

"Good to hear."

"Is your bed not comfortable?" She yawns through her words.

I chuckle. "It is, just cold."

Her eyes are on me, her gaze heated. "We have room for one more."

I glance at the floor, biting my lip. I take a step toward the bed, she shifts, then watches me through narrowed eyes as I climb in on the other side.

WRECKING US, SAVING YOU

"Nice boxers," saying as I lay my head down across from her. Her arm lays on the pillow over Silas' head, resting on it. I mimic her pose, scooting my hand under hers.

"Thank you, I've been meaning to wear them."

She cocks her brow. "You've been meaning to? Do you not usually?"

"Not around the house, suppose that needs to change."

Desire boils over between us. "Please, don't change for me."

"I wasn't planning to." She licks her lips. "Just wanted you to decide if you were making this your home before I break you in."

A line forms between her brows. "Are you asking me to move in?"

"No." Her eyes fall. "I'm asking for you both to move in, I want to be a family."

Her eyes snap to mine. "We're gonna have to work hard."

I nod. "We always have."

She raises her head. "Are you sure? You're positive you want us?"

"All those stories you told Silas, did you believe them?"

Her brow furrows. "Yes, I knew you'd find us one day."

"What did you think would happen, Sarah?"

She licks her lips. "I didn't think about what would happen, I thought about what I hoped would."

I raise my head, gazing into her eyes. "What did you hope for?"

"That we'd be a family. Have a home together. Be safe and happy."

I reach over, caressing her face. "Everything I've done in my life was to prepare for when I found you both. So we could be a family, have a home, be safe and to live happily ever after."

"You did a great job." She releases a heavy breath.

"So did you." I glance at our son sleeping between us. "I dare say, better than I did."

"You already love him so much, don't you?" Her tears build.

"From the minute I read you were pregnant, this just makes it perfect."

Her eyes flicker between Silas and me. "Are you sure? No one's ever wanted me, us."

"You're all I've ever wanted, he's just the silver lining." I lean in, taking her mouth. There's no resistance, nothing stands between us now.

"We'd love to." She places her hands on my face, kissing me wildly.

"Ohhh, y'all are kissin'." Silas' raspy voice floats up between us. We laugh, scooting back down in bed, and we lay laughing for hours.

We stand side by side, cleaning the kitchen. "You wanna shower first? I can stay with Silas."

"Would you mind?" I glare at her. "Old habit, I'll go shower."

"We'll keep working on it." I chuckle as she sits down at the bar, digging through her purse. "Oh and there's no charge for a shower." I smirk.

WRECKING US, SAVING YOU

She purses her lips. "A swanky place like this and I don't gotta pay to shower, Big Daddy?" she says in her best Southern twang.

"Smartass." I narrow my eyes. "Keep the 'Big Daddy' for later." I waggle my brows.

She shakes her head, pulling her phone out. "So not funny." She looks down. "Piece of shit. I need to charge my phone." She pulls out a charger, stuffing her papers back in her purse.

"Here." I reach for it. "You're more than welcome to use mine," I offer as I check out her ancient means of communication.

"Thank you, I might if mine hasn't charged by the time I get out." She stands, putting her purse back in the seat.

"Alright, it's here. Unless you want me to call Luke or work. If it's work, can I tell them you quit?"

She stops in her tracks, and her mouth hangs. "I need to quit my job, find a new one, tell Luke we're moving out."

"Why do you need to work?"

She puts her hands on her hips. "First, I'm not letting you take care of me. Second, I have bills, and third, I want to do my part."

"What bills do you have?"

She rolls her eyes. "I have half a year on my apartment, I can't stick Luke with that and other stuff." She sighs. "I'm gonna take a shower, can we pick up a newspaper when we go out?"

"We can. Don't worry, we'll be fine." Silas walks up beside me.

"We'll be fine, Momma, Chorwd's a good man." We do a double take at him. "It's what she's always told Unc, I'm just saying it." He walks toward the family room, and we laugh.

Sarah holds her hands up. "You're repeating it and you shouldn't, it's rude. Alright, I'm going." She hightails it upstairs, and I follow Silas.

160

"Hey, buddy. If I were to surprise your mom, do something to make her happy, what do you think that would be?"

He taps his chin, holding his mouth lopsided. "She wants a new wardwrobe and a chocolate shake." He smiles.

"We can do that. Is there anything else, like anything she might have said to Uncle Luke?" I'm making my son a conspirator, bad dad.

He nods. "She told Unc she will be so happy when the hospital bills were paid, and she said she wished we all could live rent free. Does that help?" His gazes at me, eyes wide.

I ruffle his hair. "You are a superhero." He stands, flexing his arms. "I'll be right back, you sit here and finish your show." I hop up, hurrying to Sarah's purse.

That's right, I'm about to commit a crime. I'm going to search a woman's purse, breaking all the rules. I'm going in and no one's gonna stop me. I grab her bag, searching it for the paper she had with her phone.

Pulling it open, I see it's what I suspected. A hospital bill for Silas. She's been paying as best as she can over the years. I reach for my wallet, dialing the number and hit call.

After paying the hospital bill, I go a step too far but if I don't, she'll never tell me. My gut twists and I know I'm crossing all the lines now, but I'll be damned if they live from week to week or worry about money.

I pull her checkbook out, calling my bank to make a transfer. As I close the book, something catches my eye. A realty company, gotcha. I shove everything back in, Googling the reality place.

"No, we'll just keep it between us for now. Thank you, I appreciate your time." I end the call, turning to find Sarah.

"Who was that?" She folds her arms.

I open my mouth, closing it again. "Business." I wrinkle my nose.

WRECKING US, SAVING YOU

"Are we telling her now, Chorwd?" Silas runs up to us, throwing his arms around Sarah.

She cocks her head. "Telling me what, baby boy?"

"Oh, it's totally nothing. I wouldn't worry, are we ready to go?" I wave it off, yanking my keys from the counter.

Her eyes blaze a trail down my body. "Think you might to want shower and dress first?"

Fuck. I look myself over, still in a t-shirt and boxers. "Uhh, yeah. Give me ten minutes." I hold up both hands.

I take the stairs two at a time, going over my conversation as I rush through getting showered and dressed. I need to swing by the office, check on my test. I also need to go by Walker's.

I button my vest as I head down the stairs, adjusting my tie as I turn the corner of the kitchen. Sarah sits on a barstool, hands in her lap, face red. Shit. I'm about to explain myself when her eyes roam my body, sighing heavily.

She stands, biting her lip as she walks toward me. Her hips sway, her eyes glint. My cock grows as my mouth waters. She stands before me, toe to toe. Tilting her head, our lips are mere inches apart.

Her chest heaves. "Looking this fucking hot makes it really hard for me to be mad at you."

I lick my lips, swallowing hard. "You think I look fucking hot?"

She slides her hand between us, palming my cock through my dress pants. "What man, as goddamn built as you, in a three-piece suit, wouldn't be? You make me wet."

I grow solid in her hand. "Sarah, I'm gonna bend you over the counter if you don't back up."

She squeezes my shaft, running her lips over my jaw to brush her mouth against mine. "And if you ever pay my bills without my permission again, you'll never get to sink so deep into my pussy you

162

come on contact." She releases me, glaring before sashaying away. "Silas, let's go, sweetheart," she yells out the door.

"Motherfucker." I rest my hands against the counter. "She did not just leave me with blue balls."

"I want a blue ball," Silas says, bouncing into the room.

"Well, your mother is an expert at handling them."

He peers up at me. "I'm sorrwy you'rwe in trwouble, you should apologize. Momma says it's imporwtant when you make a mistake."

I squat beside him. "Silas, I'm probably going to make a lot of mistakes, but I want you to know, I love you. Nothing will ever change that or the love I have for your mom. Now, I need to tell your momma."

"You already did." My eyes snap to hers. "She loves you too, but you should've talked to me."

I stand, reaching for her. "I'm sorry, I should've asked, but I knew you would've never told me or let me help."

"Listen to yourself. You're sorry for getting caught, not for doing it." She places her fist on her hips.

I shove my hands into my pockets. "You're right again. Would you like for me to cancel everything?"

"No," she huffs. "no, I don't want you to do that either." She walks up to me, laying her hand on my chest. "I want us to talk, like we used to, about everything. I want you to know, I appreciate the fact you want to take care of us."

"I am sorry." I wrap my arms around her. "I've missed so much, I want to do what I can to help. If we were together, I would've helped pay the bill."

"You can't spend the rest of our lives making up for what you missed; no one can do that, Chord. Especially when you weren't at fault." She slips her hands under my jacket.

WRECKING US, SAVING YOU

"I get it, you're right." I press my lips to hers. "Wait. Did you say, you love me?"

Her eyes gleam. "Did I? I'm not sure."

I nod my head. "I heard it, I heard 'I love you'."

"That's because I do, I love you." My heart thunders in my chest.

"I love you most."

Sarah

Chord helps Silas from the backseat, taking him by the hand. I don't have it in me to tell him Silas can walk on his own. Chord has carried him or held his hand everywhere we've went. I can't break his heart by telling him.

Chord holds the door open, allowing Silas and me in first. The office has a receptionist area with offices down both sides of the building. The conference rooms are located just behind the main desk.

"Hey, anyone around?" Chord calls out as he walks around the desk, searching the mail.

One walks out of the office to the left. "Hey, have you checked your emails yet?"

"No, I was about to," Chord answers, turning to the computer.

One walks over, hugging me. "Hi, Sarah."

WRECKING US, SAVING YOU

Silas tugs on my shirt. "Can I go around there with Chorwd."

"Come on, buddy," Chord answers before I can.

I roll my eyes at One. "He's gonna spoil him rotten."

"Is there another way?" One shrugs, beaming at his little brother.

Chord helps Silas up on his leg. "There it is, passed it! I'm officially a Real Estate Agent." Chord holds his hand to Silas for a high five.

"Congratulations." I reach over the desk, caressing his face.

"Congratulations, now get to work." One chuckles, and I wink at him as he smiles.

Chord nods. "I'm on it. Is Lea here, I need an update on a few things."

"Lea's here, so is your desk." She comes around the corner.

"We're gonna be making a run to Charleston tomorrow, will that give you enough time to finish the house?" Chord winces.

"Plenty, I have your office almost finished." She jerks her head toward the hall.

"What are y'all going to Charleston for?" One pulls his brows down low.

Chord's eyes flicker to mine, and I smile. "Chord asked us to move in."

"You should've just brought it when you came." Thayer walks in, giggling.

"Right? I was waiting for him to ask, and he was waiting for me to speak up."

Chord narrows his eyes. "It wasn't nothing like that, I didn't want to rush her."

166

"Whatever, we knew y'all would be back together. It was just a matter of time." Thayer puts her arm around me.

"Thayer, have you looked at any of the applicants for the receptionist? We keep growing, and we need the help," One says.

"Umm, we need a receptionist. A family-owned business needs help. I happen to know someone who wants a job." Chord stares at me.

"I've never been a receptionist. I wouldn't know where to start or what to do." My eyes widen, and my stomach flip flops.

"There's nothing to it, you answer the phone and take messages. We'll all be around to help." Lea raises her brows with a smile.

"And who can say they have a job with full benefits? You can also bring your child to work with you anytime. We have cribs in our offices." One inclines his head toward his office.

"Seriously? You want me to work here, with you all?" My mouth hangs open.

"Think about it this way, it'll keep us from having to chase Chord while he runs around checking on you all day." One laughs.

I look from person to person, they seem genuine. "I'd need a week to get settled. I still need to check on schools, and we need to fix Silas' birth certificate."

"Oh, yeah. I forgot to mention a small, tiny thing." Chord smiles at Silas before his eyes dart to mine. "Sarah's a Hamilton."

The entire room drops their jaws. "Y'all, not like that. We're not married, I took the name to work and for Silas." Ahhs and Ohhs spread throughout, and I glare at Chord.

"Well, with the way you two do things, we were comin' along for the ride." Lea giggles.

"Is there anything we can do to help to get y'all ready? With the move, school, or work?" Thayer asks.

WRECKING US, SAVING YOU

My stomach has developed butterflies, it's just fluttering. "I think we may be good. I do need a couple of things to start work in, and I need to plan a birthday party." I wink at Silas, who turns to smile at Chord. Chord gazes at him, his eyes glossy. I lay my hand across my stomach, Thayer slips her arm around me.

"They look so good together," she whispers.

"Perfect." Chord's eyes flicker to mine.

"Another first, I'm not sure I can take all of this in a matter of weeks." He rubs Silas' head. "Just a little information, Aunt Lea has the most money, go for gold and kiss up to her." My eyes are wide as everyone laughs.

"Aunt Lea, can I have a plane?" Silas asks as he giggles.

"I tell you what, we'll plan a trip and you can take mine." Lea tweaks his nose.

"You have a plane?" I think my eyes bug out like a cartoon character.

"You've missed so much." Thayer bumps my arm. "We need to go shopping, sounds like a girls' day!"

"Friday, we'll make a day of it." Lea winks.

I pick at my nails, glancing at Chord as his mouth twitches. "We'll be fine, you should go."

"Just like old times, you can even slip into your favorite store." Thayer bumps me with her shoulder.

"You remember that?" I grab my chest as it skips a beat.

"What favorite store?" Chord quirks his brow.

Thayer giggles. "Oh, I bet you remember. I'm thinking it was white, maybe with lace?"

My face goes from rosy to red in two seconds. Chord's eyes smolder, mirroring mine. "Yeah, I remember."

168

"Me too." My core tightens as the memory of him entering me flashes in my mind.

"Wowza, Mommy and Daddy need a playdate." Lea fans herself.

Chord sets Silas down and stands as he watches me. "Sorry."

I give a half shrug. "It's true."

"We need to get over to Walker's. I'll drop the key off tomorrow before we leave. I need to make a few copies so we have spares." Chord scratches his head.

"Hardy can let Lea in and then go get some copies. Please let Mom know you're headed out of town. I'm sure she's wanting to see Silas again soon," One says.

Chord stands beside me and I slip my hand into his, earning me a squeeze. "Will do. Hate to run, we'll get together this weekend. Thanks y'all." He turns, tugging me along with Silas in the other hand.

Chord drives a few lights down, turning into what looks like an old bank but it says law office. He parks, turning to me. "Are you okay with this? I feel like all I've done is railroad you since you got here."

"I hate we have to do this. I wish like crazy we didn't." My palms are sweating, and I feel sick at my stomach.

He takes my hand. "There's nothing you could have done about it. I know one thing, we've got to push past our regrets. None of them were our fault."

"Silas, this is our last stop and then we'll do something fun." Chord smiles at him, erupting my butterflies.

Chord stands to the side as Silas and I walk in front of him. He moves to the front once we're in the door. "Hi, Chord Hamilton."

"Walker's expecting you, go on in." His secretary is the sweetest.

"Thank you, Donna." Chord takes my hand, leading us to the back office.

He knocks on the open door. "Chord, how are you?" Walker extends his hand, shaking Chord's hand. He's tall, big, and handsome.

"Good." He smiles. "I'd like you to meet, Sarah. Sarah, Walker Pennington." He reaches for my hand, and I take it, gawking at Chord.

"It's good to finally meet you." He grins. "All these years, I thought he was delusional." He closes the door behind us. "Please, have a seat."

Chord takes Silas' hand and we take a seat across the desk from Walker. "Sarah and I have decided to move forward. One of the ways that will help us do that is to have me added to the birth certificate."

Silas tugs at Chord's arm. "Chorwd."

"One minute, buddy," Chord whispers.

"Alright. Do you have the original?" Walker asks as he takes out a file.

"I do but there's another problem."

"Chorwd." Silas pats his leg, and Chord moves him to his leg.

"What's the issue?" Walker leans forward.

"Sarah had to take on an assumed identity but never had any paperwork. She added my name and Silas was born a Hamilton," Chord explains as Silas taps his arm.

"Chorwd."

"So it's as though her name is Hamilton and there's no father listed." Walker goes over the paper.

"Chorwd." Silas pulls on his arm. "Chorwd." He pokes him. "*Daddy!*" Chord's eyes grow wide.

"You called me daddy." Chord's face glows. "I'm sorry, what is it, buddy?" Chord's eyes are filled with tears.

"He looks like Thor and he's got his hammer." He points to the table by the couch, his eyes are about to pop out of his head.

Chord laughs, hugging him close. "Actually, Walker, you do have an uncanny likeness. Are you sure you're not Thor?"

"Positive, I'm better looking." Walker laughs with Chord. "Let's see what we can do with this. I think we're going to need to petition the court and have a family law judge sort it out."

"I thought so." Chord sits back in his seat.

"What is it? Why a family law judge?" My head bounces between Walker and Chord.

Walker stops taking notes to explain. "When you gave birth, you were Sarah Sutton Hamilton. You are neither, Sarah Hamilton or Sutton Hamilton which means you have no way of proving you're his mother. Nor is there a record he's the father. A family law judge will hear it privately, and we can skip over some of the technicalities of the story."

"We might have a better, maybe easier, chance of getting it fixed." Chord takes my hand.

"There's always marriage." Walker shrugs.

"Excuse me?" My chest tightens.

"Since your given name is on there, it would be like you dropped Beth and kept your maiden name. You two get married and it's done. He signs he's Silas' father, and they issue a new certificate," Walker says as matter of fact.

"Oh, that's it. We'll just get married." I tremble at the thought.

Chord's gaze drops, fuck. "We'll try this way first."

WRECKING US, SAVING YOU

"Alright, I'll get to work on it right away." Walker stands, moving around his desk. He picks up the toy hammer before kneeling in front of Silas. "This is for you, it was good to meet you, Silas."

Walker's taken by surprise when Silas throws his arms around his neck. "Thank you, Thorw."

Chord fist bumps Walker, mouthing 'thank you'. "Hit me up if you need anything."

"No worries, we'll get this worked out." Walker holds his hand out. "Congratulations, I know how much this means to you."

He turns to me, hand extended. "Sarah, I hope to get to see more of you. I hear you're an exceptional mother." My heart thrums, there's only one person who could've told him that—Chord.

"I'm sure you will and thank you, but I think he's biased."

"I am, she's amazing." Chord wraps my hand with his, grinning.

Chord

"Have you talked to Luke?" I glance at her.

She picks at her shirt. "No, I haven't. I know, I should've called."

"Why didn't you?"

She turns in her seat to see me better. "I love him, I do. He's my best friend, besides you and Thayer. But he's so damn judgmental."

"Yeah, he kinda read me the riot act before we left. Don't get me wrong, he was doing it because he loves you and I appreciate anyone who has y'alls back."

She leans against the headrest, the little v forming between her eyes. "I know he does, he has for six years."

"What do you think he's gonna do?"

"I'll hear a hundred times how this is too soon. That we need more time. It's insane to think we can make it," she grumbles.

WRECKING US, SAVING YOU

"Sarah, how do you feel about this? Us? Rip off the band-aid and tell me what the hell you're thinking?"

"I've told you, I love you. Am I scared? Yes. There's no way I'm walking away. I've waited my whole life for this love, and I'll be damned if I don't fight for it." Her brows hang low over her eyes.

"You know, that's the first time I've heard you say you'd fight for us." My heart's so full, my chest may rupture.

"When Walker mentioned getting married yesterday, you wanna know the first thing that popped into my head?" She gazes at me.

"Of course." I take her hand, laying it on my thigh.

"I love our son, I don't want him to be the reason we get married or the only bond we share. A marriage, the one we wanted, should be more. A child shouldn't keep someone in it, and they should never end one." She shakes her leg, waiting for my thoughts.

"I agree. I love him but I want you to marry me because you want to spend the rest of your life with me. I'll wait until you're sure we can withstand the test of time."

"Haven't we though? To be apart six years and still have my knees go weak when I hear your voice. To have butterflies take flight when I hear you say I love you." She laces our fingers.

"I think you know your heart and mind, tell him."

She takes a deep breath. "I'm going to, after I tell the club to fuck off."

"One of these days, he's gonna be awake and repeat one of us." I chuckle at her choice of words.

"I know." She covers her mouth. "Why are we waiting?"

"Waiting?" I glance at her, holding my breath.

She closes her eyes. "To get married?"

"I have no clue, why are we?" I raise her hand to my lips, kissing it.

"Once we're settled, how about we plan a small wedding? Maybe on the beach? Is that cliché?" She scrunches her nose up.

"If you want a beach wedding, I'll buy the damn sand. Tell me when and I'll be there, waiting." I kiss her hand again as my pulse races, telling me I'm alive again.

"Luke's gonna flip shit." She winces. "Is he still asleep?" She leans over, staring into the backseat.

"No, Momma. I heard what you said." Silas glares at her, shaking his finger.

"Silas, we may need to talk about bad words." She laughs. "For the first time in a long time, I feel perfect."

"That's because you are, to us anyway." She unbuckles her seatbelt and kisses me. "And you've lost your mind, get your seatbelt back on." I swat at her ass when she sits back down.

We drive into Charleston around noon, knowing Luke will be awake by now. We brought boxes and a few suitcases. Sarah told me they don't have a lot to move, which just upsets me more.

"Hey, where you at?" Sarah calls out as we enter the apartment.

Luke stumbles from his room, still half asleep. "I had to cover for Meagan last night, which you would have known if you'd get a decent phone. Texting, it's this incredible thing." He kisses her cheek.

"Chord has threatened to get me a new one." She elbows Luke.

"She's getting one soon, we can only do so much at once."

"What are you doing here?" Luke's head bounces from the suitcases to Sarah.

"I'm sure I know how you'll feel about this but, Luke, as much as I love you, I have to do this for us. I will never be able to repay you

175

for saving Silas and me. I don't want to lose you. We're moving in together." She fumbles for my hand, and I grip hers tight in mine.

Luke scoots close to her, holding her face in his hands. "Sarah, I love you. You're my sister, the only family I've had. You say you owe me. Not true, I owe you. You brought me back to life. You and Silas did that for me. You're never getting rid of me."

Sarah pulls him into a hug. "Thank you."

"Luke, we have two extra bedrooms, you're welcome anytime."

"It has a beach view like you won't believe." Sarah snickers.

Luke gazes at me. "I have to hand it to you, I thought for sure she would've come back by now. You must be doing something right."

"We're taking our time, planning a wedding and loving life as it comes." I shrug.

"I'm happy for you, honestly." Luke hugs her this time. "Now, what can I help do?"

"There's some boxes downstairs, I guess we'll start with the clothes first." Sarah looks over her shoulder at me.

"I'll grab the boxes."

We work for two hours, getting them packed in no time. On one hand, that's great but the other, it means they did without. I try to keep the anger at bay thinking of what they didn't have.

"Please, if you need me, call. I'm a bus ticket away." Luke hugs her close.

"Luke, if she needs you, my sister-in-law owns a plane, we'll come get you."

"Damn." He slaps his hand over his mouth. "I mean, dang. What's this house look like?" Luke places his hand on his hip.

"Four bedrooms, three and half baths, four-car garage..." Luke belts out a loud laugh.

"You, a four-car garage? Are you planning to learn to drive?" He chuckles at her, Sarah's face is red.

"I am and the Mister's gonna buy me a nice ride." She elbows me.

"We'll start tomorrow." I kiss her cheek.

"Spoil her but good. She deserves it." Luke smiles.

"If she'll let me, we've already fought over paying bills. By the way, thank you, your rent is paid until the new year." I reach for his hand, but he has other ideas. He pulls me into a hug.

"He is a good one." Luke eyes me.

"He is." Sarah slips her arm around me.

We have a late lunch with Luke and Sarah gives her notice. Everyone is thrilled we found each other again. We hit the road around four, hoping to make good time. Silas has had a crazy week with little rest.

"We need a few more things from the grocery store, is it okay if we stop?" Sarah grimaces.

"Why are you asking? And what's with that face?" I turn my nose up.

"Going to the store used to be fun, now it leads to arguments." She squints at me.

"Only because you won't let me pay."

"Fine, you can pay," she murmurs. This woman.

We get to the store and decide to split up, she takes Silas to grab his stuff. I run to get what we need. We're ready to get home. I turn down aisle five and run into trouble.

"Chord Hamilton, where have you been?" Tiffany slides up against me. I take two steps away, swallowing hard. She's wearing the lowest top known to man with her cheeks hanging out. It's a grocery store for the love of God!

"Life, it's been crazy busy lately. It's good to see you, gotta go." I throw my hand up, only for her to wrap it with hers.

"Hold up, now. You haven't called, I want to know why? We were about to get hot and heavy when you shut it down." She runs her hand down my stomach.

I back away, hoping to make my escape. "Chord, did you get everything?" Fuck me. I spin to find Sarah giving Tiffany the once over.

"Not yet, I'm working on it." I know my eyes are as round as baseballs.

"Who's the welfare case?" Tiffany leers at her.

Sarah steps around Silas, blocking his view. "Who's the slut? You know what, I don't give a fuck. Keep your damn hands to yourself."

"Huh! Who does she think she's talking to?" Tiffany curls her lip.

"Don't, this will not end well. This is Sarah, my fiancée, and our son, Silas."

"Funny, he just proposed to me last week," Tiffany snarls.

"Proposed what, to get an STD test? You best take your ass on down the road." Sarah gets in Tiffany's face, and I wrap my arm around her, pulling her back.

"Let's go before Silas gets upset," I beg. "Sarah, please."

Sarah spins on her heels, taking Silas with her. I'm on her tail before she can get too far. "I guess this is what I can expect the rest of my life, your old girlfriends touching you and talking shit."

"I'm sorry." I shake my head as we unload our items. As I pay for our things, Sarah walks out.

Sarah and Silas make it to the SUV ahead of me, she's so mad. I think I see fire coming out of her ears. The ride home is silent, even Silas is afraid to talk. I can't even argue this one with her.

I pull into the garage, and she's out the door before I can get parked. "I'll get our things out tomorrow, if I decide to stay." She helps Silas out, taking several bags as she goes. I get the rest, following them inside.

"Sarah, I need you to calm down."

She glares at me. "Do men know anything? Telling a woman to calm down is like throwing a cat into a tub of water."

Huh? I lean against the counter while she walks around me. Angry cleaning. "I'm not sure why you're so mad at me."

"Because, damn it!" she yells.

"I'm going to get Silas ready for bed." I head toward the couch, where he's watching television. He's sound asleep. I pick him up, carrying him toward the stairs.

"Is he out?" Sarah rushes to us.

"He is, I'm going to change his clothes and tuck him in."

"I'm going to shower." She throws her towel in the sink.

I get Silas down, taking time to enjoy this beautiful child. He may be the sweetest kid ever, and I love spending time with him. Placing a soft kiss on his forehead, I head to bed.

I'm hoping to get out of Sarah's way before she gets out of the shower. I get to my door as the bathroom door opens. "Oh, sorry. I didn't want the light from the other door to wake him." She stands there, wet, with only a towel on.

"No problem." Here's the thing, I'm a man. One who's deliriously in love with the woman standing in front of me, a towel separating me from heaven. Yes, I'm going to gawk.

WRECKING US, SAVING YOU

"Sorry about the store." She chews her lip. "She made me mad as hell."

I step toward her, desire pooling in my blood. "Why did it bother you?"

She averts her eyes. "I was jealous."

"I love you, Sarah. I want you."

"You want me?" Her eyes smolder. I hover over her, watching her tremble.

"Yeah, Sarah. It's been a long damn time since I've spent quality time inside you."

She bites her lip, turning it crimson. "I remember, my thighs were sore for days."

"I'm bigger now." Her eyes lock onto mine as her breasts heave.

"You are?" She drags in a ragged breath. "Show me."

I lean down, lifting her mouth to mine. I brush her lips, tasting her. "Tell me, what do you want?"

"You, Chord. I want you, I can't wait another minute." She wraps her arms around my neck.

I pick her up, and she locks her legs around me. Carrying her to our room, I take her mouth. She moans as I push the door almost closed. I sweep my tongue over hers, and she battles me back.

I lay her on the bed, opening her towel slowly. "Damn, baby. Is it possible, you're more beautiful?" Her hips are fuller, and her breasts sway when I put my knee on the bed. Her tats are fucking hot, a tribal on her arm and a butterfly on her foot.

I lay over her, nipping her bottom lip. She mewls with need. "I never thought I'd see tattoos on you, they're sexy." The tip of my tongue sweeps the parting of her mouth. She opens, allowing me to take her hard. Our mouths slowly work out what our bodies want.

180

I kiss down her jaw, on her neck, traveling to her breasts. Her every breath, rocking and swaying her. Her nipples, hard and pink, in need of me. I swirl my tongue around her, sucking her breast into my mouth.

She bucks from the bed, and I take a ragged breath. I nibble on her, kneading her opposite breast in my hand. My mouth trails down her ribs, over her belly. I drag my hand from her breast, fingers touching lightly here and there.

"Hips." She raises them as I pull the towel free, dropping it on the floor. She sits up on her elbows, watching me leave kisses on each side of her pussy. Placing a soft kiss on her, I replace it with a swift lick of my tongue through her center.

Wrapping my hands around her thighs, I pull them open. Rewarding me with her moan, she squirms beneath my tongue. I swirl her clit, sucking it into my mouth. Releasing it, I flatten my tongue and lick her completely.

I slide a finger into her, and her thighs give way. I brace my legs, pushing them open as I dig in. I add a second finger, she's tight and ready. I can't help but to lick her one last time.

I sit up, dragging my shirt over my head. Her hooded eyes blaze a path to my cock. I pop the first button, watching her gasp with each release. Standing, I drop my pants on the floor. Climbing between her legs again.

"Chord, take me." I do just that.

My mouth on hers, I push into her. Filling her until I stop, waiting for her to acclimate. Her pussy clinches, holding me. My cock grows harder being inside her. It's what dreams are made of. I pull with a slow, intense drag through her wetness. Pushing back in before I'm out.

Her hips rise and fall with my rhythm. Our thrusts becoming more defined and determined. The pace, heating to a boiling point, I rock into her as she meets me with her warmth.

181

WRECKING US, SAVING YOU

Our bodies meeting in perfect motion, I pull her from the bed, resting her on my thighs. Her ass slaps against them as we race to our climax. My arms wrapped around her waist, hers around my neck.

The sweat building between ours bodies helps us slide as her breasts rub against my chest. I pick her up, thrusting into her. She raises, slamming down on me. Our eyes lock as a bright light flashes behind mine.

Sarah calling my name as an anthem, I pledge myself to her. "I love you," she murmurs.

"I love you, Sarah. Most." We crash to the bed, sated and hopelessly in love.

20

Sarah

"No, I can't." I eye him sternly.

"Why not? We're just going for a test run." Chord falls back into the couch. "You have to learn at some point."

"It's not that, I can't today."

He narrows his eyes. "Why not?"

"Chord, please drop it."

He gets on his knees, crawling toward me. I put my foot out, holding it on his chest. "Why can't we go?"

He moves my foot like licorice, laying between my legs. He grinds into me, igniting a fire deep in my core. "Please." I sigh, not sure if I'm begging for more or him to stop. His hips swivel, and I discover I want more.

WRECKING US, SAVING YOU

"Let's go take care of this." He jerks his head toward the bedroom.

I shake my head. "And do what with our son?"

"Just a quickie, we can say we're getting dressed." He kisses my neck, making me groan.

"Argh, stop it." I hold his face, kissing him.

"That's not stopping, that's going." I giggle. "Well, then you need to practice."

"I'm so fucking sore, I can't move. Okay?"

He tilts his head. "Are you now?"

"Yeah, I know you enjoy hearing it. I think your dick's bigger both ways, longer and thicker," I whisper against his mouth before kissing him.

His devilish grin appears. "I think so too," he quips, and I can't help but roll my eyes.

"You're so cocky." I pinch his side.

"That's what I hear." He hunches me, making me laugh harder. Chord starts tickling me until he's attacked.

Silas jumps on his back. "Thorw to the rescue."

I cackle as Chord pretends to fight with him. Wrestling all over me, the couch, and onto the floor. My chest swells, making my heart race. I have my family, mine. No sharing or asking, they're mine.

Chord peeks up from the floor. "Come on, let's go practice. We also need to plan a party." He pounces on Silas again, they have the best giggles.

"Fine! Silas, I'm gonna get dressed." I stand, and everything south of my belly button tightens. "I'll bring your clothes down, finish your food, please."

"Yeah, I guess I better find some clothes." Chord waggles his brows.

I stop at the bottom of the stairs, biting my lip. "You can help find mine."

"I'm on my way." Chord jumps up, chasing me up the stairs.

Two hours later, Chord worked my soreness out and we head out. I hate this. I've never done it for a reason, I don't own a car. Chord, of course, wants to buy me one but after just leaving the phone store, I'm not sure I'll let him.

"I'm never gonna learn how to work this thing."

"The car or the phone?" Chord cocks his brow.

"Both." I snicker.

"You will, momma. I can help you. I love mine." Silas chirps from the backseat.

I lean around, watching him play with his iPad. "You're gonna go broke, spoiling us."

"Is this a bad time to tell you, I'm adding you to my checking?" He raises his brows.

I narrow my eyes. "How can you just do that stuff without me?"

He shrugs, focusing on the road. "I have a few places to show you, maybe we can plan a party of sorts. Maybe, two."

"The wedding is simple, point me toward the beach." I smile. "Silas, I'm not sure. We've always been at home, small and simple."

"He's never had a party, like at a park or anything?" Chord cuts his eyes at me.

"No, we had to budget. And he hasn't started school to have any friends, so we can keep it small."

"Me and small don't go together." I quirk my mouth.

"Tell me about, baby." I shift in my seat.

WRECKING US, SAVING YOU

He makes a right turn, then another, parking. "You ready?"

My eyes are round. "Seriously? You realize what this thing costs, right? What if I break it?"

"Then I'll buy me a new one and this one can be yours." He chuckles, removing his seatbelt. He walks around, opening my door. I swivel, facing him. He stands between my legs, kissing me.

"This is getting us nowhere," I say against his lips.

He sighs. "I was trying to get to first base but now that's off."

"You've been there, years ago." I roll my eyes.

Chord lifts me from the seat, setting me on my feet. He turns me, swatting my ass. "Go. Drive, woman."

I stomp around the back of the SUV, trying my best to pout. Climbing in, I release my tension with a long breath. "Ughhh, okay."

"Stop being so dramatic. Alright, let's go over the basics. Under your right foot is the gas, the long bar in the middle is your brake. Once you've started it, pull the arm here into the letter D.

"You'll want to ease off the brake until you get a feel for the wheel and how it drives. After that, I want you to work the gas, get an understanding of it. The thing is with both the gas and brake, some vehicles will need you to push them hard and others won't.

"That's the main thing, knowing your car and how it reacts under you. Then, we'll tackle parking." His lopsided grin may be the best thing in the world, well almost.

"You can do it, Momma. I can't wait until you can drive me to school if Daddy can't." Chord's hand lands on his chest.

"Still getting use to that, damn if I don't love it." Chord's eyes are soft and sparkling.

I take a deep breath, gripping the wheel so my hands stop shaking. "Here goes nothing."

186

Three hours later, I think I might have the hang of this. "There ya go, baby. Good job." Chord high-five's me as I park again.

"It's this car, I can see the end of the earth this high up." I run my hand around the steering wheel.

"I think you've got the hang of this. How about we go grab some grub?" Chord looks back at Silas, and I take his hand.

"I have to be honest, I often thought about you being a dad. I knew you'd be amazing, but I never imagined this, how you are with him. With us, it's better than any of the dreams I had in high school."

"I hate so badly we missed all these years, it hurts." Chord's eyes are downcast.

I scoot toward him and lean in, taking his face and lifting it up. "I love you, always have, always will. Forever." Our lips meet.

"Are y'all kissing again?" Silas bemoans.

"Fine, let's go eat." About the time I remove my seatbelt, Chord's phone rings.

"Hey, what's goin' on?" He listens, nods and turns to smile at me. "We're right up the street, be there in five."

"What?" I cock my brow.

"Mom's at the office with a full spread."

"Good, I'm starving." I slide from the seat, meeting him at the back of the SUV. He pulls me into his arms.

"I should've asked but to be clear, we don't have to go if you want us to be alone." He holds me close.

"Don't be silly, I love your family. We've had several days. Of course, after last night, I can't get enough of you. But I think, if we could control our hormones as teens long enough for dinner with your family, we can now."

187

"Our. Our family, our home, our son." He brushes his lips with mine. "Our life."

"Gahhh! This is why I fell in love with you, you've always made me feel perfect."

"Because you are." He smacks my ass. "Now, get that junk in my seat."

We drive down Seventeen, holding hands. This. This is my life. "Have I ever told you what I thought about you, my first day of school?"

He shakes his head with a lopsided smile. "Nope. I do remember smiling like a goofball."

"I remember that too but no, that wasn't my first thought. It was how sweet you were to me, the girl from the wrong side of the tracks."

"Never the wrong side, just on that side. You've always been the most beautiful girl in the world to me." He kisses the back of my hand, then turns right into the parking lot.

I shift in my seat, my chest tightening. "The first time they laid Silas in my arms, I stared at him for hours. I told him everything, right then. How he was your spitting image, that our love was epic and that one day, we'd be together."

"I love the faith you have in me. He really is perfect, Sarah. If you know nothing else, believe you did this right." He leans over, pressing his lips to mine.

"Geez, let her breathe." Hardy slaps the hood.

Chord rolls his eyes. "She was trying to choke me. She stuck her tongue down my throat, I was fighting her off."

"I did not." I slap at him, my face flaming.

Hardy opens Silas' door. "Come on, little dude. Your parents are weird."

"Tell me about it." Silas slaps his forehead.

Chord and I stare at each other, eyes wide as we burst into laughter. We head in, hand in hand, giggling. Glancing up, everyone is watching us. We stop in our tracks.

"What?" Chord asks, pulling me to his side.

"Y'all look good together, that's all." Thayer smiles at us.

"You look eighteen or, at least, how you looked at each other then." Elise touches her eye with a tissue.

One narrows his eyes. "Looks to me like they've been to Jordan Lake."

I cut my eyes at him. "Nah, Space Mountain." I wink at him and watch as he turns rosy colored.

"I don't get it, what's she mean?" One cocks his brow.

Hardy bumps his shoulder. "She got laid, explains the smile on Chord's face."

"Y'all, I can't even with you two." I practically run from them.

Lea waves me into the conference room. "Come on, sweetie. Those three will always be teen boys with raging hormones."

"I haven't decided if I like that or not."

"Because we're the ones making them rage." She pats my arm.

The guys follow me back, and we pass out plates. Sitting around the table, there's a million conversations going on. I decide to just jump in.

"Chord wants to throw Silas a party for his birthday, where's the best place?"

"My house," Elise says. "We'll rent blowups and have a blast."

"Seriously, Mom, that's a great idea." Chord looks to me.

"You're the one wanting to have a big party, I'm fine with it." I shrug. This family has taken care of me for eighteen years, no way I can tell them no; it's too much. This family. I scan the room as my heart thrums in my chest. My family.

"Silas?" He turns to Chord. "How about a party at Grandmother's with blow ups and a bouncy house?"

"Will Thorw be therwe?" He walks over to Chord.

Chord tilts his head. "I suppose we can ask him to come."

Silas jumps into Chord's arms. "You're the best daddy everw."

Chord pulls him up into his lap, holding him tight. The room is silent as we all bear witness to the most perfect moment.

"When did he start calling him dad?" Thayer dries her eyes.

"About the time he became the coolest dad ever. His friend looks like Thor, according to Silas." Thayer's face turns to Lea's.

"Walker," Lea and Thayer say in unison. Hardy grumbles something under his breath, rolling his eyes. It's then that it hits me, Walker and Thayer.

"Oh, yeah. We will talk tomorrow, I have lots of questions." I glare at Thayer.

"Hey, Lea has a bunch of drama too. She puts mine to shame." Lea's mouth pops open.

"Throw me under the bus." She hits Thayer with a napkin.

"The biggest thing Lea did was three kids and a shit ton of money." Hardy laughs.

"And running from One." Chord chuckles.

"I ran faster." One punches him.

"Whatever, Captain VonnWoods. We also need to plan our wedding." Chord winks at me as the room screams.

"Wedding? The ring, let us see it." Thayer lunges forward, grabbing my hand. "There's no ring."

"There's no ring?" Lea echoes.

"No ring?" One and Hardy say as they stare at each other, hands over mouths. Holding their laughter, I'm sure.

"No ring? Well, how's she supposed to know she's getting married." Elise leers at Chord.

Chord throws his hands up. "I'm working on it. I've had a lot to do lately, give a guy a break."

I take his hand, tugging it into my lap. "He'll get me one, when the time's right. He's always taken care of me, and he always will."

21

Chord

"Sarah, you do know we have a reservation?" I shout toward the stairs.

I cut my eyes at Silas, and he sighs heavily. "Girwls."

"Tell me about it, buddy." Shoving my hands in my pockets, I pace. A clicky clacky on the hall floor gets our attention, and our eyes snap to each other's. Silas sits up straight as her heels hit the stairs, and we rush to the door.

She turns the corner as Silas and I stare with open mouths. Sarah's wearing the hell out of a blue Bodycon dress. My mind goes blank as my mouth hits the floor, dreaming of unzipping the front of her damn dress.

Laying it open and taking her, savagely. My eyes dart to hers, burning with frantic desire. She's biting her lip, making my mouth water. I lick mine. I whirl my finger in the air without a word. She spins. That ass.

"Momma's beautiful." Silas' eyes are wide as he smiles at her.

I drag in a much-needed breath, trying to calm my raging hormones. "Yes, she is."

"Is it too much?" She wrinkles her nose, as she checks herself out in the window.

"I'll thank Lea and Thayer later." I waggle my brows. "It's perfect for now, I'll adjust it later."

She fights her wicked smile, running her hand over her plump ass. "I'm looking forward to it."

"Okay, folks. I have grandparents waiting to spoil me," Silas announces, making us laugh.

"You don't go thinking you're going to get whatever you want," Sarah quips.

"I'm not, Grandmother said it." I shrug, taking her hand in mine.

"Shall we?" I wink.

"Where are we going?" Sarah asks.

"To my parents to drop him off." I smirk to her annoyance. I close Silas' door, turning to her. I take her hand, helping her in. "I love your hair up like this." I say as I play with the pieces that have fallen around her face.

"Thank you." She presses her lips to mine.

After dropping Silas off for a sleepover at my parents', we arrive at the restaurant in the nick of time. I fucking love when we walk in. Sarah makes every man in here turn his head. As we're seated, a man drops to his knees to propose. Everyone in SeaBlue turns to them, watching the event unfold.

WRECKING US, SAVING YOU

Sarah's eyes fill as she rubs her finger, dreaming of the day I put a ring on it. She spins to me, her smile as warm as the sun. "That was so amazing."

"I'll give him props, the ring was cha-ching." I rub my fingers together.

She wrinkles her nose. "I didn't see the ring, only her eyes." Such a beautiful soul, she doesn't care if she has a penny, she wants to be happy.

"No, you wouldn't pay attention to that kind of stuff."

"What's that supposed to mean?" She scowls at me.

"Nothing. You aren't that kinda girl, you don't care about the ring and stuff." I shrug.

"Again, what kinda stuff?" She raises her chin, my breath quickens.

"I mean, you don't care if you have a big, blingy ring or if I'd propose here or in the bathroom. It's not you, romantic shit."

Her shoulders slump. "I like romance."

"Says the girl who didn't believe in love." I smirk.

Her head drops, she fumbles with the menu. "I was young and stupid, it was before you showed up."

"So you're saying you want a big proposal?"

She half shrugs. "No, not at all."

"Let's order." I try to divert her. "We can discuss it later, I don't want it to ruin the mood."

She nods, averting her eyes. She fidgets while we wait on the food, and once it arrives, she picks at it. I think I hurt her feelings, damn it.

"Not any good?"

Her head snaps up. "Huh? Sorry, too much to think about."

"Your food, does it taste good?" I incline my head to her half-eaten plate.

"Oh, yeah. It's delicious." She lays her fork down, laying her hand on her stomach.

"I can tell." A chill runs over me, knotting my stomach. She's looking everywhere but at me. I sigh. "You wanna go?"

Her chest heaves as she nods. "I think so."

I call for the check, watching her closely. Once in the car, Sarah lays her head against the window and we drive home in silence. I help her out of the SUV, taking her hand in mine.

"Tell me what's wrong?"

"Nothing. I'm just all weird tonight, you know, first grownup date and all." I lift her chin to my face.

"You know, all you ever have to do is to tell me what you want or need."

She nods. "I know." She tiptoes, pressing her lips to mine.

I release her, watching her walk to the door. "Hey, before you go up and change, can you grab me a bottle of water? I'm gonna check the back lights, they weren't working last night."

She forces a smile. "Yep, I gotcha."

I wait until she's in the door before heading out back. I check things quickly and then take the deck steps two at a time. I knock on the door until she walks up to it.

"Sorry, I thought you would use your keys." She spins just as I grip her wrist.

"Sarah?" Her head falls to the side. "Look at me. Please."

195

WRECKING US, SAVING YOU

She releases a heavy sigh, turning back to me. I step out of her line of sight, her eyes land on the tent. She beams as the light from inside glows.

"What's this?" Her brows furrow.

"Stuff." I tug at her hand.

She pauses, kicking her shoes off. "How'd you do this?"

"The same way we did it back then."

"One," we say in unison. "And Hardy helped this time."

She bends, checking it out. 'Should I go in?"

"I'm hoping so."

I lean back, watching the most perfect ass this side of the Mississippi wiggle up across the air mattress. "Now that's a fucking sight for sore eyes." I adjust myself, climbing in behind her.

She giggles as I get comfortable. "It feels a little smaller than it did before."

"A little? How in the hell did we do anything in this?" I can't help but to laugh.

"I was a contortionist and you were Houdini." She giggles.

"I was good at making things disappear." I lift the hem of her dress, running my hand up her leg.

Her breath hitches from my touch. "Look at you, still making me quiver like a virgin."

I move over her, laying her back. "Look at you, feeling like one."

She pinches my side. "Hey, asshole."

"I thought that was a good thing." I cock my brow.

"I don't even care, this is amazing. And yes, this is my kinda stuff." She locks her hands behind my head, pulling me into a kiss. I fight myself, hating to release her.

"Hold up." I throw my finger up, sitting back on my knees. I offer her my hand, she takes it and I pull her up with me.

"What? If this is about earlier, I was just being weird." She waves it off.

"No, this is about something else." I reach under the pillow, pulling the little red box out. I unfold my hand, revealing it to her.

She gasps, and her hand flutters to her mouth. Her eyes flicker from mine to my hand. "You did not."

"You have been my heart for as long as I can remember, I can even tell you when you became my soul. It was the first day I kissed you, I knew there would never be another like you.

"I will never be able to tell you how much I love you. Not only for loving me but for giving us the perfect son. Please, after all these years of waiting and wanting, answer this question for me.

"Sarah Beth Sutton Hamilton, will you honor me by becoming my wife, my best friend, my partner, the mother of our son and many more to come but most importantly, the love of my life?"

She nods before I even finish. "Yes! Yes, I will."

I take the ring out, sliding it on her finger. The two point two carat, white gold solitaire has a twisted band with diamonds imbedded around the band and the prongs. She takes my mouth with a hunger, fisting my hair.

Her tongue rolls over mine, leading the way as they fight for the upper hand. I reach between us, unzipping the front of her dress. It falls open as I lay her back. Her mouth on mine again, she wiggles free from her dress.

Her hands work the buttons on my shirt. Giving up about halfway down, she rips it open. Pushing it over my shoulders, she nips my neck before taking my mouth again. I palm her breast, running her hard nipple between my fingers.

WRECKING US, SAVING YOU

She slides her hand down my pants, fisting my cock. I groan as I watch her face when she strokes me, long and hard. Her mouth forming the perfect O. My pants unzipped, she works them down my thighs.

Leaning back, I pull them off my legs. I turn back to her, gazing at the most beautiful woman in the world, in front of me, stripped naked. Placing soft kisses, I work my mouth up her side and over her ribs to her breast.

Taking it in my mouth, I flick her puckered flesh. Sucking it between my lips, she bucks from the mattress. She grabs my face, pulling it to her mouth. She swirls her tongue around mine, nipping at my lip.

"Chord." I look in her eyes. "I know you love me, I need you to fuck me." Her chest heaves, rubbing me in all the right ways.

"I'll fuck you anyway you want, baby." I back up, kneeling at her feet. Running my hand up her legs, I grip her behind her knees, pulling her to me. Her ass rests on my thighs as her breasts sway. I slide my arm under her, flipping her to her knees.

I smack her ass. "Up, baby."

She mewls as she steadies herself. I push my legs between hers. Laying over her back, I slide my hand around her stomach. I trail my fingers down to her wet center. I pull my middle and ring finger through her pussy, over her clit.

I rub her, circling around, until her back arches. Gripping her hips, I plunge deep in her core. She cries out as I gasp. I find a quick pace, grunting with every thrust. Pulling her ass into my body as I push into her.

Our bodies falling and crashing into one another. The sound of her moaning drives me harder into her. I push her legs out, getting deeper into her pussy. I pound her from behind, meeting her every groan with my own.

I quicken my pace, pushing us higher. Her pussy grips and releases me, making my cock throb with each grind. My hips moving faster, my thighs burning as I slide in and out of her. She's slick and hot, I drive deeper.

We work toward the same goal as she pushes back and I slam forward. I reach around, circling her clit with my finger, releasing her to scream as she comes, drenching me.

I meet her, exploding into her as I call her name. I fall to her side, pulling her back to me. Our breathing, labored and sated. We slowly fall back down to earth, her in my arms. Made for me and I for her.

"I love you."

"I love you. Most."

Sarah

The sun breaks through the slit in the curtains, I blink, trying to get my eyes to open. Laying here in Chord's arms, I feel protected from all the bad in the world. I don't want to move, I prefer to stay here.

"Have I mentioned how much I love this." His raspy voice sends chills over me.

"Love what?"

"Holding you." He pulls me closer. "After you left, I spent days like this, holding the pillow with your scent on it."

My stomach lurches. "I had nothing. Mom didn't give me a chance to get anything."

"I don't know how you did it, how you survived it all." He presses his lips to my head.

I swallow hard, forcing the memories back. "I found those pictures of us and when I had Silas, it was like having you. The child looks nothing like me."

"Poor child, I wish he did look like you." He chuckles, shaking the bed.

"Stop it, I think you're hot." I turn in his arms. "You know, we could remedy that?"

He places a kiss on my nose. "What's that?" He kisses my brow.

"Having a child who looks like me." My gaze drifts to the ceiling.

He presses his lips to mine. "Are you saying you want another baby?"

"Yeah. I mean, not right now but yes." I sigh as his mouth nibbles on my neck. "I want to make more of us." I moan when he slips his hand between my legs.

"Care if we start now?" He rolls me onto my back.

"Not in the least."

An hour later, we trek downstairs for food. We're busy flirting while we clean the kitchen. He cooked and I said I would clean but here he is, by my side, like he's always been. A phone starts buzzing, and I continue washing the dishes.

"It's yours." Chord hands me the phone.

"I thought it was yours." I giggle.

"Hello."

"Hey, sister." Thayer sounds bright-eyed.

"How are you?" I giggle. Chord is behind me, kissing my neck.

"Tell him to leave you alone for five minutes." She laughs.

"She said to leave me alone for five minutes."

"You're taking her away later, I have to make up for lost time," he mumbles through his kissing.

"I'll be over around two, does that work?" Thayer asks.

"I think Chord's going over to Lea's with Silas, so we can leave from there. We need to get some yard toys he can play with."

"Okay, we'll meet at Lea's," she chirps. "Later."

Chord runs his hands over my hips and around to my breasts. "Let's work on baby number two again."

I spin on him. "I didn't mean pregnant today, just sometime. We haven't even gotten married yet."

"There were no guidelines earlier, Sarah." He presses his lips to mine.

"Guidelines?" My jaw clenches, and I step under his arm to leave. I lived by everyone else's rules my entire life, why is he acting like we have them now?

"Hold up." He grabs me, lifting me to the countertop. "I'm joking."

I stare at my hands, picking at my nails. "I know, I'm all over the place. One minute, I want it all right now and the next, I'm afraid we're going too fast."

He nudges my chin up, waiting for my eyes to meet his. "I get it, it feels like we're moving fast but at the same time, standing still and watching it all happen."

"And here you are, all Joe Cool."

"Not in the least, I'm freaking out. I don't want to push you, yet. I want to somehow be where we would be if we had never lost each other." A line forms between his eyes.

"You mean as if we had finished college, we would've been married already for like, two years?" I half shrug.

"Exactly. I want us to be working on our second child, our lives going the way we dreamed and you, to be the happiest girl in the world." He presses his lips to mine.

"So you think had things not happened the way they did, our lives would be like that?" I search his eyes for any variation of the truth.

"Yes, I do." He believes it, I can see it.

I push at his chest, trying to not laugh. "You just want me for sex."

"Six years without you. I jacked off a million times thinking of you, don't cock block me now." My mouth drops to the floor. "That'll work too."

"There were a few times you weren't alone." I hate myself the minute it leaves my mouth.

"Three times, Sarah. Is it fucked up that I betrayed you when you stood strong? Yes, and I hate myself for it. But there's no way I wasn't telling you. We've always been honest with each other, and I wasn't letting you hear it from anyone else."

"You had no clue what the hell was going on or if something had happened. For all you knew, I was gone." The pain in my chest is suffocating me.

"Nevertheless, I'll regret it for the rest of our lives." He hangs his head, shame written all over him.

"Stop, I don't want you feeling this way. I hate I feel this way." I wipe my falling tears. "I know something that would help me feel better."

"Please, tell me. I'm willing to do anything." He places his hands on the counter, caging me in.

"When I'm at my lowest, doubting everything, love me fiercely." His eyes float to mine.

"I do, baby. More than my own life." He hauls me into his arms, taking my mouth and owning me. Body and soul.

"I need a shower, you need a shower." I drag his shirt over his head.

"So what are you saying?" Desire teeming in his eyes.

"I've never had sex in the shower." I watch as his mouth turns into his boyish grin.

"Me either." He puts my legs around his waist. "Time to check off another dream of mine." He pulls me from the counter, carrying me upstairs.

I stand in the bathroom, drying my hair. I scan the room, the blues and neutral tones are beautiful. The color palette carries throughout the house, except three rooms.

Laying the dryer down, I walk into the extra bedrooms. There's furniture but no color or bedding. I wonder why Lea didn't finish these rooms?

"There you are..." Chord wraps his arms around me. "What are you doing, besides standing naked in the middle of the room?"

I giggle. "Like there's an inch of my body you're shocked to see. Why aren't these rooms done?"

"I was waiting for you." He shrugs. I turn, looking at him. "I had to do downstairs, it would've been weird to have a couch and television, and nothing else. Well, that's what Lea said."

"I was..." I trail off, hesitating.

"You were?" He's going to make me say it, isn't he. He is. I roll my eyes.

"I was wondering if you mind, can I decorate them? Maybe paint, some bedding?" He pulls me closer when I shiver, but I'm not cold.

"Absolutely. If there's anything you want to change, we can do that. Lea and Torrie have a ton of samples at the office." My brow furrows.

"Seriously?"

"This is our home, do what you want. You don't need to ask for a thing, except the bank card but only because we don't have yours yet." He cocks his brow.

I tug at his hand, leading him to Silas' room. I pull clothes from the drawer as he watches. A line forms between his brows.

"Not sure I'll ever get past taking your money." I slip into my panties, glancing up to find Chord glowering. "What's that face?"

"Why are your clothes still in here?" He shoves his hands in his pockets, making his pecs flex deliciously.

"Should I move them?" My stomach flips when he raises his brows. "I'll move them. Any particular spot?"

"Yes, our closet."

"No shit. I mean, dresser, chest, which side of the closet? Do you use a particular sink or side?" I hook and spin my bra as his eyes follow my every move. I snap my fingers. "Here, babe." Pointing to my eyes. "I'm here."

"I hear you. I like seeing you." He hooks his finger in my bra, yanking me to him. "Why do you need to wear clothes?"

"We have a son, and there's this thing about nudity in public places."

"Oh, yeah." He sighs. "Listen, this is our home. If my clothes need to be moved, do it. If you want the sink closest to the outlet, take it. If you want to paint something, I don't care."

"I love you."

"Wait a second, you may change your mind." He takes a deep breath as my palms begin to sweat. "I haven't earned most of my money. I have an inheritance from my parents and a brother who always thought the best investment he could make would be for Thayer and myself.

"I had more money in high school than most of the parents did. This house was my second purchase from that money, my car the first. My college was paid for by my parents, and One bought my first SUV for my birthday."

"And you're telling me this because?"

"Stop acting like it's my money. If it weren't for my family, we'd be living on noodles and Kool-Aid. But as long as you were by my side, I wouldn't care."

"Your point, dear?" I ask, my hands on my hips.

"There is no 'your money, my money' from this point on; it's our money." He crosses his arms.

"Is that so?" He nods. "Is that an order?"

"Nope, but it sure would make life easier and another hurdle jumped." He rubs the back of his neck. He's so sweet and yummy and maddening, but he's also right.

"For the record, I win the next argument." His eyes light up, a smile growing on his mouth.

"You bet, baby." He reaches for me, but I slap his hand away.

"Oh no, big boy. That look in your eyes will get us both in trouble and we're already late. Now, scoot. I'll move my clothes after I get back with all the new ones you're buying me today." I wink.

"I'll grab a shirt and make room in the closet." He slaps my ass before jetting out of the room.

"Smartass," I grumble with a smile as my heart skips a beat.

I've spent the afternoon shopping with Thayer and Lea. I have several new outfits to wear to work on Monday. I'm so excited to be doing something Silas can be proud of.

We walk along the mall, window shopping, when I spot something on the other side. I don't say a word, making a beeline to the window. I peek inside the store as I look at the dresses up front.

"Are we needing one of these?" Lea nudges me.

"Not yet, but a girl can look." I smile as my stomach knots.

Thayer grabs my hand, tugging me through the door. "Let's get a closer look."

There's racks upon racks of dresses, wedding, bridesmaids, and flower girls. I just want to marry Chord, not have the world in it. Simple, low-key, and family. His family, but they're the only one I have.

I giggle as Thayer and Lea try on veils when something in the corner gets my attention. I work my way around the stands, glancing at the girls and then the material until I reach it.

I pull it from the rack as my heart hammers. It's the most beautiful thing I've ever seen.

"Try it on," Thayer whispers in my ear.

I fight back tears when I turn to them. "It's perfect."

WRECKING US, SAVING YOU

"Oh, you have to try that on; if you're about to cry, you have to do it." Lea takes the dress, plodding to the changing room.

Thayer hooks my arm. "I can't wait to see you in it."

I take my time, making sure everything's where it should be. It has lace and a flowing sheer skirt, everything I ever envisioned. I step out, easing my way to the full mirror.

"Sarah." Thayer grasps her chest.

"Oh, yeah. That's the one." Lea's eyes shimmer.

I lay my hand on my stomach as it flutters wildly. I take my free hand, fanning my eyes as I hold back my tears. "This. It's the dress. The one I have to wear to marry Chord, he deserves a dress like this."

Lea puts her arm around me, looking at me in the mirror. "You deserve to marry Chord in a dress like this, Sarah."

"I've always wanted to say this—are you saying yes to the dress?" We giggle like little girls.

"I am." I dab at my eyes.

Thayer helps me from the dress while Lea gather's our bags. She walks with me to the front of the store, where a lady begins ringing me up.

"Will that be all?" She smiles.

"For today."

"That's $1685.00 Is this cash or credit?" My jaw goes slack. I cut my eyes to see where the others are, standing by the front window.

"Oh, my. I forgot to look at the price. Would you happen to have a layaway?" I run my hand through my hair.

Her face softens. "We do. Can you pay two hundred dollars today, it's a little more than ten percent."

I think back when I checked my money on the way here, I have two hundred and thirty dollars in my account, and I haven't spent anything. "I can." I hand over my debit card.

"Is there a problem?" Thayer steps close to me.

I wave her off. "No, I'm going to lay it away until I start working."

"Would they not take Chord's card or check? I know there's no problem with his." Thayer glares at the clerk.

"Thayer, I'm buying it. I refuse to marry your brother in a dress he bought."

"I'll pay for it." Thayer reaches in her purse.

"No, you will not. I've got it."

"What's going on?" Lea pops her head in the door.

"Sarah's putting her dress on layaway so Chord won't be buying it." Thayer side-eyes me.

"I'll buy it or let One," Lea says tossing her wallet at Thayer.

"No." I put my hands up. "Thank you, but no. I appreciate y'all, I do. But I wouldn't even let Elise buy this dress. This family has done more for me than my own. If Chord marries me, it'll be in the dress I bought for him."

"There ya go," Thayer says.

"She really does belong in this family of strong women. Well, have at it, sis," Lea says to the clerk.

On the way home, I stare at the dress receipt. It'll be easy to pay off and I'll have done it on my own. I fold it as small as possible and put it in the little secret pocket in my purse.

Chord

"Hey, buddy. Good mornin'." I rub Silas' back, waking him up the way my mom did me.

He stretches, forcing his eyes open. "Mornin, Daddy."

"Are you ready for some birthday party fun?"

He sits up with a lopsided grin. "I am. I'm so excited."

"I think your momma has something special for you to wear, wanna go see?"

"Yes." He stands, raising his arms. I grab his wrist, sliding him onto my back. It's become our ritual. "I smell pancakes."

"Yes, you do. Momma has been working hard to make today nice for you." I trot downstairs as he bounces on my back.

210

We turn the corner at the bottom and watch as Sarah plates a stack of flapjacks. The smell is to die for, she adds a little cinnamon to the mix.

"Momma, we smelled that from our room." I wink at her, when she walks over.

"Are y'all hungry?" Silas nods.

She places a kiss on his temple. "Happy birthday, Silas Jordan."

I let him slide into the chair. Leaning over him, I kiss the top of his head. "Happy birthday, buddy."

"Who wants pancakes?" Sarah yells as she sets down a huge plate.

We get busy with breakfast, finishing in no time. I know Silas is thrilled, Sarah seems anxious. She hurries down the stairs, spinning in a circle as Silas and I watch. Our heads bounce back and forth like tennis balls.

"Here's his clothes, please make sure he gets them on right." She doesn't even look at us before she's off again.

"Thor!" Silas screams when he holds his shirt out.

"Cool, dude. Momma thinks of everything."

She comes down the stairs with Silas' backpack. "He needs this on."

"Can I help you do something?"

She stops in her tracks. "Can y'all take these things out to the car?"

"Yes, ma'am."

Silas covers his mouth, snickering. "You called her ma'am."

"She's a girl, I can do that. You grab those two, I'll take these." Silas follows me to the car, and we come back in to find more bags.

"Sweetheart? Baby? Sarah!" I yell up the stairs.

211

WRECKING US, SAVING YOU

She pops her head around the corner. "Yes?"

"Is there something you want to tell me?" I fold my arms. She comes down, stopping in front of me, out of breath.

"Huh?"

"Why are we packing the SUV like you're leaving?" She gapes at me.

"What if he needs a change or I do? And we may need towels, did she say if he could wear shoes or flipflops to take off before playing? Oh, sunscreen." She jumps up, turning to run, but I grab her hand.

"Honey, we have everything we need. I'm sure Mom has some things, if not."

Her face falls, I pull her to me. "I want everything to be good for him."

I lift her chin, pressing my lips to hers. "It'll be great. We've gotta go or we're gonna be late." I throw her over my shoulder, turning the corner, I take Silas' hand. "Get the door, buddy."

The gates to my parents' home swing wide, allowing us to drive through. As we get closer to the house, we can see cars all the way around the drive.

"Who did she invite?" Sarah's forehead creases.

"Family and friends." I shrug with a lopsided grin.

She fidgets with her clothes, even fusses with Silas' once he's out.

"How do we look? Is his shirt dirty? Wait, his shoes have a frayed lace, I need to change them." She sprints to the back, digging through bags.

I lean against the back of the SUV, and Silas leans against my leg as I run my hand through his hair. I'm waiting for her to breathe. She doesn't. "Sarah?" She cuts her eyes at me. I'm not sure what flashes in them, but I can tell this is bigger than I first thought. "Talk to me. And don't say nothing."

She wheels around. "What if they laugh at him over his shoes?"

Fuck. "I promise you, that will not happen. Most importantly, he's not you. He has an amazing mom, who takes better care of him than any mother I know could."

"You think?" She crinkles her nose. I slide Silas around to face her.

"Have you ever seen anything more perfect?"

Her eyes flicker to Silas. "No, I haven't."

"Come on, let's go party." I hold my hand out to her, and her eyes lock with mine as she takes it.

I lead them around the side of the house where Mom has every blowup offered in her yard. The grill is going and there are kids playing.

Silas yanks on my shirt. "Are those my frwiends?"

"If you want them to be. Why don't you go say hi?" He takes off running, we follow behind.

"Chord, how you doin'?" Brannon throws his hand up.

"Hey, man." I shake his hand. "Brannon, this is Sarah."

"Hello, Sarah. I hate I keep missing you at the office." He offers his hand, she takes it.

"Right, you're married to Torrie."

"I am. And that little brunette next to Silas is my daughter, Andi."

"She's beautiful." Sarah beams when Andi holds Silas by the hand.

"She's her mother." Riley chuckles. "Hey, y'all."

WRECKING US, SAVING YOU

"This is Riley, Walker's brother." I incline my head at him. "Wait for it, Andi's stepdad."

Sarah's head flips from me to them. "And Walker was Thayer's fiancé?"

"Yep, good job." Brannon winks at her.

"I love it! Y'all are one big, happy family." Sarah's mouth curls into a smile.

"We all grew up together, in one way or the other. So why should that change." Riley grins.

"Sarah, my baby girl." Mom gives her a hug. "I'm gonna hug you until I get my fill."

"You know you can anytime." Sarah hugs her again.

"Why am I not allowed to get my fill of you?" I mutter, earning me chuckles from the two assholes beside me.

"What's that, Chord?" Mom asks.

"He thinks he's being cute, he's talking about sex." My head whips around to Sarah, who laughs her ass off.

Mom rolls her eyes. "You boys and sex."

I stand there, mouth on the ground. Sarah leans against me, snickering. "Don't try to embarrass me, Chord. You won't win."

I slip my arm around her, holding her to me. "Duly noted."

"More like, dayum." Brannon hits Chord's arm.

"No refills allowed, your mom said so." Riley bends over holding his stomach, cackling.

"Har, har, har. Y'all are too fucking funny." I shake my head, hoping to cool my reddened cheeks.

"Sarah?" A familiar voice to surprise my loves, calls her name. She turns, slapping her hand over her mouth.

214

"Luke? Oh my gracious." He hugs her tight, giving me a high-five.

"How did you?" He points to me.

"He's alright, I think you should keep him." Luke winks.

"Good to see you, man."

"Chord?" Sarah elbows me, jerking her head behind us. "I'll get Silas."

I turn to see Walker, trudging toward me. "Only for a kid."

"Hey, gorgeous," Riley says to Walker's fiery redheaded girlfriend, Reese.

"Walker?" Brannon's eyes are round.

"Man, do I owe you. Seriously, nothing but mad love for you." I take his hand, pulling him into a hug.

"I think he needs to keep this thing." Reese waggles her brows.

Alden turns the corner, carrying presents. "Y'all didn't have to get him anything, this is epic enough." I point to Walker.

"Do I at least resemble him?" Walker's brow creases.

"Thorw?" Silas' face is worth everything as he stares at Walker.

"I owe you big time." My heart thunders as Silas runs up to Walker, dressed in a Thor Halloween costume.

"Damn, he did it." Hardy shakes his head in amazement.

One pats Walker on the back as he joins us. "Gentlemen, we need to up our game, the Pennington's are stealing all the women with shit like this."

"Damn straight," Hardy grumbles.

"This is a helluva day, brother." I rub my chest, gazing at my life as they talk to Thor.

215

WRECKING US, SAVING YOU

We play with the kids, enjoy good food, and laugh with our friends. Sarah comes to my side, I pull her into my lap. She lays over on me, her arm around my neck.

"Are you tired?"

"I am, but this day has been worth it. Silas is still reeling from meeting Thor." Sarah pats my chest.

"His face was priceless, I can't wait to see the pictures."

"Your mom has outdone herself, this was perfect." She sighs.

"She loves you and Silas." I kiss the top of her head.

"Chord, it's time for the cake," Mom calls from the house.

I pat Sarah's ass. "Not that kinda cake, Chord." Thayer giggles.

"I'd take a bite." I cheese at her, as I walk away.

I step through the door as Mom puts the candles on the cake. "He's gonna love this, Mom. Thank you." I put my arm around her, kissing the top of her head.

"You're welcome. Are you doing anything for your birthday?" She eyes me as I light the candles.

"I haven't mentioned it, we've had a lot going on."

"She'll feel terrible if she misses it." Mom holds the door open when I pick up the cake.

"They come first, Mom. The best I could ever receive is having them here." She pats my face as I scoot past her.

"You're the sweetest."

Sarah calls Silas over as we begin to sing. "Happy birthday to you. Happy birthday to you. Happy birthday, dear Silas, happy birthday to you."

His eyes sparkle as he stares at his cake. "Blow them out, buddy."

LEAONA LUXX

He takes a big, deep breath and blows. We all cheer as Sarah hugs him. He turns to me, throwing his arms around me. I tremble, holding my son for the first time on the day of his birth.

Silas eats his cake, playing with Andi as he does. Sarah encourages him to open his presents but he doesn't come until Andi sits with him. He tears through each gift, smiling and laughing.

"This is from us, baby boy." Sarah hands him the wrapped box.

Paper flies in the air. "Oh, wow. I can rwecorwd with this. This is awesome!"

"I think that's a win." Sarah giggles. He inspects the Vtech Kidizoom, turning the box all the way around.

"Thank you, Momma." He grabs on to Sarah, and she bends to hug him back.

He glances at me and sets the box down. Running toward me as fast as he can, he jumps into my arms, knocking me off balance. I hold him tight, tears welling in my eyes.

"Thank you. I love it all, Daddy," he says with a kiss on my cheek. I lose it, tears falling like rain. This little boy owns me, just like his momma.

"You're welcome." I sniffle.

"I have a million toys," Silas announces, going over to go through his stash. Between the Legos, basketball goal, race tracks, swing set and clothes, I think he might have a million.

Sarah slides into my lap, kissing my face as she settles in for the evening. The evening goes by fast. I sit out next to the ocean, taking it all in. If anyone had told me a month ago this would be happening, I'd laughed in their face.

"How you doin'?" One hands me a beer.

"Thanks." I toss the top and take a drink. "Good."

"They look happy." We watch our family as they laugh and talk. "So why are you out here?"

"Sarah." I sigh heavily. "She's been through a lot of shit, I'm worried about her."

He cuts his eyes at me. "Worried about what?"

"I can't point my finger on it." I chew on my lip.

"She's working harder than you might think."

"Don't get me wrong, I know she's doing a great job but she's still holding back. You know what I mean?" I take another drag from my drink.

"I think I do. You know Lea and I have been through a lot of shit." One turns to me. "Chord, you once told me, 'you wanted a love worth deserving', knowing full well you already had one, but it had been taken from you. You never lost sight of it, don't now."

"I'm not, she just worries me more than she'll ever know." I run my hand over my face.

"How the fuck did you get Walker to come dressed as a superhero?"

"I asked. He's got a killer soft spot for kids." We chuckle as we plod the path through the sand.

Silas and I pace the parking lot, his hand shoved in pockets, just like mine. Sarah's inside, taking her driver's exam.

"She's been in there a while, should we go check on her?" I peer down at him.

218

"She said not to come in, cause it would make her nervous." He stretches his neck to look up at me.

"We'll give her a few more minutes, then we'll go in." He points toward the building as his mom walks across the lot. "So how'd you do?"

She smashes her lips into a thin line, my stomach drops. She holds up a paper, waving it. "Passed."

We run to meet her, embracing her between us in our arms. "Congratulations, I knew you could do it."

"Yay, Momma. You can drive!" Silas yells.

"I missed one, can you believe that, one?" she fumes.

"Oh, yeah. What question?"

"When can you pass a vehicle on the right?" She curls her lip.

"I have no clue."

"Exactly." We laugh as we walk to the SUV, hand in hand.

On our way to the office, we stop by the school Silas will be attending. We fill out his papers, and he has a look around. His teacher went to school with Thayer; she's sweet, her husband's a teacher also.

We drive on over to the office so Sarah can get a jumpstart on how things work. She's nervous, even though she's been told to not be. I let Silas go in my office to color and watch television.

"To answer the phone, pick it up. If a second call comes in, push this button, puts it on hold and here are the office buttons. Initials are beside them, hit that button. And it's 'Woods Development'."

"Can we practice?" She scrunches her face up.

I grab her phone, pulling mine out. "You haven't even set this up."

"I'm waiting for you to help me." She pouts, absolutely adorable. I lean in to kiss her plump lip.

"Practice the phone not kissing." One chuckles.

"Here goes." I dial the number, and she answers on the second ring.

"Thank you for calling Woods Development, this is Sarah." I smile, hitting call from her phone. "Thank you for calling Woods Development, please hold." She pushes a button.

"You transferred it successfully," One calls from his office.

Sarah beams, so little praise but it means so much to her. "There ya go, baby."

"Can we practice a couple more times?" she asks.

"We can, but first, let's get your paperwork filled out." I walk around the desk, opening the files.

I give her the tax papers and insurance information to let her work on them. I take time to check on Silas as she works on her personnel file. I glance at her when she puts her finger in her mouth. She's worried.

"What's up?"

"I didn't graduate," she whispers.

A pang in my stomach tightens. "Why did you not finish?"

She closes her eyes, shaking her head. "Mom wouldn't let me. It was basically house arrest until she dumped me."

The mere mention of her mom and how she was treated infuriates me. My face heats, turning my cheeks red. "Don't worry about it, it's not important. Until I'm on his birth certificate, he'll be on your insurance. Or, until we get married."

"Thank you." Her mouth quirks up on one side.

"No need to thank me, love me."

"I love you. Most." She leans in, kissing me.

"Hey, can you grab the snacks for Silas from the fridge? There's a bag on the counter to put it in."

Chord walks into the closet, leaning against the door. "I sure will, he's brushing his teeth right now and then we'll go down."

"Ughh, I've tried on three different outfits, nothing looks right." I put my hands on my hips as I scan the hangers of clothes. I cut my eyes at him. "What?"

"Not a damn thing." His heated perusal of my body sends a delicious wave of desire over me.

"Should I wear this? Is this office apparel?" I spin, modeling my black lace bra and panties for him.

His eyes lock with mine, and he fists his cock through his pants. "You better fuckin' find some clothes, now."

"Or? I feel like there's another choice." I bite my lip, drawing his eyes to my mouth.

"We're gonna fuck in this damn closet." He steps toward me.

"Scat! I need to find some clothes, not lose what I already have on." I giggle when he adjusts himself.

"Such a tease."

"Baby, I can tease you." I wink, leaning in as I rub down his zipper.

He lays his hand over mine, putting pressure on it. "You have no shame in what you do to me, do you?"

"Nope." I back away, grinning. "Go help Silas, I'm coming."

"I was about to." He shoves his hands in his pockets.

"Poor baby, maybe sex on the desk this afternoon?" I waggle my brows.

He rolls his eyes with a shake of his head. "You're killin' me." He walks out, only to stick his head back in. "I'll put you on my schedule."

"Chord!" He runs away, leaving me laughing. "Perv."

I put on a blue patterned Boho dress with sandals, hurrying down to the boys. I shove a few things in a backpack for Silas, stopping long enough to gather myself.

"Here ya go." Chord tosses me the keys to the SUV.

I toss them back. "Nope, not happening."

"Yes, it is. You've got to practice because you need to know how to drive in case Silas needs you and no one's around." He tosses them back. "You look amazing, let's go."

"Oh, don't I know." He smirks.

222

"Fine but if I wreck it, it's on you." I shrug, throwing my purse over my shoulder.

"If you wreck it, I'll go buy a new one and you can pick yours out while we're there." He holds the door open for me, carrying Silas' bags and holding his hand.

I pause, stretching to press a kiss on his lips. "You're too good to me, Chord."

"I do it all for those lips." I kiss him again, smiling as we leave.

We make it to the office in one piece, although it took us a little longer. I settle in, taking calls like a pro. Now, to master this computer. I fire it up, watching it come to life. I can do this, I can.

The scheduling screen pops up, everything this office does is on here. Who's going to what site, what supplies are coming in and when, and who's in office and available. I can't do this. Shit.

I chew on my nail, studying the layout. "What's the use, like I've used one of these in years." I bury my head into my hands.

"You'll get it." Chord's arms encase me.

"I was in high school the last time I used one of these." I place my finger back in my mouth, to have Chord lower it again.

"We can access this from the house, I can also duplicate it so you can practice." My eyes widen.

"Seriously? That would be amazing, thank you." I kiss his cheek.

He turns his face to me. "You missed."

"Oh, sorry." I press my lips to his.

"Sarah, I get so caught up in us being together again, that I forget what an adjustment you've been through. Never underestimate yourself, you're kicking ass." This time, he kisses me.

WRECKING US, SAVING YOU

The first week at work passes quickly and after a little help from Chord, I've mastered the computer. I drive to work everyday and today, Silas starts school. I'm a nervous wreck but he's ecstatic.

"Momma, I see Andi." He tugs on my hand, pointing across the hall.

I wave at Torrie, she and Andi walk over. "Hi, Silas." Andi waves.

"Hey, Andi. Where's your class?" Silas asks.

"Two doors down." Andi smiles. She's a little older, but I don't think that matters to my little man. "We'll have recess together."

"He'll be fine, Andi loves it here. There's your mom, Andi." Torrie waves at Ava; they share custody and are best friends. Parenting done right.

"Silas, we have to go." I kneel in front of him when I see Chord walking toward us.

"You're good to go, buddy." Chord paid for his lunch.

"I love you. Be sure to smile, people like that. And don't worry if you don't make many new friends. Sometimes, one is more important than five." Chord rubs my shoulders. I pull Silas into a hug, tears welling.

"Daddy said it's better to make one friend forever than five for now." He nods.

Chord squats beside us. "Your momma and I were best friends at your age, and I've loved her ever since. Be brave, be strong, and do work. Fist bump." Silas hits Chord's hand and then wraps his arms around him.

"I love you, Dad."

Chord's breath hitches. "I love you most."

"Love you, Momma." He hugs me again, leaving us weeping fools in the hallway.

Chord sighs, holding his hand out as he stands. "Come on, babe. He's made his move."

"I think you may need to carry me out." I giggle, drying my face. I grab his hand, allowing him to pull me up.

"My chest feels like One's sitting on it. Shew, I can't breathe." Chord rubs his chest.

I sniffle. "I can't breathe outta my nose." He wrinkles his.

"Because you're snotty." He gigs my side, making me giggle as we walk out the door.

I sniffle again. "Kiss me, baby."

His face scrunches. "Eww."

"I did kiss you, snot and all."

"That's gross, but I would too." He kisses me, opening the car door.

Driving to work, my mind is with Silas. Last year, I was afraid of leaving him. This year, I can't stand to part with him. I fight the urge to turn around and get him, I can homeschool him.

"I miss him too." Chord takes my hand as we walk into work.

"Good, I thought I was being unreasonable."

I sit down at my desk, getting to work on my memos. Around noon, I'm elbow deep into scheduling when the date pops up. I'm working on Chord's appointments for the twenty-ninth.

Today's the twenty-sixth of August. Chord's birthday, fuck. What am I going to do? I don't have the money to buy him anything,

I can't even let Silas get him something. I glare at the screen, hating myself for forgetting.

"You okay?" Lea asks.

I cover my face. "Chord's birthday, I forgot about it. How in the hell could I do that, it's six days after Silas'?"

"He doesn't care, he's happy if y'all are." She shrugs.

"I have to do something, what can I do?" I stare at her, it's like a light over her head. Her face lights up.

"Didn't you dance?" She waggles her brows.

My face flames as I close my eyes. "I was a stripper."

"Oh, girl. Don't be ashamed of that, you were taking care of your son." She leans on the counter.

"Still, not my proudest moment."

"Why the hell not? I was a single mom, that's hard shit. You supported and raised a child on your own, damn right you should be proud." She takes my hand. "And what's better than a gift from the heart."

"Chord wasn't thrilled with me doing it."

"No, Chord was upset that you had to do it for his child. And if he's like his brother, he didn't want other men to look at what's his. Trust me, that man will fall at your feet if you strip for him." She snickers.

"I can bake him a cake and then give him the pie."

She smirks. "We're gonna be such good friends." We giggle until it turns into laughter.

"I need to get to the store for cake mix and icing without him knowing."

"I'm two doors down, sneak down and I'll hook you up." She smiles as Chord turns the corner.

226

"What are y'all up to?" He cocks his brow.

"Nothing, honey." We giggle again.

I hurry through the door with my bounty from Lea, hoping Chord's still working with Silas. I sneak around the corner, checking to see where they're at, Chord has other plans. He grabs me from behind, scaring the shit out of me.

"Ahhhh! Chord, damn it all to hell!"

He holds his hands up, his cheeks blown up. "I'm sorry." He says through his laughter.

"Paybacks are a bitch." I throw a dish towel at him.

"What's this?" He picks up the bag, looking inside. His eyes snap to mine.

"Did you forget to mention something?" I lean against the sink.

He shifts his position. "We've been busy."

"I call bullshit."

"Huh?" His brows draw together.

"You wouldn't allow me to give that excuse." I fold my arms.

"You're right, so what are we doing?" He comes over to stand beside me.

I lay my head on his shoulder. "I'm baking you a cake, and we're meeting everyone for dinner. I have nothing to give you, Silas doesn't either."

"You've given me everything." He puts his arm around me.

"I've got an idea, I'll be right back." I jump from his embrace. "Then I'm gonna bake you a cake."

"I heard something about pie earlier." He flashes me his mischievous grin.

"Cake first, pie later." I wink, rushing up the stairs to Silas.

We have several tables at The Grillin' Crab as the entire family joins us for Chord's birthday. As the check arrives, Cal hands Chord his birthday present. Silas pulls on my arm.

"After Grandpa Cal, okay?" He sits back down.

"Happy birthday, Chord." Cal gives him a manly hug with a pat on the back. Followed by Elise.

"We love you, baby." She pats his face.

He opens the envelope, removing the card. He smiles, lifting the card to them. "Thank you." No one says a word about the check tucked inside.

"Can I, Momma?" I nod. "Daddy, I made you something." Silas crawls under the table, springing back up with his backpack. Chord watches impatiently as Silas reaches him a handcrafted card. "Here, I made this for you."

He leans over, reading it as Chord does. "Thank you, Silas. It's the best I've been given." He hauls him into a hug.

"Let's see it," Thayer says as her eyes glisten.

Chord holds the card up for everyone to see. "It has Silas and me fishing on the front. Sarah's inside with us at the house. It says, "You are the sun to my moon, I'm so happy it lead me home. Happy birthday. You're the best dad. I love you, Silas."

Cue the boo hoos. My heart hammers against my chest. Chord takes my hand as Silas sits in his lap, and I have to take a deep breath. This man, this family, is mine. I struggle to breathe. How did I ever get so lucky?

Silas falls asleep on the way home, Chord carries him to bed giving me a chance to put my plan into motion. I cut a piece of cake and take the stairs two at a time.

I pop my head in Silas' door. "Hey, can you bring that piece of cake up? It's on the counter, but I need to pee."

"I sure will, baby. Do you need a drink?" he asks with the sweetest smile.

"Water." He nods, not even asking why I didn't use the bathroom downstairs.

I hit our bedroom, ripping my clothes off as I shut the door. I pull the chair out, placing it in the middle of the room. I fix the lights and set my phone up beside my entrance.

Closing the bathroom door, I freshen myself up. The lady bits need spruced up. I can't believe I haven't shaved her in weeks, but there's no way I'm wearing those panties with a fur coat.

In the back of my bottom chest drawer, I find my outfit. He loved my butterfly outfit, so I saved it and a couple more when I gave the others away. I tug on a pair of purple holographic panties to go with the top.

"Did you set the chair out for a reason?" Chord says when he walks in.

I take one last look in the mirror, smirking. "Show time."

Swinging the door wide, I reach around, hitting play on my phone. JT sings *Sexy Back* as I step out, I turn my back to him, bending at the waist. Giving him a glory shot of my ass before I whip around, locking eyes with my man.

His mouth hangs open.

My hips sway as I stride to the door, locking it. I slam my back to the door, sliding down, spreading my legs again, the lower I get. Groping my breasts, I push from the door, standing, as I walk toward him.

229

WRECKING US, SAVING YOU

I take his hand, leading him to the chair. I roam his body, turning to rub my ass against him. I wiggle down and slide back up, bending over to lock my hands on my ankles. I flip around, working my hands up his body.

Placing them on his shoulders, I slam him down in the seat. Straddling the chair, I ride him. His hands grab my hips, and he raises to meet my grind. I stand, walking to the bed, crawling onto it.

Working my knees back and forth, I hump and grind, wiggling my ass. His eyes devour me as I turn, sitting on my knees. I rub my hands all over my body, letting them slide between my legs.

He stands, desire rising at a frenzied rate, tearing a path through our bodies as he picks me up. I lock my legs around him as we fall to the bed. He hooks his thumbs on the side of my panties, shimmying them down my thighs.

His hands slide around my back, removing my top. I lay beneath him, bare. He stands, dropping his clothes to the floor. Climbing back on the bed with me. He lays between my legs.

"Happy birthday, Chord. I love you."

His mouth takes mine, making love to me, in his way and his pace, the way he wants to. I swear, I saw heaven at one point during the night. This man, loving me, like no other ever has or ever will.

25

Chord

"Two weeks and you can take your driver's test." Sarah lays on the other end of the couch from me.

"I suppose I need to learn to parallel park." She rolls her eyes.

I grab her foot, massaging it. "You've got this."

"Can you believe we've been here over a month already?" Her face lights up.

My heart stutter steps. "It's weird, like you never left but then it feels as though y'all just got here."

"Exactly." She crosses her eyes.

"How about we get cleaned up and go to the movies?"

She lays her head back against the arm of the couch. "I don't know, I'm kinda tired."

WRECKING US, SAVING YOU

"Dude, The LEGO Ninjago movie is playing. How can you say no?"

She throws her arm over her head. "Did he hear you?"

Her question is answered as little feet slapping on wood echoes through the house. He lands at the bottom of the stairs, Thor hammer in hand and cape on. His eyes round as baseballs.

"Did you say LEGOs?" He runs as fast as he can, diving on top of me. "Please oh please, Daddy, we have to go. Please."

I stare at Sarah, and she slowly covers her face with her pillow. I push on her ass with my foot, and she slaps it away. I do it again as our son climbs me like a tree. She peeks out from under the pillow.

"Mom, it's LEGOs for the love of all that's holy."

Her eyes widen. "No! Not The LEGO movie?"

Yeah, she's sprung too. "Yes, Momma. Only the bestest, most amazing movie everw."

"Better than Thor?" She raises her head, quirking her brow.

He chuckles. "You'rwe silly. No. But it's still LEGOs!"

"Yeah, Mom. LEGOs."

"As long as we go early, eat out, and come home so we can go straight to bed." She narrows her eyes.

"I prwomise." He grabs my hand, holding it up with his. "Dad prwomises too."

"Fine, let's get dressed. Buy the tickets, Dad." She smiles, knowing the entire time she'd let us win.

It's raining now. I'm in line to pick up the tickets, so Sarah and Silas are waiting in the car. People are going in and out as the other movies end. Once I have ours, I wave to them.

232

I stand to the side, waiting on my two to get over to me. When someone slides up next to me, putting their arms around my neck. No doubt, Sarah sees it all as she walks toward me.

"Hey, there handsome. Where have you been?" Mandi whispers in my ear.

I pry her off me, stepping away. "Mandi, how are you? Ladies." I nod at her company as she tries to get close again. I look around her for Sarah.

"I'm good, baby. When you gonna call me again?" Mandi pulls on my shirt.

"Never." Sarah places Silas in my arms. "Now, get your fuckin' hands off him before I take it off for you." I reach for Sarah's arm, but she ain't having it.

"Who the hell are you?" Mandi curls her lip.

Before Sarah can answer, I do. "Mandi, I'd like to introduce my fiancée and son. Sarah and I were lucky enough to find each other again after being separated for years. She's the love of my life."

"Congratulations, I suppose," Mandi sneers as she walks away.

Sarah takes Silas by the hand, walking in without me. I follow, standing behind her. I reach her the tickets when we get closer, she snatches them from me.

"I'm sorry," I murmur, she glares at me over her shoulder.

"Why? Hopefully, I can go to the ladies room and run into your other lover. Ya know, pour salt and all." Shit, she's mad.

"I hate you have to run into any of them." My stomach turns.

"I hate it too. You have no idea how much I hate it." She doesn't say anything else.

Silas sits between us during the movie, and Sarah doesn't talk as we eat at the restaurant. She's silent, and it scares me. Silas goes up

233

for a bath when we get home, I tidy up downstairs as Sarah puts him in bed.

By the time I head up, she's in bed, her back to me. I climb in behind her, slipping my arm around her waist. I pull her to me, snuggling her close. Her body trembles, she's crying. She lays her arms over mine, and I hold her until she falls asleep.

I feel a tug on my arm, waking me. The bed shifts when I rouse, I find Silas lays against my side. Sarah's on the other side with her arm around me. I close my eyes again, but something is nagging at me.

A pang in the pit of my stomach hurts so much, I wake fully. Silas is hot. I raise up on my elbow, touching his head with the back of my hand. This can't be good, Silas is on fire.

"Sarah, baby, wake up." I rub her back.

"Hmm, what is it?" She forces an eye open.

"It's Silas, he's hot."

She sits straight up. "Where is he?"

I point beside me. "I just found him." She touches his head, then his body.

"Let me get the thermometer."

She slips out of bed, hurrying into his bathroom. She leaves the light on as she sprints back. She places it on his head, he doesn't even move. As soon as it beeps, I stare at her, waiting.

"This can't be right, can this be right?" She turns the screen to me.

"102.5." My eyes cut to hers. "Is that bad?"

"They say if it's 103, take them to the doctor. Let's start him on ibuprofen. Can you wake him while I get it?" She takes off downstairs.

"Hey, buddy. Si, wake up for daddy." I place my hand on his stomach, rubbing it.

"I don't feel good," he says, scooting closer to me.

"I can tell. Come here, Mom's bringing you some medicine." Sarah comes through the door as I get him into my lap.

"Here you go, baby. Open up." Sarah dumps the liquid in. He swallows it and wallows into my chest. "I'll get a cool cloth."

I lay back with Silas on my chest. "You're cool, daddy."

"His temp may not go down if he's staying warm by your body heat," Sarah says as she climbs back into bed.

I roll over, laying him between us. She touches the cloth to his head as he dozes back off. We lay there, watching him sleep. I reach over, taking her hand from her hip, holding it.

"I'm sorry."

"It's okay, just hard." She laces our fingers.

"You think he's gonna be alright?"

"It happens, it may be nothing. Rest while he does, it's gonna be a long night." She tightens her grip on my hand.

We're up and down for hours, even Sunday is spent monitoring Silas. We stay in bed with him all day, only leaving long enough to find him some soup that he doesn't eat.

Silas dozes between us, laying without anything but a t-shirt and underwear. Late that night, we lay watching television. I'm running my hand through his hair, when Sarah catches my eye.

"What?"

"I think we need to take him in, it's been twenty-four hours and there's no change." A line appears between her eyes.

"Emergency room or office?" My stomach feels like it has rocks in it, it's so heavy.

"I'm not sure, I've always taken him to a clinic. He's never had a regular physician." Her bottom lip trembles.

"Should we wait, or call Lea or Thayer to see who they go to?" My words are low and quivering.

"Let's just go. Don't you think?" Her eyes plead with me to decide, and the hair raises on my neck, giving me my answer.

"I'll get dressed, grab him some clothes and dress him, while you get ready." We scramble from the bed.

Sarah sits in the back with Silas on the way to the hospital. I trot my leg at every stoplight; it's four in the morning, why are they even on? Sarah and I haven't said another word to each other, she's as worried as I am.

We're still at the emergency room at nine when I step out to call One. I rub the back of my neck, pacing like a caged animal.

"Hey, brother. What's up?" I swallow, hoping to not sound as worried as I feel.

"Hey, we're at the hospital. Silas is running a fever, we've fought it a couple of days. So we're having him checked out."

"Do y'all need someone to come over?" His words waver.

I roll my shoulders to relieve the tightness. "Naw, we're good right now. I wanted to let you know, we'll be in once we have him checked out."

"Keep us updated."

"Will do." My voice cracks.

I walk toward the room just in time for the doctor to walk in. I jog to get there, pushing the door open as he starts speaking.

"We've ran a panel of tests, right now we're not seeing much. His stomach is slightly distended and the fever returns when the ibuprofen wears off. I'm inclined to think it's a virus," Doctor Owens says.

"A virus?" I question quietly.

"Yes, some viruses can be just that and run their course with no more than a fever. Others can be bacterial and range from fever to vomiting and diarrhea, he has neither. Most can be detected and others not, leaving us with no way of knowing what kind it is," he explains with a furrowed brow.

"So what are you suggesting?" Sarah folds her arms.

"Continue with ibuprofen and alternate with acetaminophen. If there's no change in a couple days, bring him back and we'll run some more tests." He signs off on some papers. "The nurse will be back to discharge him."

We get our walking papers and head to the office. I leave Sarah with Silas, to go talk with One. He's at his desk when I walk in.

"Hey, there you are. Mom was just asking about y'all." He inclines his head to the phone.

"They said it's a virus. Keep giving meds and bring him back if there's no change in a few days." I sigh as I sit down.

"Kids get viruses all the time, a school is a petri dish for them," Mom says.

"That's what they said. If you don't mind, we're gonna stay home today. We'll be in tomorrow, he can stay in my office if he has to stay home again."

One nods, holding his hands up. "No worries. If any of you need anything, let us know."

"A pediatrician. We hadn't thought about it until last night, and she only had clinics down there, no regular physician."

"I can ask Lea." One shrugs.

"That's what I was thinking, so if he isn't better tomorrow, let's do that."

"I'll let her know." One hugs me. "Get some sleep when he sleeps."

"Chord, I'll bring dinner over and order you all some lunch around one, so you can get a nap in," Mom says.

"Sounds good, Mom. Thank you."

"You're welcome. Give my sweet boy a kiss from Grandmother, we love you all." She blows a kiss.

"Love y'all."

"Tomorrow, unless you need us before then, just call," One says.

"Thank you, brother."

I grab a few files and head back out. Once home, we return to our positions in bed with our baby. Napping on and off all day, we only move for the necessities. Mom has food delivered at exactly one, with a text about dinner.

Tuesday morning brings nothing new, Silas is still not feeling well. Sarah's helping me with a few things in my office while we wait on the others to get in.

"Hey, y'all are early. How's Silas?" One eases over to his sleeping nephew.

"The same. I had a few things I need to follow up on for us, so we decided to bring him with us."

"I'm gonna text Lea and let her know." One pulls his phone out.

"Yeah, we're thinking of checking out the pediatrician y'all use."

"She's on the way over, she was out running errands this morning while Em stayed with the kids." One rubs the back of his neck, making the hair on my arm stand up.

Lea walks through the door within ten minutes, setting her purse down, and she's by Silas' side in no time.

"How long has he ran the fever?" She turns to us.

"Saturday night, he came to our bed late." Sarah walks over to them.

"The ER doctor said a virus, right?" Lea asks with a furrowed brow.

"He did." I nod.

"It's been four days, I'd take him in." Lea stands, taking her phone out. "Do you want to go to our doctor?"

"Yes, please." Sarah's brows knit.

"Don't worry, I'm sure he's fine, but a second opinion is always good." Lea offers a smile, but her eyes say something different. Mine cut to One, he gives me a tight smile.

"I'll get his things together." I grab his bag from the chair, putting his drinks in from the fridge. My chest feels heavy, I take a deep breath where no one can see me.

Sarah

"Do you have to fill a hundred of these out each time?" Chord's forehead creases as he holds Silas in his lap, and I complete his registration.

"No but for school, we'll be getting more soon."

"We did those already." His brow cocks.

"There'll be more, always are." I return the clipboard, checking Silas' forehead with a kiss before sitting back down.

Chord's hand finds mine as we wait. Silas is draped over him, and Chord hasn't even so much as broke a sweat. Silas hasn't either for that matter, but he's still warm.

"Hamilton," the nurse calls from the door.

Chord follows me, with Silas on his shoulder, as we're directed to a room. Chord lays Silas on the bed, sitting beside him. I chew on

240

my nail, waiting for the doctor. I hate going over this a million times, especially if it's nothing but a virus.

There's a knock on the door and then it opens. "Mrs. Hamilton, I'm Doctor Perri." She's a petite woman, older with brown hair.

"Hello, thank you for seeing us." My eyes dart to Chord's when he snickers.

"No problem at all. So Lea tells me your six-year-old son has had a fever for about four days now, is that right?" She writes as she talks.

"Yes, it started Saturday night. We took him to the emergency room early yesterday, and they told us it looks like a virus."

She stands, moving to Silas. Chord slides from the bed, staying by his side. She checks his eyes, his stomach, and his mouth. "What was the temperature?"

"It's the same when the medicine wears off, 102.5. There's been no change," Chord explains.

"Has he eaten?" She turns, asking.

"A little here and there." I lick my lips.

"Let's do a full blood panel and some x-rays, just to rule anything else out." She takes her seat, writing the orders up. "Until we get everything back, continue to treat the fever as you have been."

"How long does it take to get the results?" Chord shoves his hands in his pockets.

"I'm asking for a rush on them, tomorrow at the latest." She stands, checking Silas one last time. "The nurse will be right back with the orders." She leaves the room, and I panic.

"Chord, his insurance hasn't kicked in." My gut turns, this isn't good.

He steps over to me, squatting as he takes my hand in his. "Don't. I've got this, you know that. He comes first, always."

241

WRECKING US, SAVING YOU

I fall over, my head on his hands, tears springing to my eyes. "He has to be alright. He has to be."

Chord presses his lips to the back of my head. "He will be, baby."

The nurse comes in, interrupting us. "I'm sorry. Here's the papers you'll need; just go to the hospital, and they'll take care of it. As soon as we have any information, we'll call."

I take the papers as Chord gets Silas. We go straight to the hospital. After all the tests, we take him home, putting him back in bed with us. Wednesday morning, he's still not feeling well.

"No, Sarah. He needs to be here, resting, and so do you." Chord sighs as he slips his shoes on.

"I don't want to let anyone down, Chord. Everyone has been so good to us."

Chord hooks me by the loop of my shorts, yanking me to him. "They're good to you because they love you, and they're your family. Sarah, you don't have to be with me for this family to love you both. They love you, always have."

"I know." I sigh.

"Call me anytime you need me. One will probably send me home, but I need to get these proposals in today." He puts a stack of papers in his briefcase.

"Please be careful, you haven't had any sleep. Between him and working all night, I know you're tired."

"Promise." He leans in, kissing Silas on the forehead. "Call me." He presses his lips to mine.

I follow him downstairs, watching as he leaves. He waves before turning onto the road, and my heart falls. I miss him already. I pick the house up, putting the dishes in the dishwasher and throwing in some laundry.

Silas wakes around ten, he wants to come downstairs to watch television. I get him set up, joining him on the other end. I jump when my phone buzzes. I pick it up quickly, thinking it's Chord.

"Hello."

"Mrs. Hamilton, this is Doctor Perri." Her voice, low and professional, makes me jittery.

"Yes, Doctor Perri?"

"Could I have you bring Silas in. I have some results I'd like to go over with you," she says, making my chest tighten.

"What's wrong? Is he okay?" I struggle for air.

"I can explain it better once you're here," she says.

"We'll be right there. Thank you." I don't give her time to finish, I hang up, dialing Chord immediately.

"Hey, baby." Chord's voice calms me as soon as I hear it.

"Doctor Perri called, she wants to see us in the office." I take the stairs two at a time to find some clothes.

"Did she say what for?" he asks as I hear papers shuffling in the background. "One…"

"No, just to come now. Chord…" I stutter.

"I'm on my way, he's gonna be fine." He tries to calm me. "They want to see us, I'm out."

"Call me," One says.

"Will do. I'm leaving now." A door shuts.

"I love you."

"I love you both. Most." Chord ends the call as his car starts.

WRECKING US, SAVING YOU

Chord carries Silas into the office, going over to sit as I sign him in. The nurse looks up, recognizing me.

"Oh, no, you don't have to do that. She's waiting in her office for you. Come on back." She waves, walking to the door.

"Chord, she's waiting." He holds the door as I walk through, Silas still glued to him.

The nurse stands beside a door. "Right in here."

"Thank you," I say as I walk through, Chord and Silas sit to the right of me.

"Mister Hamilton, let's have the nurse sit with Silas across the hall." She stands, escorting them over there. Chord's eyes are glassy when he sits back down, wrapping my hand with his.

"We're fine. We're going to be alright," he whispers as she sits across from us.

"So I received Silas' x-ray's and wanted to wait on the bloodwork before I called. Things like these can be alarming and still turn out to be okay." She shifts through some papers.

I cut my eyes at Chord, his head is turned to the right. I lean over to see what he's looking at, it's x-rays. I can't tell what they are, but when Chord's hand starts shaking, I get nauseous.

"What did you find?" Chord's voice matches his hands.

"Honestly, I'm not sure. I don't like what I see in the tests I've had done, but I'm also not a specialist. I want to refer Silas to a Pediatric Oncologist." Her eyes flicker from mine to Chord's.

Chord freezes, making my heart to clench. "I don't understand."

"It's a cancer specialist." My head starts shaking all by itself, mimicking my entire body.

"No, you're wrong, you could be wrong. Right?" My body tingles, going numb all over. Chord slips his arm around me, saying one word.

"When?"

"She's willing to see him within the week." Doctor Perri starts writing something.

"Within the week? So soon?" My ears are ringing when I become lightheaded.

"We'll be there." Chord's hands tremble, but he seems so calm.

"I'll call her now, just a second." She picks up the phone, dialing.

I rotate in my seat, glaring at Chord. "What's going on, I don't understand?"

He lays his hand on my cheek, tears welling in his eyes. "She thinks Silas has cancer."

The room starts spinning, I feel dizzy. I fumble to hold on to the chair. "No. She's wrong. Please, Chord, please tell me she's wrong." I crumble into his arms.

"Here's the directions, they'll call with an appointment." She stands, reaching Chord the paper. "I'm hoping I'm wrong."

"Me too." Chord helps me stand as we go to get our son.

Chord carries Silas, while I lean into him. He helps us both in the car, driving us home. On the way, he calls One. His voice cracking as he speaks.

"Hey, what's going on?" One answers.

"We're going to Duke this week, they're getting Silas in quickly." His hand shakes as he holds the phone.

WRECKING US, SAVING YOU

"Duke? Why?" One's calm enough for five people, so when I can hear the concern in his voice, it sends me over the edge again. My chest heaves as I hold back the tears.

"Pediatric Oncologist." He runs his hand over his face, still pretending to be strong. "Call Mom and Dad, would you?"

"I will, hang in there. We love y'all." Chord ends the call without responding.

He drives us home, fragile yet the strongest person I've ever known. Chord helps me out of the backseat, wrapping me in his warm embrace. I'm not sure how long we stand there, but I'll be damned if I don't need it.

"Hey, guys. Are we going inside?" Silas mutters, making us giggle.

"Yeah, buddy. Your mom is the most beautiful woman I've ever seen, sometimes it's hard to let go." Chord holds his hand as he steps out.

"You feel like walking?" Silas nods, swaying as he walks. Chord and I both take him by the hand.

We get him settled, then busy ourselves picking up. I left laundry in the washer and dishes to be finished. As we pass, we touch, helping me to hold on to what little strength I have left.

I join Silas on the couch, Chord kneels in front of me as I hold our son's head. "Sarah, I promise you, I'll do everything in my power for Silas."

I dry my face, struggling to breathe. "I know." The doorbell rings, and he kisses me before going to let our family in.

Thayer slips in beside me, laying her head against mine. The rest filter in behind her, Lea, Elise, and Cal sit across from us. One and Hardy stand with Chord.

"What exactly happened today?" One asks.

"She did a blood panel and x-rays yesterday. The tests came back, and she wants him to go to Duke. She even went on to say she hopes she's wrong. I looked at the x-ray, I'm no expert but something's there." Chord runs his hands through his hair.

"Do you know when you'll be going?" One says.

"She called in a favor and we're waiting for an appointment this week with the Pediatric Oncologist. We'll drive up early, the night before." Chord begins to straighten things around the room again. I don't think my heart can take this, he's trying to keep his mind busy after thinking about the x-rays.

"You will not, driving is out of the question." Lea texts on her phone. "You'll be ready to leave when they give you the day and time, there will also be a car waiting."

"Thank you," I gasp, and Thayer holds me closer.

"Let's wait, see what they tell us and we can go from there," Cal says, holding Elise's hand.

We get a call the next day for the beginning of the week. Four more days of this, I suppose we're only beginning, but the thought of waiting a week feels impossible right now.

The weekend drags by, and I'm at the end of my rope. I want answers, and they can't come soon enough. I pack Silas a bag, still numb. Later, I watch as Chord sets a bigger bag on the end of our bed.

"You runnin' away?" I wrinkle my nose.

"Don't you wish you could get rid of me that easily?" He turns, taking clothes out of the chest.

WRECKING US, SAVING YOU

"Can we run away? Let's just pretend no one said anything and runaway," I beg, my stomach turning.

He sits beside me, laying back to cuddle. No words, just the sound of our son breathing.

I wake to the sound of vomiting. I reach for Silas, but he's not there. I hit the floor, running to the bathroom.

Chord kneels beside Silas, holding him up as he vomits. My stomach revolts, not feeling nauseous but for my child. I take one shaky step after the other until I'm behind him.

"I'm sorry, I must've dozed off." I rub Silas' back. "Let me get you a cold cloth, sweetheart."

"We're alright, even made it before it went anywhere." Chord's face doesn't reflect his upbeat words. The wrinkle in his forehead says it all.

"I think I'm done." I wipe his face with the washcloth. "Can I have a popsicle?"

"You better believe it." Chord follows him back to bed. "I'll be right back, you want anything?"

"I think I may want one too." I squeeze his hand.

"Three popsicles coming up." He jogs to the stairs.

Silas scoots close to me, snuggling into the crook of my arm. "Daddy scooped me up like Superman." He giggles.

"He did? Maybe we need to find him a cape." Silas laughs louder.

"Find who, what?" Chord runs through the door, jumping on the bed with popsicles in hand.

"You, a cape so you can be Superman." Silas reaches for his treat. "I want the red."

Chord gives it to him. "Momma?"

"I want blue." He hands it over.

"That leaves me with purple." He pops it in his mouth. "Oh, Grandmother said she's going to the store tomorrow, do we need anything?"

I wince. "We need a hundred things since I didn't go this weekend."

"Text her a list, baby." I cut my eyes at him. "Yes?"

"It's a long list."

"Make sure it has popsicles on it." Silas holds his in the air.

"Did you get that?" Chord smiles boyishly as I reach for my phone.

27

Chord

"Here it is." I point to the door for Sarah.

"I need to go pee." Silas hasn't done much of anything the last few days.

I scan the hall, seeing a restroom at the end. "I'll take him, you check us in."

Holding the door, I allow Sarah to walk through and then take Silas down the hall. "Here ya go." I stand back, allowing him room.

"I can't." He sighs.

"That's okay, I do that too." I help him with his clothes, pointing him to the sink. "Get in there, let's wash up."

Once we're done, I turn to the door. "I'm tired." Silas stands against the wall.

"How about I piggyback you?" His face lights up, and I think my chest caves in. What in the hell am I gonna do?

We walk in the door to find Sarah filling out more papers. "They want insurance information." Her face is pinched up as I sit Silas down.

"Are you finished with it?"

"Just the insurance." I hold my hand out for the clipboard.

I walk over to the window, knowing there's no privacy. "Here's what we have, he doesn't have insurance."

"We'll need a payment today and you'll need to arrange future payment with billing." The receptionist's face falls, she knows it's bullshit too.

I pull my checkbook out, staring at her. "How much? And I'll let billing know it's cash."

"One minute, Mister Hamilton." She turns to the computer, types something and turns with her eyes wide. "There's no charge. Apparently, you have a line of credit."

"By the name of Hadlea Woods, I'm sure." My breath hitches. "My sister-in-law."

"You must have a great family." She hands me a receipt.

"We do. Thank you." I take my seat next to Sarah. She's staring off into the distance, mind wandering, waiting for an answer.

"We're gonna break your inheritance, aren't we?" She chews her lip. I reach up, tugging on her chin until she releases it.

"No, we're one of the lucky ones, we have Lea." My heart skips a beat as I take out my phone. Sarah draws my attention, giggling as she holds up her phone.

"Lea?" I nod. "We're gonna owe her a million dollars."

"All worth it." I lean over, checking on Silas, his head in Sarah's lap. "You doing okay, Si?"

He sighs heavily. "Yeah, I wanna go home."

"Me too, buddy. Me too."

"Hey, y'all aren't leaving me here. Me three." Sarah messes Silas' hair up.

"Hamilton," the nurse calls from the door. Sarah raises Silas up, but he reaches for me.

"You want a ride?" He smiles, nodding his head.

The nurse weighs Silas and takes his temperature, then she seats us in room eight. I sit Silas on the table, he tugs at my shirt.

"Stay with me." His round eyes, pleading.

"I wasn't going anywhere." I hop up on the table, and he leans against me. Sarah turns her head, my chest feels so heavy.

A knock at the door makes us jump. "Hello, Hamilton family. How are we doing?" A tall, lanky woman with dark hair walks through the door. She stretches her hand out to Sarah. "Mrs. Hamilton."

"Sarah's fine." She takes her hand.

"Momma's not a Hamilton, just me and Daddy. They might get married later." Silas puts it all out there, and Sarah's face turns bright red.

"Oh, well. Sarah it is, Mister Hamilton. Silas." She shakes our hands.

"Chord is fine."

"Alright, Doctor Perri sent me her tests. It looks as though there's a mass in the abdomen, and his blood work is concerning." She looks over more papers.

"A mass?" Sarah asks.

"Yes, it's clearly on the x-ray." She writes something in his file. "How long are you here for?"

"As long as we need to be." My eyes on Sarah, she nods in agreement.

"I'll have the nurse get you some hotel information. I'd like to do a battery of tests; I'll have them schedule most for tomorrow, and we'll do what we can today." She looks from Sarah to me.

"Can you give us an indication of what we're talking about here?" Sarah bites her lip. I don't realize I'm holding my breath until after she says it out loud.

"It could be cancer, but we're a long way from diagnosing anything." She stands, pausing at the door. "You're both doing incredibly well; hang in there, and let's get this."

"We don't have any other choice." Sarah sniffles.

"He's all we have."

"Let me get things moving." As the door closes, Sarah rushes to Silas. He's in her arms, as if she can protect him from all of this.

"I'm gonna shoot One a quick text."

Here for the night.

Will call later.

Need to find a room.

I'll tell the pilot. ~O

Thank you.

Lea said he's on standby. ~O

You have a room at The Durham. ~O

A car will be waiting. ~O

Thank you brother.

We love y'all. ~O

WRECKING US, SAVING YOU

Love you.

"We have a room and a car."

Sarah's eyes flash to mine. "Lea?"

"Yeah. Have I told you how amazing she is?"

"You did, but you can do it again." Her mouth is pressed into a thin line.

I slide from the bed, wrapping them in my arms. "We're gonna make it through this, baby. We are."

A nurse pushes the door open, but we don't move. "Excuse me, I'm sorry. We're going to take Silas for some testing. I even have a ride for him." She pulls a wheelchair in, but he shakes his head, scowling.

"Daddy can carry me." He reaches for me, to not be denied.

"He might get tired of holding you everywhere we're going." The nurse wrinkles her forehead.

"I'll be fine." She searches my eyes, smiling.

"Well then, let's start with bloodwork." She leads the way.

After a day of scans, tests, and imaging, they give us a time for a biopsy tomorrow morning. My arm is shredded by the end of the day but there was no way in hell I was going to not carry him. Holding him close to my heart is where I need him.

Sarah is helping Silas bathe, so I decide to call One and give him an update. He answers on the first ring.

"Hi, how are you?" I lose it with the sound of his voice. I step outside of the room to talk.

"I can't, I just got him. This isn't fucking fair, One. Why? God damnit." I slide down the wall, allowing the tears to fall.

"Chord, you're the best man I know, and if anyone can handle this for his family, it's you." His voice cracks with each word.

"Why? For the love of God, why? Didn't I do without him for long enough? Fuck!" I fist my hair.

"Yes, you did." He clears his throat. "You have every damn right to be angry."

"They're doing a biopsy in the morning at nine, since we're already here." I rub my eyes with my palms.

"Do you want us to come down?"

I sigh. "No, it's too late now anyway."

"Have they gave you any possibilities?"

"She thinks it's cancer, we're just trying to find out what type." I swallow past the bile rising in my throat.

"Please, try to keep us posted. I know we're the last thing on your mind, as we should be, but we love him too," One gasps, trying to stifle his emotions for me.

"I know." I blot my eyes again. "One, I don't know what I'd do without Lea. Please, please let her know, I'm eternally grateful."

"She loves you, you know that. Besides, she's a mother first." One knows he's a lucky man, but it's always good to hear others know it too.

"We love her, please tell her."

"I will, little brother. We love y'all, try to get some rest."

"We will, thank you. Love you all." I end the call, pull myself together and walk in the room.

"It's a good thing you packed a bag, how'd you know?" Sarah slips a t-shirt over her head.

"Yeah, I did such a great job, I forgot my wife a nightie."

"Not wife, our son said, not yet." She giggles. "He just busted us, right then and there."

"He sure did." I tug her to me. "He's right, we're not married. What are we gonna do about that, baby?"

She locks her hands behind my head, gazing into my eyes. "We're going to get married, as soon as heavenly possible."

"That'll work." I press my lips to hers. Finding solace in her lips, I take my time loving her.

Sarah and I both struggle for sleep, I'm not sure either of us ever do. We're up before the alarm, ready to go as the car arrives. Once in the hospital, we register and find our way to outpatient surgery to wait.

I clasp Sarah's hand as the elevator dings, opening the door to our floor. She offers me her best smile, weak but loving. We step around the corner to find my parents.

"What are you doing here?" I stutter as my breath hitches.

"Do you three honestly think we'd let you be alone?" Dad hugs me, kissing Silas' cheek. Mom has Sarah wrapped in her arms, she's trembling.

"I needed this so much today, thank you." Sarah's lip quivers.

Mom dries Sarah's face. "You're as precious to me as he is, Sarah Beth. And Silas owns Grandmother, don't you baby?" Silas nods, clasping on to me. "Grandpa and Grandmother are taking him shopping after this, we need a new toy."

"I need a new memory card for my video camera." Silas chirps as we sit down.

"Is that all? Maybe we can find something else to go with it," Dad says to Silas' delight.

Silas shakes his head, eyes wide. "LEGOs."

"Now, you're talking." I smile at him as a nurse steps into the room.

"Hamilton."

"That's us." I swallow hard as bile rises in my throat, knowing what my baby is about to endure. I'd give anything if it were me instead.

"We'll be here," Dad says, kissing Silas again.

Mom wraps her arm around us, kissing Silas. "Praying. We love you."

Silas lays his head against my shoulder. Sarah has a death grip on my hand as we walk our son back. The staff are amazing, they let us stay with Silas the entire time, suiting us up. He giggles when I put my mask on.

"You look funny, like a doctorw."

"I am Doctor Tickle. How are you today?" I tickle his feet as he giggles.

"Good." His eyes wide, he waits to see where I'm going next.

"How are you here?" I tickle under his arms.

He laughs louder. "Good."

"What about here?" I goose Sarah, making her jump with a yelp. She play slaps my arm, Silas rolls laughing.

"Momma's gonna get you," Silas says as he cackles.

"Yes, I am." She slaps at me again. The door opens, sending my heart plummeting.

"It's time." Two words and my world spirals.

Sarah grasps my hand as we walk little man back. An hour later, I run out to give my parents an update.

"Hey." They hurry to their feet, Mom sliding her arm around me. "It's done. He has to lay on his side for a while and then we can take him home until the results come back."

"How is he?" Mom's eyes glisten with unshed tears.

"Good. I mean, I'd be out for the count but he's strong, like his mom."

"We'll be here," Dad says. "Can we get you anything?"

"No, please go eat. I'll text you when we're ready to leave."

Mom hugs me. "We love you."

"I can't tell you what it means to us you're here." I suck in a much-needed breath.

"Always." Dad hugs me when Mom releases me.

"I'll text you." I open the door, turning back to wave at them. They made parenting look so easy, I'm one helluva lucky kid.

The driver jumps out to grab the door, but I'm already out and headed around to get Silas. Sarah scoots over to the window with him, making it easier to grab him. I reach for her hand, and she looks up at me before taking it.

"Aren't your hands full enough?" Her brows are pulled low.

"Not when it comes to you, Sarah." I yank her hand, and she bumps into me giggling.

She opens the door, shoving it. "I like your hands full of me."

I do a double take. "You're a bad girl, I think I like it." I wink at her as I walk in, and she shuts the door, smiling.

"You more than like it." She waggles her brows, tiptoeing to kiss me.

"I'm gonna lay him down, then I'll grab our bags."

She walks toward the kitchen. "I'll get his meds and meet you up there."

I lay Silas in bed. "I'm gonna run and get you something to sleep in."

He looks up at me under hooded eyes. "Can I sleep in your shirt, like Momma does?"

"You sure can, let's pick one out." I take out a couple of shirts.

He picks out the blue Panthers shirt, one that means so much to me. "That one, I love football."

"Good choice, I do too. I love this shirt." I slip it over his head. "You know why?" He shakes his head as his arms pop out.

"Because I bought it for him, the Christmas before I left." Sarah wraps her arms around my waist. "I can't believe you still have it."

"Girl, that thing hung in my room like a shrine with your pictures around it."

"Yep, you're still sprung." I grab her wrist, pulling her around. Tipping her back, I press my lips to hers.

"You better believe it." I take her lips again as Silas lays back, chuckling. "What?" I cock my brow.

"Y'all are gross!"

"Speaking of gross, here's your medicine." Sarah sits on the bed, helping our little man. "Our home looks like it was hit by Merry Maids and Costco."

"Huh?" I laugh.

"The fridge is packed! There's so many popsicles in it, it's about to burst." Silas' eyes are wide. "And the place is spotless."

"Did you say popsicles?" Silas' lopsided smile is the best.

"I'll run and grab some," I say, turning to the door.

WRECKING US, SAVING YOU

"I want one!" Sarah yells as I hit the stairs. My heart may be broken but it's so full.

Sarah

The last few days have been horrendous. I don't like waiting, I hate it in fact. Chord's worn a path in the floor pacing when he's not working. Three days, there's been no word. We don't talk about it, but we can see it in Silas' face—he's getting worse.

"Have I mentioned how I despise waiting?"

Chord peeks up at me from his laptop. "Not in the last hour."

"What are you doin'?" I crawl to the other end of the couch, straddling him to peer over the screen.

He glances up at me with the most amazing lopsided grin. "Working. What are you doing, beautiful?"

"I don't know." I sit on his legs, staring at him.

His eyes flicker to mine. "You need something?"

I twists my mouth to the side. "Nope." I sigh.

WRECKING US, SAVING YOU

He hits a few buttons, closes the computer, and lays it on the table. I'm in his arms and on my back in a flash. "I think you might want a little attention."

I roll my eyes. "Why would you think that?"

"Well, the fact I've known you for nineteen years and know you will never tell me you want it." He trails his lips over my jaw, sending delicious tingles down my body.

"You know me so well."

"Better than you'll ever admit." He snickers.

"You've always just done what I need, there's never been a reason to tell you." I kiss his temple.

"True but it would be nice to hear that you need me once in a while." His lips press below my ear, and desire blooms in my belly.

"Are you trying to get something started?" I wrap my legs around him, deflecting the other topic to a later date.

"Mmm, do you think I can?" He runs his nose between my breasts.

"I think you already have." His mouth takes mine in a slow commanding kiss. "Good thing I'm not wearing panties."

Chord groans with appreciation when his hand slips between my legs. "So I see we have a situation."

My breasts heave as heat rushes through my veins. "Please, Chord."

He shifts, slipping his boxers down, sliding into me in one fluid motion. At this moment, he gives me what I need. A safe place to lose myself in, without thought of where we are and what we face.

Chord and I decide to go to work. We need a sense of normalcy at times. The wait is driving us insane, a week is seven days longer than we can take. Silas is in his daddy's office, his Uncle One bought him a mini fridge with everything he could want in it.

I love this family, my family.

"Hey, baby. I need to run this over to the courthouse to get it filed. Will y'all be okay for about thirty minutes?" Chord's brows are pulled tight, he hates going anywhere we're not.

"We'll be fine for a half hour." I smile, hoping to convince him.

"I'll be right back." He leans in with a kiss that's interrupted with a ringing phone. His face goes pale as he glares at the screen. A pang in my stomach has it bottoming out.

"It's them."

He nods, his eyes never leaving mine. "Chord Hamilton." He listens quietly as I hold my breath. "I understand, we'll see you tomorrow morning. Thank you."

I begin to tremble uncontrollably, and Chord takes my hand, hauling me to his chest. I would give anything to stay here, in his embrace. This is not my reality, it's one only nightmares are made of.

"Did they say anything else?" One's voice is low, filled with worry.

"No, I guess we'll know everything then." Chord's forehead is pulled tight, wrinkled.

"I'll make arrangements for you. Brannon can file the papers, you need to pack in case they keep you." One takes his phone out, texting like rapid fire.

WRECKING US, SAVING YOU

"Chord?" His eyes lock with mine, reflecting everything I'm feeling. Lost, confused, wrecked and yet, he stands strong.

"We've got this, together." He presses his lips to mine. "Always." I nod, choosing to let him think I believe his words, knowing we both feel hopeless.

"I'll finish here. Take the papers or we'll just go home and worry."

"Thirty minutes." He kisses me again then heads out.

"Sarah, y'all can go home and take care of what you need to do." One tilts his head, his mouth in a firm line.

"We know, but we also need to work; it's important to us both."

"Alright. Everything's ready for tomorrow, and don't hesitate to let us know if you need anything, even if it's just to talk." One slips his arm around me, hugging me like he always has, my big brother.

The last twenty-four hours have been the longest in my life. I sit here, leaning on Chord, holding our son's hand, terrified.

"Hamilton." Chord stands with Silas, his grip tightens on me as I sit there.

He turns to me. "Come on, baby. We've got to do this."

I will myself to move, clasping his hand in a vice. "You've got us?"

"I do." He holds Silas close, never letting me go. The nurse shows us into Doctor Garcia's office, taking Silas with her to the exam room.

We watch the doctor walk in, sitting in front of us. Neither of us breathing. "Good morning."

"Good morning, Doctor Garcia." Chord tucks my hand under his arm.

"I'm going to explain what you're facing and what I believe to be the best plan for Silas. Please know, you can ask any questions, interrupt me if you need, or take as much time as you need to understand everything as we start this process," she says, and we nod in unison.

"Silas has a rare childhood cancer that occurs in the liver. There are a number of things that could've been factors in the development. The cancer is in his right lobe but has metastasized to his right lung at this point.

"This disease primarily affects children early in life but as old as five to six years of age. Surgery is not an option; to be frank, I'm not sure treatment will be of any help. With that said, I feel we need to try. Every case is different, as is each patient." I sit there, the room spinning, my ears are ringing from the blood coursing through my veins.

"What are you suggesting?" Chord is shaking, but his voice doesn't match.

"Again, surgery isn't an option. We can try to stop the growth with chemotherapy, hoping it helps to shrink it and keep it from attaching to any other organs. As for the long term, there's no promise this will help.

"It will largely depend on Silas' toleration of the medication and if, at this stage, it will help. Cells have also been found in his lymph nodes. We consider this stage four and in the most serious form." We don't move when she's done.

My body revolts, I have to vomit. I spring from my chair, Chord on my heels. "Here, use this one." Doctor Garcia points to her restroom.

WRECKING US, SAVING YOU

I run, losing the contents of my stomach as soon as I lift the seat. Chord stands, holding me up as he gathers my hair. I wipe my mouth with the back of my hand, collapsing into his arms.

There, we sit on the floor of a restroom, holding each other. Our world falling apart just as it was coming together. Chord pulls himself together, helping me up. I prop myself against the door as he hands me a cold, wet towel.

I wipe my face, then my mouth. Stepping to the sink, I rinse the taste from it. Chord helps me to straighten my hair. His arm around me as we join the doctor again, no words have we spoken. There isn't any to compare to how we feel.

"I'm sorry, I deal with this every day and it never gets easier. I find myself angry most days but continue on, in hopes of making a difference in the rare chance that I can." Her voice is low, calming.

"What do we do now?" Chord's words are short and precise.

"I can set up intravenous therapy, locally for you. You would need to return here for follow-up tests and ongoing treatment. We will need more tests after a few weeks to see if there's any change, even small shifts can be promising," she explains.

"What is your prognosis? Will this help or are we up against a beast with no hope." I sink my nails into Chord's hand, he doesn't flinch. I'm not sure I can hear this, but I guess I need to.

"With Silas' particular progression and the fact it has already metastasized, I'm skeptical, but again—every situation is different." She folds her hands in front of her.

"We have to try. I want to do everything humanly possible for him. And if I need to go beyond, I damn well will. Tell me and I'll do it." Chord's resolve cracks, his armor has taken all the beating it can today.

"I'll set him up. Give me just a moment and I'll be right back with his information." She stands.

266

Chord bolts from the room. I follow him, finding him across the hall. I clasp my chest when I find him, Silas in his arms. My heart clenches. I can't catch my breath as I watch Chord hold the son he was just given but has no promise of keeping.

His knees buckle with the weight of his hurt, destroyed with pain. He falls into a chair, clutching Silas to his chest. I fist my hair, begging this to be a nightmare. Praying I'm not awake.

Doctor Garcia returns with Silas' orders. I put them in my purse as Chord stands with our son, taking my hand. We stop for a return appointment, they schedule testing, and we're ready to go home.

Chord holds Silas all the way home, I'm molded to his side. Neither of us wanting to let go of the other. We arrive home, battered and bruised, knowing our hearts will never be the same. Yet, we're together and that's all that matters.

"We need to eat, anyone want anything special?" Chord asks.

The doorbell rings, and we know exactly who it is—our family. "You didn't call."

"I forgot, they must've known when we landed. Should I tell them to go?" His frown is deep.

"No. We need them now more than ever." He caresses my cheek.

"I love you. Most." He jogs to the front door.

"No, it's fine. I'm sorry I didn't call, we're just out of it," Chord says as everyone walks in, carrying multiple things in boxes and bags.

"Food, wasn't sure what y'all would want, so it's a little bit of everything," Elise says as she kisses Silas.

"Did you bring sketti?" He raises his brows.

"We did. There's popsicles, ice cream, chicken and pot stickers. You name it, we have it," Lea says from the kitchen.

"Sketti!" Silas yells. "Momma, can I have an orange pop?"

WRECKING US, SAVING YOU

My eyes cut to Chord. "I don't care what you have, as long as you're happy." I nod, tears filling my eyes.

"Yeah, what Daddy said. You name it, you've got it." I pat his back.

"I want Doritos too." Silas narrows his eyes as if he's waiting for the 'no'.

Thayer yells from the kitchen, "Uncle Hardy's going to get some now!"

"Y'all don't have to do that, he can wait," Chord says, rubbing the back of his neck.

"Not a chance, little brother." One wraps Chord into a bear hug, his body jerking as he struggles to not completely lose his composure.

"Let's eat." I stand, picking Silas up with a giggle.

"What is it?" he asks.

"I've laughed for weeks at your dad for carrying you everywhere, knowing you can walk anywhere and here I am, packin' your butt." Chord's arms embrace us, holding us.

"So you've been laughing at me, huh?" He chuckles.

"Maybe." Silas and I stare at each other, eyes wide.

"I'll take care of that later." He gigs me in the side as he tickles Silas.

We take a much-needed break from all things doctors, tomorrow's another day. The evening is spent laughing and loving this life. Celebrating what's most important—family.

The days ahead will be long and rough, but we'll make it as we always do, together. Silas starts his treatments on Wednesday. I'm not sure who's going to take it rougher. My stomach rolls with fear.

A week into them and Silas is still as amazing as always.

"Here ya go, baby." I hand him some orange pop, it's fast become his favorite.

He takes a drink, it's cold so it has to help his belly. "That's so good." He smacks his lips. "Why did you change your mind about me having pop?"

"We want you to be happy, I mean, if you have to be sick, why not have fun doing it?" Chord scrunches nose, putting his forehead against Silas'.

Silas takes another gulp. "It's so good."

"Let me see that?" Chord reaches for his cup.

"No way, mister. Go get your own." He holds Chord off.

"You two are going to spill it," I admonish them. Their mouths form perfect o's, as if they're in trouble. Not hardly but I won't tell them that right now.

The weeks grow from one to three. Silas doesn't complain, but my heart breaks every time we bathe him.

WRECKING US, SAVING YOU

He's wasting away, and I can't bear to look at his little body some days. "Is it worth it?" Chord's words echo my thoughts.

"It has to be, Chord. It better the fuck be, if we've allowed him to be put through this for nothing." I tremble all over.

He reaches for my hand, as he has so many nights the last few months, lacing his fingers in mine. "Hold on, Sarah. Hold on."

"I'm trying." I bat the tears away. "I feel so selfish."

"No, baby. If you are, that means I am too." His grip tightens as my heart fails to beat, and I catch my breath. "Sing him your dad's song."

My eyes flash to his, searching for his reason, but all I see is love and that's good enough for me. "Standing next to him is like standing next to a thousand suns, not a cluster of stars could outshine. I knew that a part of him belonged to the world, but the world that is within him, is all mine."

Chord slips from his side of the bed to crawl in behind me. Cradling me in his arms, safe from all the monsters that torment me. I promise myself, I'll tell him all the words I've never been able to say, soon.

29

Chord

I stand, leaning against the wall, watching them sleep. Sarah has dark circles under her eyes that rival Silas'. She's up and down more than he even is, checking on him night and day.

Two months have passed since we began this hellish nightmare. Someone can wake me up whenever they want because I'm fucking over it. One minute, anger consumes me and the next, I think, why allow it to rob me of what time I might have left? So I move beyond anger for the time being.

On days I need to work, they sleep in his bed, but I can't do that anymore. Today, I told One, if his tests come back bad, I'm staying home until I have to come back. Here is the only place I have to be, need to be.

His little body is bruised and weak. His hair, once thick and wavy, is almost gone. The medicine to cure him sure does look like it's actually killing him. His port always in our faces, screaming at us that our days are numbered.

His oxygen giving him air as we find ourselves not breathing. My chest heaves, my body on the edge of convulsing as the realization sets in of the inevitable, eating at my soul every day. Hate, my new go to emotion. Now, I get it.

Fuck cancer.

"Hey." Sarah's sweet voice coaxes me from the ledge, bringing me back to them.

I kneel beside the bed, laying my head on her arm. "I'm sorry, baby. I didn't mean to wake you."

"What time is it?" She rolls toward me, wrapping her arm around my shoulders.

I gasp, trying to calm myself. "It's umm, six in the evening."

"I need to get up, we've slept on and off all day." Her eyes close involuntary as she says it. I sweep her hair behind her ear, seeing her in a different light than I ever have.

"Hi, Daddy." The sweetest little squeak in the world calls my name.

I stand, easing over to him, so as not to wake Sarah again. "Hey, Si. How are ya, buddy?"

"I'm hungry." I help him to sit up.

"Wanna go find something to eat?" He nods. I pick him up, easier than before, taking his oxygen off. My heart seizes at the mere thought of how tiny he was, and now, he's even smaller.

I lay him on the couch, replacing his breathing mask. "I want Doritos and orange pop."

"Alright, how about some of Grandmother's homemade soup?" I try to encourage him to eat more.

"Umm, sure. Can I dip my Doritos in it?" He wrinkles his nose.

"Is there any other way to eat soup?"

He giggles. "Nope."

I fix him a tray, joining him on the couch. Sarah must be exhausted, she never goes this long without coming to look for him.

"You have an appointment tomorrow, how about after, we go fishing?"

"Cool. I still want to go camping too." He dips his chips, nibbling as best he can. His stomach swollen, skin paper thin and yet, he's the most beautiful thing I've ever laid my eyes on.

"We can go camping, we'll do anything you want."

"Dad, why do you and Mom cry so much anymore? We used to laugh all the time, don't you love each other still?" A little v forms between his eyes.

"We love each other, we're just worried. We want to make things better for all of us but don't know how." My chest is heavy as the weight lays on me like concrete.

"But you told me, sometimes things happen the way they should and we have to be happy no matter what." His lopsided smile wrecks me.

"I promise you, from this point on, we'll be happy." I ruffle his head.

"Here you two are. Something smells good." I hand my bowl to Sarah, she needs it more than me. She sits on my lap, her back against the couch arm, facing Silas. "This is so good." She takes another bite as her stomach growls. It's then I notice the weight she's lost. That can't happen.

We sit for hours on the couch, talking and making plans for the future, not knowing how long we'll have together. I carry Silas to our bed that night, Sarah's brows furrow in question without asking.

273

"I need you both here." She runs her hand down my arm to clasp my hand.

"Always." Her body molds to mine, as we hold one another up.

I put Silas in the exam room across the hall from us as the nurse comes to sit with him. He's playing on his iPad when I kiss him on the head.

"Don't play poker with him, I owe him two hundred dollars; he's a shark." I wink at him, leaving him laughing.

Sarah and I sit straight when the doctor comes in with his test results. It's funny how the mind can know so much, be packed with knowledge and understanding, but in this moment, our heart springs hope.

"Chord, Sarah. I just had a look at Silas, he's his father." She smiles at Sarah.

"Tell me about it." She elbows me.

"I'm sure you both know what I'm about to say. Please, I hope you understand how hard this is. We have growth, no shrinkage. There's been no response to treatment, at this time. I'm recommending that we discontinue the medicine and allow him to remain comfortable until he passes." A train roars down the track in my head, my ears reverberate the sound. My chest tightens as I will air into my burning lungs.

"There's nothing else we can try?" Sarah's breath hitches as her words come out garbled.

I swallow hard, forcing my words out. "I was reading about a trial at Vanderbilt, does he not qualify?"

"I'm working closely with that trial. At this time, Silas would not be a candidate. My best advice, take him home and make the time you have left all that you want and need for it to be. I'm so sorry, I wish I had better options." Her hands shake as she sits at her desk.

I swallow past the bile, closing my eyes to regroup. I release a long, exaggerated breath. "Alright, okay."

"I'll continue his oxygen and pain medicines. He'll need a home health aide to come in for check-ups. I'll have him back in two weeks." She stands, walking out from around her desk. "Silas is a remarkable young man, he made his mark."

I pull Sarah up with me, trembling. "Thank you, we think so too."

"I'm sorry."

"Of course, thank you." I force a smile, shaking her hand.

I gather my family for our trip home, one we'll never forget. Silas lays his head on my shoulder, Sarah clutches my side as we walk out of the hospital. The fallen faces don't help, it's as if people know our world is ending.

Sarah cradles Silas on the trip back, their hearts speaking as they did once before, silently to one another. Hers willing to beat for him, his tired and ready to quit. I send a quick text to my brother, letting him know the outcome.

We're coming home.

Any news?~O

No hope.

Coming home to say goodbye.

I'm sorry. ~O

Love y'all. ~O

Love y'all.

275

WRECKING US, SAVING YOU

I end my text with One, turning my attention to my family. I'm not sure how we'll do this, if we can do this. I'm lost in thought as we pull up to our home, Sarah taps my leg.

"Chord, we're home." Her swollen eyes as red as her nose.

I jump from the car, hurrying around to their side. "I'm sorry, let me get him."

"Daddy, do we have any of Grandmother's sketti?" Silas peps up.

"No, but I'm sure we can get some."

Sarah types on her phone before opening the door. "I sent her a text, give her an hour." She tweaks his nose.

I sit him on the couch, setting up his tank. "Hey, how about a snack while we wait?"

"Popsicle?" He scrunches his nose.

"I'll get them." Sarah rubs my back, I grab her hand, kissing it before letting her go.

"I have an idea, y'all."

"Oh, no. Should I be scared?" Sarah giggles.

"No." I wink at Silas. "Well, maybe."

"Am I gonna regret this?" Sarah sits next to me, handing over popsicles.

"I was hoping you'd want to help." I take her legs, putting them on top of mine. I smile, wide eyed at Silas.

"What is it?" Silas grins.

"I want to plan a lot of fun things. I want us to play and laugh, do things we've never done. What do you think?" I cock my brow at him.

Silas' brows shoot to his hairline. "Yeah, let's do it."

"What are you talkin' about exactly?" Sarah narrows her eyes at me.

276

I rub her leg, smiling. "You'll like it, I promise."

The doorbell rings, and she jumps up to go get it. "As long as it's not dangerous."

My mouth hangs open as I turn to Silas, he snickers. "Me, dangerous?"

"Hey, Grandmother and Grandpa are on the way." One walks through with his hands full of stuff.

"We're never gonna eat all of this." Sarah shakes her head.

The rest of the family slowly gather, and we enjoy the night with no talk of the future. We live for today, in the moment, laughing and loving. Each family member makes their way to Silas, making sure he knows just how fucking much he's loved.

After the house is empty, I carry our son to bed. Soon, I won't have the opportunity to do it.

"He's fast asleep." Sarah rubs his belly.

I chuckle. "Man, to be able to sleep like that again."

"Seriously, no worries at all." Her face falls, and she begins chewing on her lip.

"Should we tell him?" Her eyes are round as baseballs.

She shakes her head. "No, of course not. I mean, tell him what?"

"I don't mean right now, but when it's closer. Should we tell him he's going to Heaven?"

"No." She wipes her nose. "I don't know, what if he asks?"

"Then we'll tell him, together."

"Alright, together." She reaches for my hand and we lace our fingers, holding on to all we have left.

I wake up early the next morning and begin to make a list of things I want us to do, things he needs to do before he's gone. I want him to have every experience that a boy should have, even the ones his mom might not forgive me for but will laugh when we do it.

I hit One up, explaining my idea.

"Hey, you're up early."

"Yeah, I need some help." My chest aches, thinking of what lies on the other side.

"Whatever you need," One replies.

"I have a list of things I think Silas needs to do."

"I'm in, you know this. Text me the list, we'll get started tomorrow." One is amazing, I'm blessed.

"Seriously, man. Thank you."

"No thanks needed. We're crushed, Chord. For you and Sarah, but for our family. This is all kinds of fucked up." His voice quivers.

"Man, I know. I'm trying to be strong, but I feel selfish and pissed. I'm so damn mad, One."

"Absolutely. No one can blame you, I would be." Rage builds like fire in the pit of my stomach as if it's being flamed.

"I pray I have the strength to see this through, I want our son to live his life, even if he has to do it in a matter of weeks." I rub my eyes.

"I'm on it, little brother," One reassures me.

"Alright, I need to fix them some breakfast. They've both lost all kinds of weight, I need Sarah strong."

"Let me know if we need to do anything else," One says.

"Will do, thank you. Later."

"Later." I end the call, dropping my phone on the table.

"Good morning." Sarah traipses over to me, leaning down and kissing me sweetly.

"Mornin'." I pull her down, making her straddle me.

She wraps her arms around my neck, placing her cheek against mine. "What are you doin' up so early?"

"Making plans." I slide my hands to her ass, squeezing it. "Have I ever told you, you have a perfect ass?"

"Yeah, a million times in high school and a few hundred since then." She giggles when I do it again.

"It's even better now, your hips are to die for. Gives me a hard-on just thinking about them."

"You get a hard-on at the mere mention of sex." She kisses me.

"True, but you still have a fine ass." I wrap my hand in her hair, pulling her lips to mine.

I lay her over on the couch, moving over her. I raise up, taking in the beautiful woman who means more than life. Her looks haven't changed over the years, just the wonderful things having a child does to a woman's body.

"I love you, Sarah Beth."

"Oh, Chord. I love you, so much."

"I'm not sure how to get us through this, please forgive me if I mess it up."

She puts her hands on the side of my face. "I feel the same way, baby. I can't promise to do this the right way, I won't."

"There's only one way to make it through, that's together."

She pulls my lips to hers and we get lost in this moment, knowing we may not get another any time soon, and we wouldn't want it any other way. Silas is and always will be the most important thing to us.

"Are you going to tell me what you have planned?" She peeks over at the list on the table.

"I sure can, but no telling. I want him to be surprised." I grab the tablet. "I want him to have all his firsts or at least the one's we can give him."

"Babe, this is perfect." She covers her mouth, crying. "He's gonna love this, you're the best dad, Chord. I knew you would be, but you've blown me away."

"You're not too bad yourself, Sarah. I'm blown away by your strength." I press my lips to hers, loving her the only way I know how. By loving her just as she is and always has been.

I take her hand. "Let's go make everything we can for breakfast."

"We'll have breakfast food all day." She snickers.

"And why don't we?" She smiles.

"Why don't we."

Chord

"Where are we going?" Sarah watches the street signs.

I cut my eyes at her. "Wait for it."

"Ughh, have I mentioned I hate waiting?" I chuckle at her exaggerated sigh.

"Multiple times." I peek in the rearview mirror. "Are you ready, Si?"

"Yes! I'm excited to see the surprise." He holds his arms in the air.

"How about the…aquarium?"

His face glows as his smile grows. "You're joking?"

"Oh, Silas. It's the aquarium!" Sarah points out the window.

"Yay!" They both scream, my heart swells with happiness.

WRECKING US, SAVING YOU

We spend the entire day at the aquarium, only stopping long enough to eat. Silas is exhausted but sad when we decide it's enough for the day. I have days planned every few days, and this is just the beginning.

I give him time to rest and a couple of days later, we go fishing, surf fishing that is. We spend the afternoon, and into the evening, playing on the beach and fishing. I take him to the pier so we can cast our poles in from there. He loves every minute.

After the late night, we spend a few days in bed, watching every superhero movie I can find. Eating late, sleeping later, we make the most of life. I take him on a shopping spree, allowing him to buy whatever he wants.

Early Saturday morning, Sarah's surprise arrives.

"Chord, the door, babe." I hide in the closet as she hurries down the stairs. "Chord? Have mercy." She opens the door to a delivery driver.

"Sarah?" Her eyes are wide.

"Yes?"

"This is for you." He steps to the side to reveal a Land Rover Discovery in a gray metallic.

She shakes her head. "This can't be right."

"It is, I ordered it a little while ago. It's yours when you're ready for it." She glances at it, then throws her arms and legs around me, kissing me everywhere.

"Thanks, man." The delivery guy laughs as he walks away. I shut the door, moving my hands to her perfect ass.

A few days later, we head out to the backyard. The tent is set up and a fire already going. "Camp out, anyone?"

"With smorwes?" Silas grins.

"Yes and a wiener roast."

Sarah slides her arm around my waist. "I'm loving all of these living days."

"Good, cause we're gonna do all the living we can fit in for as long as we can."

We spend the night star gazing, eating smores and hotdogs. Silas falls fast asleep between us in the middle of the tent we planned our life in together. After the camp out, we need to spend a few days just hanging out.

"Are you ready?" I whisper to Silas.

"Yes, are you surwe she knows?" His brows are pulled low.

"Dude, I wouldn't do you like that."

"My first date. Andi's so pretty." His eyes sparkle when he says her name.

"I know that look, your dad gave me the same one at about the same age. No falling in love, you're mine forever." Sarah tweaks his side.

Andi, Ava, and Riley walk through the door and Silas' lopsided grin wins him a wave. I hold my hand out to Riley.

"Thank you so much for this."

"Our pleasure." Riley takes it with a smile.

"This is simply the best thing ever." Ava kisses my cheek.

"Thanks for coming." Sarah hugs Ava.

"Come on, Andi. The movie is about to start." Silas is a little wobbly, but when he loses his balance, Andi takes his hand.

"I've got you, Si," she says with a smile.

My heart could burst. Seriously, he's having the time of his life. They laugh through the entire movie, leaving best friends. More than I can ever ask for, it's a perfect ending to the night.

WRECKING US, SAVING YOU

The weekend brings a nice surprise, we have a huge birthday party. And the weekend after that is Christmas. It's our first together, and I plan to make it the best. We have so many more things to do, but this will be my favorite.

On our way to my parents' home, we're beyond humbled to learn the town has come together to decorate for our son. Every house and storefront is filled with Christmas trees and signs for Silas.

Sarah cries all the way there, making it hard for me to hold my shit together. Mom's house is loaded to the hilt, she has lights on everything. Even Dad is wearing a sweater that lights up.

"Merry Christmas!" we yell, walking through the door. Mom runs over, hugging Silas and me. She pulls Sarah in, holding her a tad bit longer than she did us. "What's cookin'? Smells delicious."

"All your favorites, including sketti." She holds Silas' face in her hands.

"Silas, Grandpa has a big surprise for you." Dad takes him, walking to the family room.

"Your family is still as amazing as ever," Sarah says, leaning in to kiss me.

"Our family, you've been here almost as long as me, and I often wonder if One wouldn't pick you over me."

"I know Thayer would." I press my lips to hers as we join our family.

In the corner of the room, there's a life size Thor cutout. Silas is beaming. "Daddy." He points.

"Oh, man. That's gonna be killer in your room." Dad sits him in his recliner, the chair no one's allowed to use. Si is the king today.

"We're on for next weekend. Dad may have won the battle, but we're gonna win the war." One bumps my fist, laughing.

284

"Seriously, look at that thing. I can't allow Sarah to sleep in the room with him." I cock my brow.

"As long as I want your hammer, it doesn't matter who gets me in the mood, does it?" Sarah waggles her brows.

"Hell, yes." I pout.

She pulls me close. "Your hammer's been the only one to ever nail me."

I grab her hips, holding her to me. "Fuck, you need to stop or you're gonna get a Christmas surprise."

"Did you say you want my pie?"

She snickers, but I get the last laugh, whispering, "I'd eat it all night long, baby."

"Sarah, are you sick? You just turned five shades red." Thayer cackles.

I sit on the floor by Silas, helping him open gifts from our family. He gets a Thor helmet and all the extras, a Panthers jersey with his favorite player's number on it, a kid-sized four wheeler, and a new fishing rod, just to name a few.

"We can play superheroes now, Dad." Silas' eyes sparkle when he grins.

"All day long! And you have a jersey to wear for games too."

"I'm catching all the fish next time too." His eyes are wide.

I stretch my arms out. "This big?" He shakes his head. "Oh, this big!" I open my arms as wide as they'll go, and he nods wildly. His little face is lit with color in his cheeks, something we haven't seen in a while.

He tires easily, and our family settles in so he can rest. We watch as Lath pops the big question to his girlfriend, Ryver, and she says yes. Lea cries as One holds her; it's wonderful they get to experience these things.

WRECKING US, SAVING YOU

"We're gonna have weddings galore next year." Mom smiles, holding her heart.

And yet, here I sit, still single as hell. "What?" Sarah asks.

I scan the room, looking back at her. "What, what?"

"That look, you were frowning."

"More like, scowling," Thayer quips.

I shake my head. "Thinking."

"About?" Sarah prompts.

I sigh, rubbing my neck. "I had hoped we'd be married by now. It's okay we're not, but I was hoping."

Her eyes roam. "Yeah, I know." She officially puts an end to wedding talk.

We gather Silas' things, and One helps me to the car with the greater part of it. The rest my parents are bringing over tomorrow.

"So are you going to tell me what's up, or do I need to wrestle it out?" One narrows his eyes.

I shove my hands in my pockets, throwing my head back to stare at the stars. "If she loves me, why not marry me?"

"You know she loves you." He pins me with a glare.

I release a heavy breath. "I know, I just want us married. Besides, I could've already been on his birth certificate if we were."

"Does she know that?" One's brows knit.

I roll my shoulders. "Yeah, she knows. Listen, I know things are fucked up right now, but it's not like we can't do it in our backyard even. I don't know."

One places his hand on my shoulder. "Keep your focus on Silas, the rest will work out."

"He's ready," Sarah calls from the door.

"Hang in there." One slaps me on the back. "Chord, I'm proud of you."

"Thanks, brother." He follows me through the door. I pick Silas up, and he gets his twins. "Later, Captain VonWoods."

Walking out the door, I find Sarah by the SUV. Her head down, she doesn't look at me when she opens the door.

I buckle Silas in, kissing his head. "He may be the most beautiful boy, I've ever seen."

"Yeah, he's his father." Sarah sighs.

"I was just thinking how much he looks like you."

The drive home is quiet. I think we both know we're on borrowed time. Once home, I take Silas to bed, finding Sarah in the living room.

"The lights on the tree with the fire are breathtaking," she murmurs as I enter the room.

I sit with a sigh. "Yes, it is. Too bad we don't have snow."

"Chord?" I turn to Sarah, she's staring out the window. "Is that?"

I hurry to the door, swinging it wide. I walk in wonder to the middle of our yard, in the snow. "Wow."

"It's beautiful." Sarah spins in the light flurries as they fall to the ground.

I take my phone out, turning on the music. Jon Langston serenades us with *When It Comes to Loving You*. "May I have this dance?" Holding out my hand.

Her eyes flash to mine, glistening. She gives me her hand, the way she has so many times before. "Always."

I pull her to me, spinning around. She lays her head on my shoulder as we sway to the sound of our hearts beating. In this moment, we are nothing more than Sarah and Chord.

WRECKING US, SAVING YOU

The following weekend, we pack up and head into town. I have huge plans for this day. Pulling up at The Myrtle Beach Sports Center, Sarah's head spins to face me.

"What do you have planned?" Her jaw drops.

"Everything." I smile, sliding from the seat.

We walk in to find all our family and friends. I set Silas up and get ready for our first adventure.

"What are we doing today, Dad?" he asks with the sweetest smile that warms my cold soul.

"First up, baseball and then a little football. And later, if you feel up to it, a big surprise."

"I'll feel like it." He nods with a lopsided grin.

"If you don't, there's always tomorrow." My breath hitches as I say it, knowing it may not be true. I place a baseball helmet on his head.

"Baseball first, who are we playing?" he asks.

"Uncle One, Uncle Hardy, the boys and our friends are here to make teams." I point to the growing crowd. "You even have your own cheering section."

"How in the world did you get this planned?" Sarah's eyes match Silas', big and round.

"Our family, we rented the place out and have it for as long as he wants." I shrug, as I push Silas to the makeshift baseball field.

A few rounds at bat, fielding, and a run of the bases, Silas' laughter means the world to me. A homerun and catching an out, we move on. We play touch football, leaving him cackling as the older guys get into the game and really crank it up.

A few plays later, Silas has an interception, a touchdown, and a quarterback sack. He's having the time of his life, but it's not even close to being over. I save the best for last—we're making a movie.

The camera crew comes in, setting up to follow the action. Everyone taking part hurries to change. Silas won't say it, but he's getting tired; that's why I made everything as short but full as possible.

When Walker steps into the room, Sarah gasps. She slowly stands, hand over her mouth. She stares, her eyes filling with tears. I step around him, carrying Silas' Thor gear.

"Silas, I know this will make us have two Thor's, but would you do us the honor of joining The Avengers?" His eyes alight, he shakes his head.

"Yes, Captain America." We have them all, me and Thor, The Hulk, Iron Man, and even The Black Widow. Better known as Aunt Thayer.

"Let's make our own superhero movie."

And for the next hour, that's what we do. Silas' face says all anyone needs to know as we roleplay and they film it. He is a superhero for life. And now, so are our family and friends.

Laying Silas in bed, I snuggle him down after his bath. He looks up at me, his eyes twinkling. "Thank you, Daddy. Today was the best day ever."

I lean down, pressing my lips to his forehead. "You're so welcome, Silas. Thank you for being mine."

"Do we have any more adventures?" he asks with a furrowed brow.

"We do, but we can't tell Mom. She's gonna freak on the next one." I rub my nose on his, making him giggle.

"I can't wait." He throws his little arms around my neck. My stomach knots at the thought of never having another moment like this with him.

After Silas rests for a few days, I take him and Sarah on our next adventure. I pull into the lot as One steps from the car. A cruiser with a real police officer.

"What in the hell?" Sarah clutches her shirt.

"Someone needs to make their driver's license." I wink. I jump from the SUV, taking the officer's hand. "Thank you for this."

"My pleasure. No way could I resist when One explained the circumstance," Officer Cook says.

"Let's do this." One claps his hands.

"He has no clue," Sarah says at my side. "I can't believe this, you think of everything." I kiss her, running to Silas' door. I don't want to waste the officer's time.

"What are we doing?" Silas cocks his head.

"You're going to make your driver's license." His eyes are huge. "Give a few to practice and we'll be ready."

One helps me set the seat back, and he takes Silas until I'm settled then sitting him between my legs. I work the peddles as he turns the wheel, practicing in the empty store parking lot.

We give them a thumbs up when we're ready. "Let's do this."

The officer hops in, instructing us where to go and when. Silas' tongue hangs out as he navigates the cones One set up, and he parallel parks. We sent Officer Cook a picture of Silas, and he pulled a few strings and got a fake license made.

After our course, he announces that Silas has passed. "Congratulations, you are now a licensed driver. Be safe on the roads." He hands Silas his card with a smile.

"Thank you, officerw." Silas beams.

"You're welcome."

"I did it, Dad. Now, I can drive Momma around," he yells.

Sarah laughs with One. "You've created a monster."

"I have something special for this weekend, so there ya go." I point to the SUV pulling in.

"What's going on?" Sarah quirks her brow.

"Go buy a nice dress, and you'll find out this weekend."

"Come on, I have credit cards and cash, we could go to New York and shop all day," Lea says from the window. One jogs over, kissing her.

Sarah saunters over to me, stepping up on the rails. "I love you." She presses her lips to mine, to Silas' chagrin.

"Ughh, people. Y'all are always kissing." He makes a gagging noise, making us all laugh.

"Go on, I'm taking One and Silas home." She leans in, kissing Silas.

"Later." I watch as that fine ass walks away from me, but Lea catches my attention.

"What?" I plaster on my sly grin.

She shakes her head. "You spend too much time with your brother."

"We know fine art when we see it."

"Nothing wrong with showing an appreciation for quality." One smirks.

"Oh, lawd. Y'all go on, we're going shopping." Lea waves as she drives off.

"Shew, my heart." I lay my hand over my chest.

"I heard that, mine doesn't beat without Hadlea." One smiles warmly.

"Alright, buddy. Let's get you buckled in."

"Please let me drive home," Silas' begs. One's brows shoot up.

"We could go the back way home." He smirks.

"You tell your mother and I'm dead meat." I start the SUV, and we pull out onto the side street.

Silas, One, and I have the best trip home. It took us thirty minutes longer but was so worth it. The smile on Silas' face when One gave him a high-five for getting us home was priceless.

31

Sarah

"So, no one knows where we're going or no one's telling me?" I step out, checking my off white tulle skirt in the mirror. Turning, I adjust my silver sweater.

"You're gorgeous," Thayer says from the door.

"Thank you. Do you think Chord will like it?"

She quirks her lip. "I think you're good."

There's a limo waiting on us at the door when we leave the house. Elise, Lea, Thayer and myself enjoy a little champagne and strawberries on the way to wherever it is we're going.

When the car stops, the door opens to a building with a red carpet. We celebrated New Year's last week, so what can this be? I'm the last one through the doors to be greeted by my two main squeezes.

WRECKING US, SAVING YOU

"Well hello, beautiful." Chord leans in to kiss me, dressed in a three-piece gray suit, fitted perfectly to his toned body.

A rose pops up between us. "Dad, this is my night." Silas rolls his eyes. I realize he matches us, in a gray vest and slacks.

"Excuse me." Elise takes Chord's arm. He gives me his boyish grin, and I melt. They walk ahead, leaving me with Silas.

"Shall we?" Silas says. "I'm not sure what that means, Dad said I should say it."

"It means, let's go." I turn his wheel chair around, pushing him through the last set of doors.

A banner hangs high next to the stage, 'Mother Son Dance'. There's a band playing and tables are set up. He set up a dance for me and Silas. I search the room and spotting him, I rush to him.

My eyes blurry with tears, I wrap my arms around him. Clutching him to me, my chest heaves. His love fills me up, more than any words ever spoken. He holds me tightly against him.

When I gather myself enough to speak, I lean back, gazing into his gorgeous blue eyes. "I love you. I've never known a love like yours. Thank you." Tears run down my face as his mouth takes mine.

"You blow me away." He swings me around, making my body feel the way my heart does.

"Hey, buddy. You stole my date," Silas says. Thayer brought him over to us.

"I apologize, sir." Chord bows. "Madame." He presents my hand to Silas, and I clasp my chest to try to keep my heart from exploding.

Silas and I dance the night away, I push him all over the floor. Chord helps a few times before stepping back. Lea is here with her sons, and One is here with Elise. Thayer's here with Holden.

All for me to have this special night with our son. One I'll never be able to have with him, including a dance at his wedding. Chord has given us many things we might have missed; now, we'll keep these memories forever.

"Have you two enjoyed your special evening?" Chord scoots closer to ask.

I lay my hand on his thigh. "I have, thank you."

"How about you, Si? Have you had a good time?" Chord leans over to ask him.

He nods. "I have."

"You tired, Si?" Silas nods again, and we decide to call it a night.

Chord stands, making a toast. "First, thank you. It means so much to us that you took this time to help us celebrate. This night was to honor the sacrifice mothers go through and the love only you can give. So thank you all. May we rise to your examples."

I turn, kissing Silas. His sweet smile warms my soul. Turning to Chord, I press my lips to his, giving him another thank you. Chord makes our excuses, helping Silas into the car.

Once again, he carries Silas to bed, the way he has for all of these weeks, knowing our days are numbered. We lay in bed, watching Silas struggle for air. Chord's hand reaches for mine, and we lace our fingers, praying.

"Sarah, baby wake up." I open my eyes as Chord shakes me.

"What? What's goin' on?"

"Silas, I've called an ambulance." I roll my head to get a look at him, he's barely breathing. "You have clothes on the end of bed.

WRECKING US, SAVING YOU

I stagger up, the room spinning. I rip the shirt over my head, pulling on the one Chord set out. I jerk my pants on and slide into my shoes. I turn back to Chord, and it's like a rock drops into my stomach.

Silas lays on the bed, his eyes not open and his body limp. Chord is all over the place, packing a bag, then runs down to open the door for the paramedics. I climb on to the bed with Silas, holding his hand.

"Chord." I swallow hard. "Chord."

He rushes to me. "What?"

"Sit and hold your son's hand, it could be the last time." I choke on my words as bile rises in my throat.

He leans into me, wrapping an arm around me and holding our hands in his. When the emergency personnel show up, we ride in the back with Silas. We both refuse to leave his side.

Fortunately for us, today wasn't his day. This time, when Chord climbs the stairs with Silas, he takes him to his bed. The doctor said it would be easier to do any medical checks on him. They're coming to set up his equipment. He's starting hospice.

Hospice. For a six-year-old little boy.

Fuck you, cancer.

I sit on the bathroom floor for hours, losing my shit until I can pull myself together. Chord? He sits beside our son's bed, checking on me every few minutes or so, only to make sure I'm here.

I wash my face, vomit, and do it all over again. When I can handle to face life, I slowly trudge into Silas' room. Chord has dozed off, holding Silas' hand as he sleeps as well.

I crawl in bed with him, laying as close as safely possible. I watch them sleeping as the sun rises. I can't close my eyes for fear of missing the last second this incredible human being has on earth.

"I'm sorry, I didn't mean to fall asleep." Chord rubs his hand over his face.

I wave him off. "No, don't. I have a feeling this is our life for the foreseeable future."

"I'm gonna check on a recliner or something like that for in here." He stretches. "Can I bring you anything?"

"No, I'm good."

"I'll be right downstairs, no more than ten minutes." A line forms between his brows.

"We'll be here, promise." I force a smile.

His mouth pressed into a firm line, he hurries downstairs. I lay there, listening to Silas' breathing machine. We were told it would be exchanged for a different machine this week, one that could sustain him longer.

I watch as his chest raises slightly before falling back down. What was once deep breaths, now shallow and fleeting. His skin transparent and blue veins are easily spotted. His lips dry and cracked. I need to find some lip balm when Chord gets back.

"Baby Boy, I'm not sure how your daddy and I are gonna let you go. Your daddy just got you and you're all I've known for six years now." I gasp. "Signing papers for your DNR and having people here for you, it's more than I can bare. Your dad, he pretends to be strong but I can see it in his eyes. Please, we need more time."

I've asked God for so much in my lifetime, I feel ashamed knowing what I do now. Those ridiculous requests pale in comparison to begging for my son's life. I regret so many things, mistakes that I should've never made.

Is it too much to ask for his life to be spared? Am I paying for my past or is this a judgement of my parents' sins? I don't give a damn, I want my son. I want him happy and vibrant. I want him to live.

"Silas, I don't want you to go." My breath hitches, catching on the knot formed in my throat. "Please, stay."

WRECKING US, SAVING YOU

I position my ear against his side by his heart so I can hear it beat. I hold his hand on my cheek, smelling the little boy that's left in him. Fresh air and soap, the best scent in the world.

"Baby?" Chord rubs my back.

I move my head. "He needs lip balm."

"I'll get it, tell me where." His hand splays against my thigh.

"Nightstand. I have two, could you bring them both?"

"I'll be right back." Chord scurries from the room, returning in no time. "Here ya go."

He places the balm in my hand, and I clasp on. "Stay with us."

"I'm not going anywhere right now." He lays beside me. "Sarah, I hadn't thought about it but we'll need to make arrangements."

"Not yet." I hold back a sob. "I'm sorry, I know you'll probably be the one to do it, I just can't talk about it right now."

"I'm not doing it without you. I can't, Sarah." He trembles, I know he's crying.

I sweep my finger over the balm, patting Silas' lips with it. "Why do we have to watch him leave us? Witness his pain? It's unfair."

"Incredibly unfair." Chord sniffles.

"Did I ever tell you his first word was dad?"

He sucks in a breath. "No. As much as he loves you, I figured it would've been mom."

"Nope, dad." I roll my head to look up at him. "Even then, he loved you."

"I read that letter several times a week, and each time, I thought about whether we had a boy or a girl. Who they would favor or if they even would, maybe a good mix between the two of us." His body twitches.

298

I grin. "Yeah, no, babe. He's all you."

"How lucky are we, Sarah? This extraordinary young man decided that we could be his parents," he gasps, trying to hold back his tears.

"We're the luckiest people in the world, Chord."

"You people talk too much." Silas giggles.

"Just saying how much we love you." I kiss his cheek.

He sighs. "Am I going to heaven?"

Chord sits up, looking over my shoulder at him. "Why would you ask that, Si?"

"I'm sick. I had a drweam I was in heaven, watching you and momma." He grins.

"We're all going to heaven someday, buddy." Chord tells him, making my heart seize.

His smile warms my heart. "See, momma. We'll all be togetherw again one day." He lays his hand on my face as he slowly nods off.

Chord and I hold him closer tonight, our hearts hurting but full of love.

Sarah

Minutes turned into hours, hours into days, and days to weeks. He lingers because I'm selfish. Because I refuse to let him go. I hold onto him with every ounce of fight I have in me. I know I need to let him go. So tell me how to do that, why don't you.

The equipment in his room is a glaring reminder of the life we're losing. The sounds making sleep impossible; can you imagine trying to find a little peace? The whoosh and swirls going nonstop. The bleep of his heart, the only sound that doesn't annoy me.

I no longer lay in the bed with him, his breathing machine is finicky. Chord bought a recliner and put it in the corner next to the bed. I can still touch him, but I'm not close enough. I can't hear his heartbeat from here.

When Chord sleeps, he lays on a sleeping bag on the floor by my feet so he can be near both of us. He's never too far away, always watching over us. Our hearts all too conscious of the fact our son is leaving.

We're by his side, twenty-four hours a day. Well, Chord has to take care of things around the house, but then he comes back. I don't give a fuck if the place falls in. I'd love to call this some fancy name, like insomnia, but everyone knows it's a death watch.

I fucking hate cancer.

It's ripping my child apart, and I'm losing my mind. I've traced every inch of his body so I don't forget a thing. All these years I dreamed we would be the happy ones, the people who had this amazing life.

Here it is, wrapped up in breathing machines and pain medicine. I find myself crying hysterically for a minute and then, I'm talking to him as if he hears me and is going to answer the next.

"Sarah?" Chord runs his hand over mine. "You need to eat."

I glower at him. "No, I'm not hungry."

"You haven't eaten since yesterday." He runs his hands through his hair. "Please, Sarah?"

My face scrunches as I fight tears. "No, Chord. I'm not hungry."

He kneels in front of me, tears brimming. "Baby, please. I can't lose you both."

My chest ruptures as a sob escapes. "I can't."

"Maybe later." His heart is as broken as mine, and all he does is to keep trying when I don't want to.

We sit for long hours, moving only when we can't sit there another minute. Chord tends to pace, I stare into space. Even as I help Silas, it's automatic. I want to be here, in the present, but my mind tends to protect itself.

WRECKING US, SAVING YOU

Silas' body begins to stop fighting. His breathing shallow and labored. We watch day and night, wanting the last minutes of his life to be with us. His little body sensing time is near, slowly gives up.

"Mister Hamilton?" We both turn to stare at his nurse. "It's time to call the family in."

The fissure in my chest opens as if an earthquake has it. I can't catch my breath, Chord's arms are around me, cradling me. Loving me. Willing me to breathe. I gasp, dragging air into my desolate lungs.

"I'll call them. Thank you, Andrea," Chord croaks, and his body quakes as he faces the inevitable.

"I'll be downstairs." She leaves us with our dying son.

My head shakes of its own accord. "No! Not now! I won't let him go. I can't let him go, Chord! Please, please don't make me." I fall to my knees.

"I'm sorry. Dear God, I'm so sorry, Sarah." He holds me in the floor, rocking me.

"God! Please, we haven't had enough time!" I scream as Chord's hold on me keeps me grounded.

"Oh, Sarah. I'm so sorry I failed you both." Chord cries.

My heart seizes as I hold onto what sense of being I have left. Chord's arms tighten around me, the air in my lungs evaporates. God, please. I beg you, please. "I can't, Chord. I thought I could live without him, but I can't. Don't make me." I fist his shirt.

"Sarah, baby. Shhhh, don't say that. Please." Chord struggles for words. "Hold on to me, do you hear me, Sarah. Hold on to me."

I nod, staring into his eyes as he loses all hope. I know his hurt only mirrors mine, we're losing the tie that binds us. Chord's heartache is written on his face, our world is crumbling and he can't save us.

302

He takes his phone out, hitting a button. "One," he chokes "it's time." His words a garbled mess as he hangs up the phone. He picks me up, sheltering me from the world. We hold our son's hand, waiting.

"Luke?"

"There's no way he can make it in time, baby. I'm sorry." Chord's tears streak his face.

A few minutes later, we hear the doorbell, followed by footsteps on the stairs. One comes around the corner, looking like he ran from his house to get here. His arms, no bigger than Chord's, find a way to wrap us in his love. Our tears fall as our hearts break into a million pieces.

Slowly, the rest of the family begins to show up and before we know it, Silas is surrounded with all the love his little heart can hold. I look around the room, knowing his cup runneth over.

Cal kneels at Silas' bedside, kissing him. "Hey, little man. The day you tiptoed into our home, peeking from behind your mom, you stole my heart. Those big blue eyes, just like your father's, took my breath away. I knew you were ours, and nothing has made me happier. Being your grandpa was a pleasure, knowing you an honor. I love you, Silas." I squeeze Chord's hand as my chest heaves, his body trembling.

Elise replaces him as he stands by her side, clutching her hand. "Silas, baby. Grandmother's not sure she can do this." She sweeps her finger over his cheek. "You were the perfect grandson. Your spirit shone through from the first smile, your heart willing to love and doing so without prejudice. I will never be the same, Silas. Your life has changed mine, forever. I love you."

Chord's body stiffens as One and Thayer kneel beside their nephew. Thayer taking his free hand, One holding her close. "Silas, I'm going to miss your laughter. Oh, how it brightened the room. Your love of life escaping as rays of sunshine into our lives, making us all better people. I love you." Thayer's body doubles with grief.

WRECKING US, SAVING YOU

One leans over, almost whispering, "Hey, buddy. I never had the chance to tell you how much like your parents you are. Stubborn like your mom, hardheaded just like your dad. But a blessing, just as they are. You are and always will be missed. Our hearts forever marked by your love."

Chord and I sit vigil by his side. Counting the breaths, praying as we wait for the next. Our family moving from room to room. Waiting as we do for the world to stop turning as the sun goes dark.

A tug in the pit of my stomach beckons to me. I scoot closer to Silas, laying my head across from his. Though my vision is blurry, I fight the pain in my chest and sing to Silas.

"Standing next to him is like standing next to a thousand suns, not a cluster of stars could outshine. I knew that a part of him belonged to the world, but the world that is within him, is all mine."

"Silas, I love you," Chord whispers.

Silas' chest raises as his breath expels, his body falls limp. Another shallow breath as if he's fighting leaving us, slowly dropping, as our hopes crash with his lungs. His final breathe, strong and deep, like our love for him, plummets. He's leaving us.

A sob, rupturing my heart, breaks free. I scream his name, "SILAS!" expelling the air in my lungs as they burn. The cavity in my chest, devoid of life. His death causes a fracture so deep in my soul, my chest feels as if it's split open.

I scream, praying I lay here and die with my son. There was nothing before and nothing beyond, I am lost. Chord embraces me as I feel every second ticking by that my son is not alive.

Chord's grip tightens on me as he tries to hold me from leaving like our son has. My eyes focus on Silas, my baby. He's gone. A sound springs forth, guttural, as it rumbles through my body ripping me in half.

"Sarah. Sarah! Breathe, god damnit. Sarah!" Chord shakes me until I wheeze. Air fills my cavernous vessel, forcing me to breathe again. I wail as grief consumes me.

"Chord?" I'm decimated.

"Oh, baby." His arms encase me, saving me from near death. Cheating me of peace.

I'm not sure how long we sit there beside him. It's Cal who takes the task in hand to help us move. "Chord, Sarah, they need to come get him."

They? Who? No! "Chord?" I search his eyes for answers, but it's One that does.

"The paramedics," One's voice quivers.

"No. Not yet, we need a little more time." Chord's body vibrates. "Dad, please? A few more minutes. Please?" His words, my thoughts.

"Oh, son. A few more." Cal's hands shake as he leans against the wall.

Chord pulls me up beside him. He leans forward, kissing Silas' forehead. Then he places a soft kiss over his heart. "I love you. Please know that I love you."

I lay my head against his, tears soaking his pillow. "Momma loves you, baby boy. I'm so sorry I couldn't save you. I'll love you, always." I press my lips to his.

Chord drags a long, ragged breath in. He stands, bringing me with him. He leans down, sliding his arm around my legs. He holds me to his chest, as we leave Silas behind. I look back, reaching for him as my chest breaks open again.

He carries me downstairs, sitting me on his lap on the couch. My back to the stairwell so they can take our son. Chord's arms are locked around me, the only thing holding me together.

WRECKING US, SAVING YOU

"I'm so sorry. I'm so sorry, Sarah." Chord's words become a mantra to my soul.

I hold onto his words to keep from falling further into the depths of this living hell. You're told all the time, you have no clue how I feel. I pray no mother feels the way I do in this moment.

The house, once a flurry of activity, is now quiet with only the sound of a whimper. So soft, yet full of pain, the noise makes me shudder. The suffering one must feel at the hands of agony to release discomfort must be tormenting.

"So many things left to do. To say. Did I tell him I loved him enough?" Chord crushes me to his chest, weeping.

"He loved you most." His words, fleeting as they are, mean so much.

"I can't, Chord. I can't live without him."

"I wish I could take your pain." He trembles with sobs of his own hurt.

"Chord?" Thayer says. "Here, try to dry her face."

His shirt is soaked. "Wet it, Thayer, so it's cool."

"Should we call a doctor?" Cal asks as his words float over my head.

Chord shakes his head. "No, she'll be okay. I just to need to hold her a little longer."

And he does, Chord holds me for hours. The minute I think I've run out of tears, they fall harder. He cries with me, doing his best to coax me to stop. He rubs my back, plays with my hair and rocks me, trying anything to soothe me.

"Chord, is there anything we can do?" Lea sits beside me, taking my hand.

"I don't know." His words are no more than a whisper.

As the day wears on, people start showing up. They bring everything from food to drinks to flowers. Bile rises in my throat as I think about buying flowers for our son's casket.

That image alone drags me back down into the pits of hell. Cancer is a deplorable way to end someone's life. It robs you of time, dignity, and in the end, grace. Because you can't choose how you leave this world, no more than the way you came in. Not gracefully anyway.

"Hey, you wanna grab a bath?" Chord searches for anything to pull me out of the mire.

"Not right now," I mewl.

Later that night, he lays me in bed, crawling in behind me. We cry until we fall asleep, though it never takes us under long enough. His resolve to be by my side never wavers. He's my rock.

The sun rises without Silas this morning. We watch the light grow in the distance, taking our peace and ripping it apart. In our darkest hour, the sun mocks us. My chest aches, feeling like it's been riddled with bullets.

"We need to make plans," Chord's voice quivers.

My grief is so heavy, I can't bear to think of it. "Give me a little longer."

"Okay." He laces his fingers with mine, offering me the time I need.

I dry my eyes again, turning to him. "Why do people feel the need to rush and make arrangements?"

"I'm not sure, it's what has to be done." He shrugs.

"So people go into automatic?"

"I haven't thought about it. I suppose at one time, they were taken care of differently, so time was imperative." He rubs the back of his neck.

WRECKING US, SAVING YOU

"I don't want to do it at all."

"I don't either, but we have to, Sarah." I'm making this harder on him, but I don't want to rush it. I'm in no hurry to say goodbye.

"Who says? Other people? Because we're preconditioned to lay our loved ones to rest as soon as they leave. Well, fuck that." I stand, storming from the room. It doesn't matter to me, he's right.

I run toward the beach, praying the ocean will swallow me up. No such luck, my lungs burn from running and crying. I scream, releasing everything in me. I don't want to feel anymore. I want to be numb.

"Sarah?" Chord beckons me from the edge of insanity. "We'll wait as long as you need."

I spin, running into his arms. "I'm sorry. I want to die, Chord. Please, let me go with him."

"Please stay. Help me help you." He crushes me to his chest where I find a moment of solace.

"This evening, we'll go take care of Silas." I slow my breathing. "Don't leave me."

"Never." His voice is raspy.

"Do you think he knew I loved him?"

He pulls me to his side. "Never doubt that, he was so loved by you, he was complete."

Complete but not whole, that's exactly how I feel right now. I will never be without this emptiness again. My life has been altered, and I will never go back. Life changes in a split second, what will you do when it does?

I fall apart. Because I died yesterday.

33

Chord

My life has resembled a rollercoaster, and the last few months is no different. Finding Sarah and Silas has brought me the greatest joy and now, my greatest sorrow. It's a nightmare, and I'm begging to wake up.

I replay the scene as it unfolded in front me; I felt as though I wasn't present. Like I was committing voyeurism into someone else's life. Each act, real and heartfelt. Still, I watched so many things from outside myself.

WRECKING US, SAVING YOU

We watch as his chest falls for the last time. I sit here helpless, a witness to a murder. Nothing I could do to save my son from the fate of cancer. His life ripped from him, our lives shredded. How do we survive this?

The deafening silence rings in my ears. I peer over the ledge, falling into the abyss. I watch as the room moves in slow motion. Thayer crumples to the floor, Hardy holding her in his arms. Mom clutching Dad as they both cry. One and Lea embrace, trembling as they mourn. His nurse checks his vitals, calling the time of death.

I hold onto Sarah, incapable of doing anything else. My chest breaks open as I fight for air, struggling to breathe. Sarah sobs as I hold her, wracking her body with pain. Agony etched on her face. I've never felt so helpless.

The following afternoon, we make arrangements to lay Silas to rest. Sarah's hanging on by a thread. I'm not much better, but I'll never allow her to see it. She has enough on her, even being here is more than anyone should expect.

"Mister Hamilton, we're sorry for your loss," the funeral director, Mister Bower, says.

I reach his hand, keeping an arm around Sarah. "Thank you."

"Let's see how we can help you today. Please, be seated." He motions to chairs in front of his desk. One and Thayer, per Sarah's request, came with us.

"We need to make arrangements for our son." With my words, the end of Sarah's resolve falters. She clutches my shirt as her tears fall.

"Of course, do you have anything in mind?"

"Yes. We're going to have him in gray with a blue bow tie. His eyes are…were blue." My chest caves with the words.

"Service times or location?" he asks as he writes.

"The chapel will be fine and one day."

"We can have him Thursday from noon till two. Two will be the service and internment. Will that work?" He offers me a tight smile as I try to regain my composure.

"Sarah, what do you think?" Thayer prompts her.

"It's fine. Chord?" Sarah's eyes plead with me.

"Yes, that's perfect. Thank you."

"Final resting place?" The minute I think Sarah and I can make it through this, those three words send us both reeling.

"Memorial Gardens in Little River." One takes the lead as he rubs my shoulder.

"I'll notify them. Have you purchased the plot?"

I stutter, "Yes, my brother took care of it this morning."

"If you have any particular songs or pictures you'd like to share during the service, you can email those." He nods.

"We'll take care of that tonight."

"We'll need to pick a casket." He stands. "Please follow me."

WRECKING US, SAVING YOU

I stand but Sarah refuses, her eyes wide as she peers up at me. I lean down, kissing her cheek. "I'll be right back, baby." I swallow hard past the knot, I know exactly how she feels.

One walks with me as I pick my son's final bed. I spot a dark silver metallic with a blue interior as soon as we walk in, by the back corner. The fact the room has several caskets for children is a bone-chilling reminder we're not alone.

"The silver with the blue interior." I point, not wanting to get any closer.

"Would you like to pick a vault?"

My legs feel weak, and I falter. One's arm is around me before I understand what's happening. "No, we'll take the best you have."

"Yes, sir." Mister Bower adds, "We just need to write his obituary."

I turn back to Sarah, my feet trudging along from the weight I'm carrying. Thayer has her arm around her, giving her tissues. Her head snaps up, and she rushes to me.

She throws her arms around me, holding me until I'm steady. "Thank you." Sarah laces our fingers, and I follow her to our seats.

Mister Bower sits across from us. "Will you be submitting an obituary or would you like us to draft one?"

"I'll write it and send it with his photos," Thayer says.

"Alright." He pushes a business card at her. "I'll just need his name and age for the death notification."

"Silas Jordan Hamilton, he was six-years-old." One's voice cracks with emotion.

"A beautiful name." He stands when he finishes writing. "Please call if you have any questions or concerns. And I'll be looking for your email."

One stands, taking his hand. "Thayer will get back to you a little later. Thank you."

Sarah and I stumble to the SUV, climbing in the back. One and Thayer take us home so she can get Silas' things together. We're going through our phones for pictures of him, while Sarah gets his clothes.

I realize she's been gone too long and go in search for her. She's sitting on our bed, looking through a box of papers and photos. She hands me one as she sniffles.

"I had forgot about that one." She walks over, coming back with his baby book.

"He's so tiny but smiling away." I hold the paper closer. "Is he showing his teeth?"

"Yes, smiling for the camera." She hands me another. "I think this was your favorite from his book, right?"

"Oh, yeah. Check him out mean muggin'." We giggle, immediately admonishing ourselves for it.

"Will we ever laugh again without feeling guilty?"

I drop to the bed. "I have no clue." She sits against me and I wrap my arm around her as we take our time looking through his baby book.

We take his clothes and pictures down to Thayer, she's already working on his obituary.

"Sarah," Thayer winces, "do you want your mom's information in here?"

Sarah swallows hard, falling into the couch. She runs her hand through her hair. Looking at me, she raises her brows. "Do I have to?"

"Do you want to, is the question?" I sit next to her, taking her hand as she chews on her nail.

"No, I prefer never to mention her." She hesitates. "Does that mean I can't add my dad?"

WRECKING US, SAVING YOU

"You can have your dad."

She spins around to Thayer. "Steven Allen Sutton."

"Is that with a v or ph?" Thayer cocks her brow.

"A v and two l's."

"When I finish this, I'll print one off so you can check it out." Thayer offers a tight smile.

"We need a song," Sarah says as my parents walk through the door.

I shrug. "Do you have any favorites?"

"Besides my dad's, not really."

"I have no idea." I shake my head. "Does anyone have one? If not, let's check out the internet."

We sit around listening to songs for hours, until we find the perfect one. Not long after, everyone leaves for home. Sarah and I go upstairs to find our clothes for tomorrow. I pick my suit from the dance, and she decides on a simple blue dress to match his tie.

Our drive to the cemetery is short but feels like it takes us forever to get there. One and Lea are with us today. I'm not sure how we would've made it without our family.

Family viewing first with visitors allowed in after. Sarah and I both do pretty good until we see his little body laying in that thing. His image will never leave me, not in a lifetime. Sarah is shattered.

"Please tell me this is a dream?" she sobs, trembling in my arms. Her body slumps over the casket, her shoulders quaking.

LEAONA LUXX

My words fail me, I have nothing to offer but my arms and love. "I'm sorry."

My knees buckle as I watch Sarah fall apart. Nothing I can do will help, no words to offer her solace. I'm worthless to her, helpless to my son. I can't help but to wonder, is this why I didn't get them sooner.

I find enough courage to get to my feet, helping Sarah to let go… for now. We sit in the front row, clinging to our sanity. Our hearts irreparable, our lives wrecked. I don't think I'll ever recover.

"Chord?" Riley hugs me, then Sarah. "I'm so sorry, guys. If you need anything, we're here." He's followed by his wife, Ava.

The line of family and friends continue to filter through over the next two hours. Walker and Alden are among those closest to us, with Brannon and Torrie close behind. Luke slips in beside Sarah, and he holds her for the longest time. Her anguish-riddled body vibrates as she grieves. I hold her hand, trying to control my suffering.

When the service starts, Sarah tucks herself into my side. Latching onto to me as she weeps, furthering the pain in my aching chest. We asked One to read his obituary and Hardy to read a letter from us.

"Silas Jordan Hamilton, aged six years and five months. He was born six days before his father's birthday, on August 20, 2011. His battle with cancer, taking him all too soon, on January 30, 2018. Surrounded by his loving family, Silas left us forever changed as he returned to our Heavenly Father.

"Silas was a blessing, born to Sarah Beth Sutton Hamilton and Chord Averette Hamilton. His parents' love evident from the day he came into this world, until he was ripped from their arms. That love, enduring many trials, producing one many will never know. Silas was the perfect example of their love, strength, and grace.

"He was our superhero and loved Thor. He loved to take pictures and build LEGO worlds. He found joy in fishing and wrestling with

315

his momma and dad on Saturday mornings. Silas was thrilled to be with his family, laughing.

"His grandfather, Steven Sutton, welcomed him to his new home. He leaves behind grandparents, Calder and Elise Hamilton. Aunt Thayer and Hardy Turner, their son Holden. Uncle Malone and Hadlea Woods, their children Aksel and Emmerson, Hawkins and Willow, Latham and Ryver, Wren, Harlyn and Tierney. And his special Uncle Luke Caldwell.

"Let the little children come to me, and do not hinder them, for the kingdom of God belongs to such as these. Mark ten and fourteen." One steps away from the podium, tears streaking his face.

Hardy steps forward, drying his eyes before he begins. "Sarah and Chord both have written something for Silas." As Hardy speaks, the song *Jealous of the Angels* by Donna Taggart plays softly.

"Silas Jordan, standing next to you is like standing next to a thousand suns, not a cluster of stars could outshine. We knew that a part of you belonged to the world, but the world that is within you, is all ours. Our love will forever be with you. We were honored to be your parents and will grieve you until we meet again. Momma and Dad."

Hardy joins One as the funeral director calls for the visitors to pass. I help Sarah to her feet, Luke on her opposite side. As our family and friends go by for their last farewell, we stand solemnly, offering our appreciation.

As our pallbearers take their place, Walker takes our breaths away. He stands at the end, waiting to take his side, dressed as Thor. Sarah and I are crippled with heart-wrenching sobs, grateful to our friend.

We proceed to the gravesite, where my father gives a few words before his final resting.

"Our hearts are full because we were blessed with this young man. We will forever hold him in our hearts, and God will hold him in his arms. We pray for peace and healing, asking God for mercy on our weary souls. We love you, Silas."

Our family drops white roses tipped in blue, the color of his eyes, on his casket. Sarah wavers as we step forward.

"I can't do it." She shakes her head, tears spattering her face. "Chord, I can't say goodbye."

I pull her into me, crushing her to my body. Grief paralyzing us, rooting us to the spot. Her chest heaves as she gasps for air, and rage wracks my body at the mere thought of what she's going through.

I fight the urge to vomit as my stomach rolls violently. Sarah clutching me as we hold on to all we have left, each other.

"Sarah, you have to do it. If for no one else, do it for Silas. Do it for your baby."

Her body stiffens, bracing itself to do the impossible. We lace our fingers, turning to say goodbye.

"Silas, I love you. I hope you know how much I love you. My baby boy, you've meant the world to me. I love you." Sarah's words, strangled.

I lean over, kissing the top. "I love you, Si. I miss you already, little buddy."

Sarah props against me, we're both unable to move. Concreted to this spot, knowing once we walk away, there's no turning back. My body tingles, and a shudder takes over. Sarah covers her mouth as she gulps for air.

With nothing more than broken hearts, we amble to the waiting car. Our lives tattered and no will to move beyond this point, we grapple leaving him here. Clasping hands, we will one another to look ahead.

Sarah's soul is decimated, and she cries all the way home. My concern for her is beginning to move to the forefront of my every thought. I press her to my side, helping her into the house and to the couch. Thayer helps her out of her shoes as she balls up, sobbing.

I sit beside her, and she moves closer to me, placing her head in my lap. "Can I-I…"

"You don't have to ask, baby. I'm not going anywhere without you." I press my lips to hers, wiping away her tears with my thumb.

"I love you." She tugs at my arm, putting it around her.

I lean down, whispering, "I love you, Sarah."

Our family stays until late, asking us to eat and watching over us. They all make a fuss, but we just can't eat. I do get Sarah to drink a little something, and I'm afraid she's going to dehydrate if she doesn't.

"Kids, you should let me make you some food. Neither of you have ate." Mom sits across from us, worrying her lip.

"Honestly, Mom, I couldn't eat a thing."

"Sarah, sweetie. Please eat for me," Mom begs her. I have to agree, I haven't eaten today, but it's been a couple of days for Sarah.

"Come on, baby. I'll eat if you will." I coax her.

She tips her head up to me. "You're gonna eat with me?"

"I will." I wink. "Mom, whatever's fastest."

"I'll get them something to drink." Lea jumps up with Mom.

One sits down next to us. "Hadlea sent these." He sets our drinks down.

Sarah straightens next to me, she's been molded to my side for days. "So I've wanted to ask, but it hasn't crossed my mind in a while. Why do you call her Hadlea?"

One chuckles. "The same reason she calls me Malone." He raises his brows as Lea joins us, sitting on his lap.

"We like having that just for us. No one else calls us that, so it's personal." She smiles.

"That's crazy sweet." Sarah smiles.

"Here ya go." Mom brings us a plate. "I'll be happy if y'all eat one."

Sarah twists her mouth to the side as I twirl the Alfredo on the fork. I stab a piece of the Cajun chicken on the end, offering her a bite.

"You first," she says.

I tilt my head, narrowing my eyes at her. She opens her mouth slowly, sticking the tip of her tongue out. I cock my brow, placing it on her tongue. She pulls it off, chewing it with appreciation.

319

WRECKING US, SAVING YOU

I take a big bite. "Good?"

"So good," she says through a mouthful.

We finish our meal and part of her plate, and it's well after midnight before everyone leaves. We sit by the fire, not wanting to go upstairs. It's either sleep here or in the bed Silas did or walk past his room.

It's early in the morning before we fall asleep, Sarah in my arms, on the couch. Light streams through the window, too bright for my eyes. I scrub my face with my hands, feeling a chill.

I sit straight up. "Sarah?" I hop up, checking the bathroom down here first.

She has to be upstairs. I take them two at a time, rushing to our room. Nothing. I whip around, scrambling to Silas' room. I slowly push the door open, she's curled up in his bed, crying.

I ease over, so as not to scare her, and slip in behind her. She flips around, curling into my arms. "I'm here, baby."

We doze on and off for a few hours before I force myself up. Sarah's still sleeping, she needs to make up for all she's lost. I leave her, hoping she'll rest for a while. I jump in the shower and get to work on a few things that need to be done.

My phone buzzes halfway into my work. "Hey."

"How are y'all?" One asks.

"We slept some, ended up in his bed around seven this morning. Sarah's still there, she needs some rest after the last few months."

"You should catch some extra sleep too." He sighs knowing, it's going in one ear and out the other.

"I needed to make a few calls. His oxygen and other medical supplies should have gone back the other day, so I made arrangements for it on Monday." I tap my pen on the table.

"I'm sure there was time."

"Probably." I hesitate. "I needed something to keep my mind busy."

"Understandable. So how's that going?" He chuckles.

"Fucking sucks ass." I drop my head. "By the way, I never said this but thank you. I appreciate everything you and Lea did to help us."

"Absolutely, wouldn't have done it any other way. But there's no thanks needed. We love y'all, that's why it was done."

I sigh. "I know. I'll get back to work next week, if that's alright. I want to give Sarah a little more time."

"Take all the time y'all need, there's no rush," he assures me. My chest aches as I think about him.

"I'll never get over this, One. I don't have a clue how Sarah will." I rub the back of my neck.

"Time. Nothing happens overnight, everything needs time." He's right.

"I heard that. I guess I'm gonna go check on Sarah, she's been up there a while."

"Let us know if we can do anything. Love y'all."

"Love you, brother." I end the call, clean up my mess, and head upstairs.

Sarah's still sleeping, so I decide to leave her; I'm sure she needs it. I won't lie, I'm worried. She's broken, and for so long all she had was Silas. I hope she can hang on and help me save what we have left.

I head back downstairs and get to work. I check on Sarah throughout the afternoon, she must be exhausted because she's still sleeping. I make my way out to the laundry room, clearing a path to the garage.

"What in the hell are we gonna do with all of these?" Silas was sent flowers, cards, gifts and toys by so many people. We can't keep

321

them all, but I refuse to toss them. I take out my phone, pressing her number.

"Hey, babe," Lea answers.

"If I hadn't already gave my heart away, I would've gave One a run for his money."

She giggles. "I might've liked that. What's up?"

I take an exaggerated breath. "I'm working around the house a little, trying to keep my mind busy, you know?"

"Hey, you do what you need. Nobody's gonna judge."

"I hope not, it would mess with me bad if people thought I was disrespecting my baby." I chew my lip, praying no one would think that.

"People grieve differently, Chord. And no one has the right to tell you how to do it. You do what's best for you." She's right, as always.

"Yeah, that's exactly what I need to do." I sigh.

"One said Sarah was resting, how's she doing?" Her voice is soft and caring.

I shake my head. "She's still in bed, I'm gonna try to get her up in a bit."

"Give her time, maybe this is her process."

"True, I will." I sigh, sitting by the mounds of gifts. "The reason I called, I have a few ideas I'd like to get you in on. Ya know, to honor Silas."

"I'm there. What can I help you with?"

"I'm not sure, I want to do something with your foundation for single mothers, and maybe the hospital for the pediatric cancer wing." I scrub my hand over my face.

"I think you're amazing. No better way to honor your child than by helping others. So how can I help?" I love her as much as my siblings. She and Hardy are just as close to me as they are.

"Well, get some ideas for your foundation, and maybe check with the hospital?"

"I can do that, let me check and see what I can come up with. If you need any help with anything else, no matter the time or the problem, we're here." I adore her.

"Thank you."

"No problem, I'll get right on this. Later." She giggles.

"Later."

I straighten out a few other things, eventually making my way back to Sarah. I decide to wake her, maybe get her to eat.

"Sarah?" I run my hand down her back. "Sarah, come and eat with me."

She mumbles. "Tired."

I chew my lip. "You've gotta eat for me, baby."

She tilts her head to me. "Tomorrow."

"Today, you need food."

"I promise, tomorrow." She rolls over, her back to me.

I relent. "Tomorrow, I'm holding you to it." I kiss her head, leaving her to sleep.

I wander out to the beach, I have so much on my mind. Sarah's scaring the shit outta me. She didn't even want to acknowledge

WRECKING US, SAVING YOU

Valentine's Day, I hadn't planned much. She barely eats as it is, and she's losing weight like crazy.

I fist my hair, I'm losing her.

"Brother."

I startle. "Fuck, One."

"What the hell are you doing out here?" He folds his arms.

I run my hands over my face. "I'm losing her. She doesn't eat, talk, nothing. She stays in bed, sleeping."

"I know, I think we all hoped she would be fighting to survive by now," he huffs.

"What the fuck do I do? I can't make her get up." I roll my neck, trying to relieve some tension. "I don't want to make her do a damn thing that she doesn't want to, I just want her love."

"She's been rocked to the core, it's a hard road to walk."

I glare at him, eyes wide. "I'm on that fucking road with her, he was my son too."

"People handle things differently, Chord. Your way of grieving isn't hers." He drops his arms.

"Don't you think I know that? I do. I want her to be here with me." I hammer my chest with my fist.

"You need her. Say it, you need Sarah." One stares at me, and my heart pounds against my chest.

"Yes. I need her. What's so wrong with that? I feel like I've lost them both, One. I can't." Tears well in my eyes.

"Maybe it's time to tell her." He shrugs.

"For what? So she can think I'm an insensitive asshole."

"You're not being callous, you need your spouse." He cocks his brow. "Or are you afraid she doesn't need you?"

"I think it's a moot point, don't you?"

"I'm not following?" One narrows his eyes.

"She's never needed me, One. She's wanted me, but never has she needed me."

"Is that what you're upset about?" Fear rages through me like a wildfire.

"No. Yes," I growl. "I've spent a lifetime loving her. She's like breathing to me; I want air, but I need it to live. Sarah doesn't work that way."

"How does she work, Chord?" One cocks his head.

"She learned early not to depend on people. She doesn't need me, she wants me."

"Lea was like that or did you forget?" He smirks.

"Now that you mention it, I do remember." I roll my eyes. "When did she decide she needed you?"

"About the time I told her." He stares. "You need to tell her."

"Tell her? Our son passed away a few weeks ago, if I tell her I need her now, that makes me an ass." I shake my head.

"It makes you human." He sighs. "What are you afraid of?"

"Losing her."

Sarah

I close my eyes as I hear Chord walk up the stairs. He quietly walks in, kisses me, and leaves. He used to lay with me but hasn't in a few days. It's dark out, like my soul at this point.

I give him enough time to doze off before I get up. I can't believe I'm avoiding him. I'm terrible, I know. I don't have it in me to face him, to admit what's really going on in my head. I don't want to share Silas.

I've avoided him for days. Even when they came and took his oxygen, I walked into the bathroom. Came back to his bed after they left. It still smells like him, it's the one place I don't have to think.

I lay there and it feels as though he's still here. I close my eyes, pretending he's right here with me. If I respond to Chord, I'm faced with reality—he's gone. Besides, Chord knows what I need. And he has his family.

I tiptoe downstairs to grab me something to eat. I have no appetite, but I have to eat. I've been eating peanut butter. It has protein in it which helps sustain me, I learned that early in life. Nevertheless, I'm losing weight.

Dipping the spoon in the jar, I take my glass of milk to sit on the steps in the garage. I don't want to wake Chord. As I lick the spoon, I realize the garage is cleaner. I stand, walking over to check the once empty boxes.

I push the lids open, it's Silas' toys. Not the ones from us but the toys people sent to us while he was sick. "Why are they in boxes? Is he getting rid of them?" Blind rage fills me, who does he think he is?

"I can't believe you. Did he not mean anything to you? I suppose you have everything you need, don't you?" I stomp into the kitchen, throwing my spoon in the sink. I hurry up the stairs just as Chord stands at the top.

"You're up, can I get you something?"

"No, I'm fine." I push past him, heading back into Silas' room.

He stands in the doorway, shaking his head. "Sarah, I need you…"

I spin on him, full of venom. "What? What do you need, Chord? If you think I'm going to forget about my son and move on, you've lost your fucking mind."

"What in the hell are you talking about?" He steps toward me, his jaw set.

"You, wanting to move past Silas' death. You think because you've moved on, I should," I seethe.

"Are you kidding me? I want you to move on? I'm mourning by myself, not with my wife."

"See, there ya go. I'm not your wife, I'm nothing more to you than a high school fantasy," I spit at him as my stomach revolts from the lies I'm spewing.

WRECKING US, SAVING YOU

He blanches. His eyes drop to the floor. "Silas' headstone is being set tomorrow. I'm going over around four to see it. You're more than welcome to go, if you want."

That's it. No more fight, nothing. He's giving up, like everything else in my life. "Sure." I stare at him, so much space between us. Everything's changed.

"I'll let you know before I leave." He turns, walking away. There it is, the moment I thought my heart couldn't break anymore. We're already over. Before we even got started.

I sit in the recliner, watching the day break in Silas' room. I'm still trying to understand what happened last night. And what's with boxing up his things; who does that a few weeks after their son's death?

I hear Chord the minute he wakes, his breathing changes. He walks through the house, pausing by the door. I side-eye him, waiting. He turns and then right down the stairs he goes. Silent.

Fuming, I follow him downstairs. "When do you plan on leaving?"

"Good morning." He searches the cabinets.

I narrow my eyes at the back of his head. "What time?"

"Nice to see you're outta bed." He won't even turn around to look at me.

"Whatever. When?" I cross my arms, cocking my hip. I'm not sure what his attitude is about, but I can have one too.

"I suppose, three thirty." He turns, staring blankly at me.

"I'll be ready." I whirl around, stomping up the stairs.

I hurry into the bedroom, shutting the door behind me. I throw the blanket over me as I lay back down. My body quakes as tears build in my eyes. I don't understand why he's being so cruel. This isn't Chord, not the one I know.

I toss and turn but sleep evades me, like it has for weeks now. Night is a demon that haunts me when I close my eyes. Day brings more of the same, only I can't hide. I feel as though I'm dying.

Checking the clock on the wall, I see it's three-twenty-five. "Fuck. I needed to shower, I can't now." I drag my nasty ass out of bed, checking myself in the mirror. "You look like shit. Like it matters." I shrug, jerking the door open. "He'll never notice."

Chord's standing at the top of the stairs. "I was coming to get you." He turns, walking back down, then he pauses. "It's cool today, you might want something warm."

"I don't have something warm and you know it," I yell at him, dragging my sweatpants on.

I stomp down the stairs with my dress sweater in my arms. I wait by the bar as he types something on his phone. He points toward me. "Sweatshirt. You're more than welcome to it."

One of his sweatshirts hang on the back of a stool. I yank it off as I turn. "Thanks so much."

He walks past me. "I'm beginning to think I prefer you pretending to sleep." My mouth pops open. "Let's go."

I shove my arms through the hoodie, dragging it over my head. "Yeah, me too." I storm past him.

He's right behind me as I yank on the door handle, it's locked. I cut my eyes at him as he hits the button. "It's unlocked."

I close my eyes tightly, climbing in before he can help me. I grab the door to slam it, his arm is there. "I've got it."

329

WRECKING US, SAVING YOU

I fold my arms over my chest. "Fine."

He shuts the door, continuing around to get in the SUV. He doesn't say another word as he starts the car and backs out. We sit silently, like strangers, on the way to the cemetery. I have no clue what's happened to us in the last few weeks, but I don't like it.

I see the sign before he hits his signal light, and my stomach bottoms out. I grab the door handle, praying I don't vomit.

"You okay?" His voice is low, as if it pains him to ask.

"I'm fine, I'll not mess up your precious car." I cut my eyes at him.

He blows out a long breath. "Alright."

We take the next right, driving around the semi-circle to get to his place. They're just leaving as we park. Chord ordered the headstone. I told him I didn't care what he put on it at the time. Now, I wish I would've asked.

He waits on me by the front of the vehicle. We walk side by side toward our son's grave. I need to block this out. "How did you get this so fast?" My body trembles.

"Dad, he knows the company." He pauses. "I hope you like it, you said do whatever."

As we get closer, the markings come into view and my heart melts. "It's perfect." His name and birthdate with his departure date. But it's what's written on the bottom that makes it perfect.

"To our baby boy, Si. You are our sun, our moon, and all our stars." The sun, moon and star are symbols.

I gasp. "Chord, it's beautiful. Perfect, even."

His chest heaves. "Do you think? I thought it was important to have something to remind us of your dad."

My eyes lock on his, I nod. "Absolutely. I love it."

"I'm happy you like it." He sighs.

We spend some time with him, a few weeks has felt like a lifetime. I don't know what I'll do in two months. Chord stays back when I'm overcome, giving me room to grieve. When he steps toward me, I hold my hand up.

I grapple with myself, gathering my strength to get to my feet. Chord reaches for me, but I refuse his hand. He's been a stranger for weeks now, don't pretend because we're here. I'm over playing house.

He holds my door open, not offering his hand this time. Once we're back on Highway Seventeen, he breaks the silence. "I need to get some gas, is that alright?"

I roll my eyes. "Get the gas, I don't care." I prop my head up with my hand, leaning against the window.

He pulls in, parking at the first pump we see. "Do you need anything?"

"No," I snap.

He takes a deep breath, sliding from the seat. I watch him from the side mirror, he looks different. He looks like me. Am I being too harsh with him? Maybe he didn't think about the toys the way I do? It could have been innocent.

I close my eyes, banishing the forming tears. When I open my eyes, a blonde is all up on him. He steps away, glancing toward my direction. She runs her hand over his chest, and he catches her by the wrist, pushing her away.

She's all over him and all I can think is we just came from our son's grave, can't they fucking wait? I'm in sweatpants, Chord's hoodie, and dirty track shoes. My hair's greasy and in a knotted mess on top of my head. I haven't showered in days but to hell with this. I haul ass out of the SUV before I can stop myself.

"Get your fuckin' hands off him," I growl, headed straight for her ass.

331

"What is this?" Dumbass blonde points at me with her red-tipped finger.

"I'm about to show you what the hell I am, now you can move your hand or pull back a fucking nub, bitch." I push the sleeves of my sweatshirt up.

Chord steps between us when I lunge at her. "Sarah, what the fuck?"

"Straighten the trash out, Chord," the blonde talking ass says.

"Yes, Chord. Please, straighten me out." I glare at him, fury raging through me.

"Kimberly, this is my... " He swallows hard. "...the mother of my son. Don't talk to her that way."

Now, I'm just the mother of his son? I thought he said I was his wife? "Oh, I see." I narrow my eyes at him. "This is one of your fuck buddies, right?" My words teem with venom.

He blanches, sinking his teeth into his bottom lip. "Can we please go?"

"She is." My face flames. "You fucked her while you were pretending to be madly in love with me and I was raising our son," I yell, flailing my arms.

"Damn right he did, he fucked me well." She leers. My stomach turns at the thought of him with her.

"Kimberly!" Chord wheels around, growling her name.

"Kimberly, is it?" My heart shattered, I fight for saving face. "Here's the thing, you can fuckin' have him. I'm goddamn over fighting for him. Take him and keep him the fuck away from me." Tears stream down my face as Chord turns to me, his brows pulled low and tight.

"You don't mean that, Sarah." His lip quivers, but I'm in 'protect me mode'.

"The hell I don't." I whirl around, climbing in the SUV, ready to get the fuck out of here.

He spins, never looking at the bitch again. He's in the car and burning tires out of the lot. He drives like a bat out of hell back to the house. I jump out before he's completely stopped, slamming the door behind me.

"What the fuck was that?" he growls, hurrying to meet me. I stand impatiently, while he opens the door.

"You heard me." I storm past him.

"I'm sorry we're always running into them, Sarah. It's not planned." He throws his arms in the air.

"I'm sorry we're always running into them too." I whirl around. "I'm sorry that I ever loved you. That I didn't fuck every dick who hit on me, so I could erase the pain of your memory. And most of all…"

"Don't, Sarah." He lowers his voice.

"Don't, what?" I cock my head. "Don't. What?" I grind my teeth.

"Do not bring him into this, this is between us." His jaw sets.

"He's always been in the middle of this. That's the only reason you tried to find me." I clench my teeth, knowing it's not true.

"Speaking of finding people, have you ever heard of a fucking computer? You couldn't walk to a library to look me up?" He stabs his finger at me.

"I'm sorry I was raising our son and couldn't run all over the damn place to find you. What about the letters y'all had sent back?" I spit at him with disdain.

"They were marked 'return to sender', the post office did it, not us." He shakes his head as my temper flares. "Don't you dare act as if I didn't want to be with you."

WRECKING US, SAVING YOU

"Oh, you did. After you fucked everything in town. Couldn't you keep your dick in your pants two damn minutes?" I pin him with a glare.

"I guess we both had a problem keeping our pants on, didn't we?" he fires back.

"I was taking care of our son as best I could, thank you." I fold my arms in defense, that shit hurt. I will my tears to not fall.

"Don't bring him into this, this is about us," he grunts.

"Don't bring him into this? I'm not surprised, you've already forgotten about him." I glare as my stomach knots.

"Forgotten about who? Silas?" His brows knit. "You've lost your damn mind," he yells.

"Really? Why are his things boxed up outside? Why haven't you stayed with me in his bed? You want to forget him!" I scream.

"Of all the fuckin' insane things to say, I'll never forget him! It was shit I couldn't take staring at alone!" he yells, leveling me.

"Alone? Where the fuck do you think I've been?" I pound my chest.

"In bed, pretending to be asleep instead of being with me!"

"Being with you? It's my fault I'm mourning and not stuck up your ass while you pack him in boxes because you can't stand the sight of his memory?" I blast him, bile rising in my throat.

"Someone had to do something. All you've done is lay in bed." He narrows his eyes.

"You've always taken care of everything, what the fuck was there to do, Chord? You just do it," I spit at him. "And you stopped coming to me not wanting to help."

"Yeah, I take care of everything because that's what I do. I never wanted to mourn him." He throws his hands in the air. "And by the way, you call that shit mourning? Funny, it looked like you were the

334

one dying, laying there letting it kill you when all the while… I fucking needed you! I'm mourning our son too." His face distorts.

I flinch, squeezing my eyes shut. I could have sworn my heart was already broken. I guess we do learn something new every day. I back away slowly, my brows furrowed, my chest concaved.

I spin, taking the stairs two at a time. I run to Silas' room, slamming the door behind me. I lock it and the bathroom door.

What just happened? This isn't love. It's definitely not our love.

I hate myself the minute Sarah runs upstairs. This went too far, we said things we never should have. I didn't mean half of what I said, and the rest was too harsh. I'm hurt, and I took it out on her.

"I need a drink." I pull the cabinet door open and grab Jack, pouring two fingers. I replace the lid, swirling the amber in the glass. "What the fuck did I do?" I slam the drink back.

Pouring another two fingers, I don't contemplate this one, I down it. A rumble builds deep in the pit of my stomach, it rolls and dives until it forces its way out. I fist my hair as I break, falling to my knees.

"How could I hurt her like that?" I elbow the cabinet, unable to contain myself. I lean back, sitting against the base. I'm not sure I can break further, the pieces are unrecognizable. I have to beg her forgiveness.

I push up from the floor, drying my face as I amble to the stairs. My breathing labored, I stagger up the steps, heavy from the weight of my guilt. I walk over to Silas' door, turning the handle to find it's locked.

My heart crashes to the ground, burning in flames. I touch the door, contemplating knocking. I drop my hand, walking away. I fall into bed, exhausted. Thoughts swirl until the morning hours when I can't fight anymore and sleep takes me.

As day breaks, so does my head. I wake up with a pounding headache, and I'll not mention how my eyes feel. Damn, if guys knew how this hurt, we'd never make a girl cry again.

I drag ass into the bathroom, splash water on my face, and brush my teeth. I might not smell so fresh but my breath will. I traipse through the house, tapping on her door. "Sarah?"

I try again, tapping a little harder. "Sarah?" I wrap the handle, twisting the knob. As I swing the door open, I find an empty bed. I check the bathroom, she's not there. I bolt downstairs, searching everywhere.

Grabbing my phone, I call her. No answer. I try again with the same result. I shoot her three quick texts, praying she'll answer.

Sarah, where are you?

I need to know you're okay.

I'm sorry.

Ten minutes. I sit here, stone-faced and dumbfounded. I jolt, bounding from the couch. I run upstairs, looking for her clothes. She's taken some, and her bag isn't here.

She's gone.

"No fucking way." I fist my hands as the pang in my stomach turns from fear to rage. It races through my body, like an inferno. A tremor shakes me to my core, the shock of my present state, throwing me off balance.

337

WRECKING US, SAVING YOU

I stumble, falling against the wall and sliding down to the floor. I fist my hair, screaming, "How could you?" I elbow the wall as I kick the chair over that she used for my birthday.

"That damn chair." Fuming, I drag my ass up, wrapping my hand around it and flipping it over. I bust the damn thing against the wall. Gritting my teeth, I growl, "Why in the hell would you leave?"

I throw the leg, shattering the mirror across the room. "FUCK!" Turning, I pick the end of our bed up, flipping it over. My nostrils flare as my body acts as a conduit for the fury that's building in my gut.

I kick the bedpost, cracking it. The fracture splinters the wood, reminding me of the pain in my chest. I grab the top piece, ripping the appendage out as I would my heart if I could get it out of my chest.

"How could you leave me like this?" I swing the wood like a ballbat, smashing the lamp on the nightstand. Pieces fly through the air like a rocket. I stomp the other post, busting it apart.

I kick the footboard, breaking it in half, then I hammer away on it with my makeshift battering ram. I upend the mattress, smashing through the box springs and tearing them apart. By the time my rampage is finished, I've demolished our bedroom with my bare hands.

My arms fall to my side as I drop my club; the damage is done and in more ways than one. I ball my hands up, hitting my head. "What the fuck have you done?" I berate myself.

I storm from the room, taking out part of the bannister on my way down with one final kick. My breathing labored, I swallow hard, doing my best to calm down. I turn to the kitchen, grabbing the Jack and a glass.

Rolling my neck, I trudge to the couch and fall onto it. I pour three fingers and throw it back, burning as it goes down to my rotting soul. I dump another glass full, tipping it back.

"What the actual fuck, Sarah?" I hurl the glass through the air, and it hits the fireplace, disintegrating.

"Well, that answers two questions." One fists his hands on his side.

"What fuckin' questions?" I snarl at him, chugging the dark amber from the bottle.

He walks closer, stopping to peer up the stairs. He cuts his eyes to me, taking a few more steps. "If Sarah left and how you are."

"How do you know?" I growl.

"Thayer seen a taxi leave after Hardy left for work."

"Yeah, she fuckin' left," I spit at him, taking another swig as he cocks his brow. "Like she did before, without a word. Like I'm nothing. No one to her."

His chest rises, falling hard with his deep breath. "What happened?"

I flop back on the couch, curling my calming juice in my arm. "We ran into Kimberly after leaving the cemetery. At least, that's where it started." I take another pull of my friend Jack.

"Well, I suppose that was a shit show." He folds his arms. "Go on," he prompts me.

I wave my hand in the air. "That's when we said all kinds of stuff, and I yelled at her. And I hurt her. And now, she hates me." I lift the bottle, shaking it to see how much is left.

"You do realize it's eight in the morning." He narrows his eyes at me, disapproving of my medicinal needs.

"Fuck it. I don't give a damn. I give the fuck up!" shouting at the top of my lungs.

He walks over, sitting down across from me. "This isn't helping a damn thing, Chord."

WRECKING US, SAVING YOU

"You know what, fuck you. I'm so sick of you and Thayer and your perfect goddamn lives." I hurl the bottle at the fireplace, alcohol and glass flies through the air. "I have nothing. Nothing!"

One cocks his brow, he doesn't even flinch. Shit! He holds his finger up, pulling his brows tight. "That's the only one you get."

"Fuck. I'm sorry." I sit up, resting my elbows on my knees. "I tried to tell her, I did. But she was so mad, she kept picking at me and then Kimberly showed up. Sarah flipped shit, got out threatening her and suddenly, she said she could have me."

"Why would she leave?" One leans in, listening.

"We both said things, One. She blamed me, I accused her of giving up. I mean, damnit, all of it was a long time ago." I rub my hand over my face, trying to dry it.

"Things y'all should've said from the beginning." He nods.

"Yeah, things that don't matter now. But when I told her I needed her, she just left." I shake my head as I stand and stagger into the kitchen. Throwing the door back, I take the Vodka out.

"You've had enough." One takes it from me, and I turn on him.

"You have no fucking clue how much I've had enough!" I get up in his face. I just messed the hell up.

One pins me with his ire. "Let me tell you right now, you best get a hold of your ass before I do."

"I'm sorry." Fuck! "I'm dying. I've lost everything, man. I've lost everything."

My brother proves to me why he's the best. "No doubt, baby brother. Not a doubt." He fists my shirt, hauling me to him as I lose my mind. He holds me, supporting me like only a brother can.

"Damn." I roll over, holding my head.

"Headache?" One pokes at my side as I nod. "Hurt much?" I nod again. "That's what your dumbass gets for gettin' drunk at eight in the morning." He hands me a glass of water and two Advil's.

I hold them up, propping up on my elbow. "Point taken, thank you."

"Now, we're gonna talk. Because Hadlea loves your ass and I don't want you to try this shit again." He sits, crossing his legs. Just like Dad used to do.

"I thought you already kicked my ass?" I close my eyes, praying this will be over quickly.

"You may prefer that to this, I can tell you that right now." I peek at him as he leers at me. I drag my ass up, resting my face in my hands.

"Alright, let me have it because I'm sure I don't hate myself enough." I curl my hand at him, waving him on.

"Death breaks people in different ways. Sometimes, the pieces resemble. Most of the time, the pieces are nothing alike. Trying to figure out how to put yourself together again when none of the pieces fit is hard enough.

"You and Sarah were trying to do it for each other, when you weren't whole yourselves. You have to fix yourself first or you'll never be of help to your spouse." One leans forward. "Fix yourself."

"When she left six years ago, no one knows what I went through but you. She thinks I fucked around to forget her. Not one time did she ask how I made it. Not once, One." I shake my head as my face flames.

WRECKING US, SAVING YOU

"Did you ask her how she made it? Raising a child as a stripper must've been real peachy." He pulls his brows down.

I narrow my eyes at him. "I more than realize she had a hard time. It's the reason I wanted to take care of them, and look where that got me."

"Chord, I remember how broken you were when she left. Days in bed, you gave up on college. Did you even tell her that's why you were just getting a degree two years later? Because you couldn't go to college without her." He cocks his brow. "I didn't think so."

"I know everyone thought we were crazy for jumping back in head first but, One, we love each other. Honest to God, love to the core. Good and bad, poor or rich. I love that girl more than my own life." I pound my chest, trying to start my heart.

He nods. "So what happened?"

I stand, pacing. "I accused her of lying in bed, wanting to die instead of being with me when I needed her most." I fold my arms, waiting for his judgement.

"Chord, men love differently than women."

"Tell me about it." I flop onto the couch.

"We love in black and white. There's the right side and the wrong side. Women love in black, white, and gray. They'll find every avenue to make love work, rarely will a man. Women are fixers, they'll do anything, including going to the gray area to get it. In the gray area, they'll find a happy medium and love us forever, faults and all."

"I live in the gray area." I shrug.

"How so?" This time, he crosses his arms.

"Sarah never had to ask, I knew her so well I just did it. Whatever it was she needed, I did it without her asking. I tried every way to love her the way she needed to be loved, always have," I grumble.

342

"Did you ever tell her you needed her? Well, except for the argument."

"No, I was happy to take care of her. It wasn't until after losing Silas, I realized I needed her more than I'd ever admit." I drop my head.

"I get it, you think if she had loved you, like you do her, she should've known what you needed." I nod. "But I thought all you needed was her."

Fuck me. "It is," I mumble. "Well, it was."

"How so?" His brows knit.

"What if she tells me she doesn't love me after all? It's been six years, maybe we've changed more than we first thought. What if she stays gone six months? I can't live like I once did. What if I can't trust her again? What if I don't believe in our love anymore?" I fight the tears rolling down my face. "What if I'm afraid of losing her for good and prefer to protect myself, my heart, this time? What if she comes back and leaves again? I'll not live through it, not after losing Silas." I fall back into the couch, drying my face.

"What if she comes back and you lose her forever because you're afraid?" One nails me.

"I'm not sure I'll survive her either way." I would say my heart breaks again, but I think it's just the pain of my cold, dead soul.

"Chord, you can't put restraints on love. It lives by its own rules."

"Haven't you heard? I'm the good guy, I don't break the rules," I counter.

"Maybe not, but love breaks them all. Don't let fear break you or one day you might regret it." He's right, I shake my head.

"What if she never comes back? It'll kill me if I don't protect myself this time." I warn him. "She left me, One. She walked away from me!"

343

WRECKING US, SAVING YOU

"It hurt Hadlea when she left me. She later told me the pain she caused me was so much greater that she could never do it again, it would kill her." One laces his fingers.

"Well, Sarah must've taken a page outta Lea's playbook. I'm leveled." I rub the back of my neck.

"No, that's what you did to the bedroom." He pins me with a glare.

I squeeze my eyes shut. "Shit, I forgot about that."

"I'll get it fixed," he says, standing.

"No." I chew my lip. "Leave it, I want to remember the way she made me feel, so I never let her make me feel this way again." I will myself to stand.

"Strong words for a man immensely in love." He smirks.

"Yeah, look where that's got me." My tears fall freely. "I've lost my family. My son. The love of my life. I'm not sure even love can save me this time."

"Your love is one worth fighting for. Let her fight for it." One pulls me into another hug, exactly like the one I need.

37

Sarah

I faintly knock on the door. I try again, a little louder. Finally, I hear footsteps. The locks turn, the handle wiggles. When the door opens, I break.

"Sarah?" My knees buckle, and he catches me before I fall. "Oh, baby doll. What in the world?" He helps me in, guiding me to my old bed.

I fall face first, tears soaking the comforter. He takes my shoes off, tossing them in the corner with my bag. I roll over, wrapping up like a cocoon. He gives me tissues, stroking my hair until I fall asleep.

I dream of my little family, happy and playing on the beach. We smile, enjoying one another. The love we share, evident on our smiling faces. My loves sitting together as they build sandcastles.

WRECKING US, SAVING YOU

My chest heaves when a wave crashes ashore, knocking down their masterpiece. Silas begins to cry, and I stand, walking toward them as Chord cradles him in his loving arms. He adores his son.

Another wave batters the shoreline, taking Silas with it as it returns to the ocean. Chord lays bruised and broken in the aftermath. He reaches for me as the waters ebb and flow, working their way up the beach again.

The closer I get, the further he's lost to the rising tide. I struggle to get to him. He fights back, calling to me, but I can't hear him for the sound of the roaring tide. The skies turn dark, rain begins to beat down on us.

He calls to me again. I try to move, but my feet start to sink into the surf. It's like quicksand, I can't fight it or it'll take me. Chord is pulled further out in the undertow, but I'm afraid to fight for him.

I'm stuck. I can't fight the surge that's drowning Chord. If I move from this spot, it'll swallow me up. My heart races as Chord urges me to step out of the quicksand. To fight for us to survive because without me, he won't make it.

He reaches for me one last time, I shake my head. If I fight, I'll sink in the struggle. He mouths he loves me as I lose sight of him, the sand begins to cover my mouth. He begged me to move toward him, but I wouldn't.

Now, the quicksand takes me with it.

I wake with a jolt, startled by the dream, and how real it felt. I'm sweating, and I need water. It's as if I haven't had anything to drink in days. I try licking my lips, but my mouth is so dry. I crawl from the bed, wobbling on my feet.

346

I pull the door open to bright lights. Shielding my eyes, I stumble through the house. Stopping by the bathroom, I pee for what feels like thirty minutes. "No wonder I'm dehydrated."

I stagger to the kitchen, finding the biggest cup I can and filling it to the brim with cold water. I chug it down, refilling it before I can finish. I walk toward the couch, drinking as I go.

"Well hello, stranger."

I curl up, finishing my water before I speak. I set the cup down, wiping my mouth with the back of my hand. "Hey, love." I sigh.

"Are you feeling any better?"

"I am. I feel like I've slept for a month." I giggle, laying my head against the couch.

"Nah, just four days."

My eyes bug out. "What? Why would you let me sleep for four days?"

"You obviously needed it." He sits across from me. "You showed back up, looking miserable and like you hadn't slept for months."

"I haven't." Tears spring to my eyes.

"So what happened?" His face pleads for answers, things I can't give him.

I shake my head, wrapping my arms around my legs. "I don't know."

"Sarah, it's me. Talk to me."

"I had a dream while I was out." I swallow past the knot in my throat.

"Oh, yeah. What about?"

"The beach and being in quicksand. Odd, right?" I tilt my head, searching his eyes for understanding.

"Seriously, weird." He nods. "Why quicksand I wonder?"

WRECKING US, SAVING YOU

"We kept sinking, I couldn't move. No, that's a lie." I chew my lip. "I wouldn't move, no matter how much I knew I needed to, that it was perilous if I didn't. I stood there, letting it take us all." I wipe away a tear.

"What do you think it means?" He frowns with me.

I shrug, drying my face on my shirt. "I don't know."

"Maybe you need some time to think about it and what it might mean?" He narrows his eyes.

"I know, I don't want to think about it right now." I hurry back to the bedroom, sinking under the covers to hide from the world.

I sleep a few more days, my body and mind deserved a much-needed break. I plod through the house in search of nourishment.

"Well hello, Sleeping Beauty."

"Mornin'." I wave on my way to the couch.

He joins me with a sigh. "Are you not feeling any better?"

"Nope. I don't think I'll ever feel better again." My lip begins to tremble. "I miss my baby, and I'm so fuckin' mad at everything and everyone."

"I'm not sure how you've survived it all."

"Have I, because I don't feel as if I've survived anything." I dry my face with the back of my hand. He reaches me a box of tissues.

"I can't imagine, baby." He pats my hand. "How's Chord?"

"Who in the hell knows?" I shrug as the tears fall harder.

He narrows his eyes. "I was thinking you should know."

"Well, I don't. It's not like we've been talking much lately." I pull more tissues from the box.

"Why's that? Him or you?" He pins me with pointed ire.

I grit my teeth. "I'm having a damn hard time being without Silas. Okay?"

"Alright, but how's Chord?" He tilts his head.

I shrug, sniffling. "Fine, I guess."

"So can you tell me why you ran like a bat outta hell from the love of your life?" Luke glares at me.

"I didn't come here for this shit." I bite my nail as disdain churns in my stomach.

He raises his brows. "Why did you come here, Sarah?"

"I'm not sure. We argued. We've never had a real argument. Ever." My chest aches as I run our words through my mind.

"Couples argue, that's not a reason." He cocks his brow.

"What do you want me to say?" I stare at him.

"I'm gonna be straight with you because I love you, and then, you're gonna be honest with yourself." He puckers his mouth. "You ran, probably because things got real, but I have a feeling you already know that. That man you walked out on is a damn good man. He loves you, and I know for fact—you love him."

"Oh, yeah. I felt it as he yelled at me."

"Did he have a right? Don't sit there and act as if you're innocent, ole girl, you're full of attitude and a helluva handful." He smirks.

"I may have raised my voice." I roll my eyes.

"Go on," he coaxes me.

I huff, "He slept with three different women while we were apart, but I'm telling you, it meant nothing. I know it didn't, he's not like that."

WRECKING US, SAVING YOU

"Why are you defending it if that's why you got into the argument in the first place?" His brows pull low.

I slump. "We ran into them in town, and the last one was the very day we went to visit Silas."

"Did he hit on her or ask her out? Maybe relived old times?" He leans in, waiting.

I smash my lips together. "No, not exactly."

"How? Exactly." He cocks his brow.

"She came on to him." I hold my finger up. "Bu-but, he didn't introduce me as his wife, like he had been doing." I narrow my eyes.

"If it bothered you, you should've said so. Letting it fester causes needless arguments."

I cover my face with my hands. "I know, I know I should've cleared the air. I was hurt he didn't wait on me, the way I did him."

"Sarah, it's different for girls. Did you ever ask why he did it? I can't believe it was to forget about you or to hurt you. I bet, he regretted it immediately after."

"Why did he stop calling me his wife?" I fold my arms over my rolling stomach.

"Did he have a reason?" He cocks his head.

I close my eyes tight. "I told him not to do it."

"Let's fast forward. What happened after that?" He folds his hands in his lap.

I twist my mouth. "I said something about keeping his dick in his pants, and he may have mentioned me giving up and wanting to die when he was there and needing me."

His eyes are wide. "He told you he needed you, and you bailed?"

"No, not like that." I bound from the couch, grabbing my glass.

"I'm waiting." He folds his arms. "Girl, you can come clean or I can have a 'Come to Jesus meetin'—you pick."

"He gave up on me. He stopped sleeping in Silas' bed with me. He boxed up all the things people bought him while he was sick." I slam my glass down, making my point.

"So your man needed you. And you think he gave up on you?" I nod. "He boxed up gifts from people you've never met, like he might give them to a foundation that could use them. Like, his sister-in-law's, who paid your child's hospital bills. And wait, let me get it right—he gave up on you because he couldn't take sleeping in the room where his son passed away. The son he just found out about, like six months or less before he lost him forever. Did I get all that right?" He glares at me as I flinch from his honesty.

"No." I tremble, shaking my head. "Hell no. That's not even remotely close."

"He told you he needed you, and you walked away. What does that say about the amazing love you declared y'all had for years?" He's pissing me off.

"It says he always had everything. He never wanted for anything in his life." I clench my jaw.

"Sarah, do you believe your own horse shit? Who took care of you for years?" he yells at me.

"Chord did, but I didn't ask him to. I never asked him for anything, he just did things." I wave my hand in the air.

"He did things for you, without you asking?" I nod. "Because you wouldn't ask?"

"Yes."

"Was there ever a time you needed him? Or told him you needed him? I mean, it took him nineteen years to tell you, but still, maybe that's why he was afraid to tell you." He leans against the wall, proud as a peacock.

WRECKING US, SAVING YOU

"Of course, I've always needed him. I would've never survived without him." I pull my brows low.

"Did you ever tell him that?"

"No." My stomach revolts.

"Have you ever asked him if he needed anything, or did you ever do something for him because you felt he wanted it?" Who the fuck is he, Doctor Phil?

"No, what's your point?"

"When you lived here, you wouldn't take one thing from me without insisting to pay for it. We did everything fifty-fifty, your choice. The bills, the chores, even the food." He points at me.

"Yeah, it was the way Chord's family worked. They did everything together."

He nods. "Because people who love each other give and take the same amount."

"Fuck." I drop my gaze. "I think we've both fucked up."

"You think?" He stares at me. "Sarah, death and grieving is hard on a seasoned couple. Grief in itself is a beast."

"You can say that again, it's like living a nightmare, every day."

"You don't think he's been living one?" he murmurs.

I shake my head, falling onto the couch. "What the hell have I done?"

"You walked away from the man you love." He nudges my shoulder.

"Luke, I lost my dad and found Chord. I lost him and gained Silas. I found Chord again, only to lose my son." Tears break their barrier. "I'm afraid we'll keep losing things, until we've lost each other."

"You can't allow fear to drive you. You love each other, as long as you continue to work together, you'll not lose."

352

I stare at the wall. "It doesn't matter, he hasn't even called. Has he?"

"Not me, hasn't he tried to get ahold of you?" He quirks his brow.

I frown. "I'm not sure, I haven't checked my phone. Besides, he knows where I am. If he wanted me, he'd come find me."

"He's done that once, but I'm not sure he should this time." He sits beside me.

"What's that supposed to mean?"

"You left him—again—without a word. You just slipped out, kinda like your mom made you do. You tucked tail and ran when the going got tough." He smacks his lips.

I release my held breath. "It was leave or fall apart."

"Oh, honey. You fell apart or you never would've come here." He pats my leg.

"I need to see if he's called." I jump up, running to get my purse in the bedroom. Jerking it off the floor, I search through it. "Hey, did I lay it somewhere?"

"You haven't had it." He follows me, narrowing his eyes.

"Shit. I left it, he can't call if he wanted to." I run my hand through my hair. "Surely, he's called you."

"Nope. Can't say I blame him either." He turns his back on me.

My face flames. "What in the hell does that mean?"

"It means, you walked out on the best damn thing that's ever happened to you." He puts his hand up when I start to protest. "I know, *you* were mourning and needed to heal some, but you should've been doing that with him. You walked out when he needed you the most. This isn't his to clean up." He shrugs.

"How do people do this? Honestly, how?" I drop to my bed.

353

"No one has that answer but you. Every relationship is different, and how you choose to make it work is up to you and him."

"I can't believe he hasn't come to get me." My heart falls.

"He probably can't believe you left him. Again." I wince, turning away from the truth.

"Okay, I get it." I throw myself back on my bed. "How the hell am I gonna fix this?" I sit up. "What if he doesn't want me? What if he's so mad he refuses to see me?"

"What if you broke his heart and he's dying without you?" He raises his brows.

I cover my mouth. "Oh God. Luke, I have. I know this has killed him. He'll think I don't love him."

"Do you?" He waits.

"I'm so ashamed of myself. I hurt him, I did." I stand. "Yes, I love him. Always have. Always will."

"You might want to go find him."

"What if he doesn't want me now?" I chew my lip.

"Remind him he has you, mistakes and all, but with that he gets your love." I wrap my arms around him.

Sarah

I take a deep breath as I turn the key, pushing the door open. I step through, setting my bag down by the stairs.

"Chord?" I look around the bottom floor. Walking out to the garage, there's no sign of him. Maybe he's slept for days too. I hurry up the stairs to find a broken railing. "Chord?" Nothing.

I push Silas' door open, walking over to where I forgot my phone. I search the bed, dropping to my knees. I find it near the edge on the floor. I try it, knowing it's going to be dead but holding out hope.

I grab the charger from behind the nightstand, plugging it in. "You're gonna need a few." I stand, tiptoeing to our bedroom. If he's asleep, I don't want to wake him. I crack the door open to peek in. "What the fuck?"

WRECKING US, SAVING YOU

Swinging the door wide, I come face to face with the carnage I've caused. My mouth hangs as I walk in, scanning the damage he's done. "Damn, I've broke him."

I whirl around, running to my phone. "I have to find you." I pick my phone up, still dead. "Come on!" The screen flashes to life, the wait for these damn things to load is beyond my capabilities to handle right now.

It's on three percent but allows me to enter my pin. "Please, please be looking for me." When the messages pop up, I have several. My heart thrums. I click the texts, Chord.

Sarah, where are you?

I need to know you're okay.

I'm sorry.

"Oh, no baby. I'm the one who's sorry." I open the next and gasp.

I can't believe you'd leave me.

I'm broken too.

I'm so sorry I let us down.

"Shit." I close the texts and check my voicemail. One. One? "Oh, no." I hit play, waiting.

"Sarah, I have no words. I know I let you down but you let me down too. I'm sorry."

"What have I done to us?" I jerk the charger from the wall, taking it and the phone downstairs. I plug it in and try to decide what to do next. I call Luke, I need help.

"Hey, what's going on?" He's cautious.

I take a deep breath, settling my nerves. "I've fucked up so bad. So bad."

"What happened?"

356

"He's not here. Our bedroom, he fuckin' tore it to hell. Nothing survived." I tremble, knowing that's not Chord. He's the sweetest.

"Shit." He sigh. "Where is he?"

"I don't know." I blow out a breath. "It doesn't look like he's been here in days." I walk over to the fireplace, there's broken glass. "He killed a bottle of Jack."

"Killed it?" he asks.

"Yeah, considering there's no stain on the floor, I'd say it was empty before it hit the side of the brick." Damn. I've messed up.

"You gonna try to find him?"

"Yeah, I'll try to call him." I bite my lip, looking around.

"What if he doesn't answer?"

"I'll go find him." I wince. "Except, I have no cab fare." I scratch my head.

"Call first and then go from there." He's right. No sense in panicking, yet.

I swallow hard. "Let me go, I need to get my man."

"Good luck. Call me if you need me."

"Will do." I end the call. "First, let's clean up while I work on gettin' my nerve up."

I work on the house. It's a mess and the demolition zone that is now our bedroom needs more than what I could do on my own. I carry as much as I can down to the garage, putting it in a pile.

I take a deep breath and make the dreaded call. It rings before going to an automated message, 'this number is not receiving calls'. What in the hell does that mean? I text him, but it bounces back. "Is his phone not working?"

The fire I thought was dead ignites with a new found kindling. "We're not doing this, babe."

WRECKING US, SAVING YOU

I grab my purse and the keys by the door. Shutting it behind me as I stare at the machine in front of me. "Here's the thing. I need to find him, and you're gonna help. Be good to me. I might break you, but it can't be any worse than what I've done to him."

I hit the key fob, opening the door to the new Land Rover Chord bought for me. I start it up, biting my lip as I back out of the garage. I ease it to the edge of the driveway. "Yeah, I know. I don't have a license but they don't know that, so help me out here. I need to find my man."

I creep onto the road and drive carefully to the end of the street. Coming to a stop, I bite my lip again as the traffic on Highway Seventeen flies by me.

"What in the hell am I doing?" I wince as I inch out between the cars. "And I'm out. Let's do this." I'm so proud of myself. I giggle thinking of Chord helping Silas get his license. He has taken such good care of us.

Turning my signal light on a little too early, I get shot the bird as I pull off. "Yeah, whatever. I made it," I exclaim. I park at the back of the lot, trying to scope out Chord's SUV. It isn't here.

I take a deep breath before grabbing the door. "You've done harder things than this, go in and find him. He needs you, and you can't live without him." I step through the door to find the place empty.

I walk back to Chord's office, the lights are off. Flipping them on, I see Silas' fridge by the couch. He still has toys everywhere, and my heart races. Chord loves him so much. "How could I leave you?"

"That's what we've all been wondering?" I jump as Thayer's voice startles me.

"Shit, you scared me." I hold my heart as I spin around.

She folds her arms. "What do you want, Sarah?"

358

"Chord." I bite my lip, holding my hands up before she says another word. "Listen, I know I fucked up, but I love him and I will make it right."

"If that's how you show love, I'm not sure he needs it." Her jaw clenches.

"I said I fucked up. I know I've hurt him, but I'll be damned if you're gonna stop me from loving him." I fist my hands as I shake. Thayer and I have never argued, but I draw the line with Chord.

"Maybe he's better off without you." She steps toward me.

"The hell he is, he loves me."

"Not anymore," she seethes, lashing out at me. It cuts me deep and may be the worst I've ever been dealt.

I blanche, holding my tears at bay. "He doesn't?" I stumble back, finding my balance against his desk. "I've lost him?"

"Thayer, chill the hell out." Lea steps between us.

"She's not going to hurt him anymore." She points at me.

"Chord's a big boy, he can decide on his own." She turns back to me. "Sarah, sit down."

"I'm sorry, I know y'all love him and want to protect him, but I never meant it. I hate myself for hurting him." I find the seat behind me, slowly sitting.

Thayer shakes her head. "Well, that's a start."

Lea sits beside me, cocking her brow at Thayer. "Chord's pretty rough, Sarah. It's been a hard few months for you both."

I turn to her, my face wet. "I know, I do. Everything happened so fast, and I didn't mean anything I said."

"He didn't either, but the damage is done. I'm not sure it can be fixed this time, sweetie." Lea lays her hand over mine.

WRECKING US, SAVING YOU

My eyes flash to hers. "Please, don't say that. I can't make it without him."

"You may have to, if he refuses to try to work things out." I clutch my chest, and my heart hammers at my ribs.

I rub my lips together as sweat pools on my forehead. "Would he do that to me? I mean, I know he's hurt, but it's me."

"I don't think he would've ever thought you would do that to him either." Lea scrunches her nose. My stomach knots.

Thayer steps in, flopping down into a chair. "Listen, he's scared. He lost everything in a matter of weeks. He didn't know whether you were coming back or not."

"It was an argument, a horrible fight, but I never said I didn't love him." My forehead wrinkles as my pulse accelerates.

"Did you say you did? Did ya leave a note? Or maybe, you could've called in the almost two weeks you've been gone," Thayer spits at me.

I scoot to the end of my seat, looking Thayer in the eyes. "I'm sorry I hurt you when I left the first time. No matter the circumstance, I hate I hurt you. But by god, don't act as if I don't love your brother. He has been my one constant, but I lost sight of that. There's nothing I wouldn't give to fix it. I was broken and in turn, I've hurt the love of my life."

"I'm sure Thayer can understand the power of snap decisions." Lea glares at her.

She sits back in her seat. "He was shattered the first time, do you know that? Have you ever asked any of us, what it did to our family when we lost you?"

"No, I haven't because Chord wanted to move forward. Pick up where we left off. But looking back, I know we should've spent a little more time talking about how it affected us to be apart."

"Love, grief, and time...those three bitches are beautiful and hateful, we run the world creatures." Lea smirks.

"You got that right." I sigh. "Y'all, I get it. The things we said during our argument should've never been an issue, except for one."

"Which one was that?" Thayer cocks her brow.

"The fact he never told me he needs me and, once in a while, I could tell him how much I need him." I wipe my eyes.

"Shit." Thayer sits up. "So what's your plan, sister?"

Lea and I snap our heads around. "You called me sister." I grin,

"Shut the hell up, don't let it go to your head." She smirks.

"Thayer, as soon as I get my man back and locked up. You, Lea, and I are gonna have a long talk over a big glass of wine." I wrap her hands in mine.

"Wine? Hell, we're Southern girls, break out the Jack and I'll bring the Coke." Lea laughs.

"I would but my future husband cracked the Jack." We all laugh. "Oh, our bedroom is demolished. We need an entire new bed and a lamp. A chair, mirror, and maybe a light fixture."

"Malone said it was bad, damn." Lea wrinkles her nose.

I sigh. "I had no idea how hurt he was. Is."

"He's staying at Elise and Cal's." Lea presses her lips into a thin line.

Thayer twists her mouth. "So what'cha thinking? How you gonna shake him outta this and make him your man again?"

"The hell if I know, but I think I'm gonna start with an apology."

"Better place than any at this point," Thayer says.

"Well, there is something." I bite my lip. "It's a start, but I need something big. Huge."

"Sarah, if I can help, I'm there." Lea smiles. "He loves you. Malone and I both know it."

"Thank you, I'm gonna need it." I turn to Thayer, and she eyes me skeptically.

"Fine but if you hurt him ever again, I'm gonna kick your ass,"

"I'm well aware. And if you need to start getting rid of that anger, I know this chick named Kimberly. I want to hurt her." I narrow my eyes.

"Ugh, she's the worst." Thayer rolls her eyes.

"Seriously, I hate her," I seethe.

"Tell us how we can help." Lea smiles as One walks through the door. He looks from me to Lea and back.

"Ladies, are we okay in here?" He leans against the door.

"Oh, yeah. You missed the excitement. Thayer's gonna kick her ass, and Sarah's gonna kick Kimberly's ass. We're all mad, and we've all cried. Now, we're gonna make plans for Sarah to win Chord back." Lea winks at him.

He raises his brows. "Whose ass are you gonna kick?"

"Baby, I only want your fine ass." She crosses the room, pressing her lips to his.

"You fight dirty." He grins boyishly, exactly like his brother.

"Oh, shut up. You like it." Thayer giggles.

"Now I know where Chord gets it from." My cheeks flame thinking of him.

"Hey, now. Calm down over there, you gotta get him back first." Lea laughs.

"But that's a start. No man alive turns down his woman if she's willing to give him some good lovin'." One chuckles.

My face flames. "Y'all, hush. I need to talk to him before I jump him."

"It could work." Thayer's face is hysterical.

"Lea, I think we need a new bedroom suite." I bite my lip. "And we have a few repairs, One."

He rubs the back of his neck. "If he finds out I did this, he's gonna be mad."

"By the time I get him back in our bedroom, I promise you, it'll be the last thing on his mind." I smirk.

One throws his hands up as Thayer leans over and high-fives me. "Hell yes. Let's do this."

"I'm out." One backs away.

"Let's order a new bedroom suite, and you can pick the design this time." Lea settles in with Chord's computer.

"I love the blues and grays so I was thinking, a pewter wrought iron bed. Maybe he'll not break this one." I chuckle.

"Let's hope not." She sighs. "I love this one." She turns the screen to me.

"Perfect. Can we get it by tomorrow?" I frown. "I'm gonna use the money he put into my account for this. I know he's still paying technically." I shrug.

"We can, I'll have it there as soon as possible." Lea nods. "I get it. Letting go of being independent isn't easy, but it's a start of letting him know you're depending on him in a way."

"Yes, he wanted me to know he was taking care of us, but I never gave in. I think it's time I show him, I know he's a good man and can take care of his family." I sigh.

"It also helps to tell him you believe in him. And that you're together," Thayer says.

"Yep. Now, I need a big, 'please forgive me, I'm an idiot'."

"We need to ask a man." Lea's eyes are wide as we laugh.

"Good idea, but I think I might have something." I stand, taking out my checkbook. "Can I leave this with you, I need to get moving."

"Sure, this is a good thing." Lea smiles.

"Let's hope so, I love him. I'm nothing without him." I hug them both and take off. I have a ton to do.

39

Sarah

I make a couple of stops before heading home. If I'm gonna do this, it has to be done right. I'm going all out to win his heart back. I pull into the garage, walking over to some boards we have left from the build.

"This could work, maybe One can help me with it." I bite my lip, trying to see the design before I start on it. I get a brain storm, so I hurry in the house and get it down on paper.

"I'll need help. I can't do it all on my own, and I know this is the only way to bring him back." I get to work on my list, making sure I'll have everything I need. It's long and seems almost impossible, but I'll make it work.

I shoot off a few quick texts, working on my help list. I decide to call One over, I need to see him in person. No one can know about this. I dial his number.

"Hello, Sarah."

"I need you." I hold my breath.

"Funny, I thought you were in love with Chord?" He chuckles.

I giggle. "Oh, hush. I need help with the bedroom and the bannister, when can you do it?"

"Hardy and I can run over this evening, it's not as bad as it looks," he says.

"I've gotten most of it cleaned out, but you're right, it isn't that bad."

"You moved the bed on your own? You shouldn't have done that," he admonishes me.

"One, I'm responsible for it. Besides, it works into my whole 'get my man home' scenario." My gut rolls. I hope it gets him home, anyway.

"We'll be there around six."

"Thank you." I breathe a sigh of relief.

"Have you talked to him?" he asks, his voice low.

"No, I have a few more things to do first, but I will soon. I promise."

"Alright, see ya later," he says.

"Later." I hang up, making my next call.

"Pennington Law." Donna's so sweet.

"May I speak with Walker?"

"Who's calling?" she asks.

"Sarah Ha-Sutton." Shit.

"Please hold."

"Sarah, how are you?" Walker's the best. He's made me feel right at home.

"Not so good, but that's another story. I need some help."

"I'm in the business of helping," he says.

"Is there anything I can do to expedite Silas' birth certificate?" I chew my nail, waiting on him to answer.

"I actually happen to have some news on that, but Chord hasn't returned my call." I can hear papers shuffling.

"We had a fight, and I left." I roll my eyes when my stomach twists. "I messed up, bad."

"If there's one thing I know about that family, they know how to forgive." He sounds as if he knows.

"Let's hope so. I'm not sure he will though."

"Well, I hope what I'm holding in my hand helps." My heart seizes.

"You're kidding?"

"No, I can drop it off tomorrow," he offers, making me love him so much more.

"Walker, I'm not sure what you've done in your past, but dude, you're a helluva a man. I can never thank you enough for what you've done for us." I dry my eyes, trying to control my falling tears.

"I thought you'd have heard by now, I was an ass," he murmurs.

"You've redeemed yourself. And now, you're helping me to do it." I sigh. "Thank you."

"You're welcome, Sarah. I'll see you tomorrow." He ends the call, and I scream with happiness.

"Perfect." I twirl.

I head up the stairs to finish cleaning our room. I still need a big 'forgive me' but nothing's coming to mind. I work the afternoon away, keeping my mind busy. I want to be ready for when One and Hardy get here.

I stop in Silas' room to make the bed. I pick up my dirty clothes and a few of his. I can't help but smell them. I can't wash them, so I open his drawer to put them in there and find his video camera.

My chest aches as I think of my baby. "Let's go see what you have on here, little man." I pop the memory card and head downstairs. I shove the card in, but One and Hardy arrive before I can watch it.

I open the door, letting them in. "Hey, y'all. It's ready to go."

They bring several tools in, setting them by the stairs. Hardy stops to wrap me in a hug. "Hey, sister. This is a good thing."

"I hope so, Hardy. I have to get him home." My heart thunders in my chest.

"This is a good start." He walks up the stairs as I motion for One.

"Can you follow me?" His brows knit.

"Alright." He joins me at the bar. I push my rudimentary drawing at him. His eyes flash to mine. "This is for?"

"I can't tell you right now." I furrow my brow.

"We can do this." He nods.

"There are a few boards out by the garage we can use."

"No, if you're gonna do this and it's what I think it is, we're doing it right. Let's text Thayer and she can order the material." He takes his phone and grabs my pen. A few calculations later, he gives Thayer the order.

"Thank you." I beam.

"I hope you know what you're doing." He raises his brows.

"Not in the least, but hell if I ain't gonna try." I giggle.

"Lord, help us." One shakes his head.

"Hush, it's a work in progress."

"Speaking of, I'm going to help Hardy." He turns to leave, but I have one more question.

"One more thing." He pauses, tilting his head. "Do you know someone who can help me make a DVD with like, music?"

"Your nephew, Lath. He's badass." I grin. "His number is probably in your phone if I know Chord."

I grab my phone, scrolling the numbers. "Yep, here he is."

"Call him and tell him, 'Dad said help'." His smile is so big when he says 'dad'.

"Will do." I start dialing his number. "Thank you, Captain." He chuckles when Hardy bursts into laughter as he carries down the parts of the bed I couldn't.

I love having a huge family, something Silas enjoyed as well. I'm happy he got to see it. I hit dial.

"Hey, Aunt Sarah." His deep voice booms over the speaker.

"Hey, Lath." My heart thumps at his endearment. "Your dad said you could help me make a DVD with music on it."

"I sure can."

"Well, he's here now. Can you come on over, I'm at home." I pick at my nail.

"I'll see you in ten."

"Thank you." I end the call, thrilled everything seems to be coming together.

Sure enough, Lath walks through the door ten minutes later. We sit at the counter so I can show him what I want. I'm surprised by what I find on Silas' memory card but once I do, I know exactly what to do.

"You okay, Aunt Sarah?" Lath's eyes cut at me as we go through all the photos.

369

WRECKING US, SAVING YOU

I dab at my eyes. "Yeah, I'm good. It's amazing what kids see when adults don't know they're looking."

"Remarkable skills for his age, that's for sure," he says as we scroll through the gallery. "Hey, he has a video on here."

Cue the freakin' tears. "Oh, my. Yeah, put this on there too."

"I planned on it." He grins.

An hour later and a few hundred tissues, I have a finished product. Now, to work up my courage to go see Chord. I spend the night making notes of what I want to make sure I say, things we need to say.

The next morning, One and Hardy are back to help me with my project.

"What in the world, woman?" Hardy quirks his brow at my table full of notes.

I give him a lopsided grin. "Notes to win Chord back. I figured I needed to up my game."

"Improve your game or plead your case?" Walker stands at the front door.

"Come on in, I was watching for you."

"No worries, I'm glad I had time to drop this by this morning." He hands me the file and my smile couldn't be bigger.

"Thank you, this is amazing." I tiptoe, kissing him on the cheek.

"Ahh, The Pennington's strike, once again." One laughs.

"We do what we can." He winks at me. "We all deserve a chance at redemption. Good luck." One shakes his hand before he leaves, nodding at Hardy as he does. Hardy growls.

One chuckles. "Get over it, she picked you."

"Yeah, she could've picked him. Wowza." I waggle my brows.

Hardy narrows his eyes. "You're here for Chord."

"Nothing wrong with window shopping." I wink, getting a rise out of One.

"Sarah, stop poking the bear." We both laugh at Hardy while he broods.

He shakes his head, flipping us off. "Screw you both." We laugh even harder. "Let's get to work."

We get busy on my project until Lea arrives with the new furniture for the bedroom. To my shock and horror, Elise and Cal come by. Wonderful, the entire family is in on my plans before I know if he'll even take me back.

"Oh, stop with the frowning." Elise hugs me.

"I'm sorry, I messed up. I know I've hurt him and I promise I never will again," I gush in one long sentence.

"We're fine, it's him you need to talk to." She pats my back as Cal walks outside with One and Hardy.

Lea's brows are pulled low as she stares out the window. "What'cha lookin' at, Lea?"

"Shew, my man. Shirt off, manual labor. Reminds me of when we met and he was tryin' his best to impress me." Her lip quirks.

"What is that you kids say, she's sprung." Our heads snap to Elise. "It's alright, girls, I understand, they got it from their father." She elbows Lea, and we giggle.

"I miss Chord." My lip trembles.

"When are you gonna go see him?" Lea asks.

"I'm hoping to catch him alone."

"He's alone now." Elise smiles.

"Look at me, I can't go like this." My chest tightens.

Lea throws her arm around me. "We can fix that." She smiles as Thayer walks through the door.

"We can fix what?" she says.

"She's going to see Chord. I'll start your shower. Thayer, clothes. Mom, pray." Lea pushes me toward the stairs, and my knees start knocking immediately.

40

Sarah

I look up at the big house, swallowing hard. I lay my finger on the doorbell and remove it. I brush over it without pushing. "Stop being a chicken, Sarah." I tightly close my eyes and ring the dang bell.

I hold my breath. No one comes. Does he know I'm here? I step back, looking up at the windows. He isn't peeking out I don't think. I try it again. No answer. I'm getting mad by the time I ring the damn bell the fourth time.

"I know you're in there." I knock on the door. Still, there's no answer. I decide to try the handle. The door opens, and I push it wide. "Chord?" I scan the bottom floor, he's not down here.

I roll my eyes up, wondering if he's asleep. I take a deep breath and hit the stairs. The problem is, I've never been up here. I'm not sure which way to go or what room is his. "Give a girl a break." I sigh.

WRECKING US, SAVING YOU

I pop my head in this room and that one, left and right. "This has to be it." I peek in, rolling my eyes. "Another bathroom." I shake my head, continuing to the next room. I open the door, scanning the room and just as I'm about to close it, something on the far wall catches my eye.

I make a beeline to the desk, standing in awe of what's above it. Pictures of me with Chord litter the wall. From kindergarten to high school. Pictures from every moment of our life together.

"You never forgot me, did you?" I place my hand down to get a closer look at a picture. When I lift it, a piece of paper sticks to my sweating palm. "Oh, come on." I peel it off, ready to toss it down, when I see my name.

Tons and tons of letters he's written to me. Over six years' worth of love letters from Chord to me. I thumb through them, reading one and checking dates on others.

"What are you doing?"

I jump, holding my hand over my heart. "Damn it, Chord. What the hell are you trying to do, scare me to death?"

He folds his arms. "I could say the same thing, but you're in my room."

My eyes flicker around the room. "I am, and I have an explanation."

He holds his hand up. "I don't want to hear it."

I feel as though I've been hit in the center of my chest. "Wow. That hurt more than I thought it would."

"Hate to hear it. Now, if you don't mind." He steps away from the door.

Say something. Anything. "Are these mine?" I point to the letters.

His eyes dart to his desk. "Nope."

"They have my name on them." I cock my head.

"Different Sarah." He pins me with his glare.

"Oh, one I haven't had the pleasure of hearing how well you fucked her?" I wince as soon as I say it. "Sorry. Seriously, I'm sorry."

"What do you want?" He grinds his teeth.

"To talk." I sigh. "Hopefully, better than I am right now, but to talk." I pick at my nail.

"Maybe you should've answered your phone." He shakes his head again, making my stomach knot. "What about, Sarah? I thought we had said it all already."

"I didn't have it with me, it was under Silas' bed. I'm sorry." I bite my nail now. "Chord, I don't think we've said enough. We've spent months not talking about the things that happened over those six years."

"What do you need to say? Go ahead and get it over with, so you can leave." He leans against the wall opposite me.

"I held back because I was scared and I didn't know how to say what I wanted to talk about and that I need you." I swallow the rising bile. "I'm sorry I left the way I did, it was unfair and callous."

"So, we should've fought earlier. Made it easier for you to leave." He glares at me.

I take a much-needed breath. "I never meant to hurt you, Chord. Please believe me. We said terrible things to each other, and I thought you hated me."

"I'm not a fan like I once was." He's being spiteful. I cross my arms, trying to protect myself.

"I'm sorry you feel that way." Tears well in my eyes. "I still love you, that's never changed."

"Oh, I know all too well what a perfect lover you are. You would never cheat on me, I'm the asshole who does it." His words are full of venom.

WRECKING US, SAVING YOU

"Why did you...you know?" I swallow past the rising bile.

He scrubs his hand over his head. "Stupidity. Friends telling me to move on, that it would help me get over you. That, I was never gonna find you."

"I see." I lay my hand on my stomach as it pitches and rolls.

"No, you don't." He scowls.

I take a deep breath, steadying myself. "Then tell me."

He shakes his head. "What's the use?"

"I love you." I shrug. "I want to know, I need to know what you went through. I think I didn't ask because I knew I was the one that made you hurt so badly and do those things."

"I didn't go to college right away. I barely graduated from high school, Sarah. Two years. Two god damned years, I sit here, waiting. Broken. Scared to fucking death you were hurt or worse, dead!" He dries his face on his shoulder.

"I was blessed to have Silas, he kept me from losing it."

"I was so broken but I knew it wasn't you that hurt me. Not like the other day. That was cruel." His brows pull low.

"We each did things, I know, we're not proud of. I wasn't ever alone in my pain, you were always there." I can't fight the tears anymore.

He lays his head back to keep from looking at me. "Sarah, just leave. We were crazy to think we could make it work, too many years have gone by."

I shake my head, wrapping my arms around myself. "No, don't say that, Chord. I'm here, I'm trying to show you I love you."

He pins me with his glare. "You never would've left me if that was true."

"I fucked up, I'm sorry."

"You left me, the same way you did six years ago. I didn't know if I should look or wait. I did both the last time, and I don't have it in me to do it again!" he yells at me.

"I know, it wasn't fair of me." I catch my breath. "I'm here and I promise I'll never leave again."

"I don't believe you."

I bite my lip, releasing it on a pop. "You're scared, I get it. I am too."

"So why are you here?" His brows fall low over his eyes.

"Because I love you. None of the rest matters, except for Silas."

"But I don't care about him, remember?" He points at me.

My chest aches. "I never should've said that."

"But you did." He blows out a breath.

"I lashed out. I wanted you with me. I thought you had to mourn the way I did or you didn't love us." Some wounds cut so deep they never heal. And for the first time, I don't mean mine. "I lost my dad, Chord, and you were there. Then I lost you and Silas came along. I keep losing the things I love the most, I was fucking scared of losing you all together, so much so, I almost have.

"I've always loved you." He drops his head. "If you don't know that, maybe we're not meant to be."

"Oh, yes we are. You own me and you're mine." I fist my hands. "I'm here, Chord. I know leaving wasn't my best decision but I was so lost. I thought you'd come find me and when you didn't, I was hurt."

"Sarah, when I met you, you had already shut down. I accepted it and looked over it for years. But I can't anymore." His eyes glisten.

I nod. "I know. I never took the time to tell you how much I appreciate all you did for me."

WRECKING US, SAVING YOU

"I did it because I love you."

"You did it because I never told you how much I need you. You did it so I wouldn't have to tell you," I gasp. "All these years, I've never had the kind of love you give. It gets no better than you and the way you love me."

He turns his head. "Now you notice?"

"No, Chord. I've always known. I just didn't realize you needed to hear what a good man you are and how your love makes me feel. That without your love, I don't exist."

His eyes snap to mine. "Why now?"

"I tried to put myself back together, and it didn't work. I don't work without you. I can't be whole again without all of the pieces. You're my missing piece, and you're the only thing that can make me whole again." I dry my face, wiping my hands down my pants.

"What if our pieces don't fit together anymore." A tear rolls down his face.

"Oh, but we do. I have proof from the best source." I pull out the DVD. "Love comes in all shapes and sizes. Sometimes, even in pictures."

"Is this gonna be something else I have to survive?" He narrows his eyes.

I lick my lips. "I hope not but if it is, I'll be by your side."

"Sarah, I can't." He looks away from me.

"I don't want to lose you. And I'm here to fight for us because you've been doing it all this time. It's my turn now. I need you, I love you, and it will never change. Here's your proof." I lay the DVD on his bed, walking past him.

"Hey?" I turn to him, raising my brows. "How'd you get here?"

My smiles grows. "I drove."

"You don't have a license." He smirks, cocking his brow.

"There was something more important I had to do." I wink. "And the police don't know that."

His mouth hangs. "You drove your car here?"

"I did. I also made a few changes at home." I smirk.

"How?" My pulse races.

"Joint checking." I smile. "By the way, I know our foundation is good, but I'd like a say so on any and all renovations in the future." I narrow my eyes at him.

He winces. "Yeah, I guess we need to remodel a few things."

"Well, the next time you decide to break the bed, make sure it's because I'm in it, under you." His eyes blaze and when I sink my teeth into my lip, his gaze scalds me. I turn to leave again.

"Where you goin'?" He tilts his head.

"Home." I walk away from him, the second most hardest thing I've ever done.

On the drive home, I go over everything that was said and remember a few things we needed to say. Hopefully, we'll have another day. I chew my lip, nervous as all get out. "I hope he doesn't take too long, I might have a nervous breakdown."

I bound through the door, putting my plans into full swing. I send a massive text, putting everyone on notice.

I'm back.

If this works, I'll let you know.

Fingers crossed.

I'm hoping by Saturday.

How'd it go? -L

He didn't throw me out.

379

WRECKING US, SAVING YOU

But he didn't come with me.

He will. – O

Butterflies make a return to my lower belly, and I'm more nervous than ever. I get to work on my projects. I'll do anything to keep my mind busy right now. The not knowing will drive me insane.

I don't sleep, I'm wound too tight. I end up pacing around three in the morning. Exhaustion overcomes me around dawn as I crash on the couch. Waking around noon, my phone vibrates on the table.

Multiple texts from the family and Luke, but nothing from Chord. I reply to Thayer. There's no way I can repeat this or read their comments to 'hang in there'; I'm hanging. By a thread, but I'm hanging.

No word.

No sleep.

I may lose my mind.

Hold on. ~T

He'll come. ~T

"I hope she's right." I fall back onto the couch, trembling as scenarios play through my mind of why he hasn't come yet. I suppose he needs more time, he's been through so much.

I get busy, moving forward with my plans, saying a silent prayer it'll all work out. As the day turns into evening, I begin to become wary. Clouds darken my once high hopes as I sit here in the dark by myself.

I'm wracked with fear. "A day. An entire day has went by and still no Chord. Why hasn't he come home? He doesn't want me, he can't forgive me."

"Oh, I'd say he wants you." I whirl around to find him standing in front of me.

My mouth opens and closes at least three times. "You're here."

He holds the DVD up. "This is mighty powerful stuff."

I hold back my tears, nodding. "Yeah, who would've thought our son could've done that?"

"It's pretty good." He moves closer to me. "Videos and pictures of us. He captured the real us. I had forgotten you look at me that way."

"I never knew you watch me the way you do. I loved our pillow fight. He gave us that gift, Chord. He knew before he left, we'd need to find our way back to each other." My chest heaves.

"So he snuck around, taking pictures of us?" He narrows his eyes.

"Of us in love, to show us how perfectly we do it for each other." I hesitate. "It was on his video camera, the card is over there." I point to the counter.

"You made the DVD?" He swallows. "And added the song on it?"

"I had help, but I picked everything, including the song." I wipe away an escaped tear.

"That song…" He twists his mouth. "*Something to Hold Onto*, you picked it?"

I raise my brows. "I did. It's how I see your love for me."

"It's perfect. You do give me something to hold on to, I love you." His boyish grin plays on his mouth.

The room spins as my heart pounds. "Huh?" I murmur above my crying.

"I love you." He steps closer. "We're here because of our love. Look what it's already given us, Silas was perfect."

"You love me?" I gasp.

"Yeah, I love you." He chuckles, stepping closer until he's in front of me. "I'm sorry."

"No, don't be. We had to learn to talk again, Chord. To grow so we could be whole again." I gaze into his eyes as they sparkle.

He slides his hand around my waist, pulling me to him. "So we're gonna talk about everything from now on?"

"Whether we like it or not. I don't want to be one of those couples that hold back. We may have hurt each other with our words, but everything we said had to be done."

"Let's just not do it that way again, okay?" He cocks his brow.

"When it comes to you, I'll love you the way you need me to."

"You always have." He brushes my lips with his. "And I'll love you exactly the way you need."

"Sounds good." I wrap my hands around his neck.

He presses his lips to mine. "Damn good."

He takes my lips, owning me like only he can. My heart races as his mouth works mine, heat building between us. I push his shirt over his abs, running my hands under it. I slide them over his hard chest, moaning with appreciation.

"Make love to me." His eyes set me on fire. His mouth takes mine, swirling our tongues together, flaming our desire. He picks me up, and I waste no time wrapping my legs around him.

He carries me up the stairs, pausing at the door. "If we do this, it's forever, Sarah. I'll never survive if not."

I caress his face. "There's no other way for us, Chord. This, it's forever."

He searches my eyes. "I love you."

"I love you."

"There you are, I've missed you." He brushes his lips against my neck.

"Mmm, there you are." My thighs squeeze around him.

He carries me over to the bed, falling onto it. He rolls me over so I can straddle him. "I want to watch you."

"Is this one of those teenage wet dreams?" I lean down, sweeping my tongue over his nipple.

My eyes flicker to his, teeming with desire. "Hell yes." His answer earns him a giggle.

"Well, let me make that happen since you've always fulfilled mine." I drag his shirt over his head, tossing it to the floor.

He does the same with mine, filling his hands with my breasts after tossing the shirt. His hips buck from the bed when I circle mine. Stripping teaches you more than taking your clothes off.

I slide my hand down the front of his pants, fondling his cock. I stroke it as I lean over, taking his mouth with mine. His groan makes everything between my legs wet. He slips his hand between my breasts, unsnapping my bra.

I raise up, slipping it off. I stand, sliding my jeans down my legs. He unbuckles his as he watches me. I grip the pants legs, he raises his ass and I pull. One more yank and he's unsheathed.

I lick my lips, crawling on top of him. I lift up, placing him at my center. Our eyes lock as I slide down on him. He fills me so completely, I gasp. I take a minute to adjust, biting my lip. "It's been too long," he whispers.

"Definitely." I raise my ass as he slides out. I fall back down, wanting him deep. I rock my hips, swaying as we slip and slide in one motion. Sensual and heated, desire pools in my core.

He sits up, wrapping his hand around my neck. He smashes his mouth to mine, filling his hand with my breast. He bucks as I ride him, my orgasm building from the delicious way our bodies rub against one another.

He flips me over, thrusting into me as I arch my back. His slow drag from my core makes me pulse around him. I'm lost in his love as we rock together to find our ultimate ending.

He rolls to his side, taking me with him. "I don't think it gets any better than that," he pants.

"I would have to agree." He wraps me in his arms as sleep takes us quickly.

I slip downstairs to get the day moving. There's so much to do, but I'm thrilled to say this day is finally happening. By noon, the house is bustling. Luke came up to help with the big stuff, and the rest of the family are all helping in any way they can.

"The pergola is finished and the cake is set up. I'm going to get dressed." Luke kisses my cheek about the time Chord walks down the stairs. "Hi, bye," Luke says as he leaves.

"What?" Chord's brows draw together.

"He's going to his hotel to get dressed."

"For what?" He tilts his head.

"Oh, yeah." I point to a paper on the counter. "We're getting married today." I smile at him.

"Huh?" His forehead wrinkles.

"No, don't give me that. I've almost lost you twice, so you're marrying me—today." I place my hand on my hip, staring at him.

His eyes glisten. "You're serious? You're marrying me?"

I walk around the bar, embracing him. "Your clothes are down here because I'm getting dressed upstairs. I was so scared you'd find my dress."

"You have a dress?" His brows furrow.

"I laid it away because I wanted to buy the dress I married you in. But things happened, and I hid it once I picked it up. I've had it for months."

"You already bought a dress? You knew all this time you were gonna marry me." He leans in. "Why the hell didn't you tell me?"

I giggle. "Surprise. You knew we were going to, it was when."

"I love you." He kisses me.

"Hey, break it up. We're not there yet." Thayer snaps her fingers as she heads upstairs.

"Yeah, we are." Chord waggles his brows.

"Go get dressed. I need you to meet me at the big brown thing outside in an hour." I shyly grin.

His eyes fill with tears. "I've waited so long for this, Sarah."

I sigh. "Me too."

"I promised you forever. I'll do everything in my power to make you happy." He kisses me.

"You already have."

"Let's go, people, we have a wedding in t-minus fifty seven minutes," Thayer yells down the stairs.

"Meet me at the alter?" I cock a brow.

"I'll be the one in…" His eyes grow wide.

"Gray, you're wearing gray." I snicker.

"I'll be the one in gray." I bite my lip when he gives me his devilish grin.

"Please, you're wasting time." Thayer stands at the base of the stairs.

I wave. "Bye."

"No." He shakes his head. "See ya, later." He winks. I narrow my eyes, sticking my tongue out at him. "Definitely, later."

"Oh, my god. Did you just reference a blowjob? No, don't tell me." Thayer covers her ears as we burst with laughter.

"Go, you're damaging your sister." I laugh.

"As long as I get to damage you later." Chord fists himself through his shorts.

"Ahh!" Thayer screams as she runs up the stairs. One walks around the corner.

"What the hell, put that away and get through the house, son. Geez, y'all calm down," One admonishes us.

Chord and I can't stop laughing. Our eyes lock and I run toward him. He catches me in his arms, bending me backward to kiss me. "I love you."

"I love you. Most." He kisses me again before standing me up straight.

"I'm totally for this, but if we don't get dressed, Thayer may have an aneurysm." One chuckles.

I start up the stairs as Lea walks in the door. "Get dressed!"

"I'm going. Chord kept kissing me," I grumble.

"That's not what Chord was trying to do." One grins.

"Sounds like his older brother." She rolls her eyes. He smacks her ass, making her giggle.

387

WRECKING US, SAVING YOU

"Yeah, Chord wants to do that too," Chord yells.

"Get dressed!" all three of them yell at us.

I stand at the double doors to the patio, waiting on my cue. I had always hoped Silas would give me away if this ever happened, but it's not possible now. I simply decided I'd walk myself.

"Are you ready?" I look up to find Calder.

"I am." Tears brim my eyes.

"Sarah, you've been like a daughter to us. We love you as we love our own, always have. Would you allow me the honor of giving your hand in marriage?" My chest aches, but this time, it's for the best reason.

"I would love it if you'd walk me down the aisle." I dab at my eyes.

"Shall we?" He holds his arm out to me.

"I've waited nineteen years for this, please." I smile.

"Let's plow." I can't help but laugh at his words.

We step out on the porch, and my eyes lock on Chord's. *Perfect* plays on a speaker as I walk toward my life. I bite my lip to keep from crying, but when he touches his eye, I break. He's crying too.

A picture of Silas sits beside his dad, and I lose it. After everything we've been through, we still found our way here. He's wearing his gray three-piece suit. It's the one I got him for the dance with Silas.

Thayer twisted my hair in a knot at the base of my neck, with wisps of hair framing my face. My dress is a fitted white lace mermaid gown with a tulle overlay that flares. Lace lays on my arms in a small detailed trim. I'm carrying blue roses the color of Chord's tie.

Thayer stands as my maid of honor with Luke as my bride's butler, and One as his brother's best man with Hardy as groomsman. Lea helps the twins, Wren and Harlyn, walk as our ring bearer and flower girl. All of our family and friends are in attendance; even with short notice, they came to celebrate us.

"Who gives this bride in marriage?" the minister asks.

"My wife and I happily take her as ours and welcome her, finally, to our family. We've been waiting a long time for her to be a Hamilton." Cal beams, making me blush. The crowd giggles and ahhs.

"Chord Averette Hamilton, do you take Sarah Beth Sutton to be your wife?"

I gaze into Chord's eyes. "No." Shocking me with his answer.

My stomach plummets as he turns, looking at One. I'm caught off guard as my heart hammers in my chest. I'm stunned and embarrassed. I scan the crowd, everyone's smiling. What is going on, I dart toward the house.

"Hey!" Chord yells, I whirl around, confused. "Where are you going?"

"You said 'no'." I hold my belly as the pain in it increases.

"Come here." He crooks his finger at me. "I forgot, we need a do-over." He takes a knee in front of me. "Sarah, will you marry me?"

"You're proposing again?"

"Yes." He grins.

"Are you insane? You scared the life outta me." I clutch my chest.

He takes me by the hand. "Will you marry me?"

"A million times over, yes."

"Hopefully, once will be enough." He leads me back to the pergola.

I give Thayer my flowers, and Chord takes my hands in his. "Sarah Beth Sutton, I first laid eyes on you when I was five, and in that moment, I knew I'd love you forever. Life gave us hell, but look at us—parents to an amazing little boy, whom taught us more in his young life than most people learn in a lifetime. I've never loved anyone else, and I never will. I promise to stand by your side, even when you don't need me to. And I'll help pick up every piece we break and put us back together. Be my wife forever because I love you, most." He slips my band on my finger.

"Chord Averette Hamilton, I've loved you forever. You're my best friend and in my weakest hour, you are my lifeline. You've held me together as much as you've held my hand. Our son was the best part of both of us, and I'll never be able to love you enough for giving him to me. Thank you for always loving me the way I needed to be, even when I didn't know what it was I needed. You were always there with all the love I could hold in my heart. Marry me because I love you and because you love me most." I slip his band on his finger.

"You may kiss the bride." The minister doesn't finish his sentence before Chord's lips are on mine.

Our family and friends gather around us, hugging and offering well wishes. It's a day nineteen years in the making. "May I have this dance?" Chord holds his hand out to me.

"Always." I lay mine in his as he pulls me close. *When It Comes To Loving You* plays as he spins me around.

Much like life, our world spins around. Sometimes out of our control, but if you can find someone like we have, you hold on until the ride's over. And trust me, the ride is worth it all.

The ups and downs of life mold us and shape us into who we are because, ultimately, who you are at the end of the ride is who you're meant to be. So when life spins out of control, hold on to the person next to you.

That's your person and the ride will be worth it.

"I've waited a lifetime to say this, I love you Sarah Hamilton. You give my life meaning and for that, I'll be yours forever."

"I love you, my husband. For all the strength and love you've given me. And the life we shared as parents, I pray there be more."

"Sarah, sweetheart, we're gonna be late," Chord yells from the main floor.

I step off the stairs, staring at him. "Babe, I will always run late. Never in the history of ever, will I not be running late. Okay?"

"Thanks for clearing that up, I'll adjust to your time." He smirks.

"Alrighty, I'm ready."

He shakes his head. "Good, cause we're gonna be late."

I laugh. "We're fine." I hold out my jacket, turning for him to help me with it.

"You're tat looks amazing." He slides my coat over it.

"I think it healed up nicely." Spinning, I press my lips to his.

Our wedding presents to one another were matching tattoos. A sun burst with a moon and stars inside. It's for Silas and the song my father wrote for me. It's absolutely perfect, making Chord an amazing husband for thinking of them.

He opens my door, helping me in. "Did we get everything?"

"I've put everything in and as soon as we're finished we can go straight there." He leans in, kissing me.

"We're gonna be late." I snicker. He rolls his eyes, shutting the door to sprint to the driver's seat.

We make the turn, circling around to Silas. Chord parks, coming to my side to grab the bag and me. He watches my every step like I'm going break. I love it and him. We walk, hand in hand, over to Silas.

"Hey, buddy. Happy birthday," Chord says as he helps me to sit beside our son.

"Baby boy, I miss you." Tears immediately spring to my eyes. "Happy birthday."

Chord sets the cupcake down, lighting the candle. He ties his balloons on as I fix his flowers.

"We brought you a new Thor, hope you like it," Chord says as he sets the action figure on his headstone. Chord joins me, taking my hand.

"Silas, we want you to know that there's not a day we don't think of you. You are the best part of us. Proof our love is a great one and can last a lifetime." I wipe my eyes.

WRECKING US, SAVING YOU

"We're hoping you know, you're always in our hearts and minds. Never far from any thought we have, you'll always be our first. We love you." Chord adds.

I take the picture out that Chord had laminated so the weather couldn't mess it up. "We're hoping you'll watch over your little sister for us. Love her and guide her through life, like we know you would have."

Chord lays his hand on my belly, and I place mine over his. "Jordan will know how wonderful her big brother was and that he was brave and kind, giving us the best gift of all. Love. Happy birthday, Silas. We love you."

"We love you, Silas."

Chord and I sit for an hour, talking to Silas as if he didn't know what was going on. Honestly, he knows. He asked for us to be whole again, knowing we would never replace him. But a love like ours should be shared and with his siblings.

Grief comes as a thief, robbing you of so much. Love comes as light, shining on the things that are most important. Don't under estimate either, nor dwell too long.

Love this life as intended. With love and to its fullest.

May your life be full of love that never ends.

Acknowledgments

To my readers, I can never find the words to thank you enough for having my back. Without people like you, I wouldn't be on this amazing journey of discovery. Your love and support of me can never be repaid, thank you.

Bloggers, bless y'alls hearts for always taking your time to offer an author an opportunity to become a favorite. I say it all the time—how you do it is beyond me.

For the Love of Pimping, Calling All Books, Reading is Our Passion, Spellbound Stories, Reckless Readers, Iamabookhoarder, and Helping Indie Authors, thank you for your undying dedication. I will forever be indebted. I love you ladies.

The Bottom Turners, I love y'all. Thank you for being the kinda people that love me for being me. Without you by my side, life would be boring. Thank you for all you do to help me or show me love. I love y'all.

Masque of the Red Pen, two years. Six books. Lessons learned. Friendship built. Love abounding.

Regina Wamba at Mae I Design, amazing photo. Thank you for being a part of my journey and giving me the inspiration for this story.

Moonstruck Cover Designs and Photography and Emma, THIS COVER!!!! Thank you for jumping in and coming on this amazing ride with me. Your hard work and dedication is astounding.

HEA PR & More: Lydia and Heidi, thank you for having patience and supporting me along the way. I value your friendship and work ethics, supporting me through every step of this journey.

Bub, your talent abounds! The song you wrote for this book is amazing…and in two minutes!! From music to lyrics to finance and beyond, your knowledge is astounding. Thank you for always being by my side. I love you oldest son.

K.K. Raines, your artistry knows no bounds!! Thank you for my chapter headers. Keep doing you and you'll succeed. I love you, baby girl.

Christina Santos. What can I say to my #spiritanimal? Thank you for your support and wisdom, but most importantly, your friendship.

My Betas, thank you for taking time away from your lives to help me live this dream. I never dreamed that, so many would help me achieve so much in such a short time. I love y'all.

My Alphas:

Lily, thank you from the bottom of my heart. Your love and guidance brought me to this point. Love you.

Doreen, thank you for all of you support and love. Your friendship means the world to me. Love ya.

Diane, from teasers to feedback, you support me any way you can, thank you. There aren't enough words to show my appreciation of all you do. Love your face!

Danielle, I love and appreciate you. Your time and energy are essential but your friendship is most important. Thank you from the bottom of my heart.

Sarah with an H! From minute one, this Sarah was you. Strong, loving and sweet. Kind hearted and always ready to help. You're amazing, just as you are. The love you give lifts me up, thank you. I love you, sweetie.

Christine Strongi, I love you. You are one of my dearest friends and forever stalker. Lol I couldn't live without you. Thank you for being there when no one else is or can be.

Silla Webb, you happen to be the greatest friend a person can have. Your support and mentoring has meant so much to me. The constant care and advice utterly appreciated but most of all, the time you take from your family to help me, goes beyond the pale. Thank you with all my heart, love you girl.

To my mom, boys and girls, I love you all. Thank you for having my back, today, tomorrow and always.

Daddy, I miss you even more today than yesterday and not as much as tomorrow. I love you.

LU, what can I say? You have my back and support me no matter what it is I'm doing. And you're always willing to try out my sex scenes with me. Thank you for being mine. Loves.

You and me… against the world.

About Leaona

Leaona (Lee-aw-na), also known as Lea, released her first book in June 2016 upon the encouragement of her father, who passed away before seeing her dream come true. She was inspired to write while raising her family, never dreaming one day, she would be published. While loving all genres of books, Lea writes redeeming contemporary romances, gritty and true to life. She draws from her life and loves to create her characters from everyday situations, proving everyone can be redeemed.

Lea and her husband, Lu, have three sons and daughters in law. She a proud fur momma to Kayelea a Calico and Frankie, a beagle. The Cove Series was followed by the Highway 17 Series, all are standalone family sagas and intertwine.

LEAONA LUXX

The Cove Series

Cherry Grove

Still Creek

Highway 17 Series

Changing Lanes

U-Turn

Collision

Made in the USA
Columbia, SC
27 March 2020

Have you ever wanted to go back?

I've contemplated it everyday for the last six years.

Knowing once I did, I'd wreck everything all over again, but still—I dream.

Until last night.

My past came back to me.

After I finish my set, looking through the smoke and flashing lights, I see him. The wreckage still written on Chord's face, tells me hell's coming. I can't erase the hurt my leaving caused, and I'll be damned if I let him wreck us even more.

But when I utter one word, I know we're finished before we can even begin to pick up the pieces.

Silas.

ISBN 9781981686087

90000

9 781981 686087

Made in United States
Troutdale, OR
12/09/2023

15605211R00056